Savage Winter

Savage Winter

❄ ❄ ❄

A Story of Wilderness... and Survival...

Butch Denny

ISBN: 0692568840
ISBN 13: 9780692568842
Library of Congress Control Number: 2015918422
Bent Sun Productions, Lockhart, TX

For

Bart Schleyer
A friend from Cheyenne, Wyoming, and a kindred spirit
1954-2004

and

E.C.S.
1948-1974

"The Service, recognizing the scientific value of wilderness areas as natural outdoor laboratories, would encourage those kinds of research and data gathering which require such areas for their accomplishment."

—National Park Service Wilderness Management Criteria

❄❄❄
Preface

MY FIRST JOB out of college was writing obituaries for a newspaper in West Yellowstone, Montana. The reporter on the paper, Doris Philips, was only sober when at work, and I remain forever grateful to her, for my big break came on March 15, 1974, when she was too drunk to cover the story. My article was picked up by UPI. In August of that year, I wrote a follow-up article picked up by AP. My editor was impressed with these successes; he promised to submit the latter article to the Pulitzers for consideration. He never did.

A year later, the Billings Gazette hired me. Six years after that, I moved to the Denver Post. I was nominated for a Pulitzer in my thirties. A couple years after that, I bought a newspaper in eastern Montana. In the 1990s, I was active during the controversial reintroduction of wolves to Yellowstone, a plan that resulted in a revitalization of flora, fauna, and even the landscape. Today, I own two ranches, a small newspaper, a motel, and a real lively café, especially at breakfast. During legislative sessions, I am a powerful voice in regional politics.

I have, you see, an agenda. I am against snowmobiling in a national park. Outnumbered and out-financed by commercial interests, I continue to speak out, and people do listen. Perhaps it's because I recall the winter of 1973-74 and the virginal snows then. Buffalo did not have the hard-packed trails of snowmobiles to follow out of the park, and the elk were not chased off their feed. The roads and buildings were buried under much deeper snow back then. And it was cold, very cold! It was the last great winter in Yellowstone, and I often look back on it.

For years afterward, my late-wife and I would go over to Yellowstone. We always stopped at the Hayden Valley Museum and Visitors' Center. It was usually packed. Most popular was the river otter exhibit, with mechanical otters sliding down artificial snow banks into a realistic-looking river, but today few tourists check out an alcove to the right of the information desk marked "Savage Winter." It was not always so.

Facing the river in front of the visitor's center is a larger-than-life Thomas Kimble bronze sculpture set on a red granite base. It's been a generation since its popularity waned, but I remember summer days when every tourist had a picture taken there. Forgotten now, the statue has grown black from sulfurous vapors that drift in from the valley, some say. The Park Service doesn't maintain the sculpture, and it looks run down. Strangely, ravens never land or poop on it.

A sad end for the biggest adventure to grace my life. I only got to stand twenty feet away that cold, snowy day in 1974, but I have never forgotten the experience. Some of the places mentioned in these pages went up in flames in the fires of 1988, but the Savage Winter stands proudly in my memory, and I continue to speak out whenever Yellowstone is in the news.

——Butch Denny
Miles City, Montana

CHAPTER 1

❄ ❄ ❄

The Experiment

"WHAT HAPPENED TO you out there?" the old man asked, looking up from the file spread open before him on a folding table.

The man standing before him was ragged and dirty, his face unshaven and cheeks sunken. "Dr. Garner, I couldn't take it," he answered. Looking down at his chapped hands, he added, "I couldn't catch what I needed. I used more energy hunting than I gained by eating. I grew weak and slow."

"You were one of our best prospects, and all you have to say is you couldn't take it?" the old man asked peevishly.

"I couldn't get dry, couldn't stay warm. I couldn't keep a fire going, and when I did, I got smoke and no heat. I was … I was sometimes scared."

"Scared?" the old man scoffed, sitting back to relight his pipe. "You? Of all people?" The new smoke drifted blue into the grayness of a roomful of old exhale.

"Yes."

"Of what?"

"Of things that go bump in the night," the ragged man admitted. "It wasn't the bears; it wasn't accidents. It was being alone, unprotected, especially at night. There are sounds in the dark," the man said, glancing out the window with haunted eyes. "Sounds I've heard before but never listened to. Squirrels chattering for no reason, birds that won't settle down, trees that creak when there's no wind. At first it wasn't bad, but after a while, my imagination…. It became unnerving."

1

The old man nodded. He had heard it before. Glancing at the file on the table in front of him, he said, "You lost thirty-four pounds in three weeks. I'm surprised you didn't die."

"I wanted to," the man answered.

"But you have a family, a career, things to live for!"

"I couldn't take it, sir. I tried my best." The ragged man seemed on the verge of tears. His cracked, red hands shook, and then he looked _beyond_ the old man, out the dirty window at the snowy pines in the distance. "I tried."

"I know you did," Dr. Garner said sympathetically. "Failure is the norm here." He closed the file. Yes, he thought, failure was normal. Garner was a dealer in failure, but he mustn't let it break the man standing before him. "Sign in with Dr. Chamberlain. Get something to eat, and then take a long, hot shower. When you're ready, I'll have you debriefed."

"Thank you," the man said, his eyes brightening at the thought of food. "Do I need to … "

"Yes. Take stool and urine specimen bottles with you," Garner said. "We'll pick up the samples later. But take care of yourself first. I'll handle the paperwork. Has someone called your wife?"

"Yes. She and the kids are on the way."

"I'll bet she's glad this is over, eh?"

"I don't know if it will be over," the ragged man said sadly. "I feel I've left something important behind."

"Only a sense of accomplishment," Garner smiled. "Your pride'll return as soon as you realize few people alive today would attempt to survive these conditions in the name of science. G'wan, see to your needs."

"So what do you think?" Garner asked Dr. Britt Chamberlain, a tall, willowy blonde, as she entered the room moments later, her high heels clicking like castanets across the waxed wooden floor. It was one of her few triumphs in this God-forsaken wasteland. The board-and-batten bunkhouse, which they had rented for their headquarters, had probably not had its floors waxed in thirty years. Everyone around her wore Vibram-soled boots and jeans, but _she_ would not give in to this wilderness. Britt had demanded the old floors be waxed, the toilets spotless, the windows clean, and the trashcans emptied every day.

"Reese's beaten like all the rest," she replied, taking a seat at the table. "He's disillusioned. Most of our volunteers risked reputations as outdoorsmen to do this, but none more so than Ranger Reese. Having devoted his life to the wilderness, Reese still failed as badly as anyone else. True, spring is late this year. We have only seven subjects left from the original forty-eight, but it's a shock when they find out we considered their failures predictable. Reese will take it especially hard."

"Our volunteers only had theoretical survival skills," Garner said coldly. "Few people have such experience on a practical level, and then only by accident. Trust me, I know. I've been studying survival for NASA for forty years."

"Yes, I know," Britt said indulgently, having read all of Garner's books and articles outlining a theory that humans, with a growing reliance on technology and modern medicines, were in evolutionary danger in the event of a rapidly changing environment.

"There is a question of determination, too," she said. "This test is merely a challenge for our volunteers. Failure means a hot bath, but there's no reward for success except another miserable day out there in the wilderness."

"Reese lost thirty-four pounds. That's a lot of determination," the old man said as he relit his pipe.

"Dr. Garner, I wish you wouldn't smoke in here," Britt complained. Someone who described herself as a "double-ist" (feminist scientist), she hated pipes and cigars. They were symbols of an outdated, unhealthy masculine world, but in answer, the old man gleefully exhaled an annoying cloud of aromatic, blue smoke, and despite her convictions, she sniffed lightly, and it was good. Her grandfather had smoked a pipe; she recognized some of the subtle nuances tobacco blends had, but she still didn't appreciate being exposed to the smoke.

Men and their repressive attitudes toward women were what Dr. Britt Chamberlain was writing about in her spare time—but among the gifted scientists here at Project Snow, she didn't _feel_ repressed. Britt believed she was considered an equal, yet most of her peers and all of the volunteers were men, so even here, there was an insidious bias at work.

"What did you think of my note?" the old man asked, peering at her over the top of his glasses. Putting aside a pencil a beaver would have been proud of, Dr. Garner opened another folder in front of him.

"That Ranger Reese act as our liaison with the Park Service as soon as he recovers?" Britt asked, sidestepping the real issue. She had already read the latest surveillance report but hadn't had time to form an opinion. The report detailed the movements and activities of just one of the remaining volunteers, the one the scientists referred to as HVTS, the Hayden Valley Test Subject.

"Of course I want Reese to work with us," Garner said. "No, I'm talking about the report on that kid, the HVTS."

The two of them had been through six experiments together—Projects Jungle, Desert, Grassy Plains, Oceanic Float, Woodlands, and Ice, so she knew what Garner wanted. Time after time, cultural inhibitions had interfered with what he termed "pure" survival, that is, survival over the long term completely dependent on the abilities of the subjects. Now, Dr. Garner's focusing on _one_ surveillance report out of dozens worried Britt. Of all the volunteers, HVTS was the only one who had demonstrated much initiative in this experiment.

"I think HVTS is doing well, which is surprising since he's the subject we didn't brief beforehand," she said. "He seems to have no problem making a fire, telling direction, constructing traps—"

"You missed the point," Garner pressed. "What do you think of his move?"

"I wouldn't call it a 'move,'" Britt answered, remembering the tension between them when Garner had abandoned his normal research procedure of directly observing his subjects, instead hiring mountaineers to report on the volunteers' activities. At first, she had felt such amateurish surveillance was an invasion of the subjects' privacy and therefore scientifically unethical. She had argued Project Snow was allowing the subjects too much freedom in too large an area, but she and Garner had compromised on a schedule of monthly examinations with somewhat less haphazard surveillance.

At the time, there was no proof this was the measure called for in these harsh conditions, but now, here it was: HVTS had left an assigned area and moved ten miles southeast. This potentially dangerous variable was reported promptly, and Britt had to agree surveillance was, indeed, justified.

"What would you call this move out of his assigned area?" Garner asked.

"Gosh," Britt said, hating to be put on the spot. A better writer than speaker, she felt that writing gave her more time to think. She had just signed a contract for her tenth book, _The Urban Hermit_, destined to be a classic study of the surprising number of individuals in our society who prefer to live alone, unknown in the midst of a bustling society. The book had taken her three years of thought and four hundred interviews, but Garner expected an answer now.

"Is there a better way to look at this unexpected move?" Garner asked. "Don't get me wrong. I'm playing the devil's advocate here."

"Thank you," Britt said, feeling reassured. "I don't think 'move' is the right word. Migration would be more appropriate. The subject's migration from an assigned area to a region more familiar to him is logical, but disappointing. I believe the Park Service chose the valley for its fertility and accessibility."

"Does the 'migration' call for corrective action?"

"What kind of action?" Britt asked suspiciously.

"Reassignment to the valley, unless you think this warrants disqualification."

"Absolutely not!" she exclaimed, her blue eyes flashing with the challenge of argument. "Migration has survival value. Birds migrate because of changing seasons; wolves follow the herds; elephants follow water supplies in a drought. We know the weather is especially bad this spring, so HVTS moves to a more accessible food supply. Why should we disqualify him for wanting better conditions?"

As he considered her point, Garner emptied sludge and slobber from his pipe into an ashtray. The ravages of time had not been kind to him. The old man's intelligent blue eyes were watery; his face had sagged with age, and his lower lip drooped permanently open, but his iron character prevented him from being embarrassed at unconscious drooling and dripping. "Good," Garner concluded, repacking his pipe. "Then we agree. We leave the HVTS alone for now."

CHAPTER 2

※ ※ ※

HVTS

TIME TICKS AWAY the biological measure of every being's life span. Tiny birds with furious pulses flit through short, eventful lives; giant tortoises plod patiently through slower and longer existences. Understanding this, Dr. Chamberlain theorized in the objectives section of Project Snow's grant-funding application, "Each being may perceive time the same way, measuring it by the passing of distances or the beating of its own heart." She continued the thought in her Mission Statement, "No one knows how each volunteer will adapt to the cold, the loneliness, or the time invested in this survival experiment."

To test her hypothesis, Britt interviewed all the volunteers before the experiment to probe their motives for risking lives and time to the Project. Three patterns were suggested to her.

There was, for example, Robert "Red" Reese, a redheaded ranger from the National Park Service, a strong, thirty-four-year-old, husband of an uncomplaining wife, a respected Mormon elder, and father of four little children. Having mastered conventional wilderness skills, Reese said, "Project Snow is the ultimate challenge."

"How do you picture the year ahead?" Britt asked.

The ranger answered confidently, "It's an uphill slope. Starting at the bottom with nothing, I hope to progress upward until success is assured, and the year completed."

After an exhaustive briefing, Reese was selected as GTS, the Gallatin Test Subject, scheduled to go afield from Highway 11, south of Bozeman, Montana. With no fanfare, he said goodbye to his family, two fellow

7

rangers, and two researchers. It was a long time before Reese stopped waving as they drove away.

Douglas Paine Hanson, a forty-eight-year outdoor writer, hoped to use his experiences in the wilderness for a book, articles, or interviews. Hanson imagined, "The year ahead is an uphill slope until survival is assured, then downhill until the end." Named LTS, the Lamar Test Subject, Hanson, a widower, began the project on May 17th at Roosevelt Lodge. Seen off by a ranger, a technician from the project, and his secretary, he walked confidently into the sagebrush.

Another volunteer represented a third school of thought, for he pictured the year ahead as a rectangle or ellipse, beginning on a short side—spring—moving through a long summer to another short side—fall—followed by a long winter.

Hurrying to interview other volunteers, Britt Chamberlain asked, "What comes next?"

The young man answered, "Summer again," and there was something about the way this volunteer said it that caused Britt to wonder later if the single, twenty-four-year-old subject had meant the eternal cycle of the seasons or the way he might conduct himself in the experiment. He went on to say, "I'm less interested in what comes after the project, than what will happen during it."

Unfortunately, Britt did not take time to ask why this young man wanted to participate. In fact, she didn't pay much attention to him at all. Chosen as the HVTS, the Hayden Valley Test Subject, this volunteer wasn't expected to last very long. He was a last-minute replacement for a better qualified volunteer who had suffered a heart attack due to the altitude the day before.

Because of the physical impossibility of starting all forty-eight subjects on the same day, Project Snow was divided into three regional groups. HVTS was in the second group, Group B, beginning the experiment at dawn, 5:06 a.m., May 15th, 1973, a Tuesday. The young volunteer waited with twelve friends, two rangers, and two scientists in a parking lot near the confluence of Alum Creek and the Yellowstone River.

It was miserably cold. A breeze whipped across the icy valley. Scarred by sagebrush swaying in the wind, the crusted snow was cracked into sheets like old, stiff Styrofoam. Many of those there that morning had thermoses of hot coffee, but even so, their teeth chattered whenever they tried to smile. Two friends, Mack Simms and a big-framed girl named Roxy Martin, sat on the tailgate of a ranger's pickup as far from the crowd as possible. Nearby, two scientists warmed their hands over a Coleman stove as they waited for the go-ahead. The young volunteer circulated solemnly among his friends shaking hands and listening to advice. Several commented how cold his hands were, but actually he felt warm, though he did admit to being nervous. Every time the radio crackled, his heart hammered in his ears, and each time, he suffered through another round of goodbyes, but finally that died away as the young man's supporters began to feel premature.

Mack and Roxy motioned for their friend to join them at the edge of the crowd. They fussed over him, straightened his clothes, and boxed his ears, and then Roxy kissed his cheek and wandered off to annoy the rangers. The volunteer's other friend, Mack, hurried away to hustle some coffee.

To others waiting in the windy parking area, it appeared spontaneous, but this goodbye had been carefully rehearsed. HVTS's pockets were now full of boot laces and clean socks, but his friends had made no attempt to slip him tools, maps, or matches, so they believed they hadn't actually broken the rules. The young man appreciated the thoughtfulness, but from now on, he intended to survive or fail on his own merits.

Taking a seat on the tailgate, the test subject swung his feet back and forth nervously. Dressed in thermals, a plaid wool jacket, new jeans, well broken-in boots, and a watch cap to hold his long auburn hair in place, the volunteer felt physically and mentally ready; he waited only for the radio signal, but that was delayed. Eager to get started, he had much to think about. Water? Not much of a problem here in the valley with its many streams and mighty river. Shelter and warmth? Something to worry about later this afternoon. Food? He would have to concentrate on that from the beginning. Five-fifteen came and went, five-twenty; finally there was no waiting any longer. Clouds had masked the dawn.

"Hayden Valley? This is West Yellowstone. Come in, over," the radio barked.

"West Yellowstone, this is Hayden Valley. You're fuzzy, but we read you," one of the rangers answered loudly, as if trying to broadcast the whole twenty-five miles to Montana without a radio.

"Hayden Valley, please see your subject, the HVTS, off, over."

"Okay, West Yellowstone. Any final instructions?"

"Negative, Hayden Valley. Good luck … ah … Eugene Carl Siegfried. Out."

"Thank you, West. We have oh-five-twenty-eight hours."

The time had come. Five twenty-eight in the morning. Several people checked their watches as if minutes would make a difference in a year, when the experiment was scheduled to end. They crowded around the young volunteer, whom they all knew as Gene, one last time. At that precise moment, attracted by the unusual noise, a flight of nine scornful ravens glided overhead, clucking and squawking outrageously at the humans collected below. Some of the HVTS's more credulous well-wishers chucked rocks up at the birds, but the ravens circled solemnly in the wind three times before drifting away as suddenly as they had come.

Grimly signing a clipboard held by one of the researchers, Gene nodded at the assembled group, and then abruptly walked away, neither looking back nor waving, but it was a long time before anyone started a car and drove off.

"Will he will … or will he won't?" a ranger chuckled skeptically.

"Oh, he will," Roxy answered as she hopped into Mack's '52 Chevrolet. "Gene's tougher than any of us."

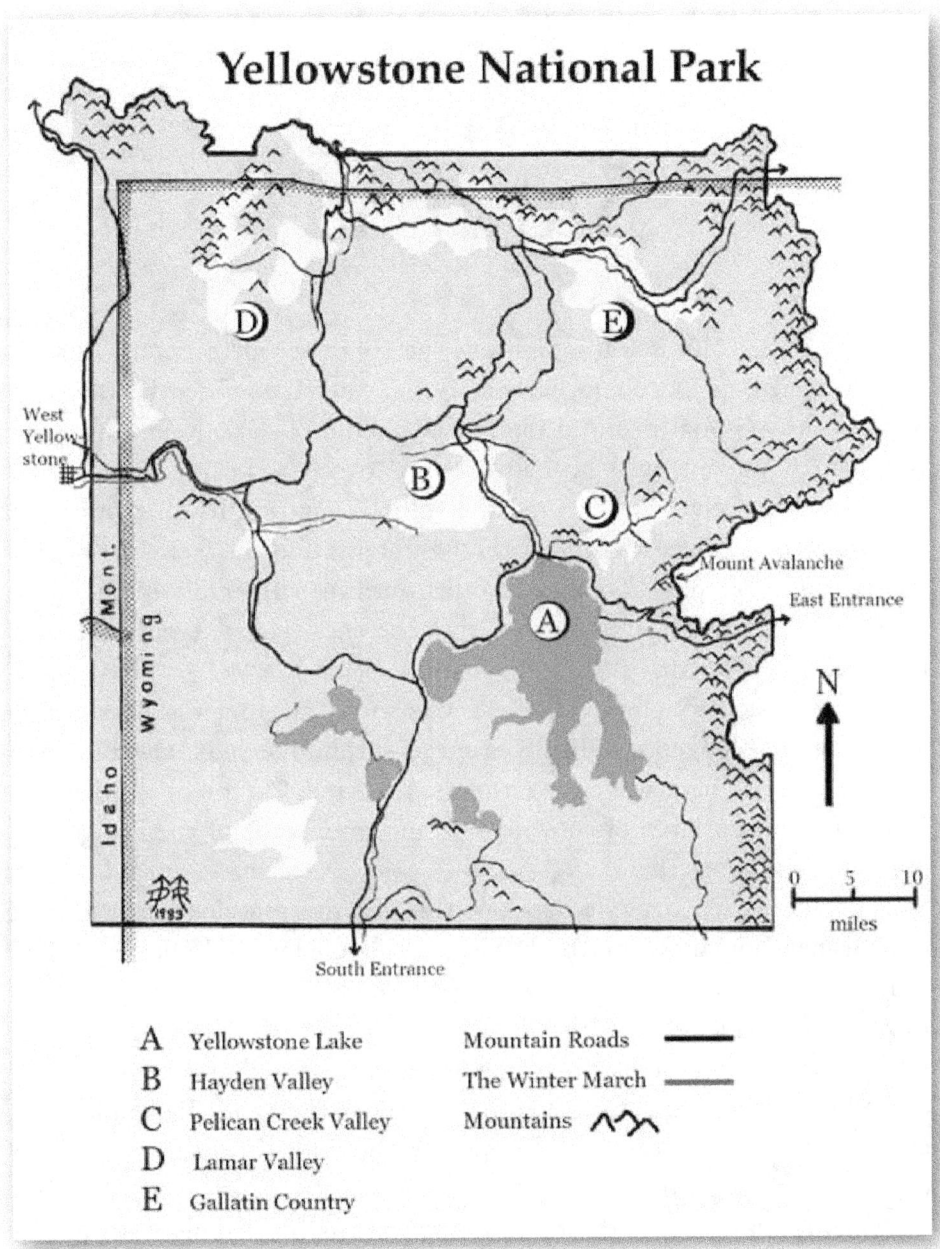

Yellowstone National Park

West
Yellow
stone

Mont.

Idaho   Wyoming

D

E

B

C

Mount Avalanche

East Entrance

A

South Entrance

N

0   5   10
miles

A   Yellowstone Lake   Mountain Roads ━━━

B   Hayden Valley   The Winter March ━━━

C   Pelican Creek Valley   Mountains ⋀⋀⋁

D   Lamar Valley

E   Gallatin Country

CHAPTER 3

─ ❆ ❆ ❆ ─

Survival

As LONG AS he could see the highway, the volunteer identified as Eugene Carl Siegfried, or more familiarly as Gene, walked confidently toward— what? With no goal in mind, he felt he shouldn't show hesitation. The young man walked until he had dropped over the near horizon, then paused indecisively and surveyed the rolling, empty hills all around. In every direction, distant vistas of the mountains and the welcome obscurity of lodgepole pine forests beckoned. Feeling vulnerable in the open sagebrush country, he bee-lined across the snow-covered valley toward the trees to the north.

The forest through which Gene was soon traveling was a tangle of young and old lodgepoles. Bushy teenagers, spindly adults, and bleached blow-downs had been woven together by the wind. On top of all this confusion lay a deep layer of snow smoothing over some of the snarl here, accenting the chaos there.

Gene Siegfried struggled upslope through this jumbled forest to look over his new domain from a high, forested ridge. Hayden Valley lay below him like a map. He could see its sagebrushed hills, looping streams, and mighty river. Except for forested areas on Sulphur Mountain and a small rise down by Alum Creek, the valley was treeless, its alluvial soil too well drained for anything but sagebrush. Somehow, the valley looked less exciting, less mysterious than the deep forests and for this reason, he didn't explore further that day.

Feeling truly alone for the first time in his life, Gene was sobered by the difficulties he faced. There was not one animal visible anywhere, though the valley had been chosen for its wealth of game. Convinced there could be no damage to the historically overpopulated elk and buffalo herds, the National Park Service had allowed Project Snow's researchers to assign him to Yellowstone National Park, but as he sat there on the ridge above Hayden Valley, Gene could not spot one buffalo, elk, or duck anywhere. Even if he had seen something interesting, he had no idea how to kill it. Raised in Trinidad, Colorado, Gene knew how to hunt deer and elk with a high-powered rifle. Stalking was no problem; he knew how to track, too, but how was he to kill an animal five times his size with no weapons, butcher it without a knife, and store the meat for winter?

Discouraged, Gene tucked his ears under his watch cap and descended the ridge to the snowy Mary Mountain Trail. That evening, soaked and exhausted, he made camp along Violet Creek in an area of sputtering fumaroles. Using a bootlace and a springy stick to make a fire drill—a trick learned as a Boy Scout—he made a nice fire. So far, the mushy crossings had only been an inconvenience and not the hardships they were to become, but Gene made his first mistake that night—trying to sleep in wet clothes. Another error took weeks to manifest itself: his wet clothes came into contact with the sulfurous ground. Before long, it looked as though they had been sprayed with battery acid—dozens of tiny holes ruined his new jeans, shirt, and jacket.

As the cold night settled over him, however, Gene Siegfried filled the primal darkness with cursing. For the first time, he wondered if volunteering for this experiment weren't a God-awful mistake. Never able to endure even a moderately cool shower, he had always been a sissy when it came to cold, and now his teeth chattered so loudly he might need a reconstructive dentist later. Analyzing the situation, he realized he was as cold giving in to the shivering, as by not allowing it to control him. Taking the lesson to heart, Gene forced himself to relax. Long before dawn, he rejoined the trail to Mary Mountain.

That morning, the azure sky had not a cloud, and the sunshine felt almost summery. Though exercise was invigorating, it wasn't long before Gene was so sleepy, he could hardly keep his eyes open. He stripped off his clothes, hung them to dry, and stretched out nude on an open patch of new, green grass to nap. It was to become a pattern for him: three or four hours sleep at night, and a few during the day, when it was warmer. Strangely, dreams came at night; daytime siestas were refreshing, black interludes.

The second night, Siegfried sweltered in front of a crackling bonfire on the shore of Mary Lake. Warm for the first time in two days, with stars blazing brilliantly overhead, he felt happier than ever before. Gene still hadn't seen much game, but he liked the area, and though he was miserable from wading through melting snow, the weather had been good all day. Confident things would work out, he was pleased that, for the first time, his own decisions ruled his life. The advantage of being alone out here was that he didn't have to worry about what his parents wanted. They had always been dissatisfied with him. They never gave him any support. Without even consulting them and having joined the survival experiment on a whim, he had unconsciously chosen the freedom to live on his own and make his own decisions.

Unfortunately, at this point, Gene Siegfried had found his time in the wilderness much like fishing alone. Every time he had fished by himself, Gene had wondered if he had chosen the wrong lure or bait. Was he in the wrong spot? Were the fish around the bend or in another eddy? Was he missing subtle strikes and unknowingly letting the big ones get away? Were there no fish anywhere near where he had cast? Was he wasting time because the fish weren't biting? He consoled himself with the fact that these "fisherman's doubts" also happened when fishing with others. Why was so-and-so catching more (or all) the fish, and he was not? Bait? Location? Luck? Technique? At least in a group, he could console himself or hear other stories. Sitting around a campfire with others, he could share the day's wonders and successes or failures, but now, alone out here in Hayden Valley, there would only be doubt.

As he enjoyed the fire that night, lazily roasting a few promising roots and nubbins on hot rocks for dinner, he worried about how to recognize lost opportunities and learn from them. He'd seen lots of sign (poop and tracks to city slickers.) Moose sign, which looked like hard black almonds, was localized. Elk—and possibly deer—looked like gluey nubs scattered everywhere in the meadows. Buffalo sign was much like cow patties. Bear sign was in turds like a human, and there was plenty of that about too. There were large animals all around him, but he wasn't seeing or hearing them. He was making too much noise. He was missing opportunities because he was too noisy. Having decided that, he ate his dinner. The roots were fibrous and tough but they had a pleasant nutty flavor; the spring nubbins were bitter. After eating, Gene pushed aside the glowing coals of the fire and lay on the warmed gravel to sleep; even so, he was up before dawn, cursing the cold.

Gene had serious doubts about his ability to survive a year in this wilderness, but when the sun rose, he forced himself to wash in the black water along the edge of the lake's receding ice. Was he doing the right thing? How could he know what to do? Was he missing opportunities just over the next hill? Where were the animals, if not here? With a companion, at least, he would have been able to rationalize poor luck and discuss alternate plans of action. Now, where every missed opportunity might mean the difference between survival and failure, he worried about mistakes. That, though he didn't understand it yet, was the main focus of Project Snow. The researchers were very interested whether a lone human could make it in the wilds. They already knew humans could survive in groups. Project Snow would come down to this: Could Gene Siegfried put aside his doubts to survive a year alone?

Late that morning, Gene found a dead elk with wildly staring eyes and a fresh, gaping wound in its neck. Hidden under a layer of grass, the carcass's blood felt tacky. Examining the area around the kill, he discovered the tracks and sign of a large bear. Should he take advantage of this good fortune and help himself to the meat, he wondered, or should he withdraw, hoping the bear wouldn't take offense at a man's scent around its kill? Consumed with doubt, he backed away.

Gene Siegfried's spirit of adventure was gone, replaced by a nagging sense of vulnerability. If a grizzly could catch and kill a winter-weakened elk, wouldn't a mere man be even easier? Would a man taste good enough for a bear to go to the trouble or did humans taste and smell so goaty he could feel a little confidence in his safety?

That night, camping along the south fork of Alum Creek, he charred and ground the end of a pine pole into his first fire-hardened spear, but it gave little comfort. Every crackle in the dancing shadows around the fire, every flickering reflection of yellow eyes in the darkness, every creak of winter-weary bough or plop of snow in the distant forest, every sigh of breeze or chatter of restless birds unnerved him, and he slept only when exhausted.

He admitted to his friend Mack Simms later, "I nearly gave up. I was terrified a bear would find me."

"What convinced you it wouldn't?" Mack asked.

"Nothing," Gene answered, looking at the distant hills. "But I don't have the energy to worry about it now."

The fact is Gene Siegfried had been so poorly briefed at the beginning—being, after all, a last-minute replacement—that he had been given no emergency procedures to follow before being placed in the most hazardous region of the project. "Doesn't matter," he had told friends later. "This is the adventure of a lifetime."

Of the things the researchers did tell Gene Siegfried, however, was the idea all of his physical needs could be summed up in four words: food, warmth, water, shelter. Water, of course, was no problem, for nearly all the running water in Yellowstone—with the exception of the sulfurous run-off from hot springs—was potable. Because of this, Gene adapted the four requirements to: hunger, cold, pain, and fear.

This first crisis, the nearness of a bear, forced him to realize how utterly vulnerable he was. The closest human was only as far as the nearest summer tourist, but in an emergency, that was a lifetime away. There would be no one to help him, care for his wounds, cover his back, share his adventures, or see that he was housed, clothed, or fed—and there would certainly be no one to find his body in this wilderness.

Overcoming fear with difficulty, he learned fear was not such a bad thing. It inspired caution and tempered daring. Only giving in to being afraid—or not admitting it—even to himself—was dangerous. This was, Gene realized later, his first step toward survival.

His second problem, hunger, plagued him from the first, but it wasn't until the fourth day that it dominated his waking hours. Gene spent less time exploring and more time searching for food. The forest near Sulphur Mountain became a temporary base, and he set out each morning to prowl the valley for edibles.

Shedding the inhibitions of civilization, Gene became bold with hunger. The spreading green rush of spring provided a veritable banquet of roots, leaves, and shoots. Small game was abundant. He surprised a Canada goose beside the river and clubbed it to death as it tried to take off. He strangled marmots with a bootlace as they emerged from their dens, and he collected grubs wherever he could. He ate raw fish, roasted fish, and baked fish. He swallowed insects whole; he waded the river flats feeling in the muck for bulbs and roots; he ate frogs, scraped flesh from grisly bones, and sampled bark and sprouts, but it was only bare subsistence. The rigors of a wilderness life demanded more, and Gene Siegfried began to lose weight.

Twice, he got sick from his culinary experiments, but fortunately, the effects weren't serious. Many of the foods Gene tried were unpalatable or bland, and he learned to rely on his senses of taste and smell to detect useless or poisonous species. Though he accidentally discovered powerful purges and laxatives, he continued to try everything, for his survival depended on flexibility. For this reason, he decided to move one day to the Sulphur Hills, ten miles southeast, in order to take advantage of spring fishing on the shores of Yellowstone Lake. By adapting and being willing to learn, Gene Siegfried hoped to come to grips with a desperate situation. It was a long day's walk to get there, but soon after relocating, he began to feel more confident he could survive a year in the wilderness.

CHAPTER 4

✳ ✳ ✳

The Scientists

By June 15th, the end of Gene Siegfried's first month in the wilderness and the day he reported to the researchers at Canyon Village for his first exam, weather conditions were improving. Daylight temperatures were moderate, while those at night were consistently above freezing. The snow was mostly gone, and the spring melt had brought on high water, deep mud, and clouds of voracious mosquitoes.

Having examined the few remaining subjects from Group A the day before, the scientists were not overly shocked by Gene's appearance as he warily entered the building, nor were they moved by his desperate condition. Siegfried looked thin and dirty. Smoke blackened his skin, and reddish fuzz covered his face; his auburn hair, parted in the middle now, was tied in back to cover his neck from mosquitoes. His cap had long since been lost in the tangled forests; his proud Pendleton jacket was frayed and torn, its collar and elbows black with soot. Looking like they had been sprayed with acid, his jeans were in terrible shape, their pockets useless, their cuffs ragged, the knees busted wide open. Worse than any of this, however, was the fact he stank. Gene Siegfried smelled of pine forests, smoky fires, salty sweat, fish, dead meat, and wet hair. His breath was awful.

During four hours of prodding and poking, he gave blood, urine, and stool samples, then suffered through an EKG, eye test, and dental exam. Only once was the testing interrupted, as another ragged volunteer was led down the hall past the examination room.

"Is that Hanson?" Gene asked.

"Yes," a technician answered. "LTS, the Lamar Test Subject."

"I didn't have a chance to meet him last month," Gene said.

"When this is over, I'm sure you'll get an opportunity," the technician replied evenly. "You two should have a lot in common.'

"That depends," Gene answered smugly, "on who outlasts whom."

Later, Siegfried was ushered into a series of rooms, and the scientists began to question him. Rangers wanted an accounting of his use of the back country, a botanist wanted to know what plants he was consuming, an anthropologist needed an outline of his adventures for a press release, and then the woman psychologist asked for an interview.

An assistant led Gene to her office in the back of the building. In the hallway, researchers were discussing their findings, but even with the thin, varnished plywood walls, Gene understood little of what they were saying. He glanced around the room, seated himself on a folding chair in front of the gray metal desk, and unconsciously straightened his hair in the mirror on the wall near him.

Dr. Britt Chamberlain entered the room, crisp and clean in a sleeveless green dress. She had abandoned high heels and was now wearing tennis shoes. She had been curiously watching through the one-way mirror as she adjusted a camera to record the interview. Though her subject looked boyish and guileless, there was something about this young man that fascinated her. She wasn't outdoorsy or athletic, but she had furnished the room with rocks and specimens to put him at ease, and she was pleased Gene held one of her props in his hands, an interesting beaver skull a ranger had given her the week before. Though she would touch such dirty things only with a tissue or gloves—bones were, after all, reminders of death—Britt Chamberlain hoped she had established a rapport with the young man for what she intended to be an intensive probing.

"I'm Gene Siegfried," he said as she seated herself behind the desk. He had been rubbing the skull's orange teeth with a cracked finger, but he rose from the creaking chair and offered her a red hand.

Loath to shake that hand, having been warned about its unintentionally powerful grip, she managed to smother a wince as he latched onto her. "Dr. Britt Chamberlain," she introduced, scooting her chair forward and arranging the files on her desk. She motioned for him to relax and took the opportunity to look him over. Hardly remembering him from the previous month, so brief was their meeting, she reminded herself he hadn't been expected to last this long.

"You're one of the psychiatrists I talked with in May," the young man smiled, appearing anything but nervous.

"Yes, in May," she smiled rather absently. Britt felt threatened, for his gaze was level and clear, his voice strong, his posture confident. He was … too masculine, too cocky. She felt the same looking at him across the desk as she did when exposed to tattooed truck drivers or foul-mouthed enlisted men. What was it that bred such coarse men, she wondered, and how could some women be attracted to them?

He interrupted her train of thought in a rumbling voice, "What happened to your helper, the little fat guy with the glasses?"

"First of all," she answered, "I'm a psychologist, not a psychiatrist. And the 'little' guy was Dr. Roger Mumsey, an associate of mine from UCLA. He was here to help get the project started. There were a lot more of you volunteers then."

"I hear there ain't so many now."

Was that supposed to be funny, or was it merely a comment? She decided to ignore it. "Let's say a few of our subjects have reconsidered their participation in the experiment. Now, if you don't mind, I have some questions. I have to drive to Roosevelt Lodge this afternoon with the Lamar Test Subject." She hadn't meant to be short; she took a breath, and made a mental note to examine what it was about this young man that made her nervous.

"The Lamar Test Subject, Douglas Paine Hanson!" Gene exclaimed, wonder in his voice.

"Do you know him?"

"I know of him, that's for sure. We've never met. He works for the Bozeman newspaper, and I think he's syndicated. He's the John Muir of our times."

"Moore?"

"Muir, John Muir."

"Oh," she said, tapping a pencil on the table. "Anyway, I do have to drive him up there later, but there's plenty of time." The young man probably chewed tobacco and went to ro-deos, she thought, and it was only with some effort she quieted her inner feelings. Such men emphasized a woman's weaknesses, not her strengths. She mustn't be defensive with him. She must relax.

"How's he doing?" the young man asked.

"Who—?"

"Hanson."

"Oh … in need of a meal, like you."

"Well, you can't eat descriptions of sunsets, can you? Even so, Douglas Paine Hanson's no sentimental dude—"

"I thought only cowboys used that word," she said, having heard it ever since coming to the mountains. In fact, the motel clerk in West Yellowstone insisted on calling her a dude whenever he saw her.

"A dude is a flatlander," Gene told her. "It's an insider's term for someone from outside these mountains. All of the tourists are dudes. You're a dude too, but give you a few months, and you'll be a savage like me."

"That'll be the day!" Britt laughed. "Did you ever hear the song *'I'm in with the in-crowd'*? You mountain people call yourselves savages; you think you're so exclusive, don't you?"

"Sure, we're exclusive," he agreed.

Realizing this interview was going nowhere, she gave her eyes something to do by glancing at his medical records. Her voice changing pitch, she said, "I see from your physical you've not only lost weight, you've shrunk an inch."

"Yeah," he admitted, looking out the window. "Those guys down the hall believed me last month when I said I was five-eight. This month, they actually measured me." Rolling his eyes, he confided, "My grandma's disappointed I ain't made six feet yet."

His face was long and sad, but there was something about his eyes that made her wonder if he weren't pulling her leg. The truth was, however, that five feet, seven inches or not, Gene Siegfried was one of the biggest men she had ever met. He had very wide shoulders and thick, but short legs—in fact, if his legs were in proportion to the rest of his body, he would have exceeded six feet. With a wide, square face, a heavy jaw and thick brows, he was not handsome, though he was attractive in the way that a farmer in a pickup with a toothpick in his teeth was attractive—attractive to _other_ women, that is.

Such men always had dirty fingernails, she thought, glancing at the young man's chapped hands. Surprisingly, his nails were fairly clean compared to the other subjects, but his nails were still chipped and scratched from hard use. The only things about Gene Siegfried not overly brawny, she decided, were his eyes, which were sensitive, jade green, and laughing at her now.

Irritated with herself, she coolly began to question him. At first, Gene was reluctant, but as he warmed to her, his answers grew more candid. She inquired how he was adjusting to the loneliness, the groveling, grubbing, and killing; he philosophized about the nature of being and the supposed superiority of man over the beasts of the field. The month before, Dr. Mumsey reported Gene was petulant and short-tempered, but Britt didn't see a trace of that now. She enjoyed the interview, and she was impressed with his attitude, confidence, and stability.

"I guess that covers it," she concluded. "Thank you. Take care of yourself. Perhaps I'll see you again in July."

"Am I finished?" he asked uncertainly.

"I don't think so. Please wait in the lobby. I've got to make some notes, then I'll check to see if anyone else needs you." Waving him out of the little room with a smile and a nod, she opened her briefcase and took out a leather-bound personal journal. "One hour, eighteen minutes. Why does this subject put me on edge?" she wrote. Analyzing her feelings further, she admitted, he was "surprisingly interesting."

As Gene walked down the hallway, he glanced into every room he passed. In one, rangers were discussing a map. One had his finger on Mary Bay on Yellowstone Lake. The other held a protractor on the Sulphur Hills. They knew he hadn't been living in Hayden Valley, he realized. His move to the lake from the valley was not secret anymore. Farther on, a lab technician was dropping a clear fluid into a sample of his blood, and a doctor was studying an x-ray of his left wrist—a traumatic injury from childhood that had been troubling him. There were no secrets here, yet no one seemed interested now that their questions had been answered.

The lobby of the wooden bunkhouse was a small, drafty room at the front of the long building. There was an oil heater in one corner, a battered map of Yellowstone on a wall, a card table with a coffee urn bubbling away on it, and several ancient, sticky, black-vinyl armchairs that had probably seen service in a 1960s dentist's office.

Gene helped himself to a cup of coffee and picked through a box of donut crumbs, then sat in one of the squeaky chairs. Across the room, an old wrinkled man was busily sucking on a pipe, but he didn't say a word. Gene sipped his coffee and looked around at the walls in boredom. For ten minutes, he and the old man shared the drafty room, the man moving only to tap drool out of his pipe or to cough.

Meanwhile, Gene crossed his legs and stared at the floor, then rubbed his eyes and yawned. Five more minutes passed, and still neither of them spoke. Finally the old man struggled out of his chair and ambled over to the coffee urn, every bone in his body crackling as he moved.

"More coffee?" he asked.

"No thanks," Gene declined. "Coffee and beer make me want to take a leak."

"Good for your bladder," the old man countered as he crackled back to his chair. Balancing his coffee on his knee, the man rummaged in his pockets for matches and tobacco. It took two minutes to load and light his pipe, then he muttered, "Good for your bladder," unaware of the time he had spent.

"Not around here," Gene sighed, getting up. He moved over to the USGS map of Yellowstone and studied Hayden Valley. "Every time I take a leak, it's got to be in one of their bottles."

"Count your blessings, son. At least they don't have a goddamn proctologist, or they'd be doing more than taking samples."

"I guess you're right about that," Gene agreed. "Do you work here?"

"Uh huh," the man answered, fussing with his pipe. "This afternoon, I've got to drive to Roosevelt, then tomorrow, up to Montana."

"Well, I wouldn't knock it, but then again, you've got to put up with all these scientific types."

"You don't like these doctors and scientists? What's the matter? They asking too many questions and poking at your privates?" the old man chuckled.

"That ain't the half of it. Those med-techs down the hall are shaking each other's hands because my blood sugar is textbook. That other guy, Doctor Capland, never said one human word to me the whole fifteen minutes I was in his office. And the rangers? They just want to make sure I'm not upsetting the balance of nature. They're afraid I'll turn into Euell Gibbons."

"Uh huh," the man mumbled as he knocked mud from his pipe into an ashtray. Looking over the top of his trifocals, he asked, "What do you think of Dr. Garcia, the anthropologist?"

"He's okay, and Dr. Fontaine, too, but they're convinced I'll give up soon. They don't know me, that's for sure."

"Do you think you'll last the whole year?"

"I'm going to try."

"Really?" the man said. "That surprises me. Everyone else quits the minute they get miserable. What's the matter, you not miserable enough?"

"Oh, I've been miserable, believe me," Gene said. "But I'm not a quitter."

"What about the psychologist?" the old man asked.

"I enjoyed talking with her, but she's never been far enough off the road to lose sight of her Cadillac. She's one of those that thinks because they have a natural, unplanted tree in the front yard, they live in the country."

"A dude, huh? Still, I understand she's done of lot of skiing—"

"In Aspen," Gene scoffed.

Suddenly, two rangers entered the room. They headed straight toward the coffee urn, and then Dr. Capland came down the hall, followed just moments later by Dr. Britt Chamberlain and a lab technician.

"You about done, Doctor Garner?" Britt asked as she sat down near a multi-paned window.

"Yes, I'm done at this very moment," the old man said, looking at Gene apologetically.

"Garner?" Gene asked in surprise. "_You're_ Doctor Garner, the guy in charge of this project?"

"Afraid so, Gene," the man said, putting his pipe in his pocket and getting up for more coffee.

"Then you had my number all along." Despite himself, Gene laughed amiably.

"I didn't get a chance to meet you last month," Garner explained, "Frankly, I couldn't understand the conflicting stories I heard, but now I see you're a fiddle in West Virginia and a violin in Boston."

"That may be," Gene laughed. A ranger nodded toward the door, and he took the hint. "The bad thing about getting my number is I've got _yours_ too. See you next month. I hope we get a chance to talk again."

Pausing at the door, he turned and said, "Since all of you are wondering what Doctor Garner and I were talking about, we were saying Fontaine and Garcia have to stop being negative, and you," he said, pointing at Britt, "have to read some John Muir. Isn't that what we were saying, sir?"

"That's exactly what we were talking about," Garner agreed.

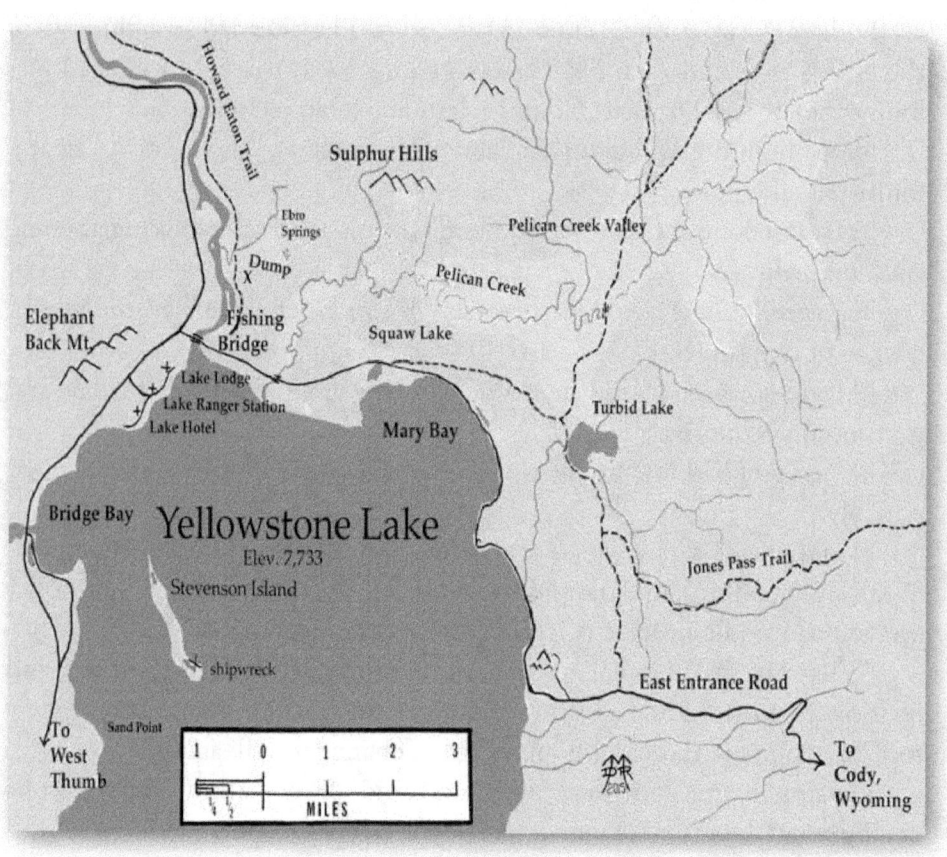

CHAPTER 5

❄ ❄ ❄

The Fisherman's Knife

By MID-JUNE, THE rotten snow had shrunk sullenly away to the highest peaks and darkest shadows. From the tiniest rills to the mighty Yellowstone River, the park was in full flood to handle the annual spring melt. Gentle breezes brushed the feathered treetops, carpets of flowers filled the open meadows, and luxurious grasses soaked up the muddy places. Roots, leaves, shoots, and the first fruits of summer could be harvested with little effort. Small game was abundant; larger animals cavorted playfully and waxed fat, including the lone man, Gene Siegfried.

Lulled into a false sense of contentment, he found himself enjoying the good weather and often napped in the warm sunshine. He forgot the desperation of his first weeks in the wilderness and rarely thought about the future. Like him, buffalo, elk, moose, and deer nibbled away the summer, but somewhere off in the trees, bears were busily stuffing themselves with 20,000 calories a day, a year's worth of eating in just eight months.

One evening, having finished a meal of tubers and sprouts, Gene sat burping on the high eastern bank of the Yellowstone River idly watching a fly fisherman work the water below. It was so quiet the fisherman's heavy line arrowed audibly across the black, mirrored surface of the river. Overhead, the sunset promised to be spectacular, and the quiet evening was full of peace and beauty, but Gene rolled to his feet and scrambled down the bank.

"Hey," he called. "Looks like it's going to be a beautiful sunset, doesn't it?"

"Yeah," the fisherman nodded, hardly glancing over his shoulder at the sky. Trying to provoke a trout to rise, the man cast a wide loop upstream. Above him, the clouds were glowing pink around their edges. To the east, a sandhill crane trilled its heartsong, and then there was a splash as a trout took the fly, rejecting it before the man could set the hook.

"You're catching quite a few fish," Gene called. "But I should warn you there are new regulations this year. You're not supposed to fish this part of the river, and the limit's been changed to two." When the fisherman didn't react, Gene added, "Besides, the season doesn't begin until July fifteenth."

"That so?" the man said, continuing to fish.

"Yeah," Gene replied.

"This is my day off," the stranger said. Stopping for a moment to change flies, he jammed the butt of his rod into the top of his waders and expertly gathered in his line. He wore a battered Stetson and when he spoke, Gene knew him as a fellow westerner by his strong vowels.

"I'm trying to enjoy the benefits of living here in the park the best I can before I go back to work tomorrow. The new regulations are okay, but they're for the dudes, aren't they?"

The man was one of Yellowstone's select working fraternity, the "savages," and Gene wondered why he chose to ignore the law. Everyone who knew the park loved it. Shouldn't the man be as interested as Gene in protecting Yellowstone's fragile resources?

"The fishing's about done for the day," Gene observed. "But if people did this every day, there wouldn't be any fish left." Sniffing the clean breeze, he thought how much better cold air satisfied him than warm. It was so beautiful here, so soothing. How could the fisherman be oblivious? Above them, the sky blazed in myriad colors, but the fisherman was unmoved and unrepentant.

Gene shook his head at the man's lack of appreciation. "The law's the law. There's a reason for it."

"Yes, there's a reason," the man replied. "The rangers want to cut down on people's enjoyment of the park. They run it like it was their own goddamn preserve. They think the more they hassle the dudes, the less likely the tourist'll be back."

"That's not right," Gene disagreed "The Park Service is protecting the park."

"Protect it!" the fisherman whooped. "Don't you believe it!" Changing subjects, he asked, "How long you worked here?"

"Four summers," Gene answered, omitting the fact he wasn't working this summer, but instead just trying to survive in the wilderness.

"How many grizzly bears did you see four years ago?"

"As a matter of fact," Gene admitted, "I used to see a few, especially up toward Canyon."

"How many black bears did you see four years ago? Couldn't drive to West Thumb for all the bears on the road, right? The tourists loved it. The park was famous. People came from all over the world. What about now? Any grizzlies? Any blacks? How many bears you hear about being shot or overdosed lately?"

Gene couldn't argue with that. He wanted to talk about fishing, but somehow the man had turned it around on him. Not only that, what the man was saying was true, and it frustrated him he couldn't respond. Though he would never admit it to anyone, Yellowstone was his heart. It was a wilderness; it was forever, but not only were people messing with its purity, they, like the fisherman, made comments Gene Siegfried couldn't imagine. There were things said about this place he didn't want to hear. These comments made him nervous and had the potential to make him sad.

"They say," the fisherman continued, "the grizzlies had artificially high numbers due to the garbage dumps that used to be here. Did you ever consider grizzlies overpopulated?"

Gene didn't know much about the politics of managing the park, nor did he understand why stuffy bureaucrats in Washington were determining the welfare of this great wilderness. At the same time, area ranchers were holding up something good for the park—reintroduction of timber wolves—for they were afraid of losing livestock, but it was not an issue directly involving him. He didn't like controversy, nor did he care about politics; he was only interested in the park as it was, and should be.

The fisherman turned his back, whipped line out of his reel, and slashed another cast over the water. Attached to the line by a nearly invisible leader, an artificial fly drifted gently into an eddy just like a real insect. A cutthroat trout took it and ran upstream, but the fisherman played it skillfully, scooped it up in a net, and dropped it into a creel with five others.

"We were talking fish," Gene tried again. "Did you know these cutthroat are a fragile population? Outside the park, they've interbred with other kinds of trout, and the hybrid offspring are sterile. In Yellowstone, the trout are isolated by the falls, so no other trout have established themselves here yet. That's why fishing out of season and taking more than your limit hurts the fishing. There's a reason for the regulations—the Park Service is trying to keep the park from getting fished out."

The fisherman looked up at the fading colors of evening. "I know," he admitted. "It's another case of too much, too late. The rangers are always behind the trends, and this is just another example." Wading to a better vantage, he slipped off his hat and scratched his balding head. Around him, the water was glassy, not even disturbed by feeding fish now.

"There was a time," the fisherman continued, "when a guy could catch a mess of twenty-inchers in this river. These regulations are intended to cut down on the number of trout taken, but they encourage people to put injured fish back, in the hope of getting a bigger one later. The result is there are more fish, but smaller, since the food supply remains the same."

"Oh!" Gene countered. "That's a classic fisherman's argument. More fish will eat less and be smaller—but how come the fish management people say the opposite is true? The population can't get any bigger because the big fish eat the little ones."

"Yeah, that's right," the fisherman conceded. "There ain't two fishermen that will agree. More fish mean smaller size each, or more fish mean plenty of little ones for the big ones. There's a good example right here in the park. Why are there fewer fish, but larger ones, at Park Point, which is relatively isolated and hardly fished, than at Gull Point, which is practically on the highway and heavily fished? On the other hand, why are there fewer fish, but bigger ones, in Lewis Lake, which is right on the road, than in Shoshone, which is remote?

"No," the man said, shaking his head, "I don't know which argument's correct, but I know the quality of fishing's gone downhill despite the rangers' up-and-down policies. No controls, and fishing gets worse, lots of regulations, and fishing gets worse. The rangers are so afraid of getting their funding cut in Washington they go pussyfooting around trying not to offend anyone by being too strict. They're bound and determined to choose the wrong policies, no matter if they go right or left, protection or use, fishing, less fishing, or no fishing at all.

"But it tells me the time for leaving this park alone," the man said, mouthing words Gene certainly didn't want to hear, "the time for grizzlies, cutthroat trout, and free-ranging bison has passed. There will always be elk and deer here, for they're a marketable resource and can be bred like cattle. An animal like the grizzly, on the other hand, can never be controlled. Nope, wilderness is done for. Wilderness and progress are incompatible. Mother Nature is doomed.

"Iowa grows corn where elk once grazed, and pistachio trees are taking over the deserts. The California condor picks at rabbit bones, and Colorado grows sugar beets where there used to be prairie dog towns. If man wanted wilderness, he'd give up a bit of his progress. He'd quit tampering with something never controlled before. I feel I might as well get in on the goodies while the getting's good. My grandkids will never enjoy them—but that's okay, because they won't know what's been lost."

Perhaps once in a lifetime, a chance conversation rings a listener's bones like this one did for Gene. He sat on the shore, unable to counter what he didn't want to hear, and whether the fisherman knew it or not, the doubts he had planted in Gene's mind would haunt him for some time. For now, though, the discussion was over. Crunching ashore, the man cleaned his fish and tossed the guts in the water for the morning gulls. After packing the trout in his creel, he walked away into the growing darkness.

Gene sat on the ashen gravel and let the peace and beauty of the evening fill him. With the sunset fading, black clouds drifted across the blue-velvet sky, and night settled over the river. Clouds of mosquitoes buzzed loudly all around him. Summer's fragile warmth seeped out of the beach, and misty tendrils of vapor rose out of the water like aimless ghosts. Somewhere a coyote yodeled in the primal darkness, but there was no moonlight, nor any light at all, for the nearest building was hidden by an angle in the river, two miles away.

Strangely depressed, Gene slapped at the mosquitoes around his head. Above him, the Milky Way was a band of brilliant white star fire stretching clear across the sky. Suddenly, Gene caught a flicker of reflected light from the beach nearby. Locating it with his peripheral vision—which is far more sensitive—he bent and retrieved the fisherman's knife, which must have fallen from its sheath when the man bent to pick up the fish. Unable to examine the knife in the starlight but liking the way it felt, Gene scrambled up the bank and headed for the nearest trees.

Out of sight of the road, Gene gathered branches, twigs, and a handful of duff. Using a hastily improvised fire drill, which he sawed back and forth on a log until he produced a glowing coal, he had a small fire going in no time at all, and in the light, he could see this was no discount-store knife. The knife was handmade, had a high-carbon steel blade, wood grips riveted to a flat tang, and no guard. The long blade had a sharp point and was curved and thin.

That the knife substantially altered the rules of the experiment, namely not to accept, borrow, or steal help, materials, or advice from the outside world, bothered him a little, and he guiltily stuck it in his belt, intending not to mention it to the researchers. With its thin, filet-style blade, the knife was unsuitable for anything but a camp tool and wouldn't materially affect his chance of survival, but the acquisition of the knife marked a turning point in his life in the wilderness.

CHAPTER 6

✳ ✳ ✳

Forge Fire

JUST DAYS AFTER acquiring the fisherman's knife, Gene was again attracted to the area north of Fishing Bridge. This time, when he peeked between the branches of a scraggly pine at the edge of a clearing, he saw bulldozers piling shattered pine trees onto guttering bonfires. As he watched, trucks darted from one side of the construction site to the other, and surveyors plotted mysterious pieces of ground. Wood smoke and diesel grime hung low in the cool mountain air.

"What are they building north of Fish Camp?" he asked Mack Simms when his friend dropped by for a secret visit. "Is it the beginning of a new road? I heard they want to build a highway over the LeHardy Rapids to bypass Fishing Bridge altogether."

"No, it's a sewage treatment plant," Mack said with disgust. "They're building it on the old landfill the Park Service and the concessionaires have used for years. It's invisible from the road, so tourists can't complain."

"How do you feel about it?" Gene asked, for he relied on Mack for opinions he was unwilling to make. This was especially true in matters of the environment. In such issues, there was never black and white, just shades of gray. What one activist said was good—the reintroduction of wolves into the Yellowstone ecosystem to control the overpopulated elk and buffalo—was viewed by another as impacting negatively on area ranchers. This kind of controversy created in him what he despised: inaction caused by doubt. Gene was the type of thinker least influenced by activism. He could see good in all arguments, so his customary reaction was a tendency not to take a stand.

His role in Project Snow concerned him. When the experiment concluded, people would look to him for hard-set opinions on wilderness issues, but he knew he was not cut out for such a role. For Mack, who had
been born into a well known ranching family in northwestern Wyoming,
it was easier. Mack saw things on an emotional level. Most of the time he
could sort through an issue and come up with an essential truth, and once
he'd decided on a course of action, he was rarely dissuaded from his opinion. So when Gene asked him, "How do you feel about the sewage plant?"
Mack answered uncharacteristically.

"Mixed feelings," he said. "They've killed a lot of timber and used a
lot of land. I don't like that, but it'll insure the purity of the Yellowstone
River, and that's good."

Unsure about the benefits of such a project, Gene waited until the
workers had stopped for the day. As the tired men drove away, the scene
regained a bit of its pristine beauty, though the air was full of acrid,
diesel smoke. Gene rose stiffly. Due to recent exertions, he was having
trouble with his left knee, but as he limped into the clearing to wander among the bonfires, it unkinked somewhat. Favoring that leg, he
walked slowly among the fallen pines and freshly compacted soil until
he stood at the edge of the old landfill. Below him lay an assortment
of jumbled mattresses, car springs, broken concrete slabs, and chunks
of iron.

The scene inspired him. Feeling more excited than he had been since
the experiment began, Gene clambered down into the pit to salvage what
he could. Before nightfall, he had collected a small mound of treasure: a
broken banister railing, a T-shaped steel plate once used as a brace in an
industrial machine, a length of three-quarter-inch flat bar stock in mild
steel, eight rusted pipe nipples, a small claw hammer head, yards of rein-
forcement bars, wire, a variety of large carriage bolts, an aluminum cooking pot filled with dried cement, a china teacup minus its handle, a pound
of nails and bolts, and a piece of plastic sheeting. After stashing the loot
nearby, he spent the next few days transporting it to his lair in the Sulphur
Hills.

Gone forever were days of frantic food search or listless grazing over plenty. For the first time, he enjoyed the challenge of survival. The whole pattern of his existence was transformed. He rose earlier in the morning to scrounge for food and worked later every night, deciding to make the tools of his survival, beginning with a forge and tongs, and ending with weapons.

Gene's father, a small-time rancher and auto mechanic in Trinidad, Colorado, had long ago taught him to weld metal and work with wood; in addition, Gene had sometimes watched a neighbor who was a farrier and blacksmith. For a short time, he had worked on the railroad in Trinidad. These were the skills that would be keys to his survival.

In front of the hovel in which he slept was a fallen pine log on which he now pegged a chunk of steel plate for an anvil. Beside the log, he dug a shallow square hole, eight inches deep. From the center of this pit, he scraped out a trench, lining the depression with clay from a parti-colored deposit he had found near Storm Point, then roofing over the trench with sticks and clay to form an air duct to the center of the hole. Finished, this forge pan, which was about the size of a small barbecue pit, was about a foot square and four inches deep. To the right of the forge, he molded a water trough to cool hot metal. Finally, he constructed a bellows from marmot hides, which he attached to the end of the flue in order to pump oxygen to the center of the forge fire. He was ready for fuel.

His neighbor in Colorado had burned anthracite coal in his forge in order to make custom hinges and other metal artworks, but there was none of that in Yellowstone. Only vaguely familiar with the time-consuming process by which wood could be reduced to charcoal and also in a hurry to begin work, Siegfried decided to salvage what he needed at Fishing Bridge Campground. In the past, he had observed that after grilling a steak or hamburger at their campsites, many tourists discarded perfectly usable charcoal rather than carry it along on their travels; it was this wasted charcoal he intended to use.

To put his plan into action, he visited the campground at Fishing Bridge one evening. At one campsite, two shivering campers lay buried under a thick pile of blankets. As Gene looted their campsite of a half-bag of charcoal briquettes, he enjoyed the dudes' suffering, noticing for the first time he wasn't nearly as wretched as these civilized people. His body and his mind, he noted with satisfaction, were adapting to cold. Not sure when the transition had taken place, or even if it were finished yet, he realized he was getting used to misery, his first major success in the wilderness.

Just after the false dawn, in the gray mists and hooting of stirring birds, he finished gathering eighty pounds of charcoal from cooled fireplaces and barbecue pits. No one had noticed him. Except for an occasional tourist walking by on a toothbrush journey to the restrooms, the only living being to spot him skulking about was a nervous poodle barking from a luxurious recreational vehicle from Indiana.

He tied the charcoal into two bundles. It took two trips to carry the bulky loads through the nearly impassable forest to his camp, but once there, he embarked on his first project: tools. Remembering how his neighbor had done it, Gene covered the mouth of the flue with a grate and built a fire in the forge; when the coals were ready, he pumped the bellows and brought the fire to heat. Dropping the battered claw hammer head onto the white-hot coals, he heated it lemon yellow, and then plucked it from the fire with two wet sticks. Smoothing its chipped face with a rock, he reheated it, and buried it to cool in a mound of powdered charcoal to harden. Later that afternoon, he mated the hammerhead to a wooden handle, wedging it in place with an old screw.

This hammer was his beginning, as it was throughout the history of industrialization. Stone fist hammers and flaked points led to copper mauls, to smelted bronze weapons, to forged iron. Iron implements led to discoveries in case hardening, damascening, and alloying. Steel hand tools built the first lathes and milling machines, which built computers and robots, and on to the next technology. It had happened over and over in American history, too. The Mayflower had brought forges and tools. Two hundred years later, New England furniture enriched the nation's antique markets. A simple hammer made chests and machines;

the nation was enriched by the crafts from before. Nothing is lost. One basic tool led to the next, becoming an antique in the process, Gene thought, as he pumped the bellows with his foot. Each tool made life easier and more complex, the whole process of development a progression. He wondered what the completion of his hammer would lead to next.

The hammer was one of the lessons of Project Snow. Gene simply could not function with stone tools, though he often tried, for the art of shaping stone was lost to him. At the same time, most of the rock in central Yellowstone is rhyolitic; workable obsidian lay thirty miles north. There are people who can replicate stone tools today, but they are rare individuals every bit as specialized as computer technicians. Gene did, in the solitude of winter, finally learn to knap, but he never hunted with stone weapons. Because he tried, and failed, to shape stone, only the achievement of a steel hammer offered a chance at long-term survival. The implication, for the experiment, was that in a hundred years, forging would be a lost art except for a few culturally elite blacksmiths, and then survival would depend on other technologies.

Siegfried used his new hammer for his next project, a pair of tongs, forged from two equal lengths of construction rebar, bent to shape, then riveted together. Next was a cold chisel, followed by a small adze and a hatchet. The cost in charcoal for these projects was enormous, however, and he was forced to resupply his stock.

Charcoal was bulky to transport, though, and it took two days to carry enough to his camp from Fishing Bridge. As was usual on one of these resupply trips, he came out on a rocky outcropping above Pelican Creek where he liked to rest. Stretching out in the warm sunshine, he gazed about sleepily. Below him, the babbling stream curved gently away, creating a wide gravel beach on its far shore and very little room on this side, which was deeper and swifter. A gentle breeze brushed his hair, and the deep grass folded around him like a blanket.

Perched high in a dead tree on the opposite bank, a young raven sonorously clucked, "Kok Kok! Kok!" at the man's intrusion. Within minutes, however, the raven changed to a devilish croak that grated on Gene's nerves like an alarm clock being wound. Siegfried tensed and rolled over onto his belly. At first, there was nothing in sight. Pelican Creek and the strand opposite were empty, but the raven was fussing in the tree across the creek, where he spotted movement.

A moment later, a barren cow elk stepped from the forest and began to drink, often turning to watch the pines behind her. Something had disturbed her daytime rest; her ears swiveled this way and that like radar dishes, sometimes in tandem, sometimes separately. Smiling grimly, Gene selected a stone and hurled it over her head into the forest behind her. At the first bump of the rock in the trees, the cow's tail came up, and she bounded noisily across the stream and ran down the strand right under the high bank where he lay.

Gene never hesitated. He launched himself over the bank and landed smack in the middle of the elk's withers, toppling her into the swift, cold water. Wrapping his legs around her body, he rode the terrified elk like a rodeo bronco. The more the cow struggled, the deeper they splashed into the stream. Gene tightened his grip on her neck, then took hold of her muzzle and began to twist her head around violently. The cow's tail flapped like a windsock against his legs. She drooled in terror, clacked her teeth, choked convulsively, coughed twice, and then her neck broke with a pop. As she died beneath him, her gentle brown eyes turned to stare up at his red face. Feeling very guilty, Gene looked away with regret, but he needed the meat. This was, he reminded himself, his first major food all summer.

"Bless you, elk," he gasped at her death, hurriedly adding, "Thank you God," lest He take offense. All great good came from God, he reminded himself, and not the least creature fell to Gene's hand, not a crayfish or a bug, without His approval and plan. Perhaps he'd been religious before, perhaps the lessons from a childhood spent in Sunday school were finally sinking in, but now that his life depended on another's creature's death, Gene became concerned with God's generosity or lack thereof. There was no need to tempt Providence with ingratitude.

Fifty yards from where he'd jumped onto the elk, the stream cast them up on a gravel strand; it was only with the greatest difficulty Gene bullied the heavy carcass ashore, but then he fell beside it, happy at the unexpected gift of meat. Shortly after catching his breath, he gave an echoing cry of victory, and then, raising his arms over his head, he gleefully danced about the dead elk like a savage gone wild. It was his first kill. No more would he eat marmots and nestlings. This was red meat! There was fat and strength here and power too, for he now knew he had it in him to take big game. From this time on, he hoped to hunt only worthy prey for sustenance. And, the elk was big enough to give him a surplus to save for the lean times of the coming winter.

Using the fisherman's slim filet knife, Gene split the cow's hide from groin to chin. The elk weighed about three hundred pounds, and butchering it was hard work, but pulling and jerking her skin from the glistening, red body, he spread the hide fleshy-side-up on the shore and piled bloody pieces of meat on it. Enjoying the rich tone and irony aftertaste, he ate some of the heart and liver on the spot, raw, but he saved everything else remotely useful. When finished, little remained but the broken skull, spine, hip, and a few scraps. Even the slimy viscera he washed to use as strips for hanging the meat out of the reach of bears. He saved the brains for tanning the hide, the hooves for glue, the bladder to store liquids, the leg bones for marrow, and the tongue, kidneys, and other juicy parts to eat later that night.

Meanwhile, the noisy raven had been hopping from foot to foot nearby, greedily snapping up tidbits thrown to it. Symbol of death and doom to some, this young male seemed to know humankind's slow reflexes and devious tricks. It showed no fear of Gene Siegfried; it was probably, he thought, the raven that had spent last spring stealing soap from the maids at Lake Lodge. With the native craftiness of a pest, the raven insolently joined him by the pile of meat, and whenever Gene wasn't looking, it pecked into the flesh, and then innocently looked away and swallowed. Protesting loudly when he kicked the remaining bones into the stream for the fish, the raven waited until Siegfried buried all trace of his butchering. Gene hung most of his booty in a tree, and then shouldering his charcoal and some meat, he disappeared into the trees. There was no reason to stay and a good reason to go, so the raven followed him back to camp.

It took three trips to transport all the meat. In the growing darkness of evening, Gene built a bonfire to deter bears. The area north of Pelican Creek and between the Yellowstone River and Pelican Creek Valley, he knew, was thick with grizzlies this time of year. He had seen their sign and once stumbled upon a track half again as long as his own foot and fully ten inches wide—good reason to be cautious.

During the night, Gene constructed racks to make jerky and laced the elk's hide onto a frame to dry. Strangely friendly, though it was wild and not a pet, the raven perched on the frame as Gene scraped the hide next morning. Since he was a convenient source of scraps, the raven began to spend time each day near his camp. With no desire to tame such a creature but liking the companionship, Gene named the bird Munin, after Odin's own raven. Each morning, he rose and looked around for the bird; each day it sat in trees at some distance, watching him. Perhaps it needed entertainment, Gene decided, and he began to study the raven as intently as it studied him.

The day after killing the elk, Siegfried started other projects. First, of course, was a hide scraper; when finished, it looked somewhat like a curved drawknife except that its beveled edge was reversed. Next, was a flensing tool followed by a loop of hardened steel to fit around his fist. This piece, a fire striker, produced a trail of sparks whenever it was struck across a rock, and it simplified his fire making. He then forged a thick wire into a gimlet, and a smaller one into an awl. He made a scriber, a small wedge for splitting wood, three knives with thick blades for hunting and skinning, four large needles, and a sickle blade.

Between projects, he scraped the drying elk hide and tended his jerky racks. He also chipped the cement out of the aluminum pot, knocked out its many dents, and then polished its interior with sand. After riveting two simple iron loops onto the pot for handles, he cooked himself a nutritious stew of elk innards and roots. Finally, late one drizzly afternoon, he began the difficult task of making weapons.

Gene had to have some way to strike large game from a distance. He decided he would hurl javelins and darts. Forge-welding carriage bolts to short pipe "nipples," then flattening the bolts to blades, he made the first of these. These were his "heavy javelins," of which he made eight. Next, he cut a piece of flat "bar" stock into two dozen blanks, hammering each into a narrow, three-inch, double-edge blade. The result were surprisingly serviceable "light dart" heads; he made three kinds: six chisels for target practice, eight "spears" for hunting, and ten "bone-breakers" for long casts. They were so easy to make he forged a large spearhead in a similar manner. He mated the spearhead to a piece of the oak banister he had salvaged earlier. The other javelin heads he mated to simple pine shafts.

Next day, the weather turned rainy, so forging stopped. Sitting under a tree for shelter, Gene occupied his time grinding the edges of his tools and weapons on a coarse, rhyolitic boulder; afterwards, he coated them with elk fat and hung them in a tree. The rain that day varied from a heavy downpour with thunder and lightning to a drizzle that reduced visibility to less than a hundred yards. Though it was July, the cold kept the mosquitoes down, something Gene appreciated.

When the rain stopped, he again collected charcoal from Fishing Bridge. His next project would be very time-consuming, for he intended to make an axe. To do this, he cut a section of leaf spring and formed it into a loop. After punching four holes through the ends of the loop with a piece of hardened rebar and then through the T-shaped steel plate, he riveted the loop and the plate together. As he beat the blade to bevel its edge, he discovered the steel naturally curved into a half-moon shape that looked quite effective as a weapon and a tool.

The final axe head, which resembled a battle-axe, was black, crusted with iron oxide from the forging, and required two weeks to be ground, tempered, and mated to a handle. It was practically useless for cutting wood, Gene learned in dismay, for the bolsters and rivets on either side prevented that, but for the very first time, he truly felt safe. Never again would he be without a serious weapon; for the rest of his time in the wilderness, the axe was rarely more than a few feet from his hand. He practiced throwing it, and there were soon marks on all the trees around his camp.

He forged only a few more tools that summer, but his most fulfilling project—at least from a personal standpoint—was the forging of carving tools. Using the last of his charcoal, he made two gouges—one wide and one narrow—two straight chisels, and a V-tool, after which he cracked and broke the forge, burned his bellows, and erased all trace of his forging operation. By next spring, he knew, it would be impossible to find any sign of his camp at the foot of the Sulphur Hills. He strongly believed in low impact, a theory of use that leaves no trace of man's having been there to spoil the wildness of a place. He came, he enjoyed, he disappeared, and only the tools would outlive him, not his tracks. Smiling in satisfaction, Gene knew that was as it should be.

CHAPTER 7

✳ ✳ ✳

Roxy

THE YOUNG PEOPLE who came to Yellowstone to work, the "savages," celebrated two major social events: the Fourth of July, traditionally celebrated in West Yellowstone, Montana, and Christmas-in-Yellowstone, on August 25th. Christmas-in-Yellowstone was celebrated with an employee banquet, small-gift exchanges, and Christmas caroling. On the Fourth of July 1973, the biggest holiday of the summer season, however, savages from all over the park converged on West Yellowstone, Montana, to drink, shout, and screw. Hundreds of people milled about the muddy, rutted streets or wandered aimlessly through headshops and souvenir stands. Others partied in the Gusher, a crowded beer and pizza joint, or in the Lariat, the wildest saloon in Montana.

Most of the partiers were dressed in jeans, T-shirts, and boots, but Britt Chamberlain, who lived in the Stagecoach Inn, West Yellowstone's status accommodation, and her date, Roger Mumsey of UCLA, both prepared for a night out in a different way. Britt dressed in a green plaid skirt, cream silk blouse, and a wool camel blazer; Roger wore an expensive sweater, slacks and loafers. They had a proper steak dinner with wine at the Inn, unaware everyone else was enjoying pizza at the Gusher, swilling it down with Olympia beer.

By the time the two "dudes" had finished eating, the little town was humming with activity. Traffic was bumper to bumper, and cars were parked wherever there was an open space. Although West Yellowstone is famous for its long, bitter winters—it often records the nation's lowest temperatures—it wasn't much of a town. In 1973, its streets were wide, poorly paved and full of potholes. Providing the needs of ranchers and lumbermen from Bozeman to the Idaho border, the town had been in decay like many other service towns across the country. It had no respectable dying brick buildings and dreams gone sour, for the town had simply never been tamed.

Beer cans lay in piles and broken wine and whiskey bottles gleamed in the corners of the night. Occasionally, a red glow from a dark alley showed friends sharing a smoke, while snatches of music from passing cars echoed in the cold summer night. Girls hung out of car windows to shout at friends. Honking, slamming doors, laughing and cursing filled the festive streets with sound and life.

It was inevitable that Britt suggest, "Let's go to the Lariat to see what's happening." She had never been there, but she had heard the bar was not one of those picturesque and memorable saloons common to the Old West. There was no Face-in-the-Bar-Room-Floor like the Teller House in Central City, Colorado; no fabulous honky-tonk like the Million Dollar Bar in Jackson, Wyoming; and certainly no legends like the Shiloh Saloon in Medicine Bow. Instead, the Lariat was famous for its wildness. Ranchers, lumbermen, savages, miners, and tourists crowded into the bar to roar, and Britt Chamberlain wanted to see it for herself.

"Okay," Roger agreed. "but if it gets too crazy, we'll leave."

"Sure," Britt nodded, for she was wary too.

The two of them squeezed through the door of the saloon. There was no ID check, and a girl that couldn't have been twelve walked out with a beer in her hand. Tables filled most of the Lariat's floor, but there was a platform in the farthest corner reserved for a band (or strippers on Saturday nights). The bar, which covered most of one wall of the saloon, was nondescript and looked like a thousand other bars in a thousand other joints. It was backed with a mirror, lined with bottles, and adorned with elk heads and dioramic beer advertisements. A garish neon sign filled the front window, and except for the glow, the Lariat was poorly lit.

Elbowing her way deeper inside the bar, Britt found a table near the front door. There was an unbelievable din inside. Cigarette smoke hung low from the ceiling; beer, ice, vomit, and broken glass littered the floor. Pulling an empty chair from a nearby table, Britt sat down in as ladylike a manner as possible, but there was no place for Roger. After leaning against the wall waiting for a cocktail waitress that never came, he finally suggested, "I'll order drinks at the bar."

"Good idea," Britt smiled. "I'd like a gin and tonic."

A drunk crashed headfirst onto the floor near her feet, and a wrangler staggered against her table, spilling warm beer on her sleeve. She felt threatened by this unruly crowd, but across the room, she spotted the wide back of Roxy, a woman she knew to be Gene Siegfried's Amazon friend. She had met the young woman briefly at the start of the experiment, and since Britt was newly fascinated with the HVTS, the Hayden Valley Test Subject, she had questions the young woman might answer. Collecting her purse and cigarettes, Britt pushed through the boisterous crowd, intending to snag Roger on the way.

By this time, Roxy was out on the dance floor, whipping her long hair and stomping her feet to a rendition of Led Zeppelin's "How Many More Times?"

Undecided what to do next, Britt stood uncomfortably beside Roxy's table. Should she try again another time? She pulled out a cigarette and abruptly sat in Roxy's vacant chair. A teenager on her left offered her a beer, but she politely turned it down.

"I'd like to talk to that young woman on the dance floor," she shouted above the music."

"Good luck," the teenager laughed.

Meanwhile, Roxy danced on, the queen bee of West Yellowstone that night. Though not a sexy person, she wasn't crude either. She was full of energy, a coarse young woman with the build of a lumber camp cook. As soon as she stopped to grab a beer from the table, Britt jumped up to introduce herself. Her head barely came to Roxy's chin. The younger woman wasn't fat, or big-boobed, she was just big—big, tall, with tanned, heavily freckled skin, brown eyes, and coarse brown hair. Her mouth was thin-lipped, her eyes wide apart. She was nowhere close to pretty, but she had an attractive presence. Dressed in Levis and boots, the sleeves of her shirt rolled past her elbows to display long underwear, she had a carabineer hung from a front belt loop, the proud badge of a mountain climber.

"I'm Dr. Britt Chamberlain, the psychologist from Project Snow," Britt shouted. "I've been trying to get in touch with you about Gene Siegfried."

"What did you say your name was?"

"Dr. Britt Chamberlain. I've been trying to contact you about Gene. I left a note with the dorm mother at Lake Lodge."

"You're that psychiatrist that keeps leaving messages about Gene?"

"YES!" Britt shouted above the noise. "But I'm really a psychologist...."

"Let's get a six-pack to go. What kind of beer you like?"

"I don't have a favorite. Maybe Tuborg, I guess...."

"Tuborg is a bit fancy for the Lariat, but wait'll you try a cold Olympia."

"Yes, let's do," Britt answered, glad to get out of the noisy bar. Roger was talking to a pretty teenager near the bar; Britt decided to leave him to own devices. It was startlingly cold outside, and very quiet now that the earlier traffic was gone. Everyone was either in the bars or going home drunk.

As the two women walked down the uneven sidewalk, they opened a couple beers. Roxy confided, "I fooled everyone this year. I took Thursdays off. I learned my lesson last year, and I'm not going to work with a hangover again. I'm part of the housekeeping staff at Lake Lodge, where you can pace yourself until you feel better, but some of them, like my friend Mack," and she jerked a thumb at a guy and both of the girls hugging him as he exited the bar and headed to his car, "work in the laundry at Lake Lodge. Miserable, hot place for a hangover."

"How'd you meet Gene Siegfried?" Britt asked to guide the conversation.

"Well, after I'd graduated from college—"

"_You_ graduated from college?" Britt exclaimed, deciding Roxy must be older than she thought.

"Yeah, Berkeley, economics, minor in business administration. Anyway, my father, who's a bigwig for Datsun USA—"

"Your father's an executive?"

"I know what you're thinking. I look like a down-and-out hippie, don't I?" Roxy laughed. "I got money in my family, have an education, what am I doing here? I've been through it all before. My dad is short and fat, my mom is tiny, and I can't remember when I wasn't bigger than both of them, my mother sitting on my dad's shoulders. I'm an embarrassment to my parents, so after college I told everyone I was going to travel before settling down. I got a job in Vegas working a blackjack table, spent time in Texas shrimping, and then decided to go to Denver to climb some mountains.

"On the way through Raton Pass, though, I blew the head on my engine," she said. "A wrecker came for me from Trinidad, Colorado, and the characters driving it! The old man had a non-stop mouth, and his son was fifteen years old and four hundred pounds. Nice people. They took my car to a garage they promised could work on a Datsun, and found me a motel. They also invited me to their house for dinner. In that family, all of them are big. Everyone of them was over six feet tall. For a change, I fit right in. During dinner, I told them I was headed north to look for work, and Mr. Siegfried mentioned his other son was working in Yellowstone."

"And that was Gene Siegfried?" Britt asked, remembering the dry notation in his folder: "Next of kin: one brother, three sisters, both parents still alive." What kind of people were they, what values had they instilled in him, and more importantly, what did they think of his participation in the experiment?

"Gene's family is really nice," Roxy said. "They called him long distance, and he talked me into coming up. The personnel office at Mammoth, Wyoming, signed me on as a maid, and I'm glad now. The laundry people are very close and have a good time together, but it's factory work, the same thing day after day—towels and sheets until you're blue in the face."

"So when did you actually meet Gene?" Britt asked.

"I needed help unloading my gear from the car—I'm a mountain climber, y'know and have lots of equipment—and he came over to help me into the girls' dorm. My suitcase still had an old airline tag with my name, Anita, and he—"

"Anita?" Britt asked in surprise, for she thought "Roxy" suited the young woman better.

"Anita—but he christened me 'Rocks Anne' and it stuck. Later, people shortened it to 'Roxy.' Anyway, he helped me get settled. I was expecting somebody fat like his family. Gene's big across, but even his sisters are taller than him."

"This is the kind of thing I've wanted to know," Britt interrupted. "I didn't have a chance to talk with him before the experiment—he was a last-minute replacement, you know—so we had better records on the other volunteers." Suddenly apologetic, she added, "We didn't expect him to last this long...."

Looking back on it, Britt wondered if her early skepticism hadn't been simple prejudice. Didn't their subjects fail because the scientists expected them to fail? Was this the reason Gene Siegfried was so fascinating—because he wasn't programmed to give up? Would she lose her objectivity as her interest in this young man grew?

"Are we talking about the same Gene Siegfried?" Roxy laughed. "Mountain streams run in his veins! He's hiked Yellowstone more than anyone. Rangers used to ask _him_ questions about the backcountry. He's seen a dozen waterfalls that aren't even shown on maps. He knows thermal features no one else has ever seen. He's climbed both summits of Top Notch Peak and found still-standing petrified trees six feet in diameter that no one knew about." Clapping Britt on the shoulder in a most unfeminine way, the younger woman predicted, "He'll outlast all of us."

By this time, they had walked back to the Stagecoach Inn. "Y'know," Roxy said, "Where you're staying is nice, but what you'll need this winter is a place with character as well as clean sheets and indoor plumbing."

"You believe this experiment will last until winter?" Britt asked in surprise. "Do you really think Gene will still be out there when the snow comes?"

"Sure he will," Roxy laughed. "That's why you need a comfortable place to spend the winter." Since they still had a couple beers apiece, Roxy guided the older woman by the arm to the Madison Hotel, across the street from the depot and around the corner from the Lariat. It was small and far less modern than the Stagecoach Inn. Bear hides hung from the walls, mounted heads and antlers were on display, while traps and old guns proudly decorated the stairwells and halls. "The most important thing in this kind of accommodation," Roxy told Britt, "is the color television in the lobby. When winter comes, you'll need human contact to break the monotony; with only one TV in the hotel, you'll have to leave your room to be with everyone else."

Britt appreciated the advice. She was also happy she had finally made a friend in these mountains. To repay Roxy's kindness, a week later she rented a boat to go sightseeing on Yellowstone Lake. The two stopped for a picnic lunch at Stevenson Island, where the blackened ribs of a shipwreck could be seen in the shallow water along the island's north shore. "This was a steamer named E.C Waters, designed to carry tourists on the lake," Roxy said, "but it was never licensed by the park service and ended up being abandoned here. Someone burned it to the waterline in the winter of 1930."

Even after more than forty years, parts of the ship still showed; there were rusty bolts littering the beach and a piece of the engine protruded from the sand.

Sitting near the wreck, Britt asked, "Tell me more about Gene. He built a forge and made some tools, I hear."

"Doesn't surprise me," Roxy said. "He's got a creative eye. He's an excellent carver. You know he had a college deferment, so his only employment has been summer jobs. He worked as a machinist's apprentice at a railroad shop in New Mexico four years ago. The last three summers, he's worked in here in Yellowstone." Whipping off her Stetson, she showed a braided horsehair hatband he had made.

"Gene's dad tried to pressure him into a marketable education like accounting or engineering, but Gene's always done poorly in college. He has something like a hundred credits, but he's changed majors so often, he's nowhere near graduating. A year ago, he dropped out of CSU, got a winter job in a lumber mill in Hyrum, Utah, then took art classes at Utah State at night."

"Really?" Britt said, for there was no mention of his education or experiences in any of her records. She was beginning to understand the more she heard about the Hayden Valley Test Subject, the less she could judge him. Maybe Roxy was right, and maybe her intuition was right too. Perhaps her scientist's mind and all her peers were wrong, for Gene Siegfried might actually feel committed to surviving a year in this endless wilderness.

CHAPTER 8

✳ ✳ ✳

The Rangers' Plans

STILL SOMEWHAT OF a mystery to Britt Chamberlain when he arrived for his second monthly examination on July 15th, Gene Siegfried looked much better than before. He sported a thigh-length elkhide vest, worn with the hair inside and closed with carved antler buttons. His beard had filled in, he wasn't so swollen from mosquito bites, and he had regained nine pounds. Although he still smelled pretty rank, he was cheerful and full of information. The scientists were impressed with his confidence and attitude. His debriefings went smoothly. Afterward, though there were VIPs visiting the project, Gene insisted on taking Doctor Garner aside to talk privately. Finally, when his obligations were finished for another month, he hurried out into the sunshine.

Instantly, three tourists ran up and confronted him as he exited the research center. "It's wrong the kill animals for food," one shouted, then a woman cracked him over the head with a sign and all three pummeled him. Several rangers rushed up and separated them. "You alright?" Jimmy Downes asked.

"I'm okay," Gene said. "The wilderness doesn't do that to me. Only civilization does."

Nearby, another ranger was leaning on an official green pickup in front of the building, speaking with Dr. Britt Chamberlain and a lab tech. Perhaps curious to talk, Siegfried sauntered over, for the tall ranger was Red Reese, now back in uniform after failing to complete his part in the experiment. Clean and well groomed, he was not long separated from the amenities of a supermarket.

"What you got to say?" Reese greeted him, taking off his official green campaign hat and laying it on the hood of the pickup.

"Not much," Gene answered, shaking his hand. "How about you?"

"About the same," the ranger answered. "This man that just helped you is Ranger Jimmy Downes, the naturalist from Fishing Bridge. I guess you know Doctor Chamberlain, our psychologist?"

"Yeah," Siegfried answered, giving her a nod. "I hope I gave you some useful data today."

"You did," Britt said. "Our meeting was very interesting." Interesting was an understatement, for she had spent the interview questioning him about his forging. Strangely opposed to his devoting two-thirds of his time to making weapons, she wanted to know what it was he feared so much. At the same time—despite herself—she was fascinated he so wanted to _kill_ and _eat_. It was ... savage ... to use Siegfried's own word. She wanted him to tell her it wasn't part of his nature prior to the experiment, but on being pressed, he shrugged his shoulders and smiled noncommittally. Now, as she stood there with the rangers, she tried to see something in his eyes to give her a clue into a gentler, artistic character she had learned was within, but there was nothing but a faraway twinkle in his green eyes.

The younger ranger interrupted her train of thought when he abruptly reached between them to offer his hand. "How do you do," he said. "I've heard a lot about you."

"Really?" the young man answered. "How about you, Reese?" he asked, pointedly turning away from Downes to speak with the older man directly. "The Gallatin country pretty bad this year?"

"The snow," Reese admitted. "I lost thirty-four pounds in three weeks, they tell me. I guess I've gained most of it back." He patted his belly humorously.

Putting her hands in the pockets of her pink windbreaker, Britt leaned against the truck like the men and wondered if Gene weren't trying to rub the ranger's nose in his failure. She had heard Reese was still depressed. He was a competitive, ambitious man, and to be "beaten" at something he considered his specialty must be galling. She knew Reese belittled the experiment to other rangers, and she could see he didn't like Gene Siegfried.

"It was worse than I expected," Reese confessed. "I've crossed that country before but it's different wading in the snow twenty-four hours a day. I couldn't get dry, couldn't keep warm. I guess I had psyched myself up for a ski trip, and it ended up being a lifestyle."

"I know what you mean," Gene sympathized, suddenly scratching his crotch. He slept on the ground, he sat on the ground, he ate on the ground, Britt thought, wondering what manner of ant or tick or bug was irritating him. She looked away, a bemused look on her face, and when she turned back, he didn't show any sign of embarrassment. "I froze my tail off too, not that I'm doing better now. They tell me most nights this month it's been in the high thirties, but at least it's not so wet. I do better when I'm dry. You know that other doctor in there?"

"Capland?"

"Yeah, him. He says my tolerance for cold is measurably increasing." Turning to the younger ranger, Siegfried explained, "You see, they put electrodes on my skin and chill me to test my reactions. You wouldn't believe the personal questions these scientists ask."

"Oh, but I would!" Downes laughed. "I've seen the reports on you."

A shadow crossed Gene's face, but he held his tongue. What was he thinking? Britt wondered. He seemed to be measuring Downes, testing him. She was afraid the ranger might say too much. Reese tapped the side of his foot against Downes' boot; the younger ranger contented himself with chuckling.

Ignoring Downes, Siegfried told Reese, "Part of my adaptation to cold is psychological. Not only do I tolerate cold better now, I've learned to control my goose-bumping reflex."

"I thought goose-bumps were natural reactions to heat your body," Reese said.

"No, goose bumps increase your surface area and make you colder. They used to work when humans were hairier because bumps raised the hair and trapped air underneath as insulation," Gene said. "These scientists don't seem to know why Hanson and I've adapted so much better than you—what I meant to say is…"

"That's okay, Gene. I'm not sensitive," Reese smiled magnanimously. "You're doing better than I did." Surprised at the comment, Britt searched his face but could detect no insincerity.

"They tell me I'm the only one who's had no trouble making a fire," Gene said. "That's supposed to be an advantage."

"I had trouble," Reese admitted. "I couldn't take the cold. My fingers were stiff. It sometimes took hours to get a fire lit, and when I did, I got mostly smoke."

"Where'd you go after you left the highway?" Gene asked. "I remember you started on Bacon Rind Creek."

"I went over Fawn Pass to Gardiner's Hole. I made a lean-to east of Quadrant Mountain, next to a lake, but I didn't do any good. Killed a beaver in a deadfall, but that's the only luck I had. I moved closer to the Gardner River, then called it quits."

"You looked pretty miserable when you came in," Britt said, remembering how utterly _wet_ and ragged the ranger had been.

"I couldn't imagine them putting you in that area anyway," Gene sympathized. "Lots of elk in the fall and winter, but in the summer, all you got is moose, and you know how cantankerous they are. What about bears? Up there, if the mosquitoes don't carry you off, the bears will!"

The rangers and the psychologist exchanged a meaningful look, for there _had_ been a bear incident, but the younger ranger tactfully changed the subject. "Did you know only you and Douglas Paine Hanson are still afield?"

"Yeah, me and the Great Outdoorsman, imagine that!" Siegfried laughed. "They tell me Hanson actually gave a news conference in the field. Garner warned me not to talk with reporters because they'll do anything for a story. He says he wouldn't be surprised if they tried coming into the back country to see me."

Again the rangers exchanged glances. Earlier, Britt knew, Reese had been put in charge of security to prevent such incidents. "Gene," the ranger said, "There was something I'd like to ask you. We were hoping we could visit your camp later this week." He spoke hastily, for Doctor Garner and a man in a suit were coming out of the research center.

"I don't know. What'd Garner say?" Gene replied. "He didn't mention it on the schedule." Looking suspicious, Gene seemed to sense a nervousness come over the rangers as the other men approached. Standing next to the men, Britt was just as surprised by the suggestion as Gene was.

"No, it's not on the schedule," Reese admitted, lowering his voice. "It's my personal curiosity. You see—as a former volunteer—I was interested in how it might have been." By now, Garner was almost close enough to hear.

"I don't think it would be a good idea," Gene decided. "You have access to my records. That should be enough. I wouldn't be comfortable with you poking around my campsite." Spinning around to greet the doctor, he said, "I was just leaving."

"Good, it's time you were off," Garner smiled, clapping him on the shoulder, which made a sound remarkably like thunking a hollow log. "G'wan, get out of here. We'll see you next month."

"Catch you later," Siegfried yelled over his shoulder as he jogged away.

"Jimmy?" Garner said as soon as the young man was gone.

"Yes sir?" Downes replied.

"What were you talking about?"

"The kid was asking about Reese and the Gallatin country."

"And that's all you were discussing?"

"Of course. He doesn't have the slightest idea who I am or what I'm doing," Downes said confidently.

"Izzat so?" Garner remarked, tapping his pipe against the bottom of his shoe, then picking at its bowl with a key. Almost casually, he added, "He wants the surveillance team pulled off."

"What?" Downes choked, his jaw dropping to his collar. "He knows?" For her part, Britt was surprised too, and she immediately wondered who told Siegfried he was being watched. "He knows about me?" the ranger asked.

"Yep. He knows how long you've been there, knows your voice, how much you weigh, and that your left boot heel is worn twice as much as your right. He knows all about the two men who've been with you, and he knows they're both back there on the trail waiting for him. He's seen your binoculars hanging from a tree branch, seen your fires at night, and even heard you laughing in the trees. You're a bunch of goddamn amateurs. Naturalists, indeed! Just because you can identify seventy types of wildflowers doesn't make you a woodsman."

"Sir, I can assure you that it won't—"

"I know it won't happen again! I want you and your amateurs out of the back country this afternoon," Garner ordered. "I'm leaving you in command of surveillance, but only for coordination. If _you_ go into the backcountry for any reason, I want to know about it first. You got that?"

The old man spat brown goo onto the gravel at his feet and then indicated the distinguished man to his left. "Senator Mansfield and I have arranged for a new surveillance team. We've got four tough Crow Indians from Montana, all trail-experienced men who don't leave tracks or show fire. They won't make mistakes like you did. They'll be here on the eighteenth, Wednesday. You put 'em on the payroll and have 'em in the field by Thursday."

"Yes sir," Downes mumbled. "I'm sorry I let you down. There's just one thing, Doctor Garner. If I'm supposed to put four scouts on Siegfried, three on and one off to rest—and I'm only authorized a total of six in my budget—does that mean to cut down on Hanson?"

Britt looked at Garner and shook her head imploringly. She had become convinced these difficult circumstances required surveillance.

"No," Garner said, agreeing with her look. "We're letting most of our technicians go. We've only got two subjects afield, and both of them are looking long-term, so I have to plan for the future. We'll allocate funds for an extra scout on LTS Hanson. I want four on HVTS Siegfried. Surveillance goes on. I think it's imperative we take as few risks as possible with these men. I also think surveillance inhibits our subjects' actions. I want you to double or triple the distance from our subjects. This increases our margin for error, and I know it makes losing them a possibility, but I want no more mistakes. Besides, I think the kid's the only one who'll give you trouble. Hanson's more sedentary; he doesn't wander the distances Siegfried does."

"Yes sir. There won't be any mistakes," Downes promised. "I'll have the new men oriented and in position by Thursday."

"Good. We'll see you tomorrow at Hanson's physical." Turning to the senator, Garner said, "The best steaks in Yellowstone are at Roosevelt Lodge. I guarantee a chuck-wagon cookout like none you've had before."

In a rolling radio voice, the Senator Mansfield disagreed, "I've had some mighty fine steaks in my own Montana, let me tell you—"

"Oh, I'm not saying these are the best in Wyoming, just the best in Yellowstone. The best beef in Wyoming is in Cody—"

"At the Green Gables?" the senator asked.

"Yes, that's the one. Cattleman's cut prime rib." The senator got in the old man's battered station wagon and slammed his door, but before Garner got in the driver's seat, he looked back and gave the rangers a hard look.

"Damn!" Reese said under his breath. "Guess that blows the deal for pictures of the kid's campsite."

"To hell with that," Downes muttered, "I didn't like it anyway, but it was a way to keep the reporters out by doing their work for them."

"Surely you're joking," Britt said, but there was something about the way the two men looked at each other that told her differently. "I don't want any reporters out there and Dr. Garner doesn't want any mistakes. Do you understand?"

"Yeah," Downes agreed, "but I don't like the sound of this increasing our distance and hiring new people. There's trouble coming," he predicted.

The rangers and woman had hardly driven away, before Gene Siegfried emerged from the trees, thankful they were finally gone. After retrieving the fisherman's knife from a stump where he'd hidden it near the research center, he hurried straight west to avoid the surveillance team waiting for him on the Howard Eaton Trail. Trotting across the busy highway, he scrambled up a steep slope just as a car skidded to a stop, and a tourist jumped out with a camera.

"Stop!" the dude yelled. "I want a picture."

"Why?" Gene said, posing impudently at the edge of the forest, then bolting into the trees. Behind him, the tourist grinned in triumph, not realizing until several months later that he had taken the only unofficial photograph of Gene Siegfried in the wilderness. It would also be the only one ever published.

The afternoon was warm and pleasant, the sun bright, not a cloud in sight. Making good time, Gene jogged and jumped through the tangled forest like a buffalo calf. For the first time since the experiment began, he felt really alive and happy. Things were going well, and it was time to plan for the future. By mid-afternoon, he was sitting naked in a pool beneath a small waterfall on Violet Creek. Although the water was sulfurous and gritty from the hot springs upstream, he took time to wash his clothes, hanging them from a tree to dry. Using a piece of wood as a scraper, he cleaned his skin in the foaming water and soaked contentedly for over an hour, thinking of his next move.

From his previous explorations, he knew the ridge behind him was steep and too exposed to casual hikers. The meadows and reaches of Mary Mountain to his right would be deeply drifted in winter, and every migrating buffalo and winter bear would travel through, so somewhere on the southern fringes of Hayden Valley, there had to be an open area, easily defended, hidden, yet close to the southern trail and good water.

By late afternoon, he had found such a place on the far western fork of Trout Creek where an intermittent stream emerged from the forest. Beyond the brook, a gentle meadow was hidden by an angle of the trees. This meadow sloped northeast toward the valley, but a small rise and finger of the forest on its western and northwestern edge would protect it from winter's worst.

Scouting into the forest on all sides of the meadow, Gene found buffalo tracks, but no trace of bears. That was a good sign, he thought, for bears were his most important concern. About seventy-five yards into the forest, he located four stout pines a foot in diameter whose nearest live branches were fifteen feet above the ground. The trees were perfect for building a cache. Gene returned to the meadow to dig through the deep grass at the foot of the slope. The soil was good volcanic gravel, dry and cindery to the touch, though it had a vague sulfurous smell. After careful consideration, he decided the area would make a good home, so to christen it, he lit a fire and fixed a dinner of mashed jerky and a roasted root.

So it was that having deliberately eluded the amateurish surveillance team, Gene unintentionally caused the researchers to miss their best opportunity to discover the site of his winter cabin. Although he didn't have a block and tackle, chains, or a proper woodsman's axe, he admitted to Doctor Garner later the only thing he regretted not forging earlier that summer was a pair of hinges for the door. It was one of the few times he admitted a mistake.

CHAPTER 9

‹ ❄ ❄ ❄ ›

Surveillance

A COLD WIND blistered Ranger Jimmy Downes' eyes as he looked through binoculars at the gray-blue feature on the horizon. What attracted his attention represented one of the biggest disadvantages facing him as head of the surveillance team. He was not looking at an identifiable mountain. Though it appeared physical, what he was seeing was a product of his imagination. He was staring at the Sleeping Giant, which resembled an enormous head from Easter Island laid on its back. As he did so, he wondered how a lone man in the wilderness kept a straight course through tangled forests using such ephemeral clues as this.

The Sleeping Giant is not shown on a contour map, for it's an illusion, a combination of prominent landmarks. The feature is not visible from the north, or from the east or west; it can only be viewed from a few scattered meadows between Elephant Back Mountain and Lake Butte. Unreliable as an indicator of distance, the Giant was an example of how inadequate maps really were.

A map might show a trail switchbacking eight times up a thirty-degree slope of four hundred feet, but what does it say about the trail itself? Is it gravel worn into the soil, or a vague trace across the forest floor? Is it shaded from exposure to the sun and likely to have relict snow banks even in July? Is it relatively easy, or a lung-buster that strains knees and jams toes into boots? No, the ranger decided as he lowered his binoculars, simple lines on a piece of paper couldn't compete with the reality of ground experience, and that he simply did not have.

His new surveillance team had the most up-to-date contour maps divided into labeled quadrants, laminated in plastic, and marked with grease pencil. They had two-way radios for coordination, plus compasses, range finders, and binoculars. They could get weather information and resupply any time they needed, and rangers could be called upon for assistance. Thousands of tourists roamed the highways searching for movement that might be a wild animal. Cameras recorded the minutest details, hikers moving down every trail reported everything interesting or unusual—yet the Hayden Valley Test Subject, with none of these advantages, would soon give them a lesson in woodsmanship. Unwittingly, Gene Siegfried was going to elude them every time he was tracked, and he would surprise them every time he seemed predictable.

The Crow Indians assigned to watch Siegfried were good hunters and trackers. Though not inherently better outdoorsmen than others, these men, like most Native Americans, had a reputation and worked hard to maintain it. They were tough, confident, and mature. Responsible not only for reporting Siegfried's movements but also protecting him from emergencies, they were, at the same time, expected to be unobtrusive. They didn't like the rule increasing their distance from the subject, but after a quick orientation hike on Wednesday and an evening of briefings and map study, they decided to establish three small camps near Gene's. He would have no reason to travel or forage north of the Sulphur Hills, so the men arranged camouflaged bivouacs—one to the east which Downes code-named "Vermillion," another to the south, "Pelican," and the third to the west, named "Ebro." To simplify communications, the ranger used these designations as identifiers for whichever man rotated to that site.

On Thursday, the ranger and the four scouts surreptitiously packed in their gear and made camp, taking all possible bear precautions. On Friday, since their quarry still hadn't shown, the Indians explored while the ranger drove up to Canyon Village to talk to Professor Garner. On Saturday morning, Downes set up a radio on a table in a cramped room in Fishing Bridge's natural history museum. Hoping to coordinate his men's movements by radio, the ranger did not want any mistakes from now on.

Being called an amateur by the professor had been the worst insult of his career, and Downes had promised there would be no more slip-ups.

"*Camp-Com, we have the subject,*" one of the men reported by radio Saturday afternoon. As expected, Gene had emerged from the forest to the west and walked nonchalantly home to his campsite at the base of the Sulphur Hills.

"Roger," Downes said, smiling in satisfaction as he pressed a red marker onto a map to indicate the HVTS's location. From this time on, he hoped, there would be few times Siegfried was not under surveillance. The ranger ordered one of the men to rotate out to wait as a replacement, and the other three to settle down in their bivouacs.

Early Sunday morning, Gene fixed a light breakfast of trout and greens, and then set off on a hike. Soon afterwards the western picket reported the subject moving southwest into a grassy meadow near Ebro Springs. Hearing this, Ranger Downes ordered Pelican, the southern outpost, and Vermillion, the eastern man, to intercept him. "Don't lose him," he ordered.

To make as few tracks as possible, both men cut through the forest paralleling Gene's line of travel. Pelican had an especially difficult route to follow, for the area between Pelican Creek and Ebro Hot Springs is full of meanders, quagmires, and tangled blow-downs. Vermillion took a northerly approach up the crumbly ridge of the Sulphur Hills, across the crater and down the cindery slope to the meadow, but when the three scouts linked up at the edge of the forest, there was no sign of their quarry.

"What?" Downes shouted over the radio. "Well, find him—but don't let him know you're there."

"*But he could be anywhere,*" one of the men complained by radio.

"I know that, but find him anyway," the ranger snapped.

Searching the area, the men were ready to give up when Vermillion crossed Gene's trail in a meadow. Hastily regrouping, the scouts tracked their quarry only to discover he had scrounged Everts thistle roots and returned to camp, oblivious to men passing through the trees on either side of him. When they spotted him again, Siegfried was quietly boiling a soup in his pot while polishing his ax with a pumice-like stone.

Squatting just out of sight of the squalid camp, the scouts vented their frustration over the radio. "Our mistake," the ranger decided, "was losing sight of him while linking up. In the future, whoever spots the subject will stick with him; the others will have to catch up the best they can. This way, there shouldn't be a need for tracking."

The next morning, without making a fire or eating breakfast, Gene wandered past Vermillion's camouflaged campsite and headed east toward Pelican Creek Valley. This time, Vermillion followed after him, and the other two scouts converged, exhausting themselves in the process. Together, the three men forded the waist-deep water of Pelican Creek and patiently worked their way closer. They practically stumbled upon Siegfried kneeling at the edge of the forest.

He was digging up a bed of tubers. Minutes after he had gone, the scouts took samples, noted the location on a map and took pictures. Downes ordered them to be sure to erase their tracks. Then, while heading back to the Sulphur Hills, one of the men noticed Gene's tracks were going in the opposite direction. He hadn't headed for home; he was going somewhere else! The surveillance team had lost sight of him again, and this time, Siegfried had a long head start. Expecting to see him at any moment, the scouts trailed after, curious what he was up to next.

By five p.m., it was clear HVTS could not make it back to camp by nightfall; at six, Downes ordered one of the men to walk five miles back to Vermillion's camp for food and a propane stove. The other two kept moving, lost Gene's tracks at sundown, regrouped by radio in the dark, and made camp at ten. "Damn!" the ranger swore. "What the hell's that kid doing out there?"

It rained that night and drizzled all the next day, but, by splitting up and following the tendency of the evening before, the scouts discovered an obscured campsite near Turbid Lake. Indications were that Gene Siegfried had then walked down a muddy service road toward Squaw Lake.

Hurrying after him, the scouts were sure they had lost him again, but about noon, Downes radioed, "A dude spotted him near Mary Bay on Yellowstone Lake. I'll meet you with a car and a fresh scout." Breaking out of the trees, the men ran to the highway to meet the ranger.

Surveying his men after this, their first excursion, Downes shook his head irritably. They were muddy, soaked to the skin, famished, and scratched raw by the forest. Since the Ebro scout was in the worst shape, Downes rotated him out for a rest. The other scouts then moved along the windy shore of Yellowstone Lake, locating their subject by the sound of chopping wood. Before long they spotted him splitting an alder log near Butte Springs.

The yellow wood was obviously difficult to cut, for neither Gene's curved ax nor his small hammer and wedge were suited for heavy logging, but once quartered, the log seemed to split more smoothly. By early evening, he had roughed out a dozen straight poles an inch thick and four feet long. Making camp in the lee of a wind-beaten pine, he used what remained of the alder tree for a comfortable fire. Satisfied he would not move before dawn, the scouts ran back to the highway and hitched a ride to Fishing Bridge, where they rented a cabin, showered, washed clothes, and ate.

Back on the scene by five the next morning, the men watched Gene clean up his campsite and tie the pieces of wood into a bundle for the trip home. This time, the scouts anticipated his destination perfectly; they hitched rides to Pelican Creek Campground and hiked north from there. Gene wandered into camp exactly as predicted, early that afternoon.

For four days, Siegfried did not move from camp, for he was busy fitting the alder shafts onto his javelins. Later, he began to practice throwing at a stout log target; before long, he could hit a plate-sized target three times out of five at a range of twenty-five feet. That wasn't very good, but he learned rapidly; by the end of the week, he could hit the target sixty percent of the time at any range up to fifty feet. The scouts reported the javelins carried enough punch to sink two inches into the pine, enough power to kill a large animal when the time came.

Siegfried then fitted handles on some of his other tools and utensils. Straight chunks of oak left over from the salvaged bannister railing were hammered onto the tangs of his carving tools, and then he riveted grips on his scraper, and elk antler onto a camp knife and awls. While cutting one of the antlers to size, however, he paused and hefted it in his right hand. A yearling's spike he had picked up at Storm Point, the antler was about three feet long with a rough knob where a brow tine should be. The antler curved slightly, and Gene hefted it by this bend, raised it over his head, and swung it swiftly back to front.

Apparently inspired, he laid the spike across his anvil and lopped off the point of the antler with a hatchet. After carving into the knob at its lower end, he trimmed the antler until he had a straight shaft with a hook at one end and an angled handle at the other. The finished product was about two feet long, less than an inch in diameter, and weighed about a pound.

This _atlatl_, or spear thrower, immediately caused a controversy among the scientists as to its inspiration. Where did Siegfried's version of this ancient tool originate? Was it a primal memory, a cultural achievement of long ago locked within the instincts of all humans, or was it unconscious retention of a forgotten documentary on television? Even more incredibly, several of the scientists wondered if the HVTS might have reinvented one of the great weapons of history.

It pointed out, of course, one of the weaknesses of Project Snow. Garner had already observed by the time the subjects were debriefed at the end of the month, the volunteers might not remember their exact inspiration nor be able to express it. So it was that Gene Siegfried's spear thrower became a mystery, a surprise, an unknown variable that caught the researchers unprepared.

For his own part, the young ranger was impressed. "You know," he told Reese one drizzly evening as they drank a beer while sitting on the verandah at Lake Hotel, "There's something extraordinary about this kid, the HVTS."

"What's that?" the older ranger asked.

"I think he's going to last the year."

"Bullshit!" Reese snorted. "We don't know if he can hunt, let alone if he can kill. There's leather to tan, clothes to make, snow to survive."

"Maybe," Downes allowed, "But I have a feeling Siegfried is passing the test in front of our eyes."

Truly, the achievement of a spear thrower was only a first step, but Gene sweated over its best use. Although he would experiment with other *atlatls* during the course of the summer (finally settling on just a simple leather amentum), this first thrower taught him the most important lesson: timing.

Holding the spear thrower with three fingers while gripping a javelin shaft between thumb and forefinger in such a way as to keep the spear's butt engaged in the thrower's hook, Gene taught himself to snap the weapon back, then hurl his arm forward, transferring all five fingers to the thrower as the force of the thrust powered the javelin ahead.

In just days, he developed accuracy and increased his range dramatically. The extra length added to his arm by the *atlatl* magnified the power of his cast, and he soon needed to rebuild his targets. During the next two weeks, Gene practiced until he could maintain accuracy at ranges up to 100 feet. Some of his farthest hurls would strike near a target at 125 feet, but his accuracy was so limited Jimmy Downes doubted he intended to hunt at such ranges. Altogether, however, it was a phenomenal achievement for a lone man in an unforgiving wilderness. Downes was very impressed, though he had learned to hold his tongue around other rangers.

A week after making his first spear thrower, Gene prepared for a trip to his cache. He loaded a pack frame with dried fruits, the last of his smoked trout, his large stock of roots, and most of his tools. As soon as the scouts reported these preparations, Ranger Downes decided they had little chance of following him successfully, so he ordered, "Let's get ahead of him this time."

The moment Siegfried left camp, Vermillion and Pelican dashed through the forest to link up with Ebro. Figuring they had a ten-minute head start, the men broke cover and sprinted west for the Howard Eaton

Trail. Obviously, their subject would never turn south toward Fishing Bridge and its crowds of tourists, so the three men, with Downes' approval, hid in the forest on either side of the trail north of the bridge complex.

Siegfried moved slowly under the heavy pack. When the scouts spotted him again, he was laboring across the grassland toward the trail, but then—to their simple amazement—he did turn south, and they were again in the position of following him. It should have been easy, for the dusty trail paralleled the high, forested bank of the Yellowstone River as it neared the noisy tourist complex. His tracks were easy to follow, especially when he marched through the dusty Fishing Bridge Campers' Cabins. Seen by at least two hundred people, most of whom mistook him for a rougher-than-usual hippie, he passed through the crowd, walked down a busy sidewalk along a bumper-to-bumper highway and disappeared somewhere on the far side of the river.

Jimmy Downes and his scouts wasted a half hour looking for someone who had seen where he had gone. Across the timbered bridge, there were many trails, a thousand footprints fanning out in every direction, any one of which could have been his. While one of the Indians worked his way along the rocky beach of the Yellowstone River, another investigated the deep grass and sagebrush on either side of the road. The ranger and the third scout searched the forest. About an hour later, Jimmy Downes found a weak trail leading north toward Hayden Valley.

None of the scouts could say if the trail were Siegfried's, but they had also found another, slightly stronger trail, the prints of a man under a heavy pack mounting the river bank south of the bridge and meandering toward Lake Lodge. These tracks seemed similar to Siegfried's, and since Downes already suspected the young man planned a permanent residence in the Lake area, he told the scouts, "We'll follow this trail."

The tracks petered out north of Lake Lodge, but the ranger guessed at their tendency, finally deciding, "The path leads toward Elephant Back Mountain Trail. The mountain is perfect for a winter hideout. He knows this area well, because he's spent a few summers working at Lake Lodge."

Pointing up the mountain, he predicted, "Siegfried's up there somewhere. Let's go find him."

Two days later, the ranger told Professor Garner, "I'm convinced HVTS has selected a permanent campsite near the base of Elephant Back Mountain, but we haven't found it yet."

"Do you think he's begun building a cabin?" the professor asked.

"No. He hasn't had time."

"It's imperative we locate this site soon," Garner said.

"Yes sir," the ranger agreed. "I think we've learned enough about this subject's moves that we should have no problem following him in the future."

"I certainly hope so," the doctor said.

CHAPTER 10

❄ ❄ ❄

The Plea

THE RESEARCHERS EAGERLY awaited the Hayden Valley Test Subject when he reported to Canyon Village for his third monthly physical on August 15th. Though he was making important progress in the field, the only contact they'd had with this fascinating subject had been long-range and impersonal. Though the HVTS was still swollen from mosquito bites, the scientists were glad to see he had gained weight. The doctors were pleased with their arcane tests and samples, but in the end, the anthropologists, rangers, and botanists were disappointed with his moodiness. Finally, it was the psychologist's turn.

"Hello," Britt Chamberlain greeted Gene Siegfried as she breezed into her office. After plopping a thick medical folder on a table, she took off her dove cashmere sweater and seated herself at a small desk. As she did so, she looked her subject over and noted a change in him since their last meeting. His green eyes looked narrower and more cunning, but that came, she decided, from sun and smoke. He was quite filthy and smelled, but his beard had filled in and now covered his wide face with a pleasant, reddish wool. At the same time, his hair looked cleaner, probably due to the recent rainy weather, she decided. Nevertheless, he was changing; the daring college boy of just weeks before was different somehow. She felt uneasy in his presence, though she could not put her finger on the reason.

Saying nothing while she reviewed his medical data, Siegfried contented himself with looking around at the plain, plywood walls. He didn't seem nervous, but he didn't appear interested either, and the woman wondered what he had on his mind. She looked up from the folder and said, "You're in better shape than last month."

"I should hope so," he answered with a twinkle in his eye. "Otherwise, I'd be downright miserable."

"Do you think you're miserable now? The first time I interviewed you, I thought you were about to give up."

"No, I'm having too much fun. I may be cold and my stomach may rumble, but I'm coming into my own." Pausing for a moment to let that sink in, he leaned forward in the squeaky metal folding chair and said, "As I understand it, Project Snow is based on the premise you can't dump an unequipped man in the snow and expect him to survive. Is that correct?"

"Yes. There was a previous test in the Garner Experiment called 'Project Ice,' designed to test how quickly the average human could adapt to winter conditions. It was very short-term. Ninety subjects were dropped throughout the arctic north in Canada. It did not last a week."

"So you didn't learn much...."

"Sure we did. We learned we couldn't place the average human in those conditions and expect him to survive for any length of time."

"Very funny."

"We didn't expect to learn much," Britt said. "Survival in those conditions requires highly specialized skills that took generations to develop. An ordinary individual cast into that situation doesn't have time to develop the techniques and tools of survival."

"That's what I figured," Siegfried nodded. "That's why, as a control or whatever you call it in the science business, you had to determine how long it would take for someone to dredge up the necessary survival skills, right?"

"Um huh."

"And what about Project Snow? You had ninety subjects in that other experiment. Why so few in this one?"

"We didn't need so many," she answered. "The purpose of this project is to measure the _time_ of development. Obviously, humans have survived winter conditions as a group, but we needed to know more about the individual. At the same time, we were limited in the number of potential sites, so we decided to run the project closer to home, in the continental United States. The National Park Service, the Bureau of Land Management, and the Forest Service have been very supportive, which has been appreciated because our budget was smaller this year. On the whole, however, I think we got subjects who were better qualified. The average person from our society, when cast into this situation, would not survive for long, so we chose volunteers with experience—except for you." Looking away in embarrassment, she admitted, "You have always been an unknown entity, especially now that you're doing better than everyone else."

"Which brings me to my point," he said. "In this project, there's been plenty of time to develop the skills and means of survival—that's the anthropologist's interest, isn't it? Even so, as much as you guys are beginning to admit I'm doing well, none of you understands what's really going on."

"What do you mean?" Britt asked, wondering why she felt at odds with this fascinating young man.

"You're a psychologist. What are _you_ doing here?"

"I think I've explained that. I'm here to chart your personal growth. What effect is this experiment having on you? How will you adjust? What decisions do you make, and how and when do you make them?"

"That's what I mean. You see, my cultural and mental adaptations are nearly complete. I have what I think I need for survival. I've had time to construct my tools and get myself ready, and now the experiment really begins. All of the misery I've been through was preliminaries. The winter is coming. It's time to shift your focus."

"When you put it that way," she admitted, looking down to brush a spot of lint off her wool skirt, "You're right. The winter is the major focus of the experiment."

"There's much to be learned," Siegfried laughed. "Fall's coming. You scientists act like this is winding down, but it's beginning to get interesting. You want to know if a lone man can survive a winter, given the fact he's had time to prepare himself, so this has been, up to now, a training exercise. None of you will know until spring if you've learned anything about the human animal. I've made steel tools, but is metal the key to success?

"And what if I fail? Doctor Garner thinks that means people cannot do it alone anymore. He believes we can only survive in a group. He tells me humans have come to rely too much on thought, language, memory, and culture—all of which are relatively untried in the grand scheme of things.

"If I succeed," Gene persisted, "you think you've _learned_ something, but if I fail, you think you've _proven_ something. But it won't prove anything," he continued, "except my choice of tools was not proper, or my reliance on certain food sources wasn't correct, or—well, any of a thousand variables. There are too many things you're not taking into account."

"Like what?" Britt asked, feeling very uneasy. What was he driving at, and why did she feel so tense around this young man? Why—and how—was the HVTS so different from everyone else?

"What are you, the psychologist, prepared to learn?" Gene asked. "Have you devised tests to gauge my adaptations? No, you're wasting time theorizing about survival or failure," he told her. "It's all so neat for you. I can do it, or I can give up—that's what you think. For you, this is a game."

"It's not a game…" she answered lamely.

Jumping subjects, he asked, "Have you seen the winters in Yellowstone?"

"No, I haven't," she answered, wondering what he was trying to tell her. "But I've heard—"

"How determined do you think I really am?" he interrupted. "How determined am I to go through with this?"

She sighed audibly. "Very determined, probably to the point of foolishness."

"Foolishness!" he laughed. He obviously hadn't expected that, and he chuckled like a child over it. "Yeah, maybe, but even so," he said, "the focus of this winter's study won't be survival or giving up; it's living until spring … or dying in the snow. The wilderness is unforgiving of mistakes, and since I'm pigheaded enough to give this my best, quitting is not going to be an alternative.

"Stop talking about possibilities and statistical chances," Gene said. "The other scientists probably argue until late at night about survival, but this is not about survival. It's important that you, the psychologist, understand this. The whole thing is going to boil down to one thing: the effects of trying, against all odds, to live, but there are levels of living. What's going to happen to me out there in the snow? Only _you_ can appreciate my progress down the ladder of civilization. I hope you will understand...." He stopped, disappointed at the confusion in her face.

Britt was touched by his appeal, but she didn't know what this young man needed. Why did Siegfried have to be so different from the others? The psychologist's mouth opened and shut helplessly. She simply didn't understand. At the same time, she was convinced the HVTS was doomed to fail. At some point, now or later, Gene Siegfried would give up.

Gene sighed and sat back in his chair. Gene had missed an opportunity of some sort, but then he changed subjects again. "If it came to the point where I had to give up or die," he said, "and if there were time, I would do it, but I'm on the brink of circumstances so alien to you I might not be able to explain them. I don't know what's going to happen to me, except I have to survive because I'm thinking in terms of adapting."

He stopped to collect his thoughts, then continued in a quiet voice, "But you've got a man who cannot think beyond a full belly and leather for his shoes. Douglas Paine Hanson's brilliant—did you ever read his articles?"

"No, I'm not into sports literature."

"Oh, Hanson's far beyond that! He's famous for his ability to give you the feel of the outdoors. I've never met him, but he's stubborn and proud, and Hanson thinks this is some kind of competition. It's a game to him; you survive or you quit, but the time for quitting has almost passed. It'll be September soon. You scientists have an obligation to take him out. Give him an excuse—his blood sugar's too low, his reflexes too slow—give Hanson something to fall back on so he has his self-esteem."

Siegfried has been in the trees too long, Britt decided. He's rambling; he needs to talk; it doesn't have to make sense, it only has to comfort. She looked up from her papers to give Gene another topic to discuss. "What about your friends?"

"My friends?" he snorted in disappointment. "It's time I made like a bread truck and hauled my buns out of here." Putting his hands in his pockets, Siegfried jumped up and stood over her just a moment too long. "See you next month," he said rather sadly.

"Wait," she apologized. "I'm sorry. I still have—"

"No, it's time to go." Gene Siegfried looked uncomfortable. Turning awkwardly, he hurried through the door and walked down the hall to the lobby. Doctor Garner was waiting for him with another man, a tall, pale stranger with skin like cookie dough, whom Garner introduced as Rogers Morton, the Secretary of the Interior. Gene sat with the men, had a cup of tea, and talked for more than an hour. Although the Secretary had little feel for the vast lands under his care, he was an experienced infighter, jealous of budget and with eyes open to Congressional inquiries and environmentalists' claims. The choice of Yellowstone as a site for three of the test subjects—though only two were still afield—was already being called into question in Washington. The Secretary had come to meet the HVTS and LTS test subjects and seemed satisfied Siegfried was not the killer-of-game some in the media were calling him. Instead, the Secretary focused on Gene's failures. He seemed happy with the course of the interview.

Down the hall, a low hum of conversation came from the anthropologist's office, med-techs worked over Gene's samples, and a manual typewriter clacked away in Dr. Capland's room. The scientists were busy, and Siegfried was forgotten for another month. After taking leave of the two men, he escaped into the clean air and bright sunshine and vanished into the pines. Soon thereafter, Britt emerged from her room and walked down the hall for a cup of coffee.

"How'd it go?" Garner asked, lighting his pipe and motioning for her to sit next to him.

"I didn't get much," she confessed. "I certainly didn't get anything like I expected. I've been reviewing my tape of the interview, and I'm more confused than ever."

"Really?" the Secretary said. "We had an informative conversation with him."

"Yes," Garner agreed, "but earlier, before you joined us, I probably had the same conversation with the Hayden Valley Test Subject as Dr. Chamberlain." He pulled his pipe out of his mouth, wiped his lips on his sleeve, and said, "I think Gene's finding out how thinly civilized we really are."

"That sounds like what he was trying to tell me," Britt agreed.

"And he mentioned Douglas Paine Hanson?"

"Yes, that too."

"I think he's right. If Hanson doesn't strengthen by the first snow, we'll have to bring him out."

"Trouble?" the Secretary asked anxiously.

"Just a precaution," Garner smiled. "Hanson's been minimally successful; he doesn't have the necessary surpluses to tide him over the long winter. I'm told Siegfried's making great progress there. He has several hundred pounds of dried fish, meat, roots, and seeds. I'm beginning to believe he's got exactly what he needs."

"You mean he might make it all the way?"

"Yes," Garner admitted. "I'm beginning to think he's going to do it."

"Dammit!" The door banged open suddenly, and Jimmy Downes ran into the research center. "We've lost him again." The ranger hurried down the hall to his radio as Garner looked apologetically at the Secretary, cradled his head in his hands, and sighed.

CHAPTER 11

✳ ✳ ✳

The Grizzly

THEY HAD, INDEED, lost Gene Siegfried again, for in his random way, he had not started directly for home after his physical, but instead disappeared into the scattered lodgepole pine trees west of Canyon Village. Intending to scout the northern trails of Hayden Valley the following day, he made camp beside Cascade Creek, where he knew he would find raspberry bushes. As evening settled in around him, he started a fire and roasted tubers over the coals. Feeling tired after all the stress of debriefing, he unkinked his back and lay down in the long grass. Around him, the normal daytime sounds changed to the eerie rustle of a mountain evening, then the hush of night. As the air grew humid, the scent of mountain flowers filled the air. Occasionally, he heard a car growling down the distant highway and what seemed like laughter echoed from a campground far to the northeast. Birds whispered in their roosts in the pines; bats fluttered silently overhead.

Gene caught himself staring vacantly at the fire, mindlessly lost in the shadow of a thought. "Huh?" he said aloud, brushing hair away from a suddenly ticklish brow. What a beautiful night, Gene thought as he looked upward, a night more beautiful than any so far this summer. Millions of twinkling stars glimmered in the velvety sky. The Milky Way was a brilliant band of white across a black-velvet sky, and other stars—red, blue, silver, green—twinkled high above his head in a splendor never matched.

Swaying slightly, Gene leaned forward to look into the fire—the most magnificent flames he had ever seen. A drop of saliva dribbled out of his mouth and down his bearded chin, finally dripping onto his jeans.

"What?" he said in amazement, for it was the coldest spit he had ever felt. Siegfried reeled drunkenly and put a hand to his chin. Wait! Was his chin numb—or his hand? Shaking his head violently, he slumped over and groaned. What was happening? The ground rippled like a snail beneath him. Throwing his head back to get the ticklish hair away from his brow again, he glanced at the trees around him. Yellow eyes shone from a thousand shadows, but when he reached for a javelin, it slithered away from his fingers like a snake.

"Aaaaah!" he screamed, and the cry echoed a thousand times, forcing him to cover his ears. Somehow, he got to his feet, but he fell immediately. Siegfried's tongue was swollen and beginning to hang out in the dirt, his heart hammered like it would beat a hole through his ribs, and his fingers twitched uncontrollably. What was wrong? He scrabbled back to the fire, picked up a red coal, and crushed it in his fist. There should have been pain, but Gene didn't feel a thing as he showered the sparkling ash back into the fire. Struggling to sit upright, he became hypnotized by the flames again.

The night was full of strange noises. He could hear not only the flapping of bats but also their sonar whistles, and somewhere behind him, there was the trepidacious patter of a small animal, possibly a mouse or mole, its ears beating the air in search of sound. Surely, the little one could hear him breathing—HE WAS BREATHING, WASN'T HE? Yes, he reassured himself, his chest was still moving shallowly.

Straightening up with difficulty, he punched himself in the face. "THINK!" he shouted, and it seemed to echo in his head, *"Thinkinkinkinkink."*

"DO SOMETHING!" Gene thought, and it echoed back, "Do something... thingthinginging...."

"I'VE GOT TO THROW UP!"

"Upthrowupthrowupupupupowup...."

Coming to his feet like a puppet on a string, he forced two fingers as far down his throat as he could and vomited his dinner into the fire. Sparks popped away into the night, and a pink mist rose all around him as his belly convulsed. Dry-heaving and choking on the bile, he moaned, "WATER," and again, the sound echoed,"terwaterwatererter."

Worse than any commode-hugging drunk, his malady took him. Neither crawling nor walking to the little stream burbling near his campsite, he managed to wallow in the shallows to drink and heave and drink and heave again. His head thumping painfully, he explored his teeth with his tongue, spitting out bits of food trapped there, and then he retched and vomited on the aftertaste. Silver minnows nipped his swollen hands in the water. Tears poured down his cheeks and into the corners of his mouth, making him gag on the salt; blood ran from his nose and congealed in his mustache and beard.

Siegfried forced himself to drink again, but he threw the water right back up, still cold. Around the fire, tall trees leaned over to watch this misery; there was a whine coming from the stars, and Gene's feet seemed so shrunken he worried his boots might come off in the stream. Moments later, the boots felt so tight, he thought his swollen feet would surely break the laces. Slowly realizing it wasn't good to lie in the icy stream for any length of time, he crawled back to the fire, wrapped himself around the bleached trunk of a fallen pine, and hid his face in the runic trails of long-dead bark beetles.

The next time Gene looked up, it was daylight, about ten in the morning by the angle of the sun. The fire had burned away and was now sifting white fly ash in the breeze. Crawling back to the stream to wash his face, he scraped water bugs aside and drank his fill. Still wobbly, he decided he felt a bit better. Gene dusted himself off, retied his boots, picked up the javelins he had brought, and staggered away from the campsite, not knowing nor caring where he went.

A strange paranoia seized him as he dared to walk alone in this trackless forest. Every shadow in the trees, every creak of wood and rubbing of branch among the ship-mast pines, even the tapping of woodpeckers, or the chattering of squirrels, the unexpected plop of a pine cone, sometimes even the silence was enough to set his nerves on edge. Hypersensitive to such stimuli, Gene found every sound terrifying. He saw danger in every shadow, and he moved slowly, testing the wind and searching the trees for movement.

Eventually, Siegfried came to an open glade. Feeling danger behind him, he dashed across the grass and hid in the trees beyond. There was nothing back there, he saw with relief, but the pines mocked him; squirrels laughed from above, but he didn't care. Wait! Gene thought. Was there movement back there? No, he decided after staring at it for ten minutes. It was nothing but a breeze sweeping through the grass.

A few minutes later, he discovered an abandoned roadway in the trees. Grass grew in the middle of the track and small pines rose like sentinels on either side of the road, but Gene felt safer here, and he moved cautiously westward, stopping to drink from ponds that shone through the trees like black mirrors. Small clearings tempted him to stray, and stray he did, but each time, he returned to the road because it seemed safer than the forest. About noon, he stopped to rest next to the bole of a huge, wrecked pine, one of few hereabouts in this forest. After sleeping peacefully for three hours, he felt better, but still with a nagging paranoia. What was wrong? Why did he feel so strange? The afternoon sky was gray and brooding, and Gene could sense danger.

Confused, he wandered down the cracked asphalt looking for meaning. He found it in a pile of dung. It was brown, fresh, and looked like a man's, but each turd was thick as his wrist. Bear sign—grizzly by the size of it, he realized. It was full of grass and what looked like cardboard. From the way the stools were pointed, the bear had been traveling the same way he was.

Gene picked up a stool and squeezed it between his fingers, wondering if he felt any heat in it or was it only the warmth from the asphalt? Still stinky, the grizzly sign had few flies on it, so it was fresh. Scared, he straightened up and looked around, but there was nothing to see but trees and grass in every direction. Wiping his messy hand on his jeans, he set off toward the west.

Within minutes, he discovered the reason for a bear in the area. A garbage dump was hidden deep in the trees, its electric fence humming with menace, but there were at least three places where bears had simply dug under the wire to get to the trash. Dozens of ravens and seagulls sitting among the piles of trash greeted him with their cackles, but he turned away and continued up the road.

This was all so strange. Gene tried to think, but something important kept slipping away just as he was about to discover it. Oddly, the harder he concentrated, the slower he walked. Confused, but feeling he was in danger, he decided to walk and not think, but then a musky smell came drifting by on the breeze. He looked around at the forbidding forest. A headache crept up the back of his neck and hammered inside his skull. CONCENTRATE! Looking around, he knew there was nothing here to fear, but he was afraid anyway and despised himself for it. Cold sweat rolled down his chest, and his upper lip and palms grew moist. A highway must be nearby, he figured, and since he had just come from the east where the road was worse, the highway had to be to the west.

The scraggly trees got shorter the farther he moved away from the dump. There was gray, brooding sky visible between the spindly treetops, and he scanned the horizon for landmarks but couldn't spot a familiar vista anywhere. Suddenly, without conscious thought, he whirled around and looked back. Did he see something? No. There was nothing there, but his hackles rose, and his palms dripped sweat. CONCENTRATE, he ordered himself, and the headache knocked inside his skull. Moaning, Gene fell to his knees and vomited until he thought he was going to turn his socks inside out. A minute later, he was on the move again. Thinking he heard a slight noise behind him, he whirled around a second time and peered down the road. NOTHING! It was just a hallucination. There is nothing back there, he told himself. Turning away, he walked on, but then the scent of musk drifted past again.

He spun around. Was that a shadow, a shape of some sort? Yes, Gene decided. There was something there. The scent was stronger now. A small pine off to the right twitched as if something had brushed past. Back down the road, he could see in his peripheral vision something coming toward him, but it was at least three hundred yards away. The musk was strong—a bear was near.

Fitting a javelin into his spear thrower, Gene backed slowly up the road. It was hard to tell where the scent originated, so he chose to crowd the left shoulder of the cracked asphalt rather than exposing himself in the middle of the road. He had no illusions how long he might last in a charge, for any animal that could move fifty miles a day through this rough country—and that was not unusual for a bear—could clear the width of this road in a bound. Step by step, he crept backward, eyes darting from side to side. He listened and sniffed as hard as he could, but he sensed nothing. When Siegfried glanced back down the road, he could see a man running toward him.

There was a tingling at the base of his neck; his hackles rose like they had a will of their own. He could hear the running man shouting into a radio, "*Ebro, come in Ebro. This is Pelican, over*," and then he knew, without knowing how or why, the bear was behind him.

There are two kinds of bears to fear in Yellowstone: black bears, which can be almost any color, and grizzlies. Blacks normally weigh between two and three hundred pounds—though that depends on the season, for a bear's weight fluctuates wildly—and they are sometimes teased and tormented like overgrown dogs, but dogs they are not. Humans bred dogs and have been their masters for thousands of years, and no friendly dog can look a human being in the eye for long, but a bear, like a man, has a will of its own, and it shows in its eyes.

Grizzly bears are much bigger than blacks. Grown sow grizzlies can weigh four hundred pounds. Boar grizzlies can weigh twice that, and some legendary bears weigh over a thousand pounds. Such grizzlies might be eight feet long, nose to rump, and stand nine feet tall.

Such was the bear Gene Siegfried faced when he turned around. He was looking straight into the belly of a shaggy boar standing not ten feet away. If he had continued walking backwards, he might have bumped into it.

The bear's shoulders appeared round and droopy as it stood there, its rib cage looked grossly narrowed, its front legs seemed to bend in mid-forearm where its enormous paws dangled over its pooched-out belly, but Gene's first impression was one of coarse strength. Each of its straight, yellowed claws was as long as a man's fingers. The grizzly squinted at him out of bloodshot eyes, its sloppy nose held high as it sniffed the cold air. Apparently, it had been playing with him, testing him, silently jockeying him into position. Perhaps it was the bear's perverse sense of humor that made it sneak up behind him so quietly—and that's the trouble with bears. They are too intelligent to be controllable or predictable. A moose would attack in a tense situation, an elk would react hysterically, but a bear might stand there plotting its next meal or grinning at a good joke.

Not far away now, the other man was whispering into his radio, "*Affirmative! Boar on the service road. HURRY!*"

The bear glanced at the interloper, and then blinked to better see the little man standing in front of it. Its long, pink tongue snaked out of its mouth to lick its squarish snout, but otherwise, it didn't move anything but its eyes, and it made no sound at all.

Gene slowly inched his right arm back, a javelin ready in the spear thrower. Knowing he would not have much time, he raised another javelin in his left hand to point at the boar's throat. Siegfried was ready for the throw, but suddenly he stubbed his hand into a six-foot sapling growing behind him. Startled, he fumbled the javelin, and it fell clattering to the gravel—a lifetime away now, he realized. He raised the second javelin in his left hand and took its butt firmly in his right as he aimed at the boar's windpipe. Somewhere off to the north, a siren moaned, and Gene could hear gravel scattering, a car door closing, and a clanging of metal. The man behind him stood stock-still. Gene could hear radio traffic and the pounding of his own living heart.

Turning to its right, the bear dropped to all fours, stepped into the stunted pines beside the road, and disappeared as a green ranger patrol car came squealing down the broken asphalt.

"You all right?" the ranger asked as he jumped out of the vehicle, a mean-looking shotgun in his hand.

"Yeah, no trouble here," Gene answered. His knees were trembling, and he felt sick to his stomach.

"Biggest bear I've seen in two years!" the ranger exclaimed. Looking over Gene's head at the other man, he asked, "You okay, too?"

"I'm ... fine," the man puffed.

Spinning about, Gene extended his hand. "Thanks, I was lucky you happened along."

The man, an Indian with long thin braids hanging from beneath a baseball cap, glanced at the ranger meaningfully and said, "I was doing a timber survey on damage done by bark beetles ... and I happened onto your camp. It looked like you were in trouble—"

"Both of you okay?" the ranger interrupted diplomatically. "I know there are people in Canyon on pins and needles right now, so how about I give you a ride back?"

"Sure," Gene agreed, relieved the adventure was over. "I've been sick. I think I should talk to the botanist."

"And you?" the ranger asked the other man.

"No, thanks. I have a ride coming for me already. I'm supposed to meet it up on the highway." He gave the ranger another look and then shouldered his rucksack. "I'll be okay. That bear isn't anywhere near here now."

"Okay, suit yourself," the ranger said.

"I appreciate what you did. It took a lot of courage to come up behind me like that."

"To tell the truth," the man said. "I never saw anybody with more balls! I was pissing my pants, but you were ready to kill that goddamned bear—"

"I don't know who would've been killed, me or the bear," Gene admitted as he opened the car door. "I'm just glad we didn't have to find out."

"Even so," the scout said, "you were very brave."

Stifling a gag—probably at Gene's earthy mixture of months-old sweat—the ranger made Gene roll a window down for ventilation, then started the car. Sorry he wouldn't have a chance to get to know the Indian better, Gene stretched his head out of the window. "Thanks again," he called.

"Take it easy," the scout said, waving.

The gate barring the service road was just a short distance off the main highway, in a third-rate thermal area of gritty, pastel gravels. After locking the gate behind them, the ranger switched on his radio to check in, and Gene accidentally heard the last of a transmission on the same frequency: *"Right. I'll meet you there, and then we'd better get down by the bridge. He's on his way to Canyon Village with a ranger. This is Pelican, out."*

"That's a strange name, isn't it?" Gene commented. "Pelican. I wonder if it's an Indian name."

"What's that?" the ranger asked.

"Pelican."

"Maybe," the ranger answered as he took a mike from the dashboard. "Canyon Station? This is Mobile Four, over—"

"Mobile Four, this is Canyon. What is your situation?"

"Canyon, we had a positive bear sighting near the barrier of the dump road. Boar grizzly, prime, estimate niner zero zero pounds, classic silver tip, no distinguishing marks. All is well. Am bringing Hayden Valley Test Subject to Canyon Research Center. Estimate time of arrival in ten minutes, over."

"We'll meet you there, Mobile Four. Say again, subject okay? Over."

"Canyon, that is affirmative. Subject is fine, out."

Gene was in the examination room for three hours. Capland and another doctor prodded and tested him, but they could find nothing wrong, and in the end, they reluctantly agreed to let the experiment continue. Doctor Garner came into the room with a "Souvenir of Yellowstone Nat'l Park" pillbox on which he had soldered a strong neck chain, and he gave it to Capland to fill with a powerful purge or cathartic.

"And you," Garner said, turning to lecture the nearly naked subject sitting on the examination table, "will not poison yourself again during the course of my project. Do you understand?"

Slapping Gene's muscular leg affectionately, he continued in a more serious tone, "As you know, we didn't give our subjects emergency kits or first aid supplies. We had hoped that if there were any problems like illnesses, injuries, or infections, our subjects would come in, and we'd treat them. You, however, are an adventurer at the dinner table, and I don't want you getting sick on something that will affect your judgment. Do not poison yourself again."

"Yes sir," Gene promised. "Did you get in touch with the botanist?"

"As a matter of fact, we did. He's out at your campsite right now. He says he's found several things, but he thinks the culprit was low larkspur. Mean stuff, apparently. He'll be in with some samples. Try to remember how much you ate; that might be important. You're feeling all right now?"

"I'm okay," Gene said, though in reality he felt an odd spaciness fogging his thoughts. An occasional low-grade headache would plague him the rest of his life.

"You're sure? No complaints at all?"

"No sir. Not one."

"We're going to let you go back out there. If anything does develop later—something in your stools, a rash, a fever, no matter how minor— you get back here and have it checked out."

"I will," Gene promised, wondering if he should mention the spaciness he felt. After a moment's reflection, he decided to wait. If he still felt this way next week, he'd point it out. "I'll come back if I have to," he promised.

"Good. Capland will give you something to carry with you at all times, and he'll tell you how to use these medicines. After that, I understand Dr. Chamberlain wants to talk to you, and we both know what she wants. Be sure to consult with the botanist, and finally, I hear some rangers are here to speak with you."

"Hold on just a minute," Capland protested. "I was hoping to keep him overnight for observation."

"We'll leave it to Gene. Stay overnight, or camp nearby, what do you say?"

"I'll stay close, but I'll be gone in the morning."

"Fair enough," Garner agreed. "Now get out of here. Dr. Chamberlain's in the lobby."

She was standing in front of a dirt-streaked window watching the evening fall. "Hello, Gene," she greeted him as he entered the lobby.

"Hi," he answered. He had had the fire taken out of him in the last few hours, and the last thing he wanted was to talk about his feelings with the psychologist, but somehow her attitude and sadness soothed him. She had changed since he'd last seen her. She was wearing jeans, hiking boots and a flannel shirt. Roxy must be having some influence on her.

"Doctor Garner and I had a disagreement earlier today about this," she said, "but I want to offer you a chance to pull out of the experiment gracefully. No one can blame you for quitting now. No one will think badly of you. Dr. Garner has suggested I'm losing my objectivity, but considering how gung-ho everyone is, I think you might not be getting a fair chance."

Her face showed she didn't expect him to agree, and he didn't. In fact, he chuckled at the suggestion. "I'm more determined than ever to finish the project," he said. "I appreciate your concern, but things are going to be okay."

"Gene—" she tried, but then the door banged open and a thin, balding man entered, carrying a paper bag. Coming between them, the botanist laid a number of roots on a small table under the window; though none seemed exactly familiar, Gene pointed out three that looked similar—two of the samples were larkspur.

"You were lucky," the man said, shaking his head. "I'm surprised you weren't much, much sicker." He cautioned Gene to be careful in the future.

Minutes later, Gene was allowed to go outside, where he found three rangers. He recognized Red Reese, Jimmy Downes, and one of Canyon's rangers. "We could take care of the problem for you," Reese said, putting his hands in his pockets.

"What problem?"

"We could eliminate the troublemaker."

"The bear?" Siegfried asked incredulously. "NO! The incident—if you want to call it that—was blown out of proportion. If anyone's to blame, it's me. Besides, it was a fluke I was even up there. There's no reason for me to be in the area from Junction to the Blanding Hill. I'll never see that grizzly again."

"You sure?" Reese asked. "It's sometimes hard to figure out what's in a bear's mind. Really, it would be no problem—"

"Don't bother. I stumbled on the bear on the trail, and it took off right away. Let it go."

"Gene, it's hard for us to ignore something like this," Reese persisted. "Ever since that incident at Glacier National Park six years ago and that guy getting killed down at Old Faithful last year, there's been publicity, and too many political inquiries over our management of the bears and the park. We rangers work with grizzlies all the time, and we see what they do. We're the ones who have to live-trap the bears and keep records on them. We know what they're _really_ like. They're no good, Gene. We're concerned about you. We might not be able to help you much, but if we can be of assistance now, we would be glad—"

"Forget it, Reese. You and I got into it once before, two years ago, when you killed that grizzly cub down in Bridge Bay."

"That was an accident," Reese said, crossing his arms over his chest.

"Some accident. You had him trussed up in a culvert trap. What harm could he have done? He was just a frightened, eighty-pound cub. Reese, you're a bear-hater from way back, and I can't change that, but I'll tell you this: when I started working in Yellowstone in 1969, you couldn't walk through Hayden Valley without stepping in bear shit. But look at things now! I didn't see more'n two bears last summer. And grizzlies? You don't see them at all. Few tracks and little sign. You rangers tell everybody the bears are in the backcountry, but I _live_ in the backcountry, and I know differently. You leave this boar alone. I saw it on the trail, that's all there was to it."

"We've heard a different version, Gene," Jimmy Downes said, smiling at the other rangers.

"I'm telling you," Gene interrupted him. Though he was shorter than the other men's chins, his bulk and the look in his eyes must have made it seem as if he towered over them; the rangers leaned back on their truck, unconsciously crossing their arms over their chests. "THAT'S ALL THERE WAS TO IT."

"Okay," Downes gulped, glancing at the other men.

Gene glared at them, and then caught sight of the woman in the window. Did she know what was happening out here? Probably not, for this was unofficial and private. Weeks later, he would think of this moment when his friends Mack and Roxy met him for a visit. Roxy told him the bear had been killed only two days after the incident. It had been seen "too near" Canyon Campground and "accidentally" overdosed with a tranquilizing dart. Gene didn't ask who shot the bear. He knew.

That night, however, convinced he had won the point, he camped off in the trees where his fire could be seen from the Research Center. Next morning, he jogged south on the Howard Eaton Trail across the eastern march of Hayden Valley. He paused for a quick bath in the toy falls on Sour Creek, and then hurried to his camp in the Sulphur Hills, glad this adventure was over.

CHAPTER 12

✳ ✳ ✳

The Hunter

ONE MORNING, GENE Siegfried took three javelins and hiked into Pelican Creek Valley to hunt. Skulking along the edge of the forest in the very peach of dawn, he seemed to be searching for something in particular, but from their vantage on a low hill west of him, Ranger Downes and his surveillance team couldn't see what caused him to drop suddenly to all fours in the high grass.

After glassing the area for only a moment, one of the Indians reported, "There are three sets of antlers sticking up above the grass on the rise where the sagebrush thins. Three bull elk there two hundred yards north of our subject." He lowered his binoculars and pointed. "They're facing downslope to the northeast."

"I don't see them," Downes said, hating to admit there was something he couldn't do. Stung by Doctor Garner's accusations he was an amateur, he was embarrassed that what these experienced scouts did so easily, he could do only with effort. Moments later, the ranger found the elk, and though he smiled grimly, he was still frustrated it had taken him longer than the others.

Even at a distance, he could see one of the elk showed signs of the velvet peeling from its antlers. The bull's hormones were preparing it for the coming competition of the rut, but it lay there peacefully with its mates, three contented bachelors chewing their cud in the sunshine, blinking condensation from their long lashes. One bull lay upslope, one to the far right, the last to the left. The ranger could see the elk weighed around five hundred pounds each—not yet full size, but not small either. About eight feet long, nose to rump, the bulls would stand at least four feet high at the shoulder.

Looking them over with his high-powered naval binoculars, the ranger noticed the elks' antlers had four or five tines on a heavy beam, indicating they were probably all between four and six years old, though antlers were not a sure indicator of age. A yearling might have just a spike, a two- or three-year-olds' rack was heavier, while a full-grown bull's rack might weigh fifty pounds and be five feet across. It had always amazed him that antlers, which were not grown for protection but for the competition of the rut, were shed each year about March and grown back by August. A rack increased in size until a bull's seventh or eighth year, then diminished—if it lived that long.

Ranger Downes, whose specialty was natural history, knew fallen antlers were often gnawn by rodents, predators, and other elk starved for nutrients; the antlers were a valuable source of calcium in these deficient mountain soils. A prime bull with such antlers could satisfy a harem of fifty receptive cows and then die, too weak to survive the winter.

The bulls he was observing were big enough to challenge some harem masters later that fall, but right now, they were resting innocently, unaware a man must be crawling nearer. The wind was blowing towards them from the valley; there was no sound, no hint of danger until the flash of a javelin flying so closely over one bull it parted the hair on its withers. Jumping to their feet, the elk flashed their tails in alarm. At the same moment, Gene sprang out of the grass only fifty feet away as he hurled a second javelin. As the surveillance team gasped in surprise, he made a hit, and a bull, the shaft sticking from its rib cage, stumbled and tried to run after its companions. Hurrying after the elk, Siegfried retrieved his first spear and then ran downslope to cut the wounded animal off.

The other bulls turned to check out their pursuer, then poured on speed and disappeared over a rise on their way back into the forest, but Siegfried outmaneuvered the injured elk and forced it into the valley. The bull stopped and looked around indecisively; it then turned east into the rolling sagebrush of the open valley. Siegfried let it go. Though half a mile away, Downes could see pink froth on the elk's nose, the sure sign of a lung hit, and the ranger knew it would take some time for the bull to calm down and stiffen.

Sure enough, an hour later, following the tracks and blood trail, Siegfried surprised the elk in some sagebrush overlooking the valley. The bull awkwardly lumbered to its feet and trotted away; since it was less than a hundred and fifty yards ahead of him now, Gene ran after it, jumping the tangled sagebrush like a hurdler until he had narrowed the range to fifty yards. Stopping suddenly, he threw—but missed—with another javelin.

Once again, he had to retrieve his weapon and run after the elk, this time as it turned west toward the startled surveillance team. The ranger motioned for his men to get down. "If we move, Siegfried will spot us," he hissed, but as it was, the elk's wobbly course led downslope, closer to Pelican Creek. Gouts of blood and bubbles spotted the brush in its wake, but as it staggered along, it was apparent to the ranger the elk's slowest pace was Gene's fastest. Watching the drama unfold through his binoculars, Downes could see Siegfried was winded.

Gene had the body of a weight lifter, not a sprinter, and besides, this desperate race was at an altitude of nearly eight thousand feet. Twice he fell down, his feet tangled in the bonsai branches of the sagebrush, but despite this, he narrowed the range, threw a spear and again missed, but this time didn't hesitate. With his lungs probably on fire, he ran on until just twenty-five yards from the bull before hurling his last javelin. Remarkably, the spear was deflected by a sagebrush, slithered across the grass and bounced up, striking the bull below its left front knee.

Siegfried pulled his ax from his belt and ran after the crippled elk. Glancing over its shoulder, blood running out of its nose, the frantic bull tried to get away, but Gene caught it by snatching at the javelin shaft in its side. Circling warily, the elk fenced at him with its antlers, but as soon as the back of its head was exposed, Gene slammed his ax into its brain, dropping it in its tracks. Five hundred yards away, the three Indians and the ranger clapped each other on the back gleefully, for they had finally witnessed (and photographed) Siegfried's success as a hunter.

"By golly I think he's going to make it," Downes proclaimed over the radio.

"*You don't mean that?*" Ranger Reese answered from Canyon Village.

"I do. He can hunt. He's got everything he needs to survive now."

Reese was impressed. He had believed javelins and that silly spear thrower could not kill, but after hearing of this success, he realized the weapons were a potent combination. Give the kid more practice and he might turn into a hunter. Still a bit skeptical, Reese wrote in his surveillance log, "HVTS has proven he can hunt, but will it be enough to carry him once the snow starts flying?"

For his part, Downes figured Doctor Garner would be pleased, and he knew the other scientists at the research center would be glad to hear Siegfried was doing well too—except that psychologist, of course. She would find something wrong with this too, the ranger thought bitterly. She criticized every success, but it didn't matter. A successful hunt would almost certainly make it easier for the HVTS to last a couple more months, and it strengthened his chances for the winter. Glancing at the three Indians, the ranger saw they were also rooting for Siegfried. Yes, the ranger thought, Gene was giving it his best effort. Picking up his binoculars again, the ranger resumed his surveillance.

After sitting on the dead elk's hip for a few minutes to catch his breath, Gene finally got up, raised one of the bull's rear legs with his shoulder to lever the carcass on its back, then ripped into the tender belly skin with a camp knife. Opening the elk from penis to sternum, he broke the aitchbone and rolled the carcass on its side. The body was full of blood, and blood flowed out of the chest cavity like water from an overturned children's wading pool. A fog of steam and gas enveloped him, but he cut off the bull's lower legs, skinned the elk, and began butchering.

Almost immediately, a raven landed nearby, noisy and demanding now that there was meat. Fluttering about the kill, it was too wary to come within reach, but it was familiar enough to gobble up scraps as Gene worked. In less than an hour, the man and raven were both covered with blood.

The Indians and Jimmy Downes were intrigued by the appearance of the bird. None of the scouts had mentioned it in their surveillance reports, but looking at their faces now, Downes realized they seemed to accept the raven's behavior as normal. Wondering if they viewed it as a mystical relationship, Downes made a note to have Gene questioned about the bird next time he was interviewed. Somehow, the raven's familiarity was more than what the scientists would call a symbiotic relationship, and it worried him. Ravens weren't supposed to act this way. He remembered seeing a raven fly over the area shortly before Siegfried disappeared into the grass. Had it reacted to the elks' presence and thereby alerted him?

Producing a piece of salvaged plastic from his pocket, Gene placed the kidneys, heart, drained bladder, and liver on it. He made no attempt to save anything else from inside the bull; instead, he kicked the guts aside for the bird. Breaking through the sternum with his ax, he opened the bull's rib cage like cabinet doors, severed the head and broke open the skull for the brains and tongue. Tossing the wrecked skull to the gleeful bird to ravage its eyeballs and sinuses, Siegfried began to hack meat off the skeleton. When finished, he had a knee-high pile of lean meat weighing about two hundred pounds, plus a heavy, cinnamon-colored hide.

Several hard pack trips later, he had all of the meat back in camp; he spent the next two days slicing and hanging it from racks to dry. By now he looked like a successful hunter, for there was gore all over him. Dried blood was caked under his fingernails, blood and grease stained his beard, his ragged jeans were stiff with blood from the knees to the cuffs, and his shoulders were streaked and greasy from carrying meat to camp, but to the surveillance team, he looked happy, and he appeared full, the first time he had looked so full in weeks.

Gene built a dozen smoky fires around his camp to protect it while he jogged down to Pelican Creek to bathe and wash clothes. An hour later, just as he crossed a clearing on his way back to camp, a clatter arose from the trees to his right, and a bull elk, bigger than the one he had killed the day before, charged into the clearing—spooked, as it turned out, by one of the surveillance men paralleling Gene's course. Surprised to see another man in this untraveled area, the bull skidded to a stop, and then turned its massive, antlered head toward a different course. Before the elk could bound away, Gene's first javelin, thrown purely on instinct, struck the bull in the throat. The elk gave a bubbly squeak and swiveled nimbly around, then bounded three times, only to be hit in the rump by a second javelin. Startled, the elk stopped in its tracks, its eyes bulging in fear, then it wiggled its rump to throw the spear, its front knees bent, and it rolled on its side and died in a puddle of blood.

Two elk in two days! Siegfried danced ecstatically around the bull. He chanted something quite indistinguishable and seemed pretty proud of himself, but Ranger Downes and the Indians knew the second bull was pure luck. Most of Gene's kills would be as difficult as the first, and in the future, he would pay in sweat and blood for every pound of meat. This time, though, since the carcass was practically in camp, he saved everything remotely useful. He carried in the intestines and long bones, as well as the hooves and antlers, but the broken skull, spine, and hip were scattered for the scavengers.

Boiling the bones in his dented pot, he cracked them and scraped the marrow into the broth. He added roots and herbs, diced the brains and dropped in slivers of liver. One of the scouts in the trees muttered into his radio,

"Damn! The smell's making me hungry."

"Yeah," another answered, *"he's making me hungry too."*

While the meal bubbled over his fire, Gene cut meat for the drying racks and laced the new hide hair-to-hair with the first skin on the frame. He slept little that night, for he had fires to tend. He was obviously afraid of marauding bears, but he also kept busy with preparations to abandon camp. By this time, the scouts were sound asleep and they missed the activity, but Jimmy Downes, back in Fishing Bridge writing a report, was confident their quarry was tied to camp for at least two weeks. He decided to drive up to Mammoth Hot Springs to take care of business.

During the next four days, the scouts watched as Gene scraped and fleshed his hides. When the skins were as dry and stiff as pieces of plywood, he cut them down from the frame and, using his bare feet, he kneaded a mixture of wood lye and brains into them. Later, stretching the skins over a post to make them flexible again, he worked clarified elk grease into the leather. When the hides were as soft as old cotton underwear, he smoked them for color and smell and trimmed off the neck and extremities. The pelts were now plush, furry robes about five feet square. Never again would he have to roll himself naked into a pile of evergreen boughs for warmth at night; instead, he would sleep comfortably for the first time.

The evening of August twenty-sixth, while the surveillance team was signing off for the night and going to bed in their camouflaged bivouacs, Siegfried loaded his wooden pack frame with elk jerky, catgut, his new elk robes, and most of his tools. After hoisting the rest of his meat into a tree with a length of copper wire, lest a bear get it, he started west under a full moon. The next morning, surprised at his empty camp, the Pelican, Ebro, and Vermillion scouts moved out of their stations with full packs. Believing his course led toward Lake Lodge, the men guessed he had a cache west of the Yellowstone River near the base of Elephant Back Mountain. Jimmy Downes and three rangers joined them in a search of the area, but they found nothing, not even a track.

"We'll have to expand our search area as far south as Bridge Bay," Downes told Garner the next evening. He hoped the old man wouldn't criticize his handling of the situation. Tired of Garner's accusations, Downes was concerned with his constant failures to follow the subject.

"Yes, do that." Obviously dissatisfied with the ranger's lame excuses, Doctor Garner turned his back and walked away.

"Damn! I hope we find something soon," the ranger mumbled to himself, for the old man's displeasure was worse than any father's disappointment with a delinquent child. The Indians were good, the ranger had to admit, but Yellowstone and the kid's random nature were defeating even them. Shaking his head wearily, he vowed to find the cache, for it was the key to Gene's winter survival.

Two days later, Gene reappeared in camp in the Sulphur Hills and began packing for another trip to his cache. This time, when Ebro reported him moving west toward the river, Vermillion and Pelican hurried to Fishing Bridge and positioned themselves south of the junction—one in the forest, one in the sagebrush within sight of Lake Lodge. Meanwhile, Ebro raced ahead of Gene to cover the forest just north of the junction, in case the weak trail they had once seen there was his.

Unfortunately, Ranger Downes was busy at park headquarters, but he radioed his men, *"Don't lose him. We've got to stay with him. As soon as he crosses the bridge, get on his ass and don't lose sight of him!"*

Random, erratic, unpredictable … at one time or another, Downes had occasion to use all these words to describe Siegfried on the trail. Most probably, Gene was not trying to avoid anyone, but he rarely used the same route twice, and so it was this time. He did not cross Fishing Bridge at all; instead, in a light summer drizzle, he headed north along the Howard Eaton Trail and crossed the river by wading Buffalo Ford. The surveillance team never caught sight of him, and, due to the rainy conditions the Indians were not able to follow his trail more than a few hundred yards. They were not to see him again for four days.

Hurrying down from Mammoth, Ranger Downes raged at the three sheepish scouts for ten minutes, then he suddenly stopped, cooled off, and apologized. "I'm sorry. I had no right. I should know better than anyone," he said, "how hard it is to track someone in this wilderness. We'll get him next time."

It was, however, their last good chance to follow Gene Siegfried to his cache. Only once more would he travel north to the valley, and that trip would be the biggest surprise of all.

CHAPTER 13

※ ※ ※

The Searchers

"I HAVEN'T THE slightest idea where to look," Britt Chamberlain complained, tucking her windblown hair under a pink stocking cap, then fluffing the little ball on top. After fussing with the collar of a new down jacket, she glanced at her reflection in the car window to be sure she looked just right. It was a cold, gray day in early fall. Behind her, in Hayden Valley, the deep red grass rippled in the wind, grass that four months ago had been grazed to the mud, but which now stood three feet high and was heavy with grain.

"Neither do I, but Gene's out there somewhere," Roxy assured her, slipping on a field jacket over a wrinkled sweatshirt, then pulling her hair into a ponytail secured with a rubber band. "I don't care what anyone says. Did you read where the Bozeman newspaper says he's probably dead? Goddam scandal sheet! Gene's alive. The wild geese haven't called for him yet."

"Wild geese?"

"It's an old Indian legend I heard once," Roxy said lamely. "The geese call, someone dies. When the geese down on the Yellowstone River begin honking, it gives me the willies. Anyway ... I believe Gene's still alive."

"Yeah, he's out there," her friend, Mack Simms, agreed, changing the subject as he shrugged into his own field jacket, "but we can't prove it until we get started." Handing Britt a light rucksack filled with fruit and snacks, he pulled his own heavy pack from the car. Roxy showed Britt how to adjust the pack straps, then got her faithful Pentax camera out of the car and slammed the trunk.

"Sure is cold," Britt complained, feeling strangely excited at this, her very first hike into the wilderness. She wasn't embarrassed her pack weighed only about ten pounds, while her friends' packs were sixty pounds each. "Oww!" she screamed, jumping away from a tall thistle growing at the edge of the road.

"Have to watch that," Mack warned her. "That's an Everts' Thistle. It's named after Truman Everts—and it can really scratch you up."

"Who was Truman Everts?"

"A member of the Washburn Expedition of 1870. He got separated from the main party down by Heart Lake. He was a real dude—managed to lose his horse, gun, and blankets, even his eyeglasses. All he had was a pocketknife, the clothes on his back, and an opera glass. The only edible plant he could find sticking up above the snow was the thistle you see there."

"*That's* edible?" Britt asked, unable to imagine eating anything wild. It was one of the reasons she was so fascinated with the test subjects. She couldn't fathom them degrading themselves to eat such nasty things. Recently, she had read in a report Gene Siegfried even ate roasted tripe from one of his elk. The very thought sent shivers down her spine.

"The roots of the thistle are edible; in the spring, the young leaves are pretty good too," Mack said. "Anyway, about a month after getting lost, Everts was found crawling on his hands and knees. He weighed about fifty pounds, the balls of his feet were wore off clear to the bone, and he was burned and frostbitten."

"You wouldn't be exaggerating, would you?" Britt laughed. While she got along well with Roxy, Mack Simms had remained a mystery to her. The only thing that recommended him to her was his close friendship with Gene Siegfried.

"Not even a little bit," he answered.

"Mack's got a weird sense of humor," Roxy interrupted, "but he has a fabulous memory for unusual stories, especially the morbid ones!" Punching her friend in the ribs, Roxy urged, "G'wan, Mack, tell her the rest. It's Yellowstone's most famous survival story."

"The guy who found Everts," he said, "had been promised a reward for recovering the body, but instead, after he nursed Everts back to health and took him to the flatlands, Everts refused to reward him. He claimed he could have made it out on his own!" Slapping his leg, Mack chuckled, "Some story, eh?"

"I guess," Britt said, though she wasn't sure if the two weren't pulling her leg. She made a mental note to find out more about Truman Everts.

Mack spread a wrinkled map on the fender of his car. "Today, we'll see plenty of Everts' Thistle," he said, indicating the white valley on the map surrounded by the green tint of forest. "Hayden Valley has lots of sagebrush, every kind of grass and sedge you can think of, but fewer flowers than earlier this summer. I prefer the fall flowers myself, but I'm partial to lupine at any time of year."

"C'mon, Mack," Roxy scolded. "We've got to get started."

"Okay," he said. "Assuming he's on this side of the river—"

"Why this side?" Britt wanted to know, for she hadn't learned to trust Mack's instincts.

"Look how much grassland there is on this side of the river versus what's over there."

"Oh," she said. It made perfect sense to her, but there was more to it than that. The eastern march of Hayden Valley was rolling and cut up by streams draining into the Yellowstone River. There was less big game and vegetation, but it was also more isolated. While the eastern march was all within sight of the highway, it was separated from the rest of the valley by the deceptively treacherous river. The western march, on the other hand, was bigger and offered more, but its disadvantage was that it was accessible to tourists.

"We can figure he is at least one mile off the road," Mack said, drawing a line paralleling the highway on the map and shading the area between the line and the road. "We can forget the open parts of the valley and concentrate on the forested parts. More than likely, he's not too deep in the trees because he'll need access to open country to hunt."

"That's not so bad then," the psychologist gushed. "It leaves us with only this thin margin around the edge of the valley to search." She understood everything Mack was telling her, though it sounded as alien as the long conversations the rangers and scouts had over their maps.

Mack looked disgusted. "No, not so bad," he agreed, "Three weeks' worth if we don't do a thorough job of it."

"Oh, c'mon, Mack. We can do it in two!" Roxy teased. "I think we can forget the Crater Hills. They're too close to the road. They're apt to draw sightseers—and bears."

"Right," he agreed, shading that area also.

"And I think we can forget anyplace close to the trails for the same reason." Roxy took the pencil from his hand and shaded two more areas. "That wipes out both Highland and Violet Hot Springs, for they might be too attractive for adventurous dudes."

"You're saying he's avoiding the obvious places," Britt observed, looking at the map rather intently. Maps had always been such boring things, something to be used only when driving cross-country, but with Hayden Valley lying out in front of her now, she could see how useful a map might be. The squiggly lines within other lines were a hill, and the green tint was the trees. Actually a map was informative and even—dare she think it? —interesting.

"Wouldn't you avoid the obvious?" Roxy asked. "I mean, he's out there for weeks on end without seeing a soul, so he wouldn't want every Johnny Mountaineer dropping in for tea. You'd feel the same way living in an apartment in a big city. What if your apartment faced a stairwell? Would you leave your door open to cool the apartment? No. Everyone would look into your living room as they came up the landing."

"So he's not so much avoiding sightseers," Britt said. "as being sensitive about who drops in."

"Yeah, but he'll be glad to see us," Roxy said. "We've just got to take care not to surprise him. You see these bear bells Mack and I always wear on our belts?"

"Yes."

"I don't think anyone knows if they work or not. The sound may cause a sow bear to pull her cubs in closer, but it may attract boars to the noise. I do know you won't startle other hikers on the trail, and as keen as Gene is right now, he'll hear the bells a long way off and come looking for us."

"Oh," Britt said. She didn't understand these mountain things and readily accepted Roxy's explanations as fact. "Since the two of you have shaded in this top part of the valley, it makes little sense to look here in the trees north of—what's this? The Mary Mountain Trail?—between the thermal areas." She took the pencil from Roxy and colored in that part of the map too.

"Agreed," Mack said. "Personally, I don't think he's anywhere on the northern frontier. It's too steep. Good view of the valley, but it'll be murder in the winter."

"I think so too," Roxy said.

"This forested hill between the trail and the Crater Hills is a good possibility, and these trees too," he said, circling a hill near Sulphur Mountain. "That gives us the Elk Antler and Trout Creek drainages."

"Yep."

"That narrows it some," he said. "Let's get going."

The three hikers set off westward along the Mary Mountain Trail to investigate the forested knob near the Crater Hills. There was nothing unusual to be seen there, so they cut overland to another forested hill to the southwest, then down a brooklet toward Sulphur Mountain. Britt's curiosity dragged them out of their way to the Crater Hills, where she marveled at the mud pots and a huge boiling spring with a rainbowed plume of steam. Here, the ground actually sizzled, and there were thick sulfur deposits on the rocks. Tiptoeing across the thin crust, Britt saw places where buffalo had broken through the blistered cinder. Clouds of steam rose from the tracks, and she thought of the shades of Hades. Nearby, they found stinking bones where something big had recently died. The area had quite a few bleached bones scattered about, for a warm thermal zone attracts animals throughout the winter, many of whom die there.

Britt remembered a ranger telling her every geyser basin had dozens of carcasses in the spring. Shivering at these images of death, Britt was grateful to leave this haunted place. She followed her friends south to the old Trout Creek Service Road and a quick lunch stop. Later, the three hikers hiked overland to Elk Antler Creek and the backside of the Dragon's Mouth complex.

They found nothing, however, of their friend who had vanished almost three weeks earlier. Of course, there had been speculations, but no one really knew where Gene Siegfried was or what had happened to him. The surveillance team had observed him breaking camp the last day of August; he had buried all of his ashes, raked his campsite, and disposed of every scrap of wood, bone, and metal. After smoothing dirt over the holes of his forge and bellows, Gene planted winter grass and small plants throughout the campsite.

As soon as the scouts reported he was leaving for the last time, Jimmy Downes ordered them to take no chances. One of the men waited right on Fishing Bridge, trying to blend in with the tourists. Another sat on the high bank just north of the bridge with an easy view of the shoreline, one took a station in the trees up by the LeHardy Rapids, and the last concealed himself in the sagebrush south of the Fishing Bridge road. Downes camouflaged himself in the trees opposite the junction, while three rangers covered Buffalo Ford and Chittenden Bridge. Coincidentally, a large group of boy scouts hiked south on the Howard Eaton Trail that day, but even so, Gene eluded them.

CHAPTER 14

※ ※ ※

The Elk

GENE SIEGFRIED CAME into the meadow west of Ebro Hot Springs exactly as the scouts had predicted. Having seriously underestimated how much gear he had to carry to his cabin site in Hayden Valley, he was laboring under a pack that weighed more than a hundred pounds. Within a mile after abandoning camp in the Sulphur Hills, he had worn a blister onto his right shoulder. The blister hurt him more with every step he took, and when it finally broke, salty sweat ran under the pack strap and burned into the open wound. In a hurry to transport everything in one trip so he could get to work on his cabin in Hayden Valley, Gene tried to adjust his pack straps by padding them with wool socks and shifting the load, but he could stagger only another four hundred yards before having to stop again.

"I'm going to have to make two trips after all," he grumped. What could he leave behind? He looked around for a safe place to stash some of his gear, and then began to unload the pack. His tools had to go now, he decided, but if he stashed the jerky and other food, could he be sure no animal would get it? What would be the best way to cache things? Should he hang it in a tree or bury it? How many days would pass before he could make it back down here to pick it up? What if it rained? In a quandary, he packed and repacked a half-dozen times.

Meanwhile, a half-mile west, on the southern edge of the meadow, a sick, old elk bull wandered slowly through the scattered lodgepoles. For elk, this was the fat time of year, and this gaunt bull should have been in prime condition, but instead, pus and saliva dribbled out of its mouth. Although it was napping time, pain kept this elk up and moving, for an abscessed tooth had festered so long in its mouth, the elk's lower jawbone had broken. The elk hadn't eaten in more than a week, and now, driven by thirst, it came to drink from a tiny stream running through the open area. The cold water shocked the bull's aching mouth, and it raised its muzzle straight into the air and squeaked, a sound not unlike the high-pitched bugles of the mating season. Splashing across the narrow watercourse, the elk ambled into the warm sunshine, its eyes closed in pain.

Looking up, Gene was surprised to see the elk emerge from trees not far away. Dropping to the ground behind a clump of grass, he watched the bull move into the meadow. Twice it seemed to bugle, but then it just stood there, its head hung low. Figuring this strange behavior was part of the craziness of the early rut, Gene decided to take advantage of this unexpected good fortune. His journey to Hayden Valley could wait. After killing the bull, he could make a temporary camp at the edge of the trees, jerk the meat and continue to his cabin site in a week. That would probably be for the best, he decided, for he could pack more efficiently. Pulling three javelins from a scabbard on his pack, he stashed the rest of his gear, and then circled through the trees to get behind the elk.

Moving as quietly as an afternoon shadow, he drifted from tree to tree, testing his footing to keep from cracking a stick or making a sound. He had practiced such stalking all summer. It was called "still hunting," and it was movement and breath and camouflaged thought guaranteed to close the distance. With the pulse quickening in his ears, he felt totally absorbed in the Zen of the hunt as he neared his unsuspecting prey. At the edge of the forest, Gene lay on the ground and slithered on his belly through deep grass to the brook. The elk was out of sight over the rise. Sure now he was nearly within range, Gene decided to risk stepping over the stream, but such tiny rills are often more than they seem. While it couldn't have been more than two feet wide, the brook was at least that deep. Instead of finding firm ground on the other side, Gene stepped on a floating mass of watercress and fell facedown in the water.

Wildly splashing, he struggled to get to his feet in the strong current. The elk was long gone by now, he thought, and he was about to curse and dump the water from his boots when an odd feeling struck him that the elk might not have run very far. Looking for the raven, he found it perched in the bony top of a dead pine fifty yards to his left. It looked at him; it then looked pointedly to the left. That was a good sign, for the bird always restrained itself while he hunted. Sitting on a branch, it was eying something in the meadow. The bull might still be there. Gene rolled to his knees and silently crawled uphill.

Sure enough, when he peeked over the edge of the slope, the bull was only two hundred feet away. It looked preoccupied. For weeks he had watched cow elk banding up and the bulls polishing their antlers. Elk were on the move, many migrating south toward Jackson Hole, but others north and northwest. Early mating was happening, and everywhere, especially in the evenings, he heard the eerie, shrill bugling of bulls eager to collect harems of nubile young cows. It was natural for a bull to act strangely, so after fetching his javelins and axe, Gene strolled into full view of the elk. He tried to look as unconcerned as possible as he circled to the animal's right, even blanking out his thoughts and intentions. For its part, the elk seemed relieved the noise was only a human; it had probably seen thousands of tourists in its time. It didn't seem particularly alarmed as Siegfried drew nearer.

The bull was within range. Allowing himself a grin as he clicked a javelin into the hook of his spear thrower, Gene swung the weapon over his head and hurled it forward. The spear was right on target. It struck deep into the elk's upper rib cage, just back of its shoulder blade. Looking a bit surprised, the bull made no effort to get away. A spear killed by hemorrhage; there was no numbing shock like a bullet, just a searing pain that took precious seconds to identify as a man-caused danger. Confused, the elk hesitated long enough to allow a second throw, which hit hard at the base of its neck.

The elk stiffened, then, after a few tense moments, its front legs wobbled and bent, and it sank down, blood flowing like a torrent out of both wounds. "Ha, that was easy!" Gene exulted, gleefully running over to the fallen bull. He threw down his last javelin and pulled out a camp knife to administer the *coup de grace*.

Twitching as he grabbed its nearest antler, the dying bull groaned, struggled dizzily to its feet and slammed its antlers broadside into Gene's shoulder, catching him off-balance. Wrenching itself from his grasp, the elk twisted to the right, bounced once, twice, three times with the vigor of sparkling youth, and fell dead.

Gene was a long time collecting his wits. Rocking back and forth on the balls of his feet, he felt numb and a bit sick to his stomach. He screwed his eyes shut as pain began to shoot flaming stars into his consciousness. His knees were trembling, and the redness of his vision deepened. Redness? Reaching up rather clumsily, he felt hot globs of blood dripping onto his outstretched hands, and then his fingers found his face—or what was left of it. Recoiling in horror, he realized he was hurt.

A flap of skin hung away from his right cheek and slapped about his neck like a sail torn loose in a gale. Hot blood cascaded over his right shoulder and ran down his chest and back. "Raargh!" he screamed, trying to open his eyes, though all he could see was blood. "Waalaah!" he screamed again, louder than before.

Suddenly frightened, he explored his face with his fingers. The elk's antler had ripped his right face open until deflected by the cheekbone. The skin, peeled from his ear to his eye and down nearly to the chin, hung away from the muscles of his face and living skull. Gene screamed in horror as he understood the extent of the damage, and he felt some of that desperate cry escape out of the side of his torn face. When he tried to breathe normally, he blew bloody bubbles, and blood ran down inside his nose and down his throat, gagging him. His nose was completely flat and oddly tilted to the side.

Where was the elk? Frantically, Gene swept his hands in front of his face, but there was nothing there. He was nearly hysterical he was so scared, but he didn't give a moment's thought to seeking help, for bleeding like he was, he knew he could never make it to Fishing Bridge. Instead, he sank to his knees and pressed the skin of his face back into place. The cheek didn't fit right, but he stretched and pulled at his face despite the pain. He was relieved to find that his right eye—already glued shut with

blood—seemed intact, but it was swollen as fat as a lemon. If the elk's antler had struck an inch higher or a half-inch closer to the nose—he shud-
dered to think the dread thought.

Remembering the metal pillbox on a chain around his neck that Dr.
Garner had given him, he crushed it in his fist to pop the lid off. There
were two plastic envelopes inside; he had never taken the time to read the
labels after Professor Garner had given them to him, but he remembered
the containers held medicine for emergencies. Purge, laxative, or disinfec-
tant, they're all the same when you're bleeding. Biting the top off the little
packets, he poured them into the top of his wound. The unknown medicines stung like fire inside the torn skin of his face and ran down inside
to his mouth, but stifling a gag, Gene pressed the medicines back with his
tongue. As he worked, blood gushed over his hands with such intensity,
it ran in rivulets off his elbows and chin. He was kneeling in a veritable
puddle of gore.

Shedding his leather vest, he frantically yanked his shirttails from his
jeans with his left hand. Snapping down on the right cuff of his shirt, he
ripped the sleeve away, padded the wool over his torn face, and then pulled
the rest of his shirt over his head to cover that. The harsh ringing in his
ears, he realized rather sheepishly, was his own screaming, so he calmed
himself and bound his head with a belt. In terrible pain, he staggered to
his feet, wandered blindly back to the stream, fell to one knee, and passed
out in a stand of horsetail rushes.

If given the chance, most people would choose to die alone, for there
is no time in the last minutes to deal with affairs of life. For hours, Gene
lay perfectly still, even his breathing so shallow it made no ripple on the
muddy water near his mouth, but as close as he may have been to death he
wasn't allowed the peace to go quietly.

In the early afternoon, three ravens began to pick at the dead elk, but
a fourth raven, the young male Gene had been cultivating with scraps,
fluttered away from its mates. Death was a raven's business, and this one
seemed torn by its instincts. Flapping its wings, the raven danced down
the grassy slope to strut back and forth in front of the man's still body,

cawing as loudly as it could. When that didn't work, the bird fluttered nearer and pecked a bite of skin from the back of one of his hands.

"Ow," Gene groaned, and again, "OW!" as the larger pain struck him. He sat up and rocked back and forth like a weak kitten. At first, all he could see was blue, but then he remembered to pry back a corner of the shirt from his good eye so he could see the bird prancing in front of him. "G'wan, get out of here," he croaked, tossing a clump of mud at it. The bird did not go far, and it hopped from foot to foot in a strange dance in the long grass. A flight of four more ravens swooshed overhead and landed near the carcass of the elk, but still the bird remained near the man, too curious to begin eating yet.

Gene sank back onto the cool mud. His head was spinning as badly as if he had drunk a dozen beers. His face and head hurt, but strangely, it was his neck muscles that pained the most. He must have suffered some form of whiplash when the elk struck him, he decided. Lying there, nearly unable to roll to his right or his left due to the extreme pain in his neck, he reached behind into the stream and then dribbled water onto the bandage to saturate it. His fine blue Pendleton shirt was as thick and stiff as cardboard now, and it took an hour and a lot of gentle watering before he was able to pry the bloody wool from the wound. In agony, he forced himself to roll to his hands and knees to look at his reflection in the water.

His entire face was swollen and black, and only his left eye would open. He fixed his nose—which was flat and bent sharply to the left—by squeezing the eggshell bones together, making a sound in his sinuses similar to popping knuckles. His nose began to bleed again. He felt sick to his stomach. When he vomited, all that came up from his stomach was his own blood.

His face needed immediate attention. Washing the wound carefully, Gene encouraged blood flow all along the puffy edge of the cut. As he studied his reflection on the water, he could see his cheek was torn like a large "7" from just below his chin to a point near the eye, then two inches straight back to the ear. The wound was relatively sharp-edged, and it was much cleaner than he expected.

Quite sick to his stomach, his head spinning and stars flashing across his vision, he crawled on his hands and knees the two hundred yards to his pack. It was a terrible waste, but most of the dried fish and jerky he'd saved, a few wonderful carvings, and a few of his precious tools had to be abandoned. He salvaged a buffalo horn full of yellow crystals collected in the solfatara of the Sulphur Hills, and emptied a bladder full of seeds, saving only the bladder itself. He also kept all of his spare javelins, his precious cup, dented cooking pot, and a camp knife, but he left behind his pack frame and other odds and ends. Taking only the most necessary items, he crawled back to the slope overlooking the dead elk, since it was a convenient source of food. There was shelter and protection under a large blowdown here. After starting a small fire in its lee, he fetched a pot of water to boil.

The bladder had been sewn shut with two feet of good sinew, and Gene picked it from its stitching. The cord was as thick as mason's twine; it needed to be halved before he could use it for stitching. After softening it in boiling water, he painstakingly split it with a camp knife, and then dropped it back into the pot to boil again. Next, he found a suitable bone needle in a marmot-hide notions bag, sharpened it on a rock and put it in the water to sterilize too.

He may have slept then, for when he began to work, the sun was far to the west. Using the tiny, mirrored reflection on the fisherman's knife, which was stuck into a nearby tree, he began to stitch his face. To do this, he was forced to poke a series of holes along each side of the wound, through which he threaded the sinew into his face like the laces of a boot and cinched his cheek back together. At times, the pain was so intense he wanted to scream, but there was no one to hear him and little good to come from it; instead, he ground his teeth and kept at the work until he was finished. Next, he ground a small, clay figurine from his notions bag with water and sulfur crystals and smeared it over his injured cheek as a poultice. Then, using the long nail of his little finger, he cleared both nostrils of dried blood and bandaged his face with two clean wool socks.

In the morning, the elk was gone. A bear must have gotten it, Gene decided, for it was the only thing strong enough to move a grown elk. This was not a good sign, considering his condition. He slowly made his way to the stream for a drink, after which he washed his face again and re-bandaged it. Returning to the scene of the kill, he found a loose javelin and his leather vest. There were tracks and a disembodied lower leg nearby, but by now, he was in so much pain, he crawled back to his fire to sleep the day away.

Hours passed and a long, intense dream filled his head. There were coyotes in this dream. They were circling in snow out in front of him and behind him, coming closer and closer as they yammered to themselves. There was a great fire somewhere behind him, but he paid no attention. Occasionally, one of the bolder ones would come up and nip at him to test his strength and reactions. Strangely, he didn't feel frightened. An odd sense of the rightness of it all soothed him. This was the way it was supposed to be, the way it had happened thousands of years before humans got so civilized, and he waved at the coyotes with his axe. In his dream, his wounds were many, but his face seemed intact. Strangely, it was his teeth that felt broken, not his cheek. Despite this being the warmest season of the year, his dream featured falling snow and cold wind. Strangely, however, he was naked above the waist and reclining against a tree. He felt no desire to go towards the fire for warmth, and the coyotes didn't get him. What did it mean?

In the middle of the night, something rustled as it scratched nearby and pulled at things. Gene woke without moving, in dread of what he might find. His fingers crept across the cold dirt to the shaft of a javelin, and then he raised his head and peered into the night. A porcupine was gnawing at the antler handle of a camp hatchet, its beady eyes glaring stupidly in the red glow of a dying fire. Gene instinctively bashed the animal in the head with the javelin, giving it a stab in the throat for good measure. Nearly grinning despite the pain, he decided his luck had changed. Now he understood why the coyotes never got him in the dream. He was going to survive this injury. He skinned the porcupine, then put it aside and fetched a pot of water. As soon as it was boiling, he chunked the meat to make a stew, and although his injured face throbbed, and an enormous canker sore along his upper gum gave him problems, he ate, stopping occasionally to spit out a mouthful of his own blood.

It was, of course, his first meal in days, and it was the beginning of an orgy of feasting. He ate the entire porcupine except its quills, even splitting its bones for marrow. He boiled the last of his jerky and ate berries he discovered in the bottom of a pocket, and then he collected water plants and speared a tiny trout in the stream. Later, he scraped the inner cambium from a sapling and grubbed for roots.

He also prepared a mysterious medicinal concoction from sulfur crystals, ground elk antler, and the juice of a late flowering plant. The plant, perhaps a vulnerary such as yarrow or bistort, he found growing all over in the meadows east of the Yellowstone River. After mashing it to a juicy pulp, he combined it with the powder and packed it into a porcupine quill as a crude Syrette. Again using the fisherman's knife as a mirror, he injected this medicine into both sides of his wound and up into the canker sore in his mouth. Porcupine quills contain a natural antibiotic to prevent festering, and either this antibiotic or the medicine he invented reduced the swelling and stopped the bleeding within hours.

The whole right side of Gene's face and neck was black. His nose was crooked, and the corner of his mouth was upturned. Although his right eye looked intact, it was still swollen shut, but even taking all of this into account, he felt better. There was no trace of infection, which was nothing short of miraculous. Barely able to stand, he forced himself to get up and move. Every day he lay there recovering increased the chances of a bear finding him. Not sure how long he had been at the edge of the meadow, for he had slept most of the time, he estimated he had lost about four days.

He never considered reporting in, for looking as bad as he did, he knew the researchers would end the experiment. Instead, mile by painful mile, he stumbled north. He made it to Hayden Valley and camped in the forest under his cache, where, for the next week, he did little else but eat.

✳ ✳ ✳

Meanwhile, the scientists and rangers were mystified by his latest—and longest—disappearance. At first, they assumed he had merely eluded the surveillance team and gone into camp in the dense forest west or north-west of Lake Lodge. Figuring he must know they were spying on him, the rangers decided he had deliberately hidden his camp in some isolated spot. To discover this camp, the scouts combed the forest between the LeHardy Rapids on the north and Arnica Creek on the south, and west as far as Beach and Dryad Lakes. A helicopter scanned north to Hayden Valley, but no sign of a human was found.

After five fruitless days of searching, Jimmy Downes and two of the Indians returned to the Sulphur Hills to try to follow stale tracks. By that time, there was no actual trail left, no bent grass or broken sticks, but they followed the tendency of his path to the edge of the Ebro grass. The ranger guessed he had gone straight west to the river or the Howard Eaton Trail, but when they didn't find anything, he and his men started over and worked their way back to Ebro again. This time, they spotted a pair of ravens squabbling over something at the edge of the forest to the west, and they found a dead elk buried under a mound of pine needles. Nearby were the tracks of a large sow grizzly and two grown cubs, and it was their meat but for mark of a man: two broken javelin shafts protruded from the carcass.

There could be no doubt now that something had gone terribly wrong. Bears had hid the elk, but where had it been killed? Downes wondered if it had it escaped from Siegfried or been taken from him. He ordered his men to scour the open grassland to the north, and within an hour, they located the abandoned pack frame and other supplies. Things did not look good. Strangely let down by this ignominious end to a great adventure, the ranger felt depressed. He could see the same in his scouts' eyes, too, but there was work to be done.

It took time to organize a proper search party, but when he had assembled twenty volunteers, the ranger ordered a systematic survey of the area, foot by foot. The men soon found a pathetic campsite a quarter mile west of the pack frame, just two hundred yards from the hidden elk carcass. They also found a bloody wool shirt torn to rags, an ivory needle stained with human blood, and small pieces of sinew and porcupine hide. Carved into the side of a nearby tree were the letters ECS, which Downes took for Gene's initials, but there was no sign of a body. Had the grizzlies found him all bloody and hurt? Since the shirt was so torn, the ranger decided Gene must have suffered a crippling abdominal wound, and that gave little chance of survival.

"Doctor Garner," Downes reported at a hastily called staff meeting late that night in West Yellowstone. "I believe Gene Siegfried is dead. We'll continue looking until we find some sign."

"Damn!" Garner exclaimed. "What will we tell the reporters?"

"More to the point," Britt said, burying her face in her hands. "What will we tell his family?"

There were no tracks at all, no indications of any kind, and it certainly didn't help matters when a light snow fell that evening, a cold, wet snow that bent the tall grass under its weight. A number of volunteers joined the search for a human body, but almost everyone knew carcasses don't last long in the wilderness, and even bones disappear quickly when rodents begin gnawing. They made one final pass through the meadow looking for human bones, and then called it quits.

About the same time, the Lamar surveillance team reported their subject, Douglas Paine Hanson, was in trouble. The wet, miserable weather was too much for this man, stretched to the limits as he was. Thin, sick, coughing, and unbelievably dirty, he was spurred on only by his own courage and intensity. Day after day, Hanson struggled just to get enough to eat, and he wandered only a short distance from his wretched camp on the western fork of Slough Creek. Downes reluctantly transferred the Hayden

Valley surveillance team north to help monitor Hanson, and NASA and the Park Service began to relax, now that the end of the experiment was in sight. Permanent park employees busied themselves with preparations for winter, while seasonals packed their gear for a trip back to the flatlands.

More than two weeks passed since the disappearance of Gene Siegfried, perhaps the most critical period of the experiment up to that point, for he was far from death's door. Each day, he grew stronger. His face was healing, and he had regained much of his strength. He felt more alive than ever. There was a crispness in the air and vibrancy in his blood as fall began to chill the park. In the valley, the grass was heavy with grain. Buffalo were beginning to band up, and elk were on the move, foolish with the rut. One day, he killed a small cow elk, then later that week, an old buffalo cow with a broken leg. Broken leg or not, however, it took six hard javelins for him to put her down.

Roots bulged just below the surface of the ground, seeds were easy to gather, and fruits and berries were everywhere; he spent his days harvesting the plenty. Smoky fires glowed day and night from his hidden camp in the little meadow, and hide racks were stretched tight with new, heavy skins. In a nearby tree hung a grotesque collection of bladders, dried catgut, sinews, and hooves, as well as pieces of bone, antler, and horn.

It was the fat time of year, and a time of great fear. Hayden Valley was crowded with bears, and a day did not pass without one or two of them coming to investigate the hungry smells in the meadow. At night, there were bonfires, and the scent of man and steel, but the bears were only cautious, not afraid, of this unknown intruder. Several grizzlies stopped to sniff the cache in the forest, wondering at the delicious treasures concealed up there. A small black bear scarred the trees trying to climb into the cache, but it was defeated by downward-pointed pine spikes and swirls of loose wire.

Meanwhile, Gene busied himself with the construction of an underground home, which he thought would be warmer and easier to build than a standard log cabin. There wasn't a simple way for him to lift and notch sizable logs for a traditional design anyway, and besides, he had learned his axe was of little use cutting trees. He decided a hole would be easier to excavate, so he dug a muddy pit twelve feet wide and fifteen feet long in the steep side of the slope. In the mornings, there was a faint odor of sulfur in the pit, and a whisper of steam rose out of the rocky western wall of the hole. Smiling in satisfaction, he welcomed the warmth of the volcanic fires below, for he figured it would make the cabin more livable during the winter.

Cutting several big timbers, Gene emplaced them along three sides of the hole to frame the walls. He filled spaces between these timbers with dozens of poles pegged and tied into place. Later, he tamped dirt and rock between the walls of the cabin and the sides of the hole to tighten the construction.

A lone pine, dead for ten years, stood near the hole, its bleached trunk over a foot in diameter. Intending this tree as the main beam of his roof, Gene hacked doggedly at its base, finally toppling it across the front of the pit. Unfortunately, the tree fell so violently several of the timbers in the western wall were cracked or driven down, and the huge log itself was split along most of its length. Disappointed, Gene braced the crack and pegged the log for greater strength.

Next, he planted three logs in front of the north wall and joined them to the cabin with tie beams to form the framework of a low trapezoidal porch, after which the whole construction was covered with small poles. He covered this with a layer of branches, rocks and dirt until the roof was three feet thick. As a final touch, he gave the roof a coat of stones to discourage digging animals. The cabin was mostly complete, and Gene finally felt ready for winter.

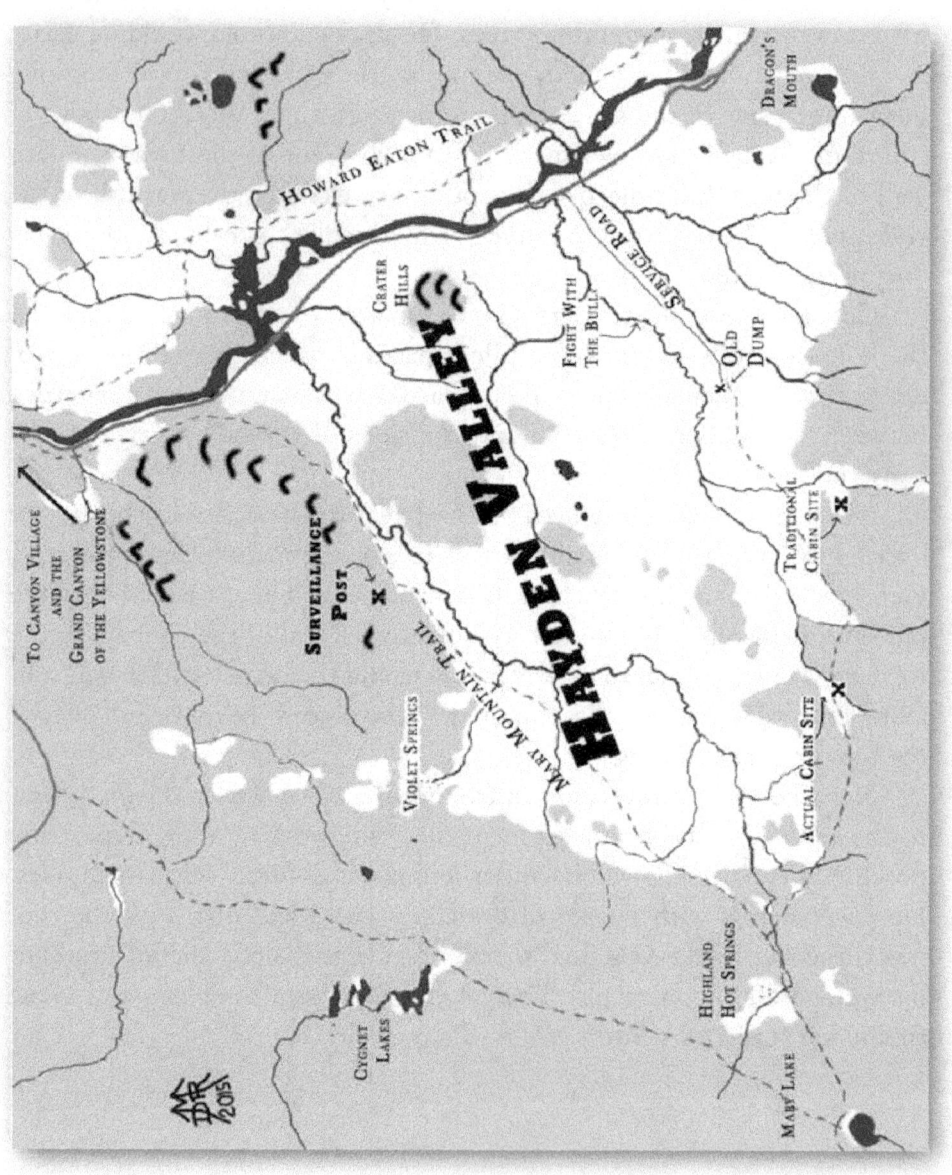

CHAPTER 15

❄ ❄ ❄

The Cabin

AFTER WALKING PAST the narrow opening to the little meadow twice, Roxy, Mack, and Britt finally traced the smell of woodsmoke to where five fires glowed under drying racks loaded with meat. Gene Siegfried's cabin was finished by this time, but rocky mounds of earth and piles of firewood surrounded it on every side. A black male raven perched in a set of moose antlers wired above the cabin's porch, but at first, there was no trace of a man. Britt felt uneasy as they drew nearer. It was like a Teutonic hunting camp, so primitive, so lost she thought, but adding to that impression, she realized, was a group of javelins leaning against the cabin and a curved axe stuck in a chopping block near the door. There were bloodstains streaking the sides of the block. What had he been chopping? What had died there? What had been butchered to pieces there?

The raven hoarsened louder the closer they approached, cackling and hopping obscenely from tine to tine in alarm at their intrusion. Back in the valley, a squadron of Canada geese rose in one of their final drills before the migration south, and the sound of their honking was a lonely echo in the trees. Walking slower than her two friends, Britt was afraid of what they might find; she felt a chill in her back, and her lips began to tremble. There was a muted clack of stone upon stone, and an ashen figure moved from the shadows of the cabin and into the light.

"Oh, God!" Britt gasped, for the figure was Gene Siegfried, and again, "Oh, God, please NO!" when she looked into his face. An angry purple weal sliced across his right cheek and disappeared into the long, wild hair over his ear. His mouth curled up on the right side. Was he grinning …

or was his mouth part of the scar too? His eyes, one still swollen half shut, were the color of emeralds, and there was a strange, wise expression in them now, a look beyond confidence ... it was competence, she realized. A goose feather flapped about the back of his head; it was woven into his long hair, and a braided leather headband crossed his brow. No, this was not the Gene Siegfried she had known ... or thought she had known.

Again the raven fluttered nervously on its perch, its eyes full of anger fire, then it silently floated away on the wind. Roxy never hesitated; she strode up to Gene, took his scarred face in her powerful brown hands and said, "God Almighty! Didn't I tell you to take better care of yourself? What's this goddamn scratch on your face, and where the hell you been the last couple weeks?" Not waiting for an answer, she wrapped her long arms around him in a bear hug. "God, I'm glad to see you."

"You mean ... still alive?" he said.

"Yes, that too," she said, "but more so just seeing you."

"I appreciate that," Gene chuckled.

Mack, more withdrawn, simply said, "Hey, guy."

"Good to see you."

"You, too," Mack allowed, leaning against one of the porch's columns. He shyly punched his friend on the arm.

For her part, Dr. Britt Chamberlain stood a few feet away, her mouth open and her hands midway between wanting to mother his scarred face and hiding the horror of it from her eyes "Oh ... oh, oh, oh!" she whispered. There was something so hurtful about scars; they could be so exotic, but they were also so frightening. She felt the same way about scars as she felt about tattoos: there was an awful hurt in them. While tattoos were voluntary, however, scars were the marks of an angry world on a human being, and scars on the face marked a man as blessed or chosen.

"I think I can manage a cup of tea if you've got some cups," Gene said as soon as Roxy released him. Before they could answer, he disappeared into the cabin to retrieve a sooty aluminum pot with iron handles. He filled the pot with cold water from the intermittent stream in the lower meadow and put it on to boil next to his biggest fire. Sprinkling three handfuls of what could have been peat moss, wood shavings, or moist duff into the water, he waved his guests to sit on a log next to the fire.

"I suppose that behind your joy at having found me there is a thought of urging me to give up," he said." I don't want to hear a word of that while you're visitors here in my camp." Dr. Chamberlain was on the point of saying something, but he cut her off. "I know as a scientist you feel an obligation to say something," he said, "but not a word now. If I had thought it necessary, I would have come in, but I'm doing better now than I have all summer. I learned some valuable lessons recently, but it was more in the spirit of preparation for what's to come." Glancing toward the horizon to the northwest, he asked, "Can you hear it if you listen hard?"

"Hear what?" Mack asked.

"The winter's coming," Gene answered. "There's a hum in the air. I can physically hear it. I can feel it, too. Sure, you know it's mid-September and winter's coming, but can you _feel_ it? I can. Maybe it's only the humming of the jet stream, but I know the sound, for it's in the fiber of my being. It's far away, but I can tell you it's to the northwest, and it's so big it's halfway up the sky. Maybe it's a mass of moving air, maybe not. Did you ever see cartoons of the North Wind as a fat face puffing storms over the frozen landscape? I can understand how primitive peoples thought there were such frost giants and malevolent gods like that. There's a physical thing coming—and it's the winter. It's what this experiment has always been about, Dr. Chamberlain," he said, looking her in the eye. "All those nights lying cold in the dirt were just schoolboy drills for what I'll soon face.

"You scientists thought I'd never last until September, but the original purpose of the project was to have a subject afield all summer getting ready for the snow. You came to believe in failure because all of your subjects failed, but I haven't—not yet, anyway. I'm stronger every day, thank God. I've come so far now I can hear something beyond your ken. There is no stopping this experiment now. Sure, I got my face cut up, and I look like something two weeks dead, but I knew you were going to find me eventually and get that look on your faces when you saw my new scar. That's why

I've been hurrying to finish this cabin. I had to prove I am a viable test subject with a good chance at survival in the snow."

"Gene—," Britt tried, but he raised his hand.

"I see you brought sleeping bags. By the time we eat, it'll be sundown. Tomorrow, Dr. Chamberlain will have to report, and the day after, the rangers and Garner'll be here. That gives me a day and a half to make it look too good to lose this chance."

"What's that you're making in the cabin?" Roxy asked, changing the subject.

"Thank you, Roxy," he said. "That will be my fire pit. I'm making it from broken stone; I'm going to raise it two feet off the floor, then build up one side to control the draft to direct smoke toward a hole I'll cut through the roof. I'm using clay from the Yellowstone River and some flat pieces of rhyolite. Hey, that water ought to be boiling by now. Let's have some tea."

As he jumped up to get the pot off the fire, Britt searched her friends' faces for any sign of how they felt. Mack looked away, unwilling to meet her eyes, but Roxy gave her a noncommittal shrug and began to play with one of Gene's tools.

"What do you think happened?" she whispered.

"He'll tell us in his own good time," Roxy whispered back.

For her part, Dr. Chamberlain didn't understand how she felt either. Did she want the experiment to end in failure? No, but neither was she happy about Gene's determination to continue. Something had to be done, something had to be decided, but was she the one to do it? She was frustrated; she was unhappy; she was very apprehensive. For the first time, Britt had a real sense of how powerful and unforgiving the wilderness could be. If Gene could suffer such a wound when practically under surveillance, what might happen in the winter snows when it would be harder to monitor him?

As she thought about it, this was exactly what Project Snow was about. Gene was right. Variables were what she and her fellow scientists called it back in their comfortable lodgings. Variables could change everything. A fluke, a misfortune, a bit of unexpected luck could alter the course of the experiment in the space of a heartbeat, and it was hard for her to deal with that as a scientist. She should relish a new variable, she should welcome new data, but instead, she was terrified. Something horrible might happen here, and she didn't want it to happen to him.

As Siegfried poured aromatic tea into their folding hiker's cups, Britt took a cracked china mug from a rock near the fire pit. "Is it yours?" she asked, feeling sad, for with no handle and a big chip missing from its lip, she would have tossed it in the trash, yet it was apparently his most prized possession.

"Yeah," Gene answered, taking it to pour himself some tea. "I found it sitting on a log a mile north of Buffalo Ford. It had been there for years and was full of pine needles and dirt."

"What is this stuff we're drinking?" Mack asked.

Gene was horsing around with Roxy, but he answered, "I don't know. It's a root. If you grate it with dried cinquefoil or spruce needles, it makes good tea. Gives you a rush, huh? I'm sure it's some kind of stimulant. The botanist will be interested in what I've discovered. Dr. Garner said that next summer, as each plant comes into season, they're going to have me show what I've learned so they can identify the plants."

Siegfried got up to stoke the fires under his drying racks, scrape hides, and clarify buffalo fat. Not wasting a minute, he later put an elk roast on a spit and hung it over a hot bed of coals, and then he was off to sharpen a stack of fire-hardened four-inch thick poles. "Except for bears digging through my roof," he explained, "I'm most worried about a buffalo walking on top. I'll plant these poles in a ring around the roof to ward off such familiarity."

"A couple of good pokes, and I'll bet anything would leave you alone," Mack agreed, jumping up. "You need help?"

"Nope. You know the rules."

"Yeah, I do" Mack said, sitting down again. "I just felt I had to offer."

Before sundown, Gene sent the two women to gather grasses for their beds, and when they returned, they found Mack and him engaged in a conversation that ended abruptly at their approach. Britt would have paid in gold to know what they had been discussing, but the moment was lost in the bustle of arranging sleeping bags and gear. In the darkness a couple of hours later, the three visitors retired for the night, and the deep chill of fall settled over them.

Britt Chamberlain had placed herself between her two friends, for she was afraid of sleeping outdoors for the first time, but she soon regretted it. Roxy snored like a sailor and tossed about all night; Mack buried himself within his mummy bag and didn't move a muscle until morning, when he emerged like a turtle from its shell, fresh and rested. Britt could sleep only fitfully. Looking straight up at the blaze of stars overhead or over at the glowing red eyes of the fires, she noticed that Gene Siegfried slept very little. For most of the night, he moved about doing chores. Once, she saw him sitting beside his biggest bonfire with an elk robe over his shoulders, but sometime in the grayness of the false dawn, he was gone.

It was seven o'clock in the morning when she woke from a warm dream to bright sunlight in her face. Mack and Roxy were sitting beside a fire, and she could smell coffee and breakfast.

"Good morning. How's our sleeping beauty?" Roxy asked pleasantly. She was very rumpled. Her face looked worn and wrinkled in the sunshine. Sometimes she looked fifty, though only in her mid-twenties, Britt thought. What would her future be?

"Okay, I guess. I'm still a little groggy. I didn't sleep well last night," Britt said, wondering if the younger woman knew what a pill she was to sleep next to.

"Only the innocent sleep well," Roxy answered, looking at her hands, looking at her nails, looking at her boots.

"Where's Gene?" Britt asked. She felt dirty after sleeping on the ground. Her back ached where pebbles had gouged what felt like craters into her while sleeping. Roxy had advised her to bring along a foam mat to sleep on, but she hadn't had the time, and she regretted it now.

"Dunno where Gene is," Roxy answered. "He hasn't been around since we've been up. Come have breakfast. Mack fixed biscuits, and we've got cheese, coffee, and jam. In the mood to eat?"

"I'm starved, though we ate like pigs last night. I had no idea elk meat was so delicious." Rolling out of her sleeping bag, Britt felt every bone in her body complain. A gritty frost covered her boots and sunglasses, and by the time she had her jacket on and got over to the fire, where Mack gave her a cup of water to brush her teeth, she was shivering uncontrollably. Although her friends were sitting in bright sunlight beside a nice fire, it was quite cold outside. Roxy poured her a half-cup of coffee, but she shook so badly she managed to spill most of it on her jeans. Ten minutes later, she was up to drinking a full cup, but it was a long time before she felt warm again.

Breakfast was good, but it wasn't pretty after being cooked over an open pine fire. Strangely, she discovered the simple fare satisfied her like no other ever had. She felt alive. The air was clear, and the sunshine and the intensely beautiful setting thrilled her. If this was why people camped, she resolved to do more of it.

"Mack's a pretty good cook, ain't he?" Roxy smiled. "He's the best campfire cook I ever met."

"Course I am," he acknowledged bashfully.

"You can do all my cooking, honey!" Roxy laughed, pinching his cheek and making him blush.

"Yes, very good," Britt allowed. "Got any soap to wash these dishes?"

"Not good in the back country," Mack answered. "Use sand. It doesn't pollute the water. There's a wide place in the brook about a hundred yards downstream. You'll have to lie on your belly to reach the water. Oh, and take a cup of coffee with you. Your fingers are going to get cold."

An hour later, as they continued warming themselves by the fire and talking, a raven swooped across the meadow and landed on its perch in the moose antlers above the cabin door. A piece of meat was waiting there, but it cawed loudly for several minutes before swallowing the treat whole.

Hopping from tine to tine in a repetitive bird's game, the raven flapped its wings in great excitement.

Gene Siegfried, his chest and legs soaked with blood and mud, was coming through the opening in the trees, a grin across his wide face. On his shoulder, he carried a javelin with two Canada geese hanging by their necks from the shaft. They had already been gutted, and gore dripped out their vents and colored the grass behind him. "Look here!" he called. "I heard these geese feeding yesterday afternoon near Alum Crick. Took me a couple hours lying in the grass before they came close enough to kill." He spread the wings of the birds to show how large they were, and then he sharpened a camp knife on a rock, skinned them expertly, and placed the meat on a drying rack. The fat from the skins he would render for use in cooking or for a lamp.

"It's about time we were on our way, Gene," Mack remarked. "We'll be back sometime tomorrow, no doubt."

"No, I don't think so," Siegfried disagreed. "You don't have any place in Project Snow; whatever you say would be taken as interference. I appreciate your concern, but tomorrow is not your day. I'll see you another time—you got my address."

Roxy may have had a tear in her eye, but if so, she concealed it by wrapping Gene in her arms and squeezing him. Again, Britt was amazed how much taller she was than him, but when the young woman stepped back, Gene's sheer bulk seemed to even things. Mack threw on his pack, patted Siegfried on the shoulder to wish him luck, and strode off toward the valley. The two women hurried to join him.

"What do you think?" Roxy asked when they were out of earshot.

"He's going to make it," Mack said.

"What happened to him?" Roxy asked.

"Elk. Bull. He thought it was dead."

"Jeez, it got him pretty good…" she said.

"Yeah, but otherwise he looks good."

"Yes."

"He's got a chance too, by the look of things. Good thing we signed those contracts, huh?" Mack grinned.

"Yep, it's beginning to look that way," Roxy agreed.

"What contracts?" Britt asked, sensing a conspiracy.

"Never mind," he warned.

"It's okay, Mack," Roxy said. "Britt, you mustn't tell anyone, especially not the rangers."

"I won't. You know I've got my own problems with the Park Service."

"Neither of us," Roxy continued, "is popular with rangers. They'd love to ship us out the gate, which is why we don't want them to find out we wrangled ourselves a contract at Snow Lodge this winter."

"What?" Britt exclaimed happily. "The two of you are going to be down at Old Faithful this winter?"

"Yep. Mack's going to do the laundry and assist me busting beds. I'm the maid. The two of us are a team, and we'll be close enough to follow what's happening with Gene."

"Then you'll be near enough that he may come over to—"

"No!" Mack said harshly. He and Roxy exchanged looks like parents over a wayward child. "At a minimum, it would be a hard day for him to reach the Loop Road at Nez Perce crossing. If he went south to West Thumb, then to Old Faithful, it would be at least three days. Straight as a crow flies, from Hayden Valley to Old Faithful? Impossible. You haven't seen the winter, but if we see Gene at all, we'll have to borrow a snowmobile and drive up here."

"Then perhaps the three of us can come visit him," Britt suggested.

"It ain't no afternoon trip," he countered. "You haven't seen it, but winter in Yellowstone is like white hell."

CHAPTER 16

✻ ✻ ✻

The Examination

WHEN THE SCIENTISTS and rangers came through the opening from the valley next morning, Gene was inside the cabin, working on a split-wood floor. During the night, he had finished framing a door, then built a wall on either side of the entranceway. Under the verandah to the left of the doorway, he had built a large kindling box, and to the right, a pantry with a door slotted to foil all but human intruders. To insulate the cabin, he had stacked four cords of busted pine on each side of the doorway. Leaning against a column under the verandah roof and surveying his work, he decided the cabin looked watertight and winter proof; he hoped the researchers and rangers would see it that way too as they came across the meadow.

As they halted before the cabin and conferred among themselves, Gene felt more confident than ever before. From what Dr. Chamberlain had told him the day before, the researchers had recently tried to convince Douglas Paine Hanson to quit, and Gene could see the amazement on their faces now at the marked contrast between their two subjects. Britt said Hanson was thin and bedraggled; Gene was thick and strong. Hanson's clothes were in rags, his beard scraggly, and his windblown hair tangled and dull. While Gene's original clothes were shot, he now wore a thigh-length, elkhide shirt and a thick, hairy vest, and he had leather pants cut out and waiting for stitching.

The most striking difference between the two men, however, was that Gene knew his new clothes weren't just practical. Hanson had only soft skins to wrap around his shoulders; Gene's shirt and vest both had carved elk ivory buttons, and he also had a wide leather belt with a real iron buckle. Hanson ate nearly everything he gathered, but Gene had a surplus of several hundred pounds of jerky, berries, fruits, and roots. He also had stocks of buffalo wool, leather, goose down, quills, bones, sinew, antlers, and horn, as well as two good elk robes, a tanned buffalo hide, and another being stretched. Even with all of this, however, he realized his injury would make it difficult to convince the researchers to let him continue the experiment.

The raven had announced their presence. There were three men from the Park Service—Jimmy Downes, Red Reese, and Gary Marlin, a ranger from the Lake area—and five scientists: Britt, Capland, Garner, Bud Garcia, the anthropologist, and another medical doctor named Tom Turner. There was a change in the breeze; the sky was gray to the northwest. There would be drizzle tonight, Gene thought. That meant they probably would not stay more than a few hours.

"Hello, the cabin!" Garner called, the effort setting him to coughing.

"Come ahead," Gene allowed from the entranceway. The raven fussed a bit as they neared, then sailed away into the eye of the breeze. Gene followed it with his eyes. It dipped down by the trees to the right of the meadow, circled once, then flew away toward the valley.

"Hi, again," Britt smiled, though she looked tired and sounded hoarse—probably from talking most of the night. She and Dr. Capland took a seat on a log near a fire, but the others stood awkwardly nearby. Capland seemed itching to get his hands on Gene's scarred face, but at the same time, he appeared strangely awestruck. Reese studied the cabin site and avoided the young man's eyes.

"You gave us a goddamn good scare!" the old man complained. "Capland, get up and let an old man sit down." Grumpily settling himself on the log, he poked the fire with his foot and snapped, "You look awful. I've a good mind to—"

"Now, Doctor Garner," Gene cooed, "I didn't come in for treatment, and I know I missed a monthly briefing, but believe me, I'm okay. I was sticking close to home until I got my strength back. You people were welcome to come see me anytime, but Dr. Chamberlain tells me you were awful quick to declare me dead. Why such a rush? None of you has credited me with half a chance, yet I'm doing better than your other subject. Hanson's your worry, not me.

"Sure, I've got a face that can use some looking after, but as you can see," he said, waving his arm at the cabin, "I'm in good shape for the winter. I've got food and fuel. I've got shelter and soon'll have more clothes. Things look good in my camp. Don't come here with a preconceived notion I've failed. I may need your intervention sometime, but I don't need you now."

Garner was obviously upset at Gene's determination, but he seemed to listen fairly. He'd probably heard it all night long from Dr. Chamberlain. As the old man looked around the camp, his wrinkled face showed he thought everything looked good, but he told Gene, "I want Doctors Capland and Turner to examine you. Garcia wants photographs of the cabin and such. For right now, we'll call this your regularly scheduled briefing. We've got a lot to talk about later."

"Okay," Gene agreed, uncrossing his arms.

As Siegfried waved the two doctors into the cabin, he overheard the old man ask Britt if she didn't think they were losing control over their subject. "When did it happen?" Garner wondered aloud. "Is this an exceptional situation with an unusual subject, or would anyone exposed to these conditions react with such tenacity? Is the Lamar Test Subject's desperate will the same as HVTS's stubbornness, and if so, are these reactions produced by the exigencies of survival or some unknown instinct deep in the human psyche?"

"I don't know," she answered. "I believe determination has survival value, though I don't know how to measure it. The project's dredging up more questions than answers."

Smiling to himself at their confusion, Gene followed the doctors into the cabin and sat on the edge of his fire pit. Outside, Britt and Garcia began taking pictures, and the rangers measured the cabin.

"Blink your right eye, if you can," Dr. Turner asked, holding up an intense light. "Again ... again. Now wink that eye slowly. Again. Can you feel any pain or tenderness here?" he asked, running his finger along the underside of the scar.

"No."

"Here?" Turner asked, reaching up to touch it directly.

"No."

"Here?" the doctor asked, running a finger north of the scar.

"That's a little sore," Gene admitted. "I lanced it a week ago, but it's still a little tender."

"Open your mouth," Turner told him. "That's it ... a little wider ... a little wider."

"Nughmm!"

"Yes, I know, but just a little wider, please. Ooh! There's a nasty canker sore along the gum here. Does this hurt?"

"Ayyaah!" Gene roared. "I didn't know it was sore until you poked it." He spat a bit of blood onto the cabin floor and pressed his hand to his cheek. "Geez!" he said. "Don't do that again."

The doctor moved toward him, however, a steel probe in his hand. "Sorry, Mr. Siegfried. Open up again. Let's have another look." With the probe, he explored next to the gum, and then he asked, "Can you raise your cheek like this?" He winced in demonstration, and Gene tried to mimic him. "Any pain?"

"Back here where I lanced it. It's good, otherwise, I guess ...."

"How so?"

"God gave two gifts to mankind: Pain to remember our mortality, and no memory of how bad the pain really was, so we can go on with our lives."

"Hmmm. There's truth in that," the doctor agreed. "So you know you were <u>hurt</u> by the elk, but don't remember how it <u>felt</u>...."

"Yep."

Dr. Turner sat back on his haunches while Dr. Capland moved in to examine the scar itself. When he finished, the two doctors had Gene strip naked, give them samples, run in place, and perform all the other routines of a regular physical.

"Okay, you can get dressed," Dr. Turner finally said.

"You done in there?" Garcia, the anthropologist called from outside. "If you are, I'd like to take some pictures."

"We're done," Dr. Capland shouted. "We'll go out by the fire to talk."

Outside, Garcia was running his hand over an intricately carved nameplate in the soffit of the lintel beam. Out loud, he read, "Desperaden," then winked at Gene as he passed and said, "The name of the cabin, eh?"

"Yep," Gene nodded proudly. He knew the nameplate was a nice bit of work.

"You carve it?"

"Yep."

"Good job."

Siegfried knew the nameplate was just the beginning. He was hoping to have a winter's worth of carving ahead, but everything depended on the course of the coming interview. Garcia had many questions, Britt had an extensive profile to conduct, the rangers wanted to ask about his recent kills, but Doctor Garner sat patiently in the same spot by the fire, smoking his pipe and thinking.

By mid-afternoon, the scientists had completed their work, so Gene put a pot of water on to boil. Within minutes, a black speck in the sky swooped over the meadow to land as a raven in a nearby tree. Gene cut it a piece of meat from a quarter hanging in his pantry, but the raven did not come in to feed. Instead, it hopped irritably from branch to branch, deathly quiet.

"I see all of you have dehydrated hikers' dinners. I'm fixing some water so you can eat," Gene said. Garner started to shake his head no, but the others immediately accepted it as a good idea. "Besides, it would make me feel good about having visitors in camp," he placated the old man. "It's no trouble."

"We'd love to," Britt interrupted, "on condition we be back on the trail before dark." Glancing at the men to make her point, she added, "I don't want to sleep out tonight. Besides, it looks like rain."

"Back on the trail before dark, eh?" Gene laughed. "Not afraid of things that go bump in the night, are you? 'From ghoulies and ghosties and long-leggedy beasties, and things that go bump in the night, Good Lord, deliver us," he quoted from an old Celtic prayer. "Don't worry, Dr. Chamberlain. You're in too large a group for bears. Besides, the bears are in no mood to cause trouble."

"You see any bears recently?" Reese asked excitedly.

"Quite a few, all grizzlies, but it's to be expected," Gene answered. "I'm intruding on the edge of one of their best feeding areas. They come to test the wind, but none have approached. I haven't seen any boars at all, just sows and cubs. I keep my fires going and'll continue until all this food's dried and put away. I'm going to bear-proof the cabin this week and clear the area of leftovers and scent."

The rangers didn't look like they believed him, and they began to argue among themselves why grizzlies hadn't raided the camp yet. Meanwhile, Gene mixed his visitors' packaged dinners in the water, stirring it into one big stew. "There," he announced, "that's plenty for the eleven of us."

"Eleven?" Reese asked, looking up in surprise.

"The two still out in the trees," Gene answered.

"What two out in the trees?" Downes asked suspiciously.

"The two down there," Gene declared, pointing to a spot in the trees to the right of the opening to the valley. "They've been watching all afternoon."

"I'm sorry, but there's no one there. We _did_ have you under some surveillance—" Downes admitted, then corrected himself when Garner shot him a look. "That is … uh … we did before your accident. We had some casual reports on a few of your activities, but trust me, we don't have anyone now."

"But you did until I left the Sulphur Hills?" Gene inquired in surprise, unconsciously complimenting the skill of the new surveillance team. "Then who are those two guys down there?" he asked.

"There's no one there," Britt swore, wondering if he weren't exhibiting paranoia brought on by his isolation.

"Oh," Gene said, shrugging his shoulders. He said no more about it at the fire, but twice during dinner, he looked up at the raven, puzzled how he had so misread the bird. Very suspicious at first, in the end, he decided to believe the scientists. The raven clucked in disgust and flew angrily away.

"Well, Doctor Capland? What did you find?" Garner asked as soon as everyone had finished eating.

Clearing his throat, the doctor reported, "Actually, I'm surprised. The eye and muscles coincident to the eye appear undamaged. As the scar tissue tightens in his right cheek, the droop in his upper lid will become more pronounced, but we can correct that next spring."

Smiling to himself—for Capland had said "next spring"—Gene knew that he had convinced the medical men. He busied himself adding wood to the fire.

"The scar looks terrible," Capland continued. "I have never seen worse stitching in my life. He seems to have gone out of his way to achieve maximum tissue buildup. We can have a plastic surgeon clean up the scar later. Siegfried tells us he's had pain something like *tic douleureux*, or trigeminal neuralgia. It may be getting worse. There is a place near his right ear that I feel should be opened and examined. I don't believe it's infected. There may be a chip of bone from the zygomatic arch that is causing pain. Remarkably, there is no major infection, due probably to thorough bleeding, rather than proper medical care—"

"And what about the injury itself? What happened?" Garner inquired.

"The elk's antler peeled the skin away from connective tissue, but caused no serious damage to muscles or bone. That's nothing short of a miracle. The injury looks worse at this stage than it really is. Of course, by spring, since this hasn't been treated by a surgeon, there will be further complications. Most likely, these problems can be alleviated in three or four surgeries, but as Mr. Siegfried ages, the right side of his face will have continuing problems."

"What kind of problems?" Garner asked.

"Neuralgia. Bell's Palsy is likely, too. Some atrophy of the muscles of the face, stiffness, perhaps some sagging, particularly around the right eye. He will always have a prominent scar—"

"He needs dental work immediately," Dr. Turner interrupted. "One molar and perhaps the premolar on the upper right jaw appear to be inflamed. I'm not a dentist, but considering the blow he took, I wouldn't be surprised if there weren't problems. He needs to be x-rayed as soon as possible, but there is nothing that will threaten his success in this project. Dr. Capland and I are of the opinion that he be allowed to continue, on condition he report for x-rays and a dental exam within the week. At that time, we will open and explore the section near his ear and put him on preventive antibiotics. He is in absolutely no life threatening or inhibiting danger we can determine. Considering what's happened, he is in good condition and seems to be recovering well."

"Um huh," Garner mumbled, sucking on his pipe, and it was hard to tell if he were happy Gene was okay or disturbed an excuse hadn't been found to end Project Snow. The old man would write later the favorable news from the doctors and the dentist who later removed two of Siegfried's teeth was the turning point of the experiment. The reports solidified the young man's intention to outlast the winter and legitimized the scientists' inability to interfere with the course of events. Siegfried had gained control over his own destiny just as winter was coming.

The long day of testing and questioning was finally over, though there were still details to be arranged. Gene agreed to visit Canyon Village for a complete physical as soon as he could secure his camp. After the exam, the Canyon Village Test Center would be closed for the winter, and Garner and a select few would wait in West Yellowstone to monitor the weather. Monthly physicals would be suspended until spring; instead, Gene promised to fill out a detailed questionnaire each month, which he would leave with medical samples in a secret stash near Dragon's Mouth.

Unbeknownst to him, Jimmy Downes was already plotting to quarter a surveillance team in a winter cabin at Canyon Village. He had decided an outpost on the high north ridge overlooking the valley—a distance required by the extremes of the coming winter—would be enough, since ninety percent of Siegfried's outdoor activities would be in the valley proper. The ridge also had the advantage of blocking the sound of the observers' snowmobiles from him.

After the researchers waved goodbye, and Ranger Downes led the group out into the valley, Gene seemed pensive, as if the enormity of his undertaking was catching up with him.

"So do you think he's going to make it?" Reese teased as soon as they were out of earshot.

"I do," Downes admitted.

"So do I," Reese agreed. "It's going to be really tough, though."

Turning away, Ranger Reese and the other ranger began to talk football. The doctors were speaking in medicalese, Drs. Chamberlain and Garner were planning their winter, and only Ranger Downes had his mind on the trail. There were logistical problems to be arranged, a winter to prepare for, a surveillance team to brief—but his eyes were on the footprints of two unknown hikers that joined the main trail from the right soon after leaving the forest to the east of the little meadow. Was this a security breach? Should he warn Reese two unauthorized people knew the location of the cabin, or was it Siegfried's crazy friends, Mack and Roxy? Interrupted in mid-thought by a question from Reese, he put the tracks joining the trail out of his mind.

Several days later, a deep, fluffy snow fell that was reluctant to melt. There was a bone-chill in the air; the fragile warmth of summer was gone for another year. It would only grow colder now, and colder still. The surveillance team watched Gene jerk the last of his meat, then scour the camp of all trace of butchery. After burning his drying racks and hide stretchers, he moved everything else indoors. Although he was now out of direct surveillance, one of the scouts got near enough to hear pounding sounds inside the cabin. Two days later, Gene went to Trout Creek for a bath, and a scout entered the cabin to see what he had been building.

Siegfried had pegged shelves to the front walls, made a stool and built a bed frame in one of the back corners. After cutting a rawhide to laces, he had woven them onto the frame. As the leather dried, it had tightened into a comfortable platform on which he had laid the buffalo hide and two warm elk robes. Careful to record every detail of the interior, the scout reported things looked good in the cabin named Desperaden, though its final touch—an abatis of sharpened stakes to protect the roof—looked barbaric.

None of the scouts or rangers took a photograph of the outside of the cabin in its final form, but Jimmy Downes described it in his logbook as strong and brooding. A meager path led through a ring of stakes to the shelter of the verandah. There was nothing homey or comforting there, no light glimmering hopefully on a dark and windy night, just a smoking, stygian hillock bristling with skewers. It was practical and safe, but the design of the cabin, Downes believed, manifested the desperation of a lone man in a dangerous wilderness—a man not nearly so confident as he seemed.

CHAPTER 17

❄ ❄ ❄

Early Winter

THERE WAS, THEY claim now, an odd ring to the wood as they nailed into it, an echoing reluctance that promised a hard winter ahead. It was probably a wives' tale, the kind that crops up that time of year. Old-timers said bears were fatter and squirrels unusually busy. The geese were migrating earlier, the pines had thicker bark, and so it went. There may be some truth to it, but then again, fall is the only time to pause and wonder whether nature is preparing for its worst, or reacting to its past.

To be sure, though, carpenters added extra nails to shutters and stiffened supports under roofs that might be subjected to undue loads of snow. Roosevelt Lodge was the first to close for the season, followed, in mid-September by Fishing Bridge Campers' Cabins and Canyon Village.

Lake Hotel, that magnificent passenger liner of a building, was next. Standing in Victorian grandeur on the high western bank of Yellowstone Lake, the hotel would take the brunt of winds coming off the ice. Old Faithful Campers' Cabins—which would reopen two months later as "Snow Lodge"— was closed about the time the boats were hauled away from Bridge Bay and Grant Village, and then Old Faithful Lodge closed its doors for the season. At the same time, Park Service crews were busily planting brightly tipped poles alongside the highways to guide spring snowplows. By the first week of October, only two Hamilton Stores, plus Old Faithful Inn and Lake Lodge were open for business.

The start of the school year had reduced the number of families on vacation, and only late fall travelers were to be seen now. This was the season for professional photographers, for all the wildlife was on the move. Moose with tabletop antlers jousted in the forest. Foolish with the rut, mighty elk bulls were fighting over harems, and bears were sleek and fat.

The land had taken on a serene beauty. Gone were the gorgeous blooms of summer and fields that changed color, week-by-week, as different flowers came into season. Now, there were only the shimmering hues of ripe grass waving in gentle breezes and the pastel gray of sagebrush. In the lower altitudes, aspen and cottonwood shimmered like gold, and scrub oak blazed such a deep red it looked like blood splashed upon the mountainsides.

One man watched the decline of Yellowstone's traffic and the changing of the seasons sadly, because for him, it was the tolling of an iron bell. Douglas Paine Hanson was in better shape than he had been all summer, but he knew he could not face the snow. He didn't have the clothes, food, or a winter-proof shelter. He had tried his best, but each harvest lasted only until the next bonanza. He never had the luck or the opportunity to go beyond a hand-to-mouth existence. He didn't have a surplus to tide him over. He knew he could never survive until spring.

One afternoon, Hanson came out on a sagebrushed hill and looked out across the rolling, glaciated valley of the Lamar Valley toward Roosevelt Lodge—and there was no traffic there, no parked cars, no crazy wranglers, no Yellowstone coaches, no horses. Feeling like his best friend had died, he sank to his knees, and the proud, the indomitable Douglas Paine Hanson wept like a child. It would have been nice to carry on his writing in a snug cabin by the light of an oil lamp, but he had never built that cabin and did not have the fat to fuel a lamp for the winter.

Walking down the middle of the empty highway, he worried this would be the end of his reputation as an outdoorsman and writer. Hours later, in an emotional press conference at the Mammoth Ranger Station, he formally called it quits. "I did not have what it takes," he said, tears washing down his face. "And it takes a lot."

"What do you plan to do now?" a journalist asked.

"I don't know," Hanson said. "I need time."

Not long afterward, however, he was invited to appear on the nationally televised Robert Faulkhiser Show. In a chatty introduction, the host said, "Douglas Paine Hanson and that other subject, the Hayden Valley guy, lived a life like Robinson Crusoe, a life we all fantasize about. Ladies and gentlemen, may I introduce one of the bravest men I have ever met—"

"Thank you," Hanson said as he came out of the curtains and awkwardly acknowledged thunderous applause with a wave of his hand. The studio lights blinded him. Tears sprang to his eyes. "I don't think of myself as particularly brave—" he said.

"Yes, but you risked life and health in the interest of science! How about that, ladies and gentlemen?" Faulkhiser asked as he eagerly shook Hanson's hand. "Let's have another round of applause—"

The audience reaction was beyond what Hanson expected. People rose from their seats, clapping and whistling. Even Faulkhiser was surprised. "Thank you," Hanson said, tears rolling down his cheeks and dripping off his chin. He had never dreamed people identified with his lonely struggle.

"Tell us about your experiences," Faulkhiser said when the applause abated.

"I was thinking about your introduction," Hanson answered. "You mentioned _Robinson Crusoe_. It's been years since I read the book. I remember it had a lot to say about one man's tendency to destroy himself just when things were going well. In his solitude, Crusoe learns to accept responsibility for his mistakes, but when he's rescued, he picks up his life right where he left it. As I remember the story, it's a quaint, sentimental tale."

"It's a classic—"

"Yes, but it frustrated me too."

"How's that?"

"After more than twenty-five years living alone, agonizing over his failures and mistakes, then finding his faith in God strengthened and learning to be patient, Crusoe finds a group of Spanish castaways living nearby. He gets them to agree to build a boat so they can escape—"

"I don't remember that part of the book."

"That's because Crusoe is unexpectedly rescued by someone else. He leaves the Spaniards behind."

"I had forgotten that too," Faulkhiser said. "So it was in character then?"

"I suppose it was," Hanson agreed. "But I never had any sympathy for the character."

"I guess that means you don't think Crusoe's experience is relevant to your own situation?" Faulkhiser asked, trying to elicit reaction from the audience.

"No," Hanson answered. There were a few murmurs from people sitting out beyond the powerful lights, but he could also see a few nods. "Robinson Crusoe had an advantage the volunteers in Project Snow didn't. He was a victim of shipwreck, and he was able to achieve the necessities of life by salvaging barrels, ropes, guns, food, and seeds. There was no question of his <u>survival</u>. He merely adapted European tools and systems to a benign tropical climate. In fact, he refused to take advantage of what the island had to offer. Here he is on a tropical island, and the only fruit he eats are grapes. He never adapted to his new situation."

"But you volunteers had to adapt," Faulkhiser said.

"Yes," Hanson agreed. "The difference between Crusoe and the volunteers in Project Snow is we started with nothing—"

"What about the other volunteer, the HVTS?" Faulkhiser grinned. "He cheated, didn't he? He salvaged what he needed—just like Crusoe!" There was a strong reaction from the audience, but it was not the sentiment Faulkhiser was trying to elicit.

Seeing the audience's response, Hanson felt reassured. He disagreed, "Siegfried jumped the gap. A piece of rusted steel offers no protection or food until it is made into a weapon. I had as good a chance as he to use scraps to make my tools, but I didn't. I couldn't. I didn't have it in me to adapt."

Surprised at his own conclusion, Hanson realized Gene Siegfried deserved to be a survivor. Hanson recalled reading a surveillance report; in it, Gene was reported picking a few maggots off a bloody bone and popping them in his mouth. Hanson had never been able to do that. He had never been able to beat his inhibitions. He had never adapted. Yes, Hanson realized, Gene had beaten him fairly. The kid hadn't cheated. He had played within the experiment's rules from the beginning.

"Don't you believe this young man—" Faulkhiser tried.

"Siegfried dredged up a cultural memory," Hanson interrupted. "He used his ability to alter steel into a useful object. It was only the superiority of his skill that gave him the edge he needed." It was a stunning change of heart for Hanson. Up to this point, he had resented Gene Siegfried's successes. He had believed this inexperienced kid had somehow bluffed his way through the experiment. Deep down, Hanson had gloated over the approach of winter to set things right, but now, as he sat sweltering under the bright lights and intrusive television cameras in New York City, he feared for Gene Siegfried's life in faraway Wyoming.

As the audience applauded, Hanson was transformed into the young man's defender. He gave an emotional description of the wilderness—the killing, the pain, the suffering, the decision-making that went into each action lest it lead to mistakes and death. In the coming winter months, much of what Gene Siegfried felt would be explained in Hanson's words. Articulate, with a wealth of observations and a style that pleased interviewers, Hanson would publish long before any of the scientists put pen to paper, and it was _his_ impressions and photos in popular magazines, not their sere data in scientific journals that would fire the public's imagination.

His major contribution, however was to focus attention on the last remaining volunteer in Project Snow, the Hayden Valley Test Subject, the HVTS. As winter closed its icy grip on the high country, Douglas Paine Hanson's appearances and writings impressed the public with the stoic courage of a man fighting to survive a dangerous wilderness alone. Gene Siegfried was noticed; he became a celebrity-in-absentia. Astrologers cast his horoscope and speculated on his success. Gossip columnists collected stories about him. Residents were asked if they had ever met him, and the beginnings of local legends evolved.

Hanson was also responsible for popularizing a native Yellowstone expression. They were all "savages," those who loved this place and knew it best—the seasonals, the permanents, the rangers—but Gene Siegfried would forever afterward be known as "The Savage."

Though he soon heard himself called so, Gene got no satisfaction from the title, for he was beginning to feel that way. Hanson could neatly express the mental transitions of failing as a hunter and being reduced to scavenging for maggoty bones, but Gene could not put into words—even for himself—the isolation he felt from members of his own species. The first snowfalls were like waving goodbye to the motherland and setting off on a voyage into the winter unknown. There were few dudes on the road now, and each time he hunted in the valley, he found himself listening for the distant thunder of tires and engines. Finally, a day came there was nothing but the soughing of the wind. He was finally alone. The winter had begun.

Even so, the big snow delayed. Gene knew the rangers itched to close the roads, and winter keepers were growing bored. He knew the Snow Lodge crew, Roxy and Mack included, were off on a brief vacation between seasons. Later, he would learn Mack spent a painful two weeks with his family in Jackson Hole and felt awkward around friends going back to college. Roxy had an obligatory three days with her parents in California and then fled to Oregon.

October faded away with only minor snows that soon melted. Once, while Gene was away hunting, his cabin received a visit from an exceptionally large boar grizzly, and his pantry was severely damaged. The bear ate, carried away, or ruined more than two hundred pounds of jerky and dried roots, but the loss was not as serious as might have been expected. Strengthening the pantry as well as he could, Gene felt certain the bear would return in the spring, when it would be desperately hungry. To deter that possibility, he hammered his last three rusty nails through the underside of the pantry door where the bear might bite first.

As previously arranged, he met a ranger on the highway and was taken to West Yellowstone for his October physical. On the way, they stopped at Canyon Village, where an isolated cabin had been set up for his use in an emergency. Inside were a radio, batteries, lanterns, food, dry firewood, matches, winter clothes, medical supplies, and blankets. Other than showing him the emergency cabin, the ranger didn't have much constructive to say, and neither did anyone else. Gene was back in the valley by late afternoon. Of his October checkup, only a few x-rays of his teeth, his white blood cell count, pulse, blood pressure, and weight remain. No one bothered to interview him or take a photo. Left to cool his heels for two hours while waiting for a ride home, he heard Dr. Britt Chamberlain was shopping for clothes in Pocatello, Doctor Garner was addressing a convention in Denver, Dr. William Capland was on vacation, and the rangers were on business in Mammoth. The experience left him feeling abandoned.

Meanwhile, the snow was coming. A great churning storm built strength in the north Pacific. Sucking cold air straight from the Arctic, the storm drew moisture from the sea and surged ashore in coastal Washington as wind-driven rain. A day later, the front eddied eastward to the Rockies, bringing the long-awaited winter snowfall. There was an eerie silence as it approached, a day of peace and tranquility as the hum of the storm rose higher over the horizon, but in the early evening of the third of November, the clouds turned black, lightning flashed, and the air was filled with falling snow.

Snowflakes—classically hexagonal crystals—drifted straight down through the chilly air. Bundles of these flakes clung together in floating collision, mixing with shattered rays and prismatic bits of rime until the snowfall grew more serious. The fluffy flakes—some as large as hens' eggs—were replaced by columns and graupel, plates and needles, irregulars, pyramids, bullets, and hollow tubes. Before long, the grass was coated, and the ripened heads of grain bent under the deepening snow.

Fallen flakes began to sublimate and re-condense, packing and rounding their own fluffiness like only warm snow can do.

Leaning against one of the supports of his verandah, Gene watched the snowfall, strangely happy now that winter was here at last. There was much to do. He had clothes to sew, wood to gather, and preparations to make, but he stood in the shadows instead and let the beauty and anger of the storm fill him. At first, the snow smelled like rain, but it wasn't long before there was no definable scent. A hundred yards away, four buffalo cows stood at the edge of the forest, grumping over the start of another winter struggle; the raven preened its feathers in a nearby tree, croaking sullenly to itself. By midnight, every bear in Yellowstone was on the move, running as if Satan himself was at their heels. It was time for denning, and the snow would bury their tracks home. It was time for him to get under cover.

But first, Gene stripped naked and went out into the storm. He raised his arms and sang something like an Indian might sing.

"Hey yay, yay, deyoda yoda yoda-hoh. Yee yee yee, deyoda yoda yoda yo. Hey de-yay, yay, de-yay deyoda yoda yoda-hoh. Yee yee yee, deyoda yoda yoda ho." It didn't matter if it was an Indian language or not. It didn't matter if it addressed a "Great Spirit," or if he'd heard it in a movie. The truth was he felt he must _accept_ what was coming, bad or good, suffering, bloodshed, cold, pain, horror, or death, he had to accept what the winter would bring. This was the heart of the experiment; it was the heart of what he had undertaken. It was the heart of what he had committed to—and again the surveillance team missed it.

The next morning, there were nine inches of clean, white snow on the ground, and it continued snowing lightly all that day. There were sixteen inches on the ground by afternoon, enough fresh snow to bury the sins of the world. Gone were the summer flowers, the deep grasses, the berries, and fruits. Only the sagebrush and trees stuck out above the white blanket, and the ground's innumerable complexities were smoothed over until spring by an unbroken porcelain cover.

The snow hadn't yet taken on its distinctive character; it lay like a sheet of paper on a cluttered desk. There wasn't enough wind in that first storm to begin the drifting and stratifying that would come later; the marks of cruel névé and sastrugi, the dangerous blue of slush, and the crackling of avalanches were in the future. There was just this first, formless blanket, and Gene found himself challenging winter to do its worst.

He should have bitten his tongue.

A cold snap followed the storm. Temperatures nose-dived below freezing, and the ponderous movements of the hiemal winds began. By day, there was a sustained breeze out of the northwest, and snow drifted unchecked across the open valley and piled in the line of trees screening the meadow from that quarter. At night, westerly and southwesterly intermittent breezes packed and rounded the drifts and started the movement back the other way. As the alternate drifting and reshaping tugged back and forth in the timeless patterns of winter, Gene watched his careful preparations for winter sawn away.

Snowdrifts breached the tree wall to the valley, marched across the little meadow and jammed into the entrance of his cabin. At night, the alternate flow sucked at the drifted snow, forcing it deep into every cranny of the cabin's face. On warm days—that is on those few days above freezing—the snow would show signs of melting, but crisp nights froze it into armored ice. The woodpile was the first casualty in this tug of war. Logs froze together so solidly he had to pry wood loose to thaw for the next day's fire. The entrance to the cabin had to be shoveled each morning, and ice built underfoot until it rose halfway up his door.

The lid of the kindling box froze shut, the pantry door was frosted over too, and then the crude leather hinges of his door cracked in the cold and failed. Snow filtered in everywhere, and when the wind was blowing, no matter from what direction, it shook the door in its frame like a banshee's death rattle. Frost filtered in every crevice, evaporated when the cabin was warm, and then refroze as sooty dew. His tools rusted, forcing him to use fat to keep them greased. What he had hoped was a winter's worth of clarified fat for his oil lamps was soon consumed. He needed much more. While the interior of the cabin was streaked with frost, and icicles grew among the herbs hanging from the ceiling, his bed grew damp and chilly, but the more fire he used to combat these evils, the more frost and cold compounded them.

The problem, he realized, was that there had to be some way to balance heat with chill, frost with damp. The secret was fire, and Gene had to redesign a better chimney damper. He shielded the chimney hole from the drifting snow by stacking firewood outside to redirect the wind. Although it was crude, the vent drew better, except of course, when the wind was coming directly from the northeast. For the first time, the chimney worked like it was supposed to, the icicles were gone, the fire burned brightly, and frost inside the cabin was reduced.

Winter had begun to take on its cake-frosting look. Sagebrush looked like giant white toadstools; pine trees under heavy loads of snow had the appearance of Christmas cards. Smooth, round drifts undulated across the valley like dunes on a beach—and the little cabin was gone! What remained was an elliptical doorway filled with smoke and a ring of miniaturized spikes crowning an anonymous white hillside.

This was nothing like anyone had imagined. It was not a cozy cabin full of warmth and boredom. Instead, Gene Siegfried found his struggle for life intensified tenfold. Every household chore took hours. When he wasn't feeding the fire or cooking, or greasing, or oiling, he was plugging gaps and chipping away icicles. His back began to hurt, especially at night. Each morning, he had to shovel snow and break ice, then chop armloads of firewood. He fought to keep dry, let alone warm, and the more he fed the fire, the more relentlessly the cold closed in around him. Winter was pitiless. It crept in at every gap, assaulted every corner. Frost and damp took hold and chilled him through and through. Twenty-four hours a day, the assault raged on, and he began to have doubts. Was he _man_ enough? Was he _smart_ enough to figure it out? Or was he too pigheaded to realize he was losing?

For others the winter was not yet so bad. Britt Chamberlain had a comfortable room at the Madison Hotel in West Yellowstone, and her days were filled with throwing snowballs at a newfound love and learning to cross-country ski. Down and wool kept her warm; electricity and gas kept her room tolerable and her bath hot. The food was wholesome, and the winter was filled with snowmobiles, skis, hot coffee, and gloves with actual fingers.

Outside the park, recreation areas were attracting hundreds of winter sports enthusiasts. Art galleries, stores, and restaurants were enjoying good business, snowshovels grated on pavement, and children laughed on the way to school.

Gene Siegfried was not laughing. He spent time floundering in knee-deep snow as he grimly battled the growing cold. Failing to make a serviceable pair of gloves, he settled for mittens, but even they were excruciatingly hard to sew. He had to exercise his fingers for an hour before he could hold a needle. In addition, the beginnings of red patterning were showing on his hands and face, a skin condition called *erythema ab igne*, a discoloration caused by prolonged contact with heat and fire. His back bowed at the shoulders, and he could straighten only with difficulty. The same happened to his knees, and the ache in his feet was becoming constant, night and day.

It was not yet high winter, and already he was having a hard time. For him, there was no adventure in this, only desperation. Douglas Paine Hanson, sitting in a warm study miles from the park, brooded over suffering he didn't need to feel to understand. On November 28th, 1973, he wrote, "This is going to be the longest winter of my life." But no one else suspected the winter was anything more than an advanced winter holiday—that is, no one except a lone skier approaching the cabin from the north.

CHAPTER 18

✳ ✳ ✳

The Visitor

"*Canyon Station?*" the radio crackled one cold December morning. "*This is Hayden Outpost, over.*"

"This is Canyon Station. Whatcha got?" Ranger Reese was assigned to Canyon this week. He'd been drinking luke-warm broth and reading a book when the call came in.

"*A skier coming out of the trees moving south-southeast along Alum Creek. Seems to know where he's going, over.*" The surveillance team was ensconced in a camouflaged, heated plywood hut high on the ridge north of Hayden Valley. On a clear day, they could watch nearly all of Gene Siegfried's outdoor activities through an enormous set of naval binoculars. On a normal day, that is, but on windy or snowy or misty, they could see nothing, much to Ranger Downes' chagrin. And so it was that "nothing to report" was normally what they recorded.

"Any sign of our subject?" Ranger Reese asked.

"*Negative, Canyon. Haven't seen him in two hours—correction, Subject HVTS has just come out of the cabin. There's no way he could possibly see anyone, but he seems to be looking in the right direction. How could he know?*"

"Describe the skier," Reese asked.

"*Appears to be experienced. Dressed in a blue snowsuit with stripes down the sleeves and legs. Hat appears red, but we're not sure.*"

"Thank you, Outpost. We'll take care of him. Out."

Having closed the highway between Lake Junction and Canyon Village to traffic that winter, the rangers still had to intercept a dozen people a week trying to sneak into Hayden Valley. Most claimed they only wanted a look at the resident savage, but enough newsmen were caught at the barricades that the ban on travel was justified.

Jimmy Downes, who was at Lake Ranger Station that week, suspected this experienced skier now moving across Hayden Valley toward the cabin was the same one stopped exactly seven days before at Lake Junction. The stranger had turned around and outrun them before he could be identified. Rubbing his hands in glee, Downes figured the man must have driven a snowmobile to Madison Junction and then skied up Nez Perce Creek to the backside of Mary Mountain to elude detection. "His machine is probably stashed along the service road," Downes decided. "Let's go get him."

As a precaution, Downes radioed rangers from Old Faithful to intercept the skier from the west or find his machine. At the same time, the ranger ordered Red Reese to catch the stranger on this side of Mary Mountain, in Hayden Valley proper. "There's no way he's going to get away from us." Downes laughed to himself.

The morning was beginning to cloud over; the forecast called for heavy snowfall that evening. Reese skied down into the valley from the Canyon Ranger Station while Downes took a snowmobile north from Lake Junction on the off-chance the stranger had outsmarted them and actually broken through from the south.

❄ ❄ ❄

The raven cawed irritably from its perch in the moose antlers over the doorway; it was the bird's warning that had alerted Gene Siegfried to the approach of a visitor. Gene had come to rely on the raven to warn him of intruders, bears, or hunting opportunities. Minutes after the raven started hopping from tine to tine in the antlers, a skier entered the meadow, stopped in front of the cabin, and pulled up his goggles. "By God!" Gene swore, slapping his knee in surprise. "How the heck are you, Mack?"

"What's happening?" Simms laughed. His face was sunburned where the goggles hadn't protected it.

"Not much, compared to you," Gene said. Noting his friend's badly crusted gaiters and exhausted face, he waved him inside. "I was about to fix stew. Want some?"

"I've got a better idea," Mack said. "I've got two freeze-dried dinners—one's chicken with rice and the other's tuna with noodles—if you can boil some water."

"I can manage. How long you staying?" Although happy to see his friend, Gene knew the weather was changing soon, and he didn't want him caught in the open during a blizzard.

"Only a couple hours. I came the long way around, and I've got to go back today," Mack said, slapping the ice off his gaiters and hanging them over the door to drip. "I borrowed a snowmobile from work. Today's my day off."

"C'mon inside," Gene said, ducking through the low doorway into the cabin. The dank interior was cluttered with tools and skins, but he knew his friend would welcome the warmth after such a long trek. Clearing a space near the fire, he threw an elk skin over a stool, then motioned for Mack to sit down.

""Geez! It stinks in here," Mack complained.

The combination of wet fur, stretched leather, blood, and smoke inside the cabin almost overcame him; he fought to control his retching. Smiling indulgently, Gene snatched a handful of herbs from a rack on the ceiling and threw it on the fire; the cabin filled with an aromatic smoke that instantly cleared the air.

"That's better," Mack said. "This the pot we're going to use?" He poked at the blackened utensil next to the flames. "Don't you ever scrub it?"

"My, my, aren't we picky today," Gene sassed him back. "If you haven't noticed, sand for a proper scrubbing is a little hard to find right now, but I do tip the pot over once in a while to burn out the residue."

Knowing his friend didn't normally complain, Gene helped him out of his parka, melted some snow, and made a cup of mountain coffee: three heaping spoons of Mack's instant coffee to a cup of warm water. The caffeine seemed to help, and before long, Mack was smiling. "I brought some whiskey," he said, pulling out two pint bottles from a pocket.

"That'll be good to ease some stiffness," Gene grinned, taking one bottle and stashing it in the rafters. "I'll save that for a bad day, if you don't mind."

"That's why I brought two," Mack said, pouring half of the remaining whiskey into his cup. He handed the bottle to Gene, who took two tiny sips and put the bottle away with its mate.

"My snowmobile is hidden under a white bed sheet on the Norris-Canyon Road," Mack said. "I tried to follow the Plateau Trail south to Mary Mountain, but it's not marked very well. I almost blundered into a couple of moose holed up in a meadow west of the mud pot on Otter Creek."

"Good Lord," Gene said, fumbling on a shelf for a buffalo horn spoon to stir the pot. "I avoid moose like the plague."

"Normally, I avoid them too," Mack agreed. "They're bad enough in summer, but in winter they're cantankerous as hell. Anyway, I cut over to Violet Springs, then circled west before entering the valley."

"Why circle west? Afraid to leave tracks across the open snow of the valley?" Gene asked suspiciously. Why hadn't Mack come straight across the valley? Gene had begun to feel uneasy lately. Was there something wrong to the east? Why had there been no winter skiers, and no snowmobiles on the distant highway? Where were the winter dudes? Had the rangers closed the park for some reason ... and yet, how could he explain two sets of tracks near his cabin recently? Were the rangers watching him? "Why come from the west?" he asked again.

"I brought you something," Mack said, ignoring the question. "Three pairs of wool socks."

"Bless your heart!" Gene exclaimed, jumping up from his seat on the edge of the bed. He had sensitive feet, and though he knew the gift broke the rules, he accepted the socks and unrolled them beside the fire. They were gray mountaineer socks, perhaps a quarter inch thick and long enough to reach his knees. "Thanks. Best Christmas present you could've given me."

He lifted his boots to show how the soles had finally broken loose from the uppers. "I have to hold my boots together with rawhide straps," he said. After unlacing his boots—something he hadn't done much that winter—he pulled off his old socks. "When the heels wore out, I reversed my socks and wore the holes on top of my feet." The old socks were full of holes and stiff as greasy cardboard. "Look at my new coat," he said, taking a large bundle from a nearby shelf.

Holding the coat near the fire, he said, "I put an elk robe on the floor, traced my outline with charcoal, then cut it large enough to come around for a double-breasted front. I made the yoke with a piece of buffalo hide."

Putting on the nearly completed, knee-length coat, Gene demonstrated how the cuffs, which would normally button out of the way, could unroll over his mittens for added warmth. On the outside, the coat was smooth, white leather; on the inside, it was hairy and warm. The lower inside edge of the coat was lined with leather to prevent snow buildup when he was wading in drifts. The coat had a slit in back, from his butt to his knees that could be buttoned against the cold or opened for movement. It weighed nearly twenty pounds, but on a man as big as him, it made no difference.

"It doesn't have fringe. A mountain man's coat should have fringe," his friend said.

"Fringe is a liability walking through these forests. I tried fringe on a shirt last summer. It catches on too many things, so no fringe, none at all." He hung the coat on a peg, and then got down another bundle. "I've got a piece of coyote skin for a collar," Gene said, "and I'm making horn buttons and a buffalo-skin hat with big ear pieces." Patting the coat proudly, he said, "This is perfect for the winter in Yellowstone."

"It looks good," Mack agreed.

"I've got other clothes," Gene said, pulling down still another bundle. "I made a pair of snow pants with suspenders, and I salvaged a piece of moose hide from a carcass near the river to make a pair of waterproof snow boots. That's the moose I got the antlers from for my doorway outside."

By this time, dinner had boiled into a glue of noodles and meat, so the two friends sat down to eat. "What else you been making?" Mack asked, holding up a buffalo-horn spoon Gene had given him to eat. Gene was eating with a wooden spoon.

"A pair of mittens connected by a leather strap to keep them from getting lost in the snow."

"Sounds like something I wore in elementary school," Mack teased.

"Me too. And then there's this," Gene said, holding up what was to become his most famous piece of winter gear: his snow mask. "The cold hurts my scarred cheek pretty badly, and the glare on the snow is bright enough to blind." Slipping on the mask, which he had made of marmot leather with a black buffalo-hair mustache and long braids, he asked, "What do you think?"

Antler tips hung like fangs from the edges of the mouth. The narrow eye slits were overhung with elk-hair brows, and in a macabre gesture, he had stitched the length of the right cheek with thick sinew to trace his own horrible scar.

"That's scary as heck!" Mack laughed. "I like snow masks. I've got a rubber one lined with wool. They're great in cold weather."

"I've made all sorts of things, but I gave up," Gene admitted, "trying to make cross-country skis. I was never much of a skier; I simply couldn't figure skis out."

"What was wrong?" Mack asked.

"The bindings. I couldn't remember how they worked, but now that I've seen yours, I realize I couldn't have made bindings without a forge anyway. Besides, I don't have anything to wax or maintain skis with, but look at these," he said, taking a pair of snowshoes off the wall. "I'm going to combine techniques and use poles like a skier."

"It's a good idea," Mack agreed. "I prefer the speed of skis, but to tell the truth, I had a devil of a time in a few places in the forest back there. You may not be as fast, but snowshoes are adaptable to these conditions."

"I hope so," Gene said, taking a piece of wood from beside the fire pit and leaning forward into the circle of light to throw it on the flames.

"God! You're going gray!" Mack said sadly. "You're twenty-five years old and your hair's going gray. How are you really? This has been pretty tough, hasn't it?"

"Yes, it has," Gene admitted. "The scientists once warned me about hypothermia—"

"What's that?"

"Loss of body heat. Being wet is a good way to lose heat, but you're in danger anytime you shiver. Your hands get numb, your speech slurred, you lose your judgment and get sleepy. It's like shock, except it doesn't come from bleeding."

"You haven't had any problems, have you?"

"No. The doctors warned me to stay dry, drink lots of water, and eat starchy foods, but there was one thing they forgot to tell me about."

"What's that?"

"The miseries," Gene replied with a straight face.

"What are the miseries?" Mack laughed. "Depression? Cabin fever?"

"Physical complaints," Gene told him. "My body was reacting to the cold by getting stiff. My back hurt all the time, I couldn't straighten my legs, and my fingers ached so badly I felt like screaming."

"What was the cure?"

"I've been taking baths in Violet Creek recently. I soaked for three hours in the hot water yesterday."

"Was the water hot enough?" Mack asked incredulously. "It must have been fifteen below zero outside yesterday!"

"The run-off from the hot springs doesn't seem to lose its heat any more quickly during the winter than it does in the summer," Gene said. "Even with all this snow, there are flowers and some insects in a micro climate next to the hot water. My muscles unkinked for the first time in a month, and the aches have pretty much gone away—"

"You're more of a man than I am," Mack said. "How's your face doing?"

"Not good," Gene answered honestly.

"What's going on?"

"I've lost another molar this month, right side. I need to get some attention."

"Have you told Project Snow yet?"

"No."

"Why?"

"They'd stop this," Gene said sadly. "My cheek aches terribly in the cold, especially up near the cheekbone. I think there's something wrong there. I think the circulation's screwed up. It looks purple sometimes. If I complain, the scientists will stop this, especially that woman psychiatrist. She gets tears in her eyes every time she sees me."

"But don't you think you've done enough? Everybody else gave up."

"I won't give up," Gene answered. "There's blood to be paid for all this fun."

"Maybe ... but I don't know that I could continue if I were you," Mack said, putting aside his empty plate and reluctantly reloading his daypack. Changing subjects, he commented, "I'll bet it was tough getting out of the hot water yesterday and back into your clothes again."

"No, my dad didn't raise no fool," Gene said. "I had a fire warming my clothes."

"You'd never catch me naked in this kind of weather," Mack confessed. "Still, it's something to remember in case I get the miseries."

"Sure is. And maybe that whiskey you gave me will help, too, huh?" Taking a small leather-wrapped packet from a shelf, Gene said, "Before you go, I want to give you something. These are Roxy's and your Christmas presents."

He held out two lengths of elk antler, both intricately carved and stained with natural thermal chemicals. One was of two elk bulls locked in mortal combat; the other was a grizzly slapping a trout from a stream. They were, he knew, quite beautiful.

"God, you're getting good!" Mack exclaimed. "Roxy's never going to believe these. Which one's hers?"

"This one," Gene answered, pointing to the bear. "I *am* getting better. It's one of the personal things I've gained from this experiment."

"The skill, you mean? I don't think so," Mack disagreed. "You've always had talent, but there's something different about these."

"It's emotion," Gene said. "I used to reproduce what I was told was good, but that's just being a craftsman. I've discovered a real artist uses not only his hands but his feelings to define his subjects."

"Aren't you describing something impressionistic? These figurines are highly realistic—"

"Selectively so," Gene corrected. "The fine points are exaggerated for effect. That's why Thomas Moran's painting of the Lower Falls of the Yellowstone will last forever, but photographs of the same scene end up moldering in someone's attic."

"Good art survives?" Mack grunted, pulling on his gaiters. "Do you think your art will?"

"Time will tell. I've been thinking the sum total of our forebears is that they were born, bred, and died. Only one thing besides genetics survives, and that's art. Someday, the Golden Gate Bridge will be scrapped for its steel because it's just pretty. The junk paintings of modern art will only last through the fad, and even Mount Rushmore depends on political stability, but Japanese calligraphy or the handiwork of a Persian carpet will always survive."

"But what about ordinary people?" Mack asked. "What happens if we don't breed or create anything? We're not artists."

"What do we remember about the market duck hunters of Chesapeake Bay?" Gene replied. "They're gone and forgotten, but their battered decoys are still around. No, a man lives on by seed or by art, nothing else survives. Anything between birth, breeding, and death is a luxury. And yet it is these things that enrich the country."

"How so?"

"If you think about it, how many tons of tools did the Pilgrims bring over on the Mayflower? Those tools built more tools, and then furniture, and houses to enrich the country. The makers are gone; but the country gets richer with each generation of tools and art."

Mack certainly didn't know what to make of all this, but it was time to go. It was mid-afternoon, and snow was beginning to fall. The wind was rising and quartering more to the west. In three hours, it would be dark.

"I'm glad you're doing alright—" he started.

"Here, I want you to take this, too," Gene said, taking his grandmother's rosary from around his neck and handing it to Mack. "I've worn this everyday since I was a child."

"But you might need it! All the time I've known you, you've worn it."

"Every time I fall down in the snow, now," Gene said sadly, "I lose something. Give this back to me next spring. I don't want to lose it."

"I'll take good care of it," Danny promised as he locked his boots onto the skis. He put the rosary around his own neck, shook Gene's hand, thanked him for the gifts, and set off on the arduous journey home. Behind him, several hundred yards too slow, Ranger Red Reese gave up the chase; by radio, he ordered the men waiting for the skier on the Nez Perce side of Mary Mountain to head for shelter, then he watched the stranger disappear into the blowing snow.

Alone again, Gene was strangely depressed; he reluctantly barricaded his flimsy door against the cold and sat beside the fire to work on his coat. Glancing at the stool where Mack had sat only a short time before, he suddenly snatched the elk hide away and hung the stool in the rafters. Even so, the cabin seemed emptier now. Not knowing how to deal with this black mood, Gene picked up a needle, sighed deeply, and began to sew by the flickering light of the fire.

CHAPTER 19

❄ ❄ ❄

The Scavengers

THE ARRIVAL OF fresh snow marked a new viciousness to the winter. Replacing periodic sunshine was an unremitting gray cold that depressed even the stoutest heart. Inching downward, daytime highs were only in the teens by Christmas, with lows of minus ten or fifteen at night. By New Year's Day, it was somewhere around forty below zero in Hayden Valley.

From the useless curses of the surveillance team stationed in a semi-warm plywood hut on the ridge north of the valley to the stoic forbearance of the sullen buffalo below, the inhabitants of the valley were assuming timeless patterns of winter survival. Under the snow, in the subnivean empire of tunnels, shrews, weasels, and foxes preyed upon mice harvesting ice-laden grasses. Between storms, moose grazed along the icy river, and flocks of wintering ducks, teal, trumpeter swans, and Canada geese fluffed themselves against the cold.

There was a harshness in the roar of the wind, and a tall plume of frozen mist rose a thousand feet above the double falls at Canyon. Similar columns of mist crowned the hot springs in the Crater Hills and at Dragon's Mouth. Unusual pops and mysterious bangs not normally heard rang through the clear air from the thermal zones. There was also a strange blue-green electricity that ran across the surface of the snow, visible only at night, and only when it was clear.

Watching the winter worsen around him, Gene decided there was an eerie beauty to all of this. The deadening effect of the snow's constant white heightened his eye's appreciation of other subtleties: the creeping, blue tint of snow underlain by slush, prismatic ice crystals gleamed like diamonds on a bright day, a streak of blood on trampled drifts, the stain of sulfur around a hot spring, or the iridescence of ice under a luminous moon on a cloudless night. From a distance, the green of the forest looked black against heavy loads of powdery, white snow. Up close, the sable mantles of buffalo appeared cinnamon, while delicate splashes of pink and raspberry glistened from fresh skeletons lying naked in the snow. Snow banks along the river were discolored with goose turd, and foam drifting downstream in the black Yellowstone River looked like lemon custard. Sometimes, the Northern Lights were visible, and its dancing colors reflected off the snow.

Gene began a series of strenuous hikes to condition himself for hunting. The winter was quite hard on wildlife, he observed, not because the weather was particularly snowy, but because of the resilience of the cold. Buffalo have a hard time sweeping their great heads in the drifts to uncover their feed, but the alternate thawing and freezing, plus the determined drifting and packing of this winter had hardened the snow, making it difficult to graze. Buffalo bands tightened up near Mary Mountain and down near the river so the bulls could do the plowing; cows and calves stubbornly followed their trail, but even so, the old, the sick, and the weak lagged behind. Opportunities for hunting were improving in the worsening conditions, and Gene began to follow the herds, hoping for a chance to kill something. Each day, the weak grew weaker and the slow lagged farther behind. Finally, on the coldest day yet, he heard a new sound in the wind, a grunt that would become common as the weeks passed—the distant commotion of death: a pathetic squeal and the yapping of wild-eyed predators around a dying grass eater.

Hurrying toward such sounds, he was rarely lucky enough to arrive in time to scavenge some meat. Usually, he would come over a rise only to find such a kill covered with snarling coyotes. Not once did he scare the predators off, so desperate were they for food, and he quickly learned to respect a territorial distance of seventy-five yards. Even after a kill was abandoned, he had to compete with ravens and bald eagles for a share of the meat, but it galled him to be scavenging this way.

One afternoon, though, Gene happened upon the carcass of a buffalo yearling lying on its side at the edge of the river. Stymied by ice too thin for mounting, but too thick to break through while swimming the river, the bull had grown tired and drowned. After drifting a mile or more, the body was cast up on an open beach, its hindquarters still in the river, the shaggy coat of its forequarters armored with ice.

He thought he needed the meat, but after a few minutes, he regretted ever starting on the enormous carcass. The slushy mud of the shoreline froze to his boots, while accidental missteps into the ankle-deep water added additional layers of ice. Unable to lever the carcass over to cut into its belly, he resorted to chopping through the frozen hide of its back. It took an hour's labor to skin the buffalo; meanwhile, the raven that had often followed him preened its feathers nearby, soon attracting more of its kind and a hungry coyote. Rather impudently, the coyote sat on the bank half a shout's distance away, but its nonchalant yawning and sly glances soon got on Gene's nerves.

The hide already weighed more than he did, but he bashed at the carcass with his axe until he broke the shoulder. By this time, there were three yammering coyotes on the bank, close enough to hear the insistent growling of their stomachs. Every time he turned his back, the coyotes slipped closer. He could see the conflict between desire and caution in their yellow eyes, and he knew that one might be a concern, but a pack this close was dangerous.

Better to lose some of the meat than all of it, he reasoned, so he repeatedly dipped the heavy forequarter into the water; as soon as several layers of ice covered the meat, he heaved it up onto the bank. To his surprise, by the time he had beheaded the bull, the coyotes had pretty well savaged the frozen quarter. With sweat on his brow and ice in his beard, he worked to sever the bull's neck at the shoulder, and then hacked through the rib cage, finding each rib as tough and as thick as an oak barrel stave.

"Lord!" he exclaimed when he looked up again. There were six coyotes and twelve ravens waiting. One of the more daring coyotes crept up behind him and took a bite out of the buffalo's neck and then another ran off with the best ribs.

He was going to lose all of the meat if he didn't hurry. The lower half of the carcass was immersed in mud and icy water, so he hacked the tenderloins free, then split the hide as close to the waterline as possible. Left with a meaty piece of frozen skin the size and weight of an iron bathtub, a few pieces of meat, both tenderloins, and some ribs, he knew it was not much for two hours' work.

Dreading the backbreaking drag back to his cabin, he realized he had learned three valuable lessons in winter survival: first, one predator waiting attracted others; second, he had to work quickly whenever he had the opportunity; and third, he must concern himself now with the threat of coyotes.

Shooing the scavengers away with a wave of his bloody axe, he grabbed hold of the frozen hide and dragged it up the riverbank and out into the valley. Two hundred yards later, he paused to catch his breath and look back. The carcass was out of sight, and so were the scavengers, but he could hear snarling as they fought over the meat. The dominant coyotes would eat first; a couple of others would have to wait their turn. Expecting these others to run after him to see where he had gone, he knelt behind the hundred-pound hide and readied a javelin in his spear thrower.

It was these less dominant, more desperate coyotes that were his greatest threat. Not only had they learned he was a source of meat—which now meant he could expect to be followed by at least one coyote all the time—but also in the spring, they would draw bears to him. Groggy but ravenously hungry after months in their dens, the bears, particularly the intelligent grizzlies, would wonder why coyotes wasted time gleaning scraps left by a mere man with a twig of a spear.

As he sat there preparing himself for action, Gene had to admit that like nothing else, he feared bears, especially desperate, lean spring bears. They wouldn't know caution; they would come straight at whatever they thought was weaker or more vulnerable. They would want whatever he had; every fight would be a battle to the death. And winner or loser, Gene would have to contend with coyotes waiting on the fringes of the combat.

Hiding himself behind the frozen skin, he took off his mittens and exercised his fingers in the cold. It was at least twenty below zero, he decided. His fingers were beet red. His knuckles couldn't have been in worse shape than if he sanded them with eighty-grit sandpaper. Every one of his fingers was cracked open near the nails. They were painful. His finger joints ached in the frozen air, but he opened his hands and squeezed them into fists repeatedly. A few minutes later, a curious bitch coyote peeked over the riverbank. She barked excitedly when she spotted the bloody hide out in the valley. Running across the snow, the coyote quickly narrowed the distance. As he expected, she didn't seem concerned at spotting him, and he allowed her to come within thirty feet before hurling his javelin.

Hit in the middle of the back, the bitch tried running away, but her spine was broken. Flopping on the snow like a dying fish, she tried to get up but her hindquarters wouldn't work. Supporting herself on her front legs, she started dragging herself back to the safety of the pack, yelping desperately for help. Feeling somewhat sorry, Gene hit her with another javelin, this time in the left front shoulder. Totally crippled now, the coyote redoubled its efforts to get away, but it was too late. He had caught up with her. Unslinging his axe from his belt, Gene brained the bitch. Looking up, he saw other coyotes peeking over the riverbank with an expression of horror on their faces. Hoping the lesson would not be lost on them, he bashed at the dead coyote, scattering blood and fur across the virgin snow. As a further macabre gesture, he lopped off the tail, held it high over his head, and stomped away howling like a madman. Later, in the shelter of his cabin, he deboned the tail and sewed it onto the back of his buffalo skin hat as a reminder, he hoped, to those who would follow him this winter.

The surveillance team, ensconced with navy binoculars and spotting scopes in their shelter far across the valley saw none of this. Instead, they reported Siegfried's next projects—improved snow gear—gave him a better chance to hunt and explore. By the middle of January, he was ranging widely. He visited the Grand Canyon of the Yellowstone, crossed over Mary Mountain to the valley of the Nez Perce, explored Dragons Mouth and hunted the eastern march. Regardless of whether the temperature was cold or freezing, the snow falling or freshly fallen, he was demonstrating a singular daring and lack of fear.

The scientists and rangers were fascinated. The surveillance team, who actually spent their time in the hut above the valley and saw it day-by-day, were impressed, but Douglas Paine Hanson, sitting in front of a typewriter in his book-lined study in Helena, Montana, was depressed. He wrote Gene's restlessness was due to moodiness and boredom more than a desire to hunt. His struggle with winter was causing him to take chances to test his new skills. Rather than survival being assured, Hanson predicted high winter would bring Gene greater risks and harder work.

CHAPTER 20

✳ ✳ ✳

The Buffalo

ABOUT TWO WEEKS after the winter solstice, when days and nights were one long, gray sameness and the temperatures moved only one direction—down—a young, sick buffalo foundered in the deepening drifts of central Hayden Valley. From a distance, its hooves looked cracked and brassy from the poisonous warmth of Sulphur Mountain, and Gene spotted strings of bloody mucus dribbling from its nose as it wheezed in pain. It was close to death, and he welcomed that death, even encouraged it by chasing the bull off its feed whenever he could, for he relished fresh meat. Recently, mice had penetrated his pantry and his even his cache—nine feet higher than the snow—and all of his best stocks of meat and fish had been vandalized; it angered him to thaw a prime elk roast, only to find it riddled with mouse bites and covered with rodent droppings, particularly since every calorie counted now. Sometimes, he had to burn big chunks in his fire pit to prevent their rot from attracting spring bears. Nearly every day now, he cooked and ate such tainted meat, but he thought if he could secure the carcass of a dying buffalo, he might be able to glaze the meat with layers of ice and suspend it in a tall pine with wire. He supposed there might be four weeks' fine eating plus a good hide.

The problem was that, though weak, the buffalo was still more than a match for him. Three times in as many days, the bull rallied its strength to chase him, and each time Gene was lucky to get away across the snow. Time was on his side, though. One day, he knew he would find the buffalo belly-down in a drift, unable to rise to its feet, and it would be safe to close around it in the death circle. Javelin after javelin would find a mark, until, like a proud Spanish fighting bull bled helpless, this buffalo would stand trembling before the blow of his ax.

And so, very early every morning he set out to test the bull. Above him, the raven circled in the sky, cawing with excitement; a dozen coyotes would peek over drifts, ears alert and eyes hungry. Gene had learned to follow such signals across the rolling snow and maze of trails to the one he and other predators most desired. If the bull didn't die naturally within the week, he would finish it, and there would be meat for all, pickings and bones.

But the bull seemed to know, for that is the natural order of things. Not ignorant of the sharp-toothed monsters on its trail, it seemed especially aware of the purpose of the thing-with-the-scent-of-steel, and there was terror on its face whenever it saw him coming across the drifts. In the world of nature, animals die soon after their prime, the way it used to be—even for humans—a few thousand years ago—so this bull did not seem afraid of death. It feared being eaten. There were reminders of this ultimate horror all around: scraps of hairy skin on the bones of a friend long gone, the horn of its very mother on the Nez Perce trail, the grunt of something disemboweled alive off in the distance. Yes, the bull knew what was going to happen and it fought to delay the inevitable.

Unfortunately, the weather was poor for such a deathwatch. Early one morning, a fierce gale tore across Hayden Valley. Blown into twisting columns, drifts danced like snow ghosts before the gale. Caught while out hunting, Gene was forced to streak for the shelter of his cabin, where he battened down his flimsy door and fed a smoky fire in the pit. During the night, an unholy storm rose over the horizon, and if there were dawn or even sunlight the next day, he couldn't tell. Pelting the roof of the verandah, snow fell so heavily the timbers and cross braces overhead groaned for the first time that winter. If the bull went down in this storm, Gene realized, there would be no finding it; it would freeze under the drifts and be picked clean by mice and spring bears. He would have to start over with a dead elk or another dying buffalo.

As he huddled over his guttering fire, an elk robe over his shoulders for added warmth, Gene Siegfried knew the fresh snow might be an advantage, for if the buffalo were not quite ready to die, the deep powder and strong winds of this storm would drain it of the strength it had left. There was a chance, he hoped, that he might still be able to locate the bull, and so, next morning, driven by meat-lust and boredom, he prepared himself to face the blizzard. Dressing in his heaviest winter gear, he armed himself with four javelins and his ax, covered his face with his snow mask, and set off into the wind.

Morning conditions were bad: intermittent whiteout and intense cold followed by wind and a killing chill factor. The valley was a ghastly ashen color unlike anything he had seen before, and the forests looked black against a sullen powder sky. At best, visibility was a hundred yards. During the worst of the whiteouts, he couldn't decide if his eyes were open or closed—it made no difference at all, and he found it impossible to navigate. Increasingly confused, he spent most of his time wandering aimlessly west of Alum Creek.

At times, he tried to hold a course by following the knife-edged sastrugi, but then they played tricks on him and lost their dimensionality. Before long, his own tracks appeared raised rather than depressed, and he caught himself stepping over shadows that looked like drifts. He happened upon a buffalo trail packed as hard as an alabaster sidewalk, but seconds later, he stepped off into the soft snow beside it and could never find the trail again. Dazed and chilled to the bone, he was finally forced to admit he had to stop. Gene was thankful he had worn a mask to protect himself from snow-blindness—which could turn the world crimson and rob him of vision—but when he tried to pull it off, he discovered it was frozen to his beard by the condensed ice of his breath.

It was the first time winter had caught him without fire and shelter but he accepted the situation stoically. Locating a wind-carved drift looming over a frozen brook, he used his snowshoes like shovels to cut a trench at the foot of the bank. He burrowed upward into the pillowy softness. It was so cold the snow wouldn't stick together, and though Siegfried was soon covered from head to foot with snow, he found it wasn't wet or miserable; slapping himself clean with a mitten, he was as dry and warm as when he started.

Digging deeply into the bowels of the drift, he tunneled through a hard layer of sugar snow, or depth hoar. About eight feet from the entrance, he dug out a room about the size of a walk-in closet. He cut a raised sleeping platform along the back wall and created a domed roof to prevent dripping. After poking a hole through the snow overhead for ventilation, he insulated the platform from his own body heat with an elk robe he'd brought along. Although temperatures outside fell to a record low that night, his snow den remained slightly above freezing.

Trapped by the whiteout, Gene remained in the snow bank for two days, eating all of his rations. The enforced ennui nearly drove him insane. The den was too peaceful for an active man, and its womb-like silence worked on him like a sensory deprivation chamber. There was nothing to look at in the grayness, nothing to hear, nothing to do except lie there and let the cold settle over him. While his backside was warm against the robe, his front was cold. He wished he had brought _two_ elk robes instead of one, but he couldn't have predicted he would be stuck like this. Fingers and toes cried out in agony as they slowly froze, then cried out again when he warmed them back to life. Sleep came easily in the darkness, however, allowing him to wander between dreams and consciousness.

He dreamed of summer, of his childhood in Colorado, of college, and his many friends, especially a girlfriend he had thoughtlessly wronged. Once again, he saw his early months in the wilderness. He remembered summer's treats and fall's feasts, gushing streams, azure mountains, coyotes mousing in ripening meadows—and green, green, green everywhere! Noisy cars clogged the roads, and the small animals—even the mosquitoes and flies-had a place in his winter dream.

In one long sequence, he dreamed the universe had begun in frigid darkness—and then there was the light of suns and living bodies. Cold was the beginning … and must ever be the end … but as he lay there in the darkness, he imagined that cold was peace too. It was only life's struggle with frigidity that produced pain. For a while, he wondered whether cold was God, but decided not, since God is a friend to life, and cold is not. So, there was cold, he decided, and there was God, and God said, "Let there be light," and there was life and warmth. The warmth was God.

Cavemen understood the cold—that's why they worshipped fire and the sun. As he lay there in the frigid darkness, Gene understood such things. He had never thought much about cavemen before this experience in the wilderness, but he was developing an affinity for them now. At first, he had wondered why early humans bothered with caves, for after all, didn't cave bears inhabit them? But during the summer, he had suffered through clouds of mosquitoes and realized a cave would concentrate smoke, driving the mosquitoes away. In the winter, though the stones were cold, a cavern concentrated heat and made the weather bearable. Without caves, without heat, without fire, Europe and much of Asia might never have been colonized. He wrote in the notebook he kept for his monthly reporting, "Cold is the end of all that is good," and "God is light," leaving it for the scientists to interpret as they would.

On the third day, the storm lessened. The whiteout was replaced by a dreary grayness. Visibility increased to as much as two hundred yards, but when he emerged from his den, there wasn't anything to see. The bitter wind was constant. It took a half hour to get his bearings, and then he quartered the wind and tramped sluggishly southwest toward the cabin. Gene Siegfried was very weary. He estimated the temperature was thirty below zero, but he guessed the chill factor was closer to seventy below. He needed to get into shelter soon. He hadn't eaten anything but jerky in two days.

Then, while making his way across the windswept wastes of the central valley, having long ago given up hope of seeing the dying buffalo, he found it again.

The cheerless light of late afternoon was fading into the grayness of evening; the horizon was an angry, festering blackness. It was brutally cold and quickly getting worse, and he was disoriented and badly iced, but as he topped the south bank of Trout Creek, he glimpsed the telltale black of a buffalo hump and a wispy breath carried away on the raw breeze. At last, he thought, the buffalo was down for good. Smiling to himself, he rolled back down the slope and jinked westward across the wind to be sure his scent would not alarm the weakened bull. Lying in the lee of the stream bank, the buffalo was probably facing the rolling sagebrush and snow to the southwest. Even sick as it was, it had remembered to protect its back with a drop-off, proof that though it was dying, it would be hard to kill.

The opportunity couldn't have come at a worse time. Gene was bone-tired from his unexpectedly long and difficult hunt. Ice clung to his snow-shoes and leggings. He hadn't eaten much in thirty-six hours, his back was bent, and his shoulders hurt. In another half hour, daylight would fail completely. The wind was rising, visibility decreasing, and the tempera-ture dropping. The kill would be difficult, though not dangerous, but the butchering could not be done under worse conditions. The buffalo's blood would freeze to a glaze wherever it touched; he would have to sacrifice the hide in his hurry to hack as much meat free as possible. During the night, he would have to pack out as much as he could carry, for as soon as the storm let up, scavengers would clean up the carcass.

Gene could waste no time. He shed the elk robe, buckled his long coat tightly and unbuttoned the slit in back. After hammering his snowshoes to clear them of ice, he unslung four javelins from the scabbard. He hung his ax in his belt. An odd anxiety came over him, but he put it out of his mind and concentrated on the killing ahead. Carefully rubbing grease off the palms of his mittens to grip the javelins better, he decided the moment had come.

Gene raced below the slope to a point directly under the buffalo. The rise was steep here, especially since he was wearing snowshoes; it took almost a minute to scramble up out of the creek bed, but once on top, he never hesitated a second. Raising a javelin over his shoulder in the spear thrower, he yelled like a banshee to frighten the downer into standing for a better target.

Startled, a buffalo bull turned its massive head toward him. There was a bass rumble of anger deep in its enormous bulk, and then whole drifts of snow were blown into the wind as it exploded out of a comfortable snow bed. IT WAS THE WRONG BULL! This was no ordinary bull either, no follower after the herds. This was a rogue outlaw, a king bull so surly few of its kind would put up with it—an enormous, black giant of a beast twice the size of the weakened buffalo Gene had mistaken it for.

"God in heaven!" Gene swore in surprise, nearly dropping his javelins.

As the buffalo rose in front of him, two other outlaw bulls, one to the left and another to the right, also jumped up. These lieutenants were slightly smaller, but all three of the bulls were more than six feet high at the hump, twelve feet long, and more than a ton in weight.

The rogue looked like the devil incarnate; its wicked, sharp horns curled upward over a frost-covered and wind-blown black mane. Its reddened nostrils flared as it sought his scent, and its hard, black eyes focused separately from the sides of its monstrous head as it inclined first one way, then another to fix him in its field of vision. Its tail cracked in the wind like a whip, and gusts of steam issued from its mouth.

To Gene, the bull's front legs looked as thick as tree trunks. Its horns were more than thirty inches across, and eighteen inches around at the base. Where most buffalo horns grew blunt and chipped with age, this bull's horns, though flattened on the outside arc, were sharp as picks. Angry eyes glared at him from about the level of his chest, and Gene was close enough to see they were bloodshot and rolling around in a crazy, uncontrolled rage. The bull splayed its naked hooves out and pawed the hard-packed ice in front of it. A strand of drool oozed out of its mouth as it coughed its first challenge, but the air was so cold the saliva was frozen by the time it splattered on the ground.

A placid grazer most of the time, a buffalo—cow, calf, or bull—has more potential for violence than any other animal in North America. Wandering through relatively long, carefree lives, buffalo have few natural enemies, and they devote little thought to defense. Surprisingly fast, they could be agile, single-minded, and overwhelming in an attack. Whether a naive tourist with a camera or a lone man with a stick of a spear—these were impertinences a proud bull would tolerate for only a short time!

Gene nearly doubled over in his haste to stop, but even so, he skidded to within twenty feet of the flaring, red nostrils of the devil bull. In the few seconds before action, he analyzed everything he had ever heard about these powerful animals. He knew the bull would try hooking him, and unlike domestic cattle, would keep its eyes open during the attack to better place its blows. It would slash with its front hooves and kick with the rear. Since a buffalo was capable of speeds faster than a running horse, Gene knew that fleeing was out of the question. Able to clear a ten-foot barrier after only a short run, a buffalo had enough power to crash through the strongest man-made fence. Two inches of bone formed an armored boss over its brain, which was then covered with an inch of skin and four inches of wool and hair. The powerful neck and shoulders contained tireless energy for goring, and the horns were strong enough to penetrate a car door.

The outlaw bull opened its attack with a straightforward charge, intending simply to run this puny challenger down. Gene avoided the first dash by scooping an armful of snow into the wind to blind the bull, but like a skilled boxer, it hooked left, right, then left again. Streamers of spit were thrown from its mouth by the force of its attack. Either by chance or design, it managed to parry a javelin Gene thrust at its nearest eye, but now, the bull was upwind of him. It cut off his retreat over the high bank, and then, in an obscene demonstration of its intelligence, the buffalo parried another pathetic thrust of his spear, this time tearing the shaft from his hand and hurling it into the wind. A moment later, it trod on the fallen javelin and pressed it into the snow.

Gene's immediate riposte, a quick stab with the javelins in his free hand, merely scratched the bull's right cheek and glanced off the ice clinging to its mane. The buffalo answered with a vicious kick from the shoulder, followed by a series of hooks as it circled in on him. Meanwhile, swirling ghosts of snow churned into the wind by the combat made the other bulls nervous, so they moved off a bit to sense the action without being directly involved.

Ducking and dodging desperately, Gene threw himself backward, but as he did so, a sudden, slashing hook by the buffalo tore at the left sleeve of his heavy coat like a knife at a sheet of paper. So far, the bull was having a hard time keeping him cornered, yet every time Gene twisted and jumped out of the way, the bull outmaneuvered him. Siegfried's only advantage so far consisted in confusing the buffalo by dodging back and forth between its eyes' different fields of vision, but even this slim margin lessened as the weak afternoon light faded into the dimness of evening. The ice on the bull's muzzle again deflected a weak thrust at the animal's face, and then the buffalo reacted with its own one-two that caught him in the left side and sent him sprawling.

Gene knew a couple of his ribs were broken, but he thanked God the horn had caught only the leather of his coat and not any flesh. As he struggled to get up, the bull tried stomping him into the snow. There wasn't any time to rise, only an instant to roll and twist. A kick straight from the buffalo's shoulder came close to decapitating him.

A few feet away, a broken javelin stuck out of the snow. Gene crawled for it, but as he stretched his fingers toward the splintered shaft, a giant hoof caught the remains of his left snowshoe, pinning his leg to the ground. Clawing at the slick shaft of the javelin with his fingernails—where had his mittens gone?—he spun around with the spear and slashed his boot out of the binding. The bull crunched the broken snowshoe like pick-up sticks, then hooked at him, giving him his first real opening: he hurled the weapon at the side of the buffalo's neck. Again deflected, the javelin buried itself high in the hump.

This time, the bull paused to saw at its own flank to remove the spear. Berserk with rage at the indignity this puny ape-thing had inflicted on it, the buffalo turned around just as Gene rolled to his feet and leapt toward his axe, twenty feet away. The bull bounded after him. As he pulled his weapon from the snow, Gene swung it with all his might at the buffalo's head. Easily parrying the blow with a horn, the buffalo hooked at his belly, one-two, one-two.

Awkwardly falling backward, Gene threw the axe at the advancing bull and rolled aside. Again his weapon was deflected, but the buffalo mistook the blow and hooked at the fallen axe in the snow. This unexpected opening gave Gene a chance to seize the twitching tail of the maddened bull and kick it in the testicles with all his might. Outraged, the beast twisted around to finish him with its horns, and as it spun, Gene was thrown from his feet and dragged in the snow only inches in front of the animal's nose. Like a belled cat, the bull whirled around and around until Gene's arms were nearly pulled from their sockets, then it stopped and started to spin the other way. In that bare instant, Gene pulled a camp knife from inside his coat and stabbed it into the bull's testicles.

Roaring like a harpooned whale, the buffalo flipped him off its tail. Blood flowed down its inner thighs as it gyrated its rump to shake the crippling steel, but only when the devil bull raised its rear leg to hook at the offending weapon did it fall out. Crushing it into the snow, the beast whirled angrily around to destroy the hated man ... but he was gone!

Gene had thrown himself over the edge of the stream bank the instant the bull was distracted. Now, with fingers stiffened from the cold, he crawled on his hands and knees back to the drift where he had stashed his elk robe and gaiters. Although they were frozen stiff and coated with ice, he desperately needed them, for his pants were split open to the crotch and his coat ripped. Wrapping himself in the robe, he pressed himself into the side of the drift and tunneled upward; in seconds, the snow thrown up by his digging settled over the depression, and Gene disappeared from sight and scent, insulated from the outside world as he tunneled deeply into another subnivean haven. Since sound travels down through the snow better than it travels up, he could hear the buffalo bellowing in the wind, but ignoring it, he created another den in the snow and shoved his arm through the ceiling to make a hole for air. Finally, when all was finished, he sat down to listen.

There was an occasional thump in the snow above, but more than two hours passed before the roaring gave way to whimpers. During the night, the bull drove off its two companions. It was difficult to get a buffalo's undivided attention, Gene knew, but a vengeful outlaw bull like this would nurse its grudges. As he lay shivering in his snowy den, he understood the bull would be very dangerous now. It had not been seriously hurt, and it would remember man-scent and seek it out next time. Rather guiltily, Gene realized the rangers would have to destroy the buffalo before summer, or some innocent tourist would get killed.

Meanwhile, he found it impossible to sleep, for every muscle in his body had been strained to the limit. He had three sprained fingers and one of his front teeth was chipped to the nerve. In addition to two broken ribs and numerous cuts, he was bruised along the entire length of his left side.

His clothing had suffered as well. His beautiful, thigh-length coat was torn and had a horn hole in one of the sleeves. His fluffy collar and all of his buttons were gone, his mittens had disappeared, he'd lost his snowmask, and the sole of one of his boots was ripped loose clear back to the heel, damage impossible to fix. The next day, however, he was able to recover a few buttons, his collar, mittens, and even the bindings of his broken snowshoes. He also located his axe head, knife, and three javelins. He was grateful he hadn't lost everything.

It took two hours to hobble the mile-and-a-half to his cabin, from whence he was not to venture for the next three weeks. Surveillance, interrupted for five days by poor visibility, resumed, and the scientists were relieved to see smoke still issued from the cabin. They did not learn until two months later Siegfried had almost been killed.

In the meantime, Gene's enforced convalescence was not wasted time. Although injuries kept him in bed for three days after the fight, and it was another week before he could wrench himself fully erect, he managed to occupy himself with handicrafts. In quick succession, he repaired all of his clothes, made a new pair of snowshoes, and sewed an incredibly beautiful, white elk-skin shirt.

The most amazing product of his active hands, however, was the beginning of the remarkable Siegfried Sculptures. He had always intended carving the interior walls of his cabin; every log chosen for its construction was purposely straight. After debarking the logs last fall, he had trimmed away the knots and scars inherent in lodgepole pine. Both the western and eastern walls would hold the bulk of his work, but in the end, every surface—the walls, beams, braces, shelves, bed, handles of his tools, as well as horns, bones, antlers, and the odd rock or two—everything was covered with carvings.

The sculptures were an intricate tattoo, a combination of techniques that demonstrated something Gene had known all along—he had the vision of an artist and the talent of a craftsman. His style was reminiscent of the decorative patterns of Celtic art, with interlacing bands of animal bodies and faces. A knot in a log became a vulva of impressions, a swelling in a roof beam became a snarling bear. There might have been some overall plan, or the carvings may have been just a collection of patterns, but Gene Siegfried did not intend them to be viewed by others. The works were merely practices to while away the time, examples of a consummate artist fooling with his palette.

Sometime after the great battle in the snow, a deep thump from above woke Gene. Jumping out of bed, he stoked his fire, dressed, and then armed himself. Two more thumps frightened him, but he never found out what the sounds meant. The vibrations, however, caused a crackling in the main beam of his roof, and it settled during the night and popped its pinning. To brace the damaged beam, he found a deformed pine in the forest with a trunk balanced by two symmetrically grown branches. He trimmed this log into a strong central post with two sinuous side supports. The central pier of this unusual log he carved into a spouting geyser that erupted into a man's burly chest and face; the two outer supports became powerfully curved arms, down which the face's long mustache flowed into the outspread hands. This post, wedged and pinned under the cracked beam, intruded on his living space. Marks of grease and fire soon stained the post's reverse side where the word "Snowdin" was carved, flanked by two buffalo horns.

Altogether, the sculptures were an intimate glimpse into the thoughts and activities of a winter-bound savage, but the support column, which ended up in a museum in California far from the wilderness where it was created, has been hailed by art critics as a stylized self-portrait, an amazing combination of nature's deformity and a man's imagination.

CHAPTER 21

✳ ✳ ✳

The Dreaded Ice

"Honesty is a virtue of men, not women," the winterkeeper claimed. "Because of that difference, answering ads in these mail-order-brides magazines is real frustrating." The keeper, a forty-year-old boilerman from Montana who took care of Lake Lodge during the winter, was giving Gene Siegfried a tongue-in-cheek description of his experiences, and Gene laughed until his sides hurt as he listened to the man's pathetic tales of answering personal ads during the long winter nights. The previous fall the keeper had started a simple quest for an unattached woman interested in having hours, days, and weeks of sex as soon as the winter was over, but as the lonely vigil in his isolated cabin at Lake Lodge dragged on, and as only a few letters came back, the winterkeeper's obsession grew.

"I discovered," he said quite seriously, "half the women don't answer—even when I enclose a stamped, self-addressed envelope. When someone _does_ write back, it's often just a woman looking for a father for her kids. Some of these ladies use swingers' ads to hustle, and once in a while, there's a bitter divorcee—but they're the kind that eat men like me for breakfast and spit out the bones."

"You've answered these ads all winter?" Gene cackled, unable to believe the winterkeeper thought he would get any action fifty miles from the nearest town.

"Yep. I subscribed to two magazines in October, when I moved here for the winter. I brought along three pen pal lists, a Russian mail order bride catalog, Mexican and Filipina correspondence magazines, the Mother Earth personal column—"

Gene's laughter interrupted the story and nearly upset the teapot and cookies on the coffee table. He gasped, "How much have you spent on this?"

"Quite a bundle," the keeper shrugged, opening a box full of letters. "Figure a dollar a shot for the forwarding fee to the magazines, a stamp for the return envelope, a hustle here, and a picture there."

The winter keeper kept the winter savage entertained for over an hour with his story, and he seemed to enjoy the company as much as his unexpected guest loved the conversation. Outside, it was bitterly cold, and a raw wind gusting from the northwest drove ground blizzards clear over the roof of the snug, little cabin. All that January, temperatures had been inching downward until the daily lows varied from zero to as much as thirty below. Out in the open, the average snow depth was around forty inches, but the drifts in the trees and behind the buildings were much deeper. In back of Lake Hotel was a massive drift twenty-two feet deep, and Lake Lodge, which also faced the lake, was buried to the roof.

The keeper, enduring his second and last winter in the park, seemed friendly and intelligent, but he was really lonely. His cabin, which was the manager's house in the summer, was comfortable, but the man confided he was sick of its varnished, peeled-log walls, cheerful fireplace, and spacious kitchen. "Last year," he told Gene, "there were a lot of winter dudes, the weather was better, the mail more regular, and there was more to do, but this year, very few people dare the East Entrance Road from Cody."

"What about your neighbors?" Gene asked.

"You mean the man who maintains the weather instruments at the ranger station?"

"Yeah."

"He keeps strange hours recording the weather data. I've seen him only three times all winter."

"What about the keeper at Lake Hotel?"

"Weird!" the man scoffed. "He's a recluse. He has a scary habit of walking the halls of the hotel looking for ghosts." Since the road north of Fishing Bridge had been closed to ensure Gene's privacy in the valley, the keeper complained, there had been few snowmobilers that winter. "And only three skiers dropped in during the whole month of December. They were in bad shape too."

"Why?"

"They battled their way north on the Thorofare Trail."

"Did you say the Thorofare? That means they came all the way up the shoreline? Why didn't they shortcut across the lake?" Gene asked.

"The ice is funny this year," the keeper answered. "Last year, it was solid, four feet thick, and too bumpy for good ice skating. This year, it's in layers of ice and slush forty inches thick, and it pops and squeaks when you walk on it. Some days, it's as smooth as a piece of glass, other times its blistered and soggy. You remember last winter three moose walked out on the ice and got caught on Stevenson Island during the spring breakup? Well, I saw a moose go out a hundred yards yesterday, stop and sniff the ice, then come running back to shore. Down near the outlet, the ice is folded in an arc by Fishing Bridge. I've never seen that in the middle of winter. Three times, big leads have opened in the lake and floes have gone down the river—and then there's been the sound."

"What sound?" Siegfried asked.

"You know, The Sound."

"Oh," Gene nodded. "_That_ sound. Y'know, I've only heard it once. My friend Mack—"

"Who?"

"Mack Simms. He's the guy who runs the laundry—"

"Oh, that son of a bitch," the keeper snorted angrily. "He issued me only twenty-five pairs of sheets and towels for the whole winter. Last year, I got all I wanted."

"Too bad," Gene said unsympathetically, thinking of the miserable conditions he himself was enduring. Shaking his head, he wanted to answer with sarcasm, but instead, he decided to let the remark about his friend go. "Well, Mack's heard the sound six or seven times."

"Would you believe I've heard it ten times this winter?" the keeper asked, a strange look on his face.

"Really?" Gene said in surprise.

""Uh huh, and it never sounded the same way twice. Sometimes it'd be like an orchestra tuning up in the sky, other times it would come chugging across the ice like a steam engine, pass overhead, and fade in the distance. It's also sounded like bees, wires whistling in the wind, or clanging pipes."

"Wow!" Gene exclaimed. "There's old-timers who've been here years that have never heard the sound once."

"I know. I was told it came mostly in the mornings, especially on clear mornings, but you know, I've heard it—well, there's just no pattern to it."

"No one knows what it is," Gene said, remembering the bright day two years before when he'd heard it. He had been fishing with a girlfriend on Sand Point. "It reminded me of a big plane flying overhead and there was a whistling of wind in its wake. I've been told the sound might be a sound-mirage carried by the wind, or electrostatic forces channeled by the Absaroka Mountains—"

"I think the government ought to investigate."

"What would they do that for?" Gene laughed. "This is a wilderness! Things are supposed to be natural here, even a mystery like Yellowstone's peculiar sound."

"Oh, you're one of those fanatics, huh?" the keeper sniffed in disgust.

"Rabid is more like it," Gene laughed amiably. "I'm going to be a wildernist when this is all over."

"A what?"

"A wildernist. I'll start wildernist groups to go out with shovels and trowels. Wherever we find unused trails, gravel dumps, and foundations without historical interest, we'll cover them up and replant."

"You're a radical, a goddamn radical."

"Maybe, but I believe it's time we did something for the wilderness. I'm tired of Johnny Mountaineers. I've sat in discussions with conservationists talking about soil formation in a fragile ecosystem, and all the while, they're tapping ashes out of their pipes onto the stonecrop. I've listened to naturalists speaking about urea production in the nitrogen cycle—while they're pulling twigs off trees and breaking them in their fingers. I know rangers who love this place but hate grizzly bears. I know people who want to pave the wilderness, cut its trees, and dam its rivers, but they're extremists with no beauty in their souls.

"I've come to the point in my life," Gene continued, "where I believe it's time to stop giving lip service to the ideals of wilderness and get down to the basics. Real wilderness exists only in the absence of man. Fifty years ago, that was a viable idea, but now there are just too many people on this planet. The idea of protection and use of the wild areas is outmoded, and today, we must protect _or_ use. I'm a protectionist myself, but I'm a realist too, because I know you can't justify using taxes to support something removed from the public domain."

"God, you've become a radical," the keeper said coolly. He gathered up the cups and teapot and dumped them in the sink, then put away the cookies.

"It's hard to stop when I get on my favorite subject," Siegfried said unapologetically.

"What brings you so far south?" the keeper asked, changing the subject. "They've been telling everyone what an awful time you're having up in the valley."

"Actually," Gene confessed, "I was getting bored. I killed an elk last week that was belly-down in the snow, and since I had some fresh meat for a change, I thought I'd come down to Lake Lodge to look around. I worked several seasons here in the laundry, you know, and I wanted to see it with ice and snow on it."

"It's completely buried under drifts, except for the roof, which I shovel off regularly."

"Oh, I know that," Gene laughed. "I thought I'd just pop in for a quick look. It's probably spooky inside, all dark and boarded up, all the equipment greased and covered. I've spent a lot of time in the Lodge too. I love those huge logs they used to frame the building, and I've enjoyed sitting at the tables, the writing desks, or out in front of the big fireplace, talking. I love the Lodge almost as much as I love Old Faithful Inn—"

"No," the winter keeper said.

Gene was stunned the keeper had refused him. "It won't be any trouble at all. I'll just take a quick look—"

"No. The doors and windows are nailed shut and boarded over. Besides, the snow's buried them."

"I know that!" Gene exclaimed, frustrated by the keeper's sudden change of attitude. "I've helped shovel the Lodge clear in the springtime, and I know once the drifts build up to the verandah roof, the snow on the porch is blown into a kind of cave all along the front windows and doors. I'll just tunnel down under the roof to get to the porch, pull off a shutter on one of the doors, and go in for a look."

"No."

"It won't be any trouble at all!"

"No. Besides, I don't have a key."

"I know good goddam well you have a key!" Siegfried shouted angrily. "I'll be in and out in twenty minutes."

"NO!"

"Why not?" Gene snapped.

"How do I know you're not gonna steal the clock, or write on the walls, or start a fire?"

"Look, I'm just going to take a look around for old time's sake," Gene said, trying another tack. "I'm not going to hurt anything or," and he said the word with distaste, "steal. I love that Lodge more than you ever will. I just want to be able to say I was inside during the winter. It's no big deal, and I don't know why you're so bent out of shape. I'm not going to hurt anything."

"No. My job is to protect the Lodge and the cabins from weather and vandals, and that's just what I'm going to do."

"VANDALS!" Gene screamed, jumping out of his seat. "I ain't no goddamn vandal. I ain't no dude. I'm a savage just like you."

"NO!" the winter keeper shouted. He was at least a head taller than Siegfried, but not nearly so big. "I SAID NO!"

"I always heard winterkeepers were strange, but now I know it!" Gene shouted. He squared off with the man, and they were probably close to blows, but then Gene cooled and shrugged into his winter coat. "Goodbye, keeper. Be careful you don't freeze or slip down this winter—I want you, next spring."

"Get the hell out of my cabin!" the man shouted. "I always heard you were …" and his words were lost in the wind and snow.

Somewhere outside in a drift by the door, Gene had left his snowshoes, but he didn't take time to put them on, instead slinging his leather rucksack over one shoulder and dragging the rest of his gear up the hill to the laundry. Behind him, the keeper's cabin was erased from sight by the blowing snow, which was now drifting so rapidly Gene's footprints were filled almost before he could lift his boot.

The eastern side of the many-windowed laundry was deeply drifted over, but he had been there so many times in the past that he easily dug down along the loading dock in front of the building to the battered access door underneath. It was black and cold down there, and Gene couldn't see much as he crawled among the pipes, but there was little drifted snow and frost inside. Nearby, there was a wisp of steam from a small black bear denned up in a far corner, but Gene crawled off to the right and found a snow-free place under one of the flatwork ironers upstairs. Wrapping himself in two warm elk robes, he wondered—before dropping off into a blissful sleep—if he weren't becoming as daffy as the winter keeper.

The morning brought ice fog, not really a precipitation and not drifting snow either, but a shifting movement of frosty shadows and a freezing breeze with enough steady sound to deaden the strongest shout. Gene scrambled out from under the building, taking care to re-close the access door so a spring snowplow wouldn't blindly take it off. He stretched his stiff joints with a few quick calisthenics and then had a simple breakfast of minced, raw elk meat.

As he stood there chewing, he felt really lonely and depressed. If anyone should have understood the isolation he was feeling during his sojourn in the wilderness, it would have been the winterkeeper. Instead, Gene had encountered hostility and betrayal. The man's refusal to let him inside the lodge made him feel very cut off from humankind.

Peeking in the frosted, dirty windows of the old laundry, he thought of all the happy times he had while working there. The maids shaking out the sheets and pillowcases for the flatwork ironers. The towels, endless towels of the hundred rooms out there in the snow. The laughter, the stories, the girls. He missed the camaraderie of the laundry. He had helped install the huge orange dryer and been the first to figure out the complex operation of the green washer named "Big Bertha." How different the laundry looked in the winter with its machinery greased and covered for protection from the cold! He had cleaned and prepped the equipment every spring, but he missed the people the most.

Greatly saddened by the pleasant memories of his summers spent there, he turned away. Nearby, the windows of Roxy's old room in the girl's dorm were buried in a hardened drift. Pulling up one of the red-tipped markers used to guide the spring snowplows, he scratched and dug at the snow until he cleared the window for a look inside. Sure enough, Roxy had left him something, a poster of palm trees and a tropical sunset glued to the window just under the shutters, but the sight only made him sadder. Turning away gloomily, he walked downhill without so much as a glance at the winterkeeper's cabin. He crossed the open meadow in front of the lodge and disappeared into a pine grove along the shoreline of the great lake.

The ice was strangely withdrawn from the gravel of the frozen strand, and at least six inches of super-cold water glistened in the space between it and the shore. Gene slung his snowshoes on his back and pulled out a javelin to test his footing. Seemingly as thin as a knife blade, the edge of the ice popped and crackled its resistance as he put his weight on it, but ten feet from shore, it seemed pretty solid. Its white, bumpy surface was broken, and there were rays and cracks petrified deep in the ice, testimony to glacial forces beyond his comprehension. It seemed to carry weight well, and though slippery, it didn't appear dangerous. Feeling adventurous, Gene headed into the frost smoke. Out on the lake, the wind gained strength and the niveous murk grew thicker. Within minutes, he had faded like a shadow in the sun's light, and even his tracks were eroded off the surface of the ice by the wind.

CHAPTER 22

✳ ✳ ✳

The Ranger Station

GENE SIEGFRIED VANISHED at precisely the moment the surveillance team discovered his absence from the Lodge. Two scouts who had followed him from Hayden Valley the day before had dawdled too long over hot coffee in the Lake Ranger Station, and by the time they learned he was not resting comfortably in the winterkeeper's cabin, he and his trail were gone.

Twenty miles north, at Canyon Ranger Station, Jimmy Downes felt a sense of urgency come over him. What had happened? Had Siegfried left the keeper's cabin and headed back to the valley? It was likely, but if he had not headed back to the valley, that opened up an even bigger mystery, where would he go next? The weather forecasts were not good at all.

After a quick check with the Lake Ranger, Downes decided on the unusual measure of committing all his surveillance team to the field at the same time. As concerned about Gene's safety as where the young man was heading, Downes decided to find Gene quickly. He dispatched two fresh scouts by way of the Lower Loop Road and two volunteer rangers south along the Howard Eaton Trail from Canyon Village. In the meantime, he ordered the scouts at Lake to search the lakeshore all the way to Bridge Bay. None of these men found a track or sign anywhere.

"The drifting is so bad," one of the scouts reported by radio, *"my own tracks are erased in minutes. We'll never find Siegfried's trail in this weather."*

By early afternoon, the ranger knew something was wrong. He ordered his men to shelter at the Lake Ranger station, then he, Red Reese, and two other rangers stationed at Canyon hurried down by snowmobile.

After an unfriendly conversation with the winterkeeper, Downes conducted a two-hour search for tracks along the shoreline.

"Damn!" he swore when he found nothing. "Reese, take two men across the river and look for tracks all the way to Mary Bay. Be back before dark." Turning to another ranger, he ordered, "Take one of the best skiers with you and head to Sand Point. Report any tracks you find."

To the Lake Ranger, he said, "We're going to take over your station until we come up with something. I'm putting you in charge of communications."

"I'm glad to have the company," the ranger said, "Since you closed the road north of Fishing Bridge this winter, there have been few visitors through here."

"And what about you?" Reese asked, putting his hand on Downes' shoulder.

"If you guys don't pick up his trail, I'll have to go out on the ice," the younger ranger answered, though the thought made him cringe. Perhaps in a hundred years, winter dudes would commonly skate and wind sail Yellowstone Lake, but today, any venture onto the vast one-hundred-thirty-square-mile surface was a terrible risk, especially with visibility limited. He glanced out the window, then opened a map and sat down to study it.

By nightfall, none of the men had found a trace, and they straggled back to the ranger station in ones and twos. Downes received each of them expectantly, but when the last man showed up with nothing to report, his disappointment was obvious to all. He sat up that night while everyone else slept; he spent the time drinking coffee and poring over maps of the region. Where had Siegfried gone this time? Gene had a day's head start, and he could be anywhere. If he hadn't started for his cabin in Hayden Valley, could he be heading south toward West Thumb to visit the thermal basin or northeast up into the remote parts of Pelican Creek Valley to hunt? That damned kid had become quite a winter tourist lately. Two weeks ago, Downes' men had followed Gene's trek over Mary Mountain, a trip for no obvious reason. Siegfried made the trek, visited a few hot springs, then turned around and headed home, nearly bumping into the surveillance team en route. In the last month, he'd made similar trips to the Grand Canyon of the Yellowstone and then over to the Ross Geyser Basin.

Not knowing Gene's intentions, Downes and his men were forced to follow each of his dangerous excursions. Why hadn't that damned winter-keeper just acceded to Gene's request to visit the interior of the lodge? The keeper should have been honored to have the kid for company, but instead he treated him like a reprobate. Now, what was Siegfried's mood? Was he reacting in anger to the keeper's refusal or was he up to something? Either way, this was not the weather to be out trekking, and Downes grew more worried with each passing hour. He glanced over his shoulder at the thermometer, looked out the frosty window and shivered. The chill factor was forty-eight below zero.

Next morning, unwilling to commit a partner to the ice with him, Ranger Downes went down to the lakeshore. He knew an unexpected dunking, a fall, an unknown crack or a blizzard out on the unexplored surface of the lake were sure death. Besides that, though they'd searched the ranger station thoroughly, they couldn't find anything to improvise as creepers for his boots. How could he have forgotten something so basic? He was acting like a goddamn amateur! The word, uttered months ago by Professor Garner, still stung.

Downes reluctantly chose one of his surveillance team to risk the ice with him. Man is only afraid of the unknown, he thought, and Yellowstone Lake was and is a complete mystery. He knew no research had been done on it except a rudimentary charting of its depths. No one knew how thick the ice might be this time of year, nor how the stresses of wind and submarine thermal action pulled and tore at the surface of the ice. No one could predict how dangerous the lake might be.

He had heard the ice changed constantly. At times, it had the consistency of Styrofoam, later it might be layered with slush, glaze ice, or névé. Great cracks might appear one day; the next, it might have the appearance of a mirror shattered by subsurface rays. Sometimes, snow covered the ice, and other times it was billiard-table smooth or crisscrossed with dangerous pressure ridges. When it pulled away from shore on the up-wind side, a skirt of frigid water was revealed; on the downwind side, huge blocks and floes piled high on the beaches. The Fishing Bridge area was subject to a flow into the river; West Thumb was heavily thermal; Storm Point took the brunt of the wind stress, and the Southeast Arm, more than twenty miles away, received most of the new water, so perhaps, he theo-rized, only the South Arm and the Flat Mountain Arm were truly stable enough to walk on.

"You don't have to go out there," Red Reese suggested by radio. "We could call in a helicopter."

"*Visibility is too poor, and the wind's just awful,*" Downes disagreed. "*Besides, the time for that has passed. If you think about this, Red, this is what Project Snow's really about. It's a chance to see if a lone human can survive an alpine winter. If we use a helicopter, he'll know we're watching him, and that will inhibit his actions in the future. Today's the turning point of the experiment, Red. It's the time for the most crucial data. We can't reveal our hand. We've got to follow. Consciously or unconsciously, Siegfried has committed to this winter. He's testing his ability to survive, and we've got to record the results and do it unobtrusively.*"

"This experiment is about survival, Jimmy, not taking chances."

"*No, it's more than survival now,*" Downes radioed back. "*Much more. It's about independence, self-reliance … courage. It's about risking your life for noth-ing. It's the only real game there is. If you win, you live to be challenged again, and if you fail, you die, but the question is: when do you commit yourself to a course of action that may have the ultimate consequence? That's what that kid's done now. Gene Siegfried could safely barricade himself in a cozy cabin in Hayden Valley and outlast the winter, in which case, we'd learn little. Or he could challenge the worst of it and triumph.*"

"He doesn't even know he's being followed!" Reese exclaimed. "If he triumphs, what good is it? It's only in his head. He doesn't even bother recording it in his monthly reports!"

"*That's exactly the point. This whole thing is in his head. We have to follow him because we don't know Gene Siegfried anymore. We don't know the value of what he does, which is, I think, one of the objectives of the research. He's become ... a savage, Red. He doesn't value what we do."*

"He may have made the wrong decision," Reese radioed. "Going out on the lake could get him—and you—killed."

"Yep," Downes admitted on the radio, looking at the howling ice, a deep scowl on his face, *"but Red, that's not important anymore—at least not to him. I don't think he worries about death. He's not concerned with mortality or injury or disability. He's reached the point where he has become a hero—"*

"Gene Siegfried's no hero!" Reese laughed scornfully.

"Oh, but he is a hero," Downes said. *"Maybe not to us, and certainly not to the media, who are trying to pretend he's a hero, and certainly not to the flatlanders who don't understand this at all—but he isn't doing this for anyone else. He's not trying to provide the project with data, not trying to prove a point, or demonstrate his masculinity. He's reached a different plane of existence. Siegfried can go out on the ice and die, and we'll always wonder why, or he can go out there and live and always be <u>different</u> from us. He'll not only have survived, he'll have pride in existence. There is something in him now that makes him better than us, Red. I didn't use to believe it, but I do now. By the time he's finished Project Snow, he will be the ultimate savage. I think this is just the beginning for Gene Siegfried."*

"I don't think he went out on the ice," Reese disagreed. "For one thing, he doesn't have the supplies for an extended trip. Figure a maximum of fifteen miles a day for five days. That'll be his trip. He's been out of Hayden Valley two days. We can expect him to double back anytime now and run for home."

"I hope you're right, Red, but in the meantime, I think we'd better get Dr. Chamberlain up here. She ought to know what's happening. She's probably the only one of us who can judge what might be going on in his head."

It took Reese and Downes two hours to decide on a course of action. They set up schedules, established lines of march, and briefed the men at the ranger station. When finished, they notified Doctor Garner in West Yellowstone. The old man's immediate reaction was that they were exaggerating the dangers, but he finally agreed to send Dr. Capland and the psychologist to the ranger station to observe the operation. Far to the north, the Park Superintendent took a more serious view. Like all permanent residents of the park, he had a profound respect for Yellowstone's winter, so he dispatched four more experienced men, four rangers, a lot of supplies, a snow coach, and a driver.

That evening, Britt Chamberlain and Bill Capland rode in a snow coach from West Yellowstone to Snow Lodge. Both had been in the park several times that winter in such a snow coach, a tracked, multi-passenger vehicle built like a tank, and both of them had forced themselves to learn to ski, but neither were enthusiastic about winter sports, and they had confined their outdoor experiences to West Yellowstone. Britt was concerned with the cold wind drying her face and hands, so she covered her skin with moisturizer and bundled up so only her nose was sticking out of her scarf.

In the crusty, black coldness of late evening, the yellow coach lurched to a stop in front of Snow Lodge. Blinded by the bright spotlights of the Lodge and some waiting snowmobiles, the two scientists were hurriedly zipped and buckled into heavy windproof snowsuits and helmets, and then Roxy rushed up behind Britt and slipped padded leather gauntlets over her gloves.

"You'll need these," Roxy shouted, nearly drowned out by the staccato roar of starting engines. Confused by all the activity around her, Britt found herself straddling a snowmobile seat in back of a broad-shouldered ranger. Fumbling for some sort of handhold and feeling disoriented, she was surprised when Roxy wrapped a nylon harness around her waist and clipped her to the driver with a carabineer.

"Just a precaution!" Roxy shouted above the impatiently racing engines. Roxy didn't even have a coat on; she wore a red flannel shirt with the sleeves rolled up to expose long underwear. "Take the bumps in your legs!" she yelled into the side of Britt's helmet.

In the beginning, it was like riding a motorcycle. Britt enjoyed the thrill of speeding along the snowy roadway with only the narrow, bouncing circle of headlights to show the way, but after crossing the Firehole Bridge, the going got rougher. The driver seemed to be endangering their lives purposefully. They jolted into depressions and bounded over drifts, then slithered around hills until she lost all track of where she was. The road between Old Faithful and West Thumb was deceptive at night, especially when viewed in the limited beam of headlights. Britt swore they were traveling in circles, first clockwise, then counterclockwise. Finally, when she knew they must be near Fishing Bridge, she recognized Craig Pass and the frozen tub of Isa Lake, not even halfway to the Thumb. The weather worsened; visibility decreased. After a while, the snowmobiles paused for a few minutes.

Britt's driver disentangled himself from her harness and shouted, "You okay?"

"Y ... yes," she croaked.

"I said, are you okay?" he shouted again.

She found it harder to answer the second time, so he yanked back her visor and repeated the question a third time. "Yes. I'm fine," she managed, glancing around at the other machines. Capland was with the men there, but she couldn't recognize him.

Her driver pulled off her gloves and examined her wrists, looking for frostbite. "Can you feel your feet?"

"Yes. They hurt."

"How bad?" he asked, pressing on her toes with his boot.

"Not bad."

"Get up and walk around. Stamp your feet to get the blood moving. We'll be leaving in ten minutes."

She needed a friend, but she couldn't recognize one. The men were busy checking each other for frostbite. One had a bright red mark on his forearm where his sleeve had gapped; the men fussed with it before deciding it was only windburn. They wrapped the man's hands carefully and used duct tape to cinch his gloves around his wrists before remounting.

How far was it to Lake? Britt wondered, hooking herself to the driver again. Twenty more miles? Another hour? The powerful machine lurched underneath her and they sped away. This time, the going was rougher, the drifts undulating badly.

They arrived at the Lake Ranger Station covered with ice. The quaint structure was full of men in bulky down jackets. She recognized Red Reese on the radio in one room, several others were comparing cross-country skis, three men were asleep, and dinner was being cooked—as it always is in gatherings like this.

Dr. Capland slapped the ice from his snowsuit and hers, found a quiet section of wall to rest against, and helped her out of her snowsuit. "Ranger Downes and one of the Indians are out on the lake. They're on foot. I guess the ice is rough."

"It was clear this afternoon before sundown. Didn't they see Gene Siegfried? Is he even out there?" she asked.

"They didn't see nothing," a man mumbled from the depths of a near-by sleeping bag. "They're in trouble."

"In trouble? What's happened?"

"Ground blizzard," the man answered. "They were blown off course after they got out there. It's been hard going. They've had a few falls and dropped their compass on the ice. They don't know whether to trust it or not—that's what they're talking about on the radio. When it cleared just before sundown, they took fixes on some landmarks. They're trying to establish the compass' deviation so they can navigate in the dark."

"Where are they right now?" Capland asked.

"That's the problem. They thought they were north or northwest of Stevenson Island and found out they were between Gull and Sand Points, southwest of the island."

"Why don't they head here? They could come back for the night," Britt suggested. "It's only three or four miles."

"They can't see the shoreline and can't keep a straight course in the wind. It's a total whiteout on the lake."

"What are they going to do?"

"Hard to say. If I were out there, I'd strike for Stevenson Island, get under shelter, and start a fire. Chances are the kid did the same thing. If he didn't ... well, it's hell out on the ice."

With the howl of the wind growing in strength outside, Britt found two sleeping bags to make herself a nest. As she slept, Capland drifted away to enjoy the camaraderie of the other men.

"*R ... Lak ... shun ... Cmn ... ver!*"

Britt woke just as Reese vaulted over her, spilling a bit of his soup on her shoulder. He grabbed the radio and shouted, "Say again, Polar Bear One, over."

"*Fmatv...k..........sh..........We............ve.........ra..............kan.........si............................r!*"

"Polar Bear, we do not copy. Repeat, we do not copy. Say again, over."

"*Lake?............its.........................this? ....rri-ble out here!*"

"We do not copy, Polar Bear. Can you get under some cover?"

"*La...?.........wind.........er!..................We got...........on the ice! ... I've—*"

"Polar Bear One. We do _not_ copy. Can you—" and Britt dropped off to sleep again.

About five o'clock in the morning, Capland shook her awake, handed her a cup of coffee and said, "Get up. The weather's changing. The wind's strong, and the temperature is dropping. The men are getting ready to go."

"How cold is it?" she asked.

"Thirty below," he answered, hustling her toward a stove in the back room.

In the outer office, Reese was briefing a few men; in the inner office, rangers were studying maps. Four other men were waiting ravenously at her elbows for something to eat. They expected her to cook breakfast, she realized in dismay.

Sucking in her breath, Britt pursed her lips, unable to admit she couldn't cook. She was frustrated she had been so blithely volunteered as a domestic for all these men. Standing before the stove clenching and un-clenching her fists, she raised her eyes and looked out the frosted window at the raging blizzard outside. It scared her. There was no way she could go out with the men. It was worse than she had imagined while in West Yellowstone. What was she doing here? she wondered. Placing an iron skillet on the fire, she poured an inch of vegetable oil in, closed her eyes, and cracked her first egg.

Men began leaving at first light. Each time a group went out, the ranger station cooled perceptively, and chilly drafts snaked through rooms recently stuffy. Two men, including the Lake Ranger, stayed by the ra-dio, two others slept on the counter in the outer office, and Britt angrily washed dishes by herself. All the others—even Capland—were gone.

Ranger Reese had several men combing the cover between Fishing Bridge and Steamboat Point; they were forbidden to cross over the highway, but told to work between it and the barren shoreline lest Siegfried double back and find their tracks. Jimmy Downes and the scout with him were moving again, having spent the night on Stevenson Island. Far north of the lake, four other men swept the forest in Pelican Creek Valley and the Sulphur Hills.

They found not one sign of a man until one-thirty in the afternoon, when one of the scouts discovered a footprint on the ice a mile south of the mouth of Cub Creek. A hundred yards on, another track in a patch of snow indicated his direction—east.

Jimmy Downes raised his eyes, and Red Reese at the other end of the radio, and the men in the ranger station and the men on the trail. They knew now where Gene Siegfried was headed, for there, due east, was the great sloping bastion of Mount Avalanche. This unmistakable peak gleamed with fresh white powder, and pale blue lines of recent avalanches scarred the slopes above timberline. It was time, Jimmy Downes realized, as he grimly gazed up at the mountain from the cold ice of Yellowstone Lake, to challenge fear.

CHAPTER 23

※ ※ ※

Avalanche

ALTHOUGH IT APPEARED from the flat expanse of Yellowstone Lake to be an enormous flat-topped butte set amidst the otherwise craggy pinnacles of the Absaroka Mountains, Mount Avalanche was actually a narrow, rocky ridgeline between a steep-walled cirque on the east and the eroded, forested highlands to the west. A trail up the mountain allows summer hikers to see one of America's great panoramas of jagged peaks, forests, and an azure Yellowstone Lake so huge in the near distance the curvature of the earth can be seen in it.

But now, as he looked up from the single footprint on the ice—the sole indicator of Gene's intentions—and gazed across the slick surface of the lake at the mountain, Jimmy Downes bellowed into his radio, "I want a weather report."

"*No update on the weather will be available for another hour,*" a ranger answered.

"Damn it!" Downes radioed back.

"*Why don't you come on in,*" the ranger suggested. It was seven miles across the ice to get back to the ranger station.

"Good idea. We're headed back," Downes agreed. "Let's stop this and get organized. Everyone return to the ranger station. We'll meet you there."

Three hours later, as the last of his tired men filtered into the warm station from outside, Downes served himself a cup of black coffee and settled into a desk chair facing the lobby. It was hard to tell what he was thinking most of the time, but as she stood a few feet to his left, Britt

Chamberlain noticed him peer out the frosted window and shiver. Twenty miles away, the flaring bulk of Avalanche could be seen soaring over the ice of the lake.

"One of Gene's friends took me up the mountain last summer," she told him. It was one of her best memories in Yellowstone. Roxy had to encourage her every step of the way. Several times she thought she couldn't go on, but Roxy had sat on a stone nearby, exhorting her to finish. Finally, as she crawled on her hands and knees onto the narrow, rocky summit of Mount Avalanche, she realized why many savages talked about the view. It was stunning up there. The sky was the most intense blue-green color. The air was clear, cold, and cleaner than she'd ever breathed before. After a lifetime spent smoking cigarettes and living in smoggy cities, her nose was so shocked by the crisp air, it started bleeding. Around her, in every direction, were the jagged, snowy peaks of countless mountains, many still capped with snow though it was July. There was not a road, power line, or building visible anywhere, though she could see as far as the Tetons, a hundred miles south.

"In the summer," Downes said, leaning back in his chair, "Avalanche is a hike. Now, it's a killer."

"Did you ever climb it in the winter?" she asked curiously.

"No," he said. "I don't know anyone who has."

"Then how do you know it's so bad?" she inquired skeptically.

"It's not called 'Avalanche' because it's tame up there." Moving over to the window, he added, "I wouldn't try it in winter if you paid me in gold, but I've seen it in the spring, when there's ten feet of snow on the lower trail. Believe it or not, it's easier to climb with snow on it, but even so, it's mighty steep, especially the last pitch of two hundred feet. The pitch'll be hard-packed now, vertical ice all the way to the top, with a big cornice overhanging the whole ridgeline."

"So why do you think Gene Siegfried wants to do it?" she asked.

"You tell me," he laughed. "You're the psychologist. You're supposed to know him better than anyone. I've never understood what he's thinking; all I can say is, it's too dangerous for me."

Some of the men standing behind them in the cluttered lobby agreed. Avalanches were only a part of it; they feared the cold as much as anything, not to mention the wind and snow. Britt looked out the window and gazed upon a scene of such incredible beauty she felt she would burst. She almost wished she could go with the men tomorrow.

Though nearly twenty miles away, Mount Avalanche was so clear she felt she could touch it. When the air was the coldest here in Yellowstone, visibility was the greatest. Because of that, she knew it must be very cold outside.

Gene Siegfried was a full two days ahead of them by now. Despite that, Ranger Reese told her they had indications he was merely ambling along. One of the scouts had found a disturbed snow bank near Storm Point that may have been his snow den; there was a track on Stevenson Island that may have been his too. What was he up to out there? The rangers were full of all sorts of speculations, but she knew exactly what he was doing. He was visiting old haunts. In spite of the cold, in spite of the danger, in spite of the wind, low visibility and quickly changing conditions, Gene Siegfried was simply wandering around, following his whims where they took him. He was playing in the snow! Who could have thought that in this experiment they'd end up with a subject like this? The young man was fearless. He was, in a word, incredible, the most astonishing subject she had ever studied in any psychology experiment.

As she stared out the window, Downes began a long brainstorming session with the men. Due to a serious lack of information about weather on the Central Plateau in the winter, the men could only guess at conditions on the mountain. After discussing all the weather reports they could get, the ranger detailed two of the men to stuff four packs with supplies for two days. He assigned another group to study available maps; after an hour's discussion, this group decided that Siegfried would stick to a standard approach: he would rejoin the highway somewhere east of the lake, most probably near Cub Creek, but perhaps as far east as Sylvan Lake, then attempt the climb along the well-known Glacier Gulch summer tourist route.

"Then what?" the ranger asked his men.

"I think he'll return the same way," one of the scouts declared.

"Why?"

"His supplies are nearly exhausted. He'll have to follow the shortest route home."

"Okay," the ranger agreed. "That means that to avoid alerting him to our presence, we must take care not to leave many tracks on the highway, nor to drive snowmobiles within earshot. It makes our job more difficult."

"You don't think he'll be suspicious when he doubles back and finds our tracks?" another asked.

"No," Reese answered, jumping into the conversation. "He may figure we're winter dudes driving through the East Entrance to Cody, Wyoming."

"I agree," Downes said. "Okay, here's how we're going to do it. Three men and I, designated as 'Polar Bear One,' will try to follow Siegfried as closely as possible. Reese will command a second group of seven, code-named 'Polar Bear Two,' with five of our snowmobiles and supplies in case of an accident or changing weather. A third group of seven, or 'Polar Bear Three,' will provide support. Communications are to be maintained at all times, and weather reports are to be monitored day and night." To accomplish this, Downes turned and asked, "Dr. Chamberlain, will you assist the Lake Ranger by monitoring the reports for us?"

"Of course," she agreed, thankful her duties weren't so arduous. Two of the men were already limping badly; most of the rest complained about various aches and pains. Dr. Capland had just spent the last two hours cleaning and bandaging several of the men's feet where their snow boots had worn blisters onto their heels. She poured herself a cup of chicken bouillon and snugged her sweater more closely around her throat. Yes, she thought with relief, she was glad she didn't have to go out in the snow with the men tomorrow.

Exactly at sundown, the clouds broke and admitted pealing shafts of bright sunshine. As she watched openmouthed through the window, the antique-glass ice of the lake blazed into holy color. Across the lake, framed by powder blue and rust clouds, the Absaroka Mountains were veiled in mysterious shades of gray and brown, presenting the overall impression, she imagined, of a vast cathedral. Strangely, she felt at peace standing there at the window, though she was surrounded by rough-hewn men in a world she little understood. As she watched in wonder, night descended, and the air filled with swirling snow.

That night, Red Reese selected three men to accompany Downes up the mountain. Of prime importance was stamina, but Reese also considered the men's character, experience, and maturity. One of the original Indians was put in charge of the radio. Reese then selected a naturalist from Mammoth and one of the Canyon rangers to go.

The support group would be composed of the rest of the original surveillance team, Reese himself, and three men from Mammoth. The reserve consisted of Dr. Capland, some rangers, a young administrative clerk from Mammoth, and a snow coach driver.

Late that night, Jimmy Downes and his surveillance team were dropped off near Steamboat Point on the northeastern shore of Yellowstone Lake. In the frigid darkness, they methodically made their way eastward along the winding, snow-covered roadway. After a brief rest and a breakfast stop the next morning, they stumbled across a fresh snowshoe trail as it entered the highway from the right, almost exactly where predicted.

Examining the tracks, Downes discovered Siegfried had moved slowly but steadily up the road, veering from it only to investigate the floundering trail of a fox. As usual, the ranger wondered what Gene was up to now. The weather was cold enough to kill a city slicker in a doorway, but Siegfried's trail proved he was taking his time, not in a hurry to get anywhere, just checking out the scenery. A broken ankle, a fall, an accidental dunking—any kind of minor crisis could occur out here, and for all Siegfried knew, he would die alone, miles from help or a hospital, yet he plowed on, acting like he hadn't a care in the world. That kid was tough, Downes decided, tougher than any of the men following him.

As he followed the trail, he realized every joint in his body ached. Downes hadn't slept well in three days and hadn't eaten a hot meal since noon yesterday. But what about Siegfried? He didn't have coffee, or aspirins, or a bath. How was he functioning out here? As he thought about it, Downes decided all his own physical complaints were rather petty. Next time he saw the kid, he'd … well … he'd show him more respect. Siegfried was not the summer troublemaker he had been told about by other rangers; Gene was teaching him lessons about survival and existence itself. Gene was living his life to the fullest, each minute squeezed for all the juice it contained. Gene Siegfried wasn't worried about incidentals like cars, money, status, or entertainment. He had somehow achieved more than anyone had imagined when this experiment began. Gene had attained a different plane of existence. He was not only happy with what he was doing, he was content, Downes realized. How could anybody be content in this cold?

As he and his men doggedly followed the trail, Downes knew the weather couldn't have been more cooperative. The official record at Lake was an observed high of twenty-two that day, a low of minus three, a trace of precipitation, and an average base of forty inches of snow on the ground. It was brilliantly clear. It was a day of sunshine and prismatic ice crystals shimmering in the air; visibility was at least twenty miles. Mount Avalanche, rising steeply off to their left and only occasionally spotted through the trees now as they moved along the East Entrance Road, was clear and sharp, but he knew that on the mountain itself, it was at least ten degrees colder and quite windy.

Apparently slogging along the snow-covered road without a care in the world, Siegfried stopped often to investigate tracks and pick at the icicled beauty of the frosted trees around him. Only a few miles behind now, Ranger Downes also stared in wonder at the haunting clarity of his surroundings. As the altitude increased, the open lodgepole forests gave way to Engelmann spruce, and the sharp mountain ridges closed in around the narrow, twisting road. He remembered driving through here on the way to the East Entrance hundreds of times in the past, but he had never known it to be so beautiful. To his right, Topnotch Peak, its split summits partly snow-free due to recent rock falls, stuck out above the storm-beaten forest. The peak would be an indicator of their progress as they followed Glacier Gulch up to the left.

Mount Avalanche, together with Hoyt Peak to the east, formed the high, northern side of Sylvan Pass. In the summer, the pass was a bony cut through the loose, gray rhyolitic talus on the north and the sheer cliffs on the south. Spring run-off created gushing waterfalls that dropped from the dizzying heights only to vanish in the scree below, and scarred tree trunks in the felsenmeer testified to the violence of winter avalanches. Today, though, as Downes and his men came into the pass, a cold wind whipped the dusty snow in a vast wheel from the south face to the north. It was a gray, brooding place, the wind moaning like a banshee through the pass, and far away, a clatter of falling rocks sounded like the tinkle of broken dishes in a clumsy cafeteria.

Apparently, Siegfried had peeked into the pass itself, but his tracks showed he approached only as close as Eleanor Lake. A sterile pond that was but a shallow interruption of the water table in the summertime, the little lake was frozen to its bottom now, its surface strewn with chunks of stone thrown down from the heights.

"We're in the Sylvan Pass," Downes radioed Canyon Ranger Station. "The subject's trail has just turned north for the ascent."

"*Roger that,*" the Lake Ranger answered immediately. "*Good luck and be careful.*"

"Will do," Downes promised. "This is Polar Bear One, out."

He knew the climb was an excellent example of Yellowstone's various habitats, the lower portion passing through pine, fir, and Engelmann spruce to the stormy territory of the whitebark pine. At about nine thousand feet elevation, natural springs at the foot of Glacier Gulch were a welcome treat for summer hikers. Carved by falling blocks of a hanging glacier, the gulch was a steep defile much worn by the trails of thousands of puffing hikers. At the top, a gravely moraine blocked the way, and beyond was an enormous bowl a quarter mile wide almost perfectly hollowed into the northwestern wall that was Mount Avalanche. Geologically speaking, the cirque was recently glaciated, and it was filled with pathetic, rolling hillocks of gravel that marked the glacier's struggles and final demise. From here, there was only one way up the mountain, but there was no trail across the rubbly cirque, only meandering tracks over the fragile soil.

At the far side of the cirque, Downes knew, was a small cairn marking Yellowstone's border with Shoshone National Forest. From here, a huge U-shaped glacial valley opened to the northeast. To the right of the cairn, Hoyt Peak, which was little more than a shell carved hollow by glaciers, sat like the empty rind of an orange resting on its side, its flaring edges thin, knife-edged arêtes. The summer trail turned west here through the stunted bonsais of tree line to the clinking rocks of the mountain's shoulder. Off to the right was a last stand of twisted trees, but the only other life above tree line on this rocky trail was the unloved Alpine Skunkflower—with a scent to match its name—and a mousy, little animal called the pika. The last rise, a gain of a hundred and fifty feet at a slope of sixty degrees, led to the ridgeline of Avalanche, which he knew was only forty feet wide.

"What's it look like?" the Lake Ranger radioed. There was a lot of static. Radio reception was being blocked by Mt. Avalanche.

"Very different from the summer," Downes answered. "We've got a dozen feet of snow over the lower trail." Out of breath and out of words to describe the grandeur he was seeing, Downes signed off. Barely able to keep up with his men, he slogged on, his lungs and legs feeling like they were on fire. Thankfully, his men paused, and when he caught up, he learned they had discovered a spot midway up the mountain where Gene had stopped, made a fire, and warmed some food or tea. Siegfried's tracks showed he often paused, perhaps to catch his breath or tighten his gear, but more likely to listen to the wind soughing through the whitebark pine and to check his progress by looking across the pass at Topnotch Peak.

About four-thirty in the afternoon, Gene made it into the rolling cirque. The flaring blue wall of Avalanche rose sheer above him to the left, cutting off the rays of the dying sun. It was already dark. An overhanging cornice the length of the ridgeline had recently avalanched, and, at the base of the cliff, huge, angular blocks of snow the size of houses lay in a monstrous pile. It was too dangerous to proceed farther that day, so he stopped near a stand of stunted trees and made a fire. Wrapping himself in an elk skin, he sat cross-legged beside the flames to wait out the night.

"Lake? We've got HVTS in sight! He's got a fire going about two hundred yards from us," Jimmy Downes reported excitedly. "I'm glad we finally caught up with him." High above Gene now on the right, the ranger and his surveillance team were tenuously dug in on the flank of Hoyt Peak, watching Gene with binoculars.

"You'd better settle for the night too," the Lake Ranger advised.

"Right. We'll do that," Downes agreed, motioning for his men to withdraw. In darkness, he and his three men descended to a level bench somewhere down by the springs, but he soon discovered their camp was entirely in the radio shadow of the mountains. Certain Siegfried would stay put for a while, Downes made a futile attempt to establish contact with Lake, then ordered everyone to humid, icy tents to weather the night.

As Downes and his men slept, they missed the greatest spectacle of winter Yellowstone: a clear, blue-velvet sky spangled with the blaze of a golden Milky Way on a cold, clear night with a full, luminous moon rising majestically over the azure mountains. Far away across the frozen lake, Britt Chamberlain watched open mouthed as the moon first silhouetted the rugged Absarokas, then rose in triumph over them. She had departed the Lake Ranger Station alone and had walked down to the shoreline of Yellowstone Lake. Dancing moonlight illuminated the face of the mountains across from her and reflected off the pale, icy lake. The snow around her reflected the light like millions of diamonds sparkling in the dark, and she sucked in her breath, afraid to break the spell of this magic night.

By now, it was as bright as daylight, but since moonlight doesn't support the prismatic rainbow like sunlight, all detail was lost in shades of blue and gray. It was the most hauntingly peaceful moment she had ever experienced, and intuitively she knew that somewhere deep in those mountains, the bare, unprotected head of Gene Siegfried was also turned upward in spiritual wonder, and he, too, was filled with awe. She was tempted to stay there the night, but in the forest behind her, a coyote yodeled, and a chorus of silly yappers soon joined in. Cursing herself for being out alone, she returned to the cheerful warmth of the ranger station.

There was a quietness later that night, a passing of shadows upon the moon, and by morning, high, scudding clouds obscured the sky. An ominous wind gusted first one way, then another, but the glazed snow, hardened by the bright sunshine the day before, resisted drifting.

At sunrise, Ranger Downes had an observer back in position on the steep side of Hoyt, but the huddled figure below was still solidly asleep beside the fly ash of his fire; it wasn't until eight o'clock that he stirred and threw the robe off his shoulders. After doing ten minutes of isometrics, Gene undid the straps behind his head, pulled at the chin of the snow mask, and slipped the leather from his face. It was the first time in two months that any of the surveillance men had seen his face.

"Damn! Did anyone think to bring a camera?" Downes asked. A camera was standard equipment for the surveillance teams, but somehow it had been left behind. Feeling a strange urgency, the ranger pulled out his notebook from an inner pocket and recorded his impressions. Siegfried's red beard looked wild and full of ice from his frozen breath, and his long, flamboyant mustache completely covered his mouth. He blew his nose upon the snow, took a long leak, and then hammered his leather robe until it was flexible enough to roll into his rucksack.

As Downes watched through naval binoculars, Siegfried ate a simple breakfast of shredded jerky, which he chewed while gazing around at the barbaric scenery of the cirque. He didn't bother to make tea and by nine-thirty, he had covered his ashes and was ready to go again. Pulling the mask back over his chin and tucking the ends of his beard under the soft folds of its throat piece, he retied the leather straps behind his head and slipped on his fur hat, letting its heavy ear pieces fall loosely to his shoulders until he needed them.

"Lake Station? This is Polar Bear One. Do you read?" Downes radioed.

"*Good morning, Polar Bear. What's your situation? Over.*" The voice was unmistakably Britt's.

"Ah, yeah, Lake," Downes answered, feeling uncomfortable talking to the woman. She was the worst cook he had ever encountered. "The subject is moving north-northeast. An attempted ascent is imminent."

Downes made a quick weather check then dispatched his radioman higher onto the flank of Hoyt Peak. Two ordinary bed sheets had been included in their supplies for camouflage in the snow, and with these, the observer made an effective observation post in the scraggly trees at timberline. From there, he could not see Siegfried's line of approach along the northern side of Avalanche's shoulder, but there would be a clear view of both the last pitch and a hint of the top of Avalanche's ridgeline.

Meanwhile, the ranger and two other men, equipped with a small two-way radio for communicating with the observer, tailed their subject as closely as possible across the rolling moraines of the central cirque. Siegfried spent a great deal of time in the saddle between the two mountains; the tiny cairn marking Yellowstone's eastern boundary was completely buried under snow, but he stood where it was and looked out over the glacial valley. After a side trip onto the incredibly dangerous arête of Hoyt's western slope to look down into its rocky cirque, he returned to the slope of Avalanche's shoulder and began vaguely following the buried trail upward.

"Snow's bad up here," Downes radioed as he waited for Gene to get out of sight before venturing into the saddle behind him. Although the day was clear, the wind was picking up. To the right, the rounded shoulder of the mountain dropped off to certain death, but he knew the hazardous last pitch, which was eight feet of ice sweeping up into the frozen belly of a cornice, was far more dangerous.

He wished he could contact someone who had ascended Avalanche in the winter. It was not an attractive or romantic climb like the traditional New Year's attempts on the Grand Teton or the fireworks ascent of Pikes Peak, in Colorado, nor was it a technical climb requiring ropes, crampons, and teamwork. Too accessible to the road to attract hard-core mountain climbers, Avalanche was a gut-wrenching challenge for a lone climber, especially in the winter.

The mountain had earned its name. Downes knew avalanches often collapsed into its cirque. Such an avalanche could have six times the force of a similarly sized ocean wave, travel at speeds of four hundred feet per second, and push a devastating wind as dangerous as an explosion ahead of it. He could see such an avalanche was there now, waiting in the form of an unstable cornice twenty feet thick, hanging over the side of the ridge. Thousands of tons of ice, dependent on the crystalline integrity of tiny ice particles deep in the base of the cornice, were suspended above the precipice, and a mere echo or even a whisper could set it in motion, though Downes realized it might also cling to the mountain until spring thaw.

"*Okay, I got him,*" the observer on Hoyt radioed when Siegfried finally moved into sight at the base of the last pitch. A slip to the left would result in an icy fall of three hundred feet, while a roll to the right meant seven hundred feet of clawing desperation to the bottom, yet Gene didn't hesitate a moment. Dismounting and binding one of his snowshoes securely upright on his pack, he tied the other lightly across his chest, purpose as yet unknown. Then, taking a javelin in each hand to probe, he began to cut footholds in the wall of snow.

Behind him, Jimmy Downes and his men moved up to the stunted trees on the right edge of the mountain's shoulder in order to see him more clearly with their binoculars. Across the lake, at the other end of the radio, he knew the woman was holding her breath, and the men in the support and reserve groups were raising their binoculars, each hoping to be the first to see a triumphant, black dot against the sky.

A quick, easy ascent was not, however, in the cards, for the snow was as gritty as an old cinder block. Big, white puffs of breath showed Siegfried's effort as he became winded, but he kept steadily on until stalled at the very base of the cornice by a lack of footing. A single, faltering misstep would have meant death, the ranger thought as he watched the figure on the mountain, but panting very heavily, Gene succeeded in trampling a solid purchase into the snow. Then, freeing the snowshoe from across his chest, he used it to hack at the belly of the cornice. He was obviously experienced at this kind of digging, Downes thought, wishing he didn't have to watch the kid do this.

Gene gradually tunneled upward into the very jaws of a potential avalanche, tons of snow looming over and around him, and as he dug, he probed the two javelins deeply into the cornice to secure his footing. Mining chunks of ice from the head of the vertical tunnel, he pressed them between his knees and allowed them to fall straight down into the void.

And finally, at exactly one-thirty on the afternoon of February 22, 1974, Gene Siegfried broke through the cornice and crawled out of the mouth of a snowy, vertical tunnel onto the narrow, ridged summit of Mount Avalanche. The altitude was only 10,566 feet, not an impressive climb by some standards, but Jimmy Downes clapped his scouts on the back, and he heard on the radio Britt Chamberlain dancing gleefully around the office with the Lake Ranger.

Siegfried stood at the highest point of the ridge, raised both fists to his shoulders in what the ranger imagined to be a shout into the wind and disappeared.

CHAPTER 24

✳ ✳ ✳

A Shadow in the Wind

MINUTES AFTER GENE Siegfried vanished from sight on top of Mount Avalanche, Downes used his short-range transmitter, patched through his Hoyt observer's radio. "Lake, you got anything from that side?"

"*Negative, Polar Bear. Too much blowing snow down here.*"

"We can't see from this side either, not from Mount Hoyt, nor here on the shoulder. Any ideas?"

"*Negative, Polar Bear,*" the Lake Ranger said.

"What about you, Dr. Chamberlain?"

"*Umm, that's a negative too,*" she answered obviously awkward speaking in radioese like the professionals.

There were ten minutes of watchful silence, and then the Lake Ranger said, "*Polar Bear One? We have a fresh update on the weather. Wind is rising here. Increased cloudiness and five zero percent chance of snow this afternoon, increasing to niner zero tonight. Temperatures are expected to drop to a low of minus one eight by morning, with chill factor varying from minus four zero to minus six zero. Estimated temperature differential based on your altitude is ten degrees.*"

"Damn! Get off the mountain," Jimmy Downes swore at the news. Another thirty minutes passed, then the head and shoulders of Siegfried bobbed into sight to the left on the ridge and disappeared once more. After forty minutes, he was again sighted at the summit, and then more than an hour slid by without any sign of him.

"Polar Bear One, Polar Bear One. It is snowing at Lake! I say again, it is snowing at Lake! Wind is west-northwest at eight miles per hour, gusting to twenty. We cannot see the mountain, over."

"Lake? This is Polar Bear One. I am declaring a priority one intervention," Downes radioed immediately. "I say again, we will intervene. Support? Move to Eleanor Lake and wait for instructions. Reserve, move to Steamboat Point. Polar Bear One will ascend; I say again, we will ascend and intervene with subject HVTS. Do you copy, over?"

"Polar Bear One, do not ascend," the Lake Ranger answered. *"I say again, do NOT ascend. Snow conditions will not—"*

"Lake? You do not have authority," Downes radioed. "We are ascending! Keep this frequency clear. Support? Reserve? You will move up as ordered."

"Polar Bear One, hold your position," the Lake Ranger shouted.

"This is Polar Bear One, out," Downes said.

"Polar Bear, wait for instructions from headquarters at Mammoth. Do you copy? Polar Bear One come in…. Do you copy? Do you copy? Over."

When he received no answer on the radio, the Lake Ranger shouted, *"Damn you, Jimmy Downes, answer me."*

In the background, Britt Chamberlain was pleading, "But he's got to go up there. Gene doesn't know the weather's closing in. He'll never be able to get down alone, especially with evening coming on. He's in great danger."

"If Gene Siegfried's not smart enough to see that snow line coming across the lake at him, then to hell with him. Too far to the left during the whiteout, and it's off into the cirque; a step to the right, and he'll be in the rocks on the other side. Better one gets killed than four," the Lake Ranger shouted. *"Hoyt. Hold your position and maintain radio contact with the surveillance team. Do not break this patch through to Ranger Downes. Polar Bear One, come in, over…."*

Jimmy Downes was not so foolish as to turn off his radio at a time like this, but he and the other two men were already pressing up through the last stunted whitebark pines at timberline. Hesitating at the foot of the last steep slope, the ranger looked up into the overhanging cornice of snow and the already clogged tunnel bored up through it two hundred feet above. Feathers of snow a hundred feet long were being blown off the trailing edge of the cornice now, testifying to the violence of the wind on top.

"Good God," he muttered. "Where's my climbing rope? Did I forget it? Does anyone have a climbing rope? We need something to harness ourselves together."

"Here, I've got one," one of the men said, pulling a rope from a pack.

"Let's get hooked together. We don't want to get separated going up that last pitch," the ranger ordered.

"*I can't see the top of Avalanche at all,*" the Hoyt observer radioed. The Hoyt outpost was beginning to lose sight of them too in the blowing snow as the three men struggled upward.

Downes was determined to get to the top quickly. It was difficult, though, and fraught with danger, especially since much of the badly drifted tunnel Siegfried had made earlier had to be re-dug by hand, but through his and his scouts' skill and professionalism, they succeeded in gaining the top without incident.

Ranger Downes was mortified to discover Gene Siegfried was not there. By this time, visibility was less than a hundred feet and declining fast, but it was easy to find a broad, butt-shaped furrow down the nearly vertical western face of the mountain. The ranger tried to recall what the slope looked like in summer: a steep wasteland of broken, gray rock crashing a few hundred feet into a stunted forest far below. He could see none of that now, but it didn't take much imagination to visualize it. The snow was chunky and uneven, and he figured it was probably studded with rocks as well. An uncontrolled slide of perhaps sixty miles an hour down the dangerous slope would be like sliding over Styrofoam studded with razor blades, and if the slide didn't kill them, the jumbled rock pile at the bottom might.

"I'm not going down that," one of the men announced, closely followed by the unnecessary question of the second, "You're not really going to try it, are you?"

The ranger pursed his lips as he stared downslope. Turning to his men, he shouted against the wind, "Chances are he's dead down there, either cracked up in the rocks or disemboweled on the slope, but there's also a chance he might only have broken a leg or his neck. If we go back now, we might as well write him off as as dead." Looking at his men grimly, he said, "Yeah, I'm going down there. I have to know what happened."

"Is there a chance he got down safely?" a scout shouted back.

"Ha!" Downes snorted "Less than one percent. Of course, when he went down, visibility was a lot better—"

"I'm not going to do it," the man declared again.

"Then go back to the cirque and link up with our outpost on Hoyt. Take our transmitter with you. You'll need it to find him in the dark. The two of you come around the mountain from the south and meet me somewhere west of the springs. You coming with me?" he asked the other scout.

In answer, the man began tightening his straps and buckles. "Good for you," Downes said, slapping him on the back. "Okay," he said, turning to the first scout, "You go back. We'll belay you down. Be careful going along the shoulder. When you get to the Hoyt radio, order the support group up to the springs. We may need them. Go ahead and bring the reserve all the way to Eleanor Lake. You got that?"

"Yeah, and don't worry about me. I'll be careful going back into the cirque," the man said, a little sadly it seemed to the ranger. "You be careful too. Don't you think you ought to take the transmitter?"

"No, we'd only break it going down that slope, and besides, it's too short-range to call Lake. Take it. When you come around the mountain, fire up a Coleman lantern, and we'll find you by the light, okay?"

"Yeah. Be careful."

"We will."

Tying the man's pack to a climbing rope, they let it through the tunnel partway down to the shoulder of the mountain, and then, while the ranger and the other man braced the line, the scout hitched on with a carabineer and slid down on his back. He finished the descent safely by foot, and at the bottom, he waved. Downes was sorry to see him go, but he couldn't blame him. The man had kids.

"Okay," he said, trying to show more bravery than he felt, "Let's get ready."

Arranging themselves for their own descent by lashing their skis and poles across the backs of their packs, he and the scout sat on the edge of the ridge with their feet facing downslope. "I hate to tell you this," Downes admitted, "but I've never glissaded before."

"Oh, shit!" the man swore. "Don't tell me that now!"

"I know the theory, though," the ranger said, looking between his feet at the nearly vertical slope. "Keep my legs together and use my ice ax to brake. Anything else I ought to know?"

"Let's not go more'n a hundred yards at a time," the man suggested. "Stop to break your momentum and steer clear of any dark spots. If you can't see where you're going, stop. There might be drop-offs down there, and we can't afford to ski-jump on our butts."

"Okay!" Downes shouted as he shoved off.

Safety was, of course, his prime concern, but it was a relative issue, for stopping was impossible. The steepness of the slope pulled him faster and faster, and within seconds, Jimmy Downes was terrified. He dug in with both feet, the result being that gritty snow was blown up both of his pants' legs and into his face, blinding him. He discovered it was a bit easier to guide than to slow down, but there was no way to tell what was ahead or how fast he was traveling. After what seemed like a mile, he skidded to a stop, unable to see the bottom yet.

At that very moment, his partner appeared out of the blowing snow, abruptly clipped a rock with his left boot, then spun around headfirst and flew downslope. Seconds later, a thud told the ranger he had made it to the bottom. Rushing downhill, Downes found the man wrapped around a scraggly pine at tree line, badly bruised and shaken, but as far as they could tell, not seriously hurt. When they looked up, ten feet to their right, they spotted a gentle skid where Gene Siegfried had come to rest ... and beyond that, another skid, and another. Obviously, he had enjoyed the exhilarating slide down the slope so much, he had climbed back up the mountain to repeat it twice! Nearby, they found a strong snowshoe trail leading into the trees, indicating he was still in good shape.

By this time, the forest was blue and hazy with falling snow in the fairy-tale fashion of Yellowstone winters. Somewhere down below them, Siegfried was probably making a comfortable fire, most likely in a snow cave, from which he would not move again before midmorning. It was time for the two men to make tracks of their own around the mountain to re-join the other rangers. Linking up in the storm proved difficult, however, and it was a long time before Downes and his men were gathered together once again. There were too many for the few tents they had brought, but they managed a miserable camp near Eleanor Lake, where some got as much as two hours' sleep that night.

The weather was changing again, and a new viciousness came into the storm. Falling snow and eroded drifting swirled dismally through the cold, black forests; it was thirty-five below zero that night with variable winds, drifts on the march, and heavy overcast, all indicators this storm would last four or five days.

Britt Chamberlain rose about midnight from her comfortable cub-byhole in a pile of sleeping bags. Unzipping one of them to drape over her shoulders like a blanket, she stood before the frosted windows of the ranger station, staring at the moody grayness outside. Occasionally, the Lake Ranger looked up at her from his desk, and then he turned to a map, which he studied like a chessboard in a match. After minutes of silence, Britt asked, "What's the purpose of surveillance?"

The ranger answered, "To watch your subject, report on develop-ments, provide security, prevent accidents if possible, and aid him if we must."

"No, that's not what I meant," she chuckled, turning back to the window. "It was a rhetorical question. Yes, of course, we have to maintain surveillance. But this kind of surveillance? What have we learned from this and at what cost?" She sat near the ranger's desk and leaned over the map. The office was dark; only a desk lamp provided light to see the map. "What have _you_ learned from all this?"

"I've never met Gene Siegfried," the ranger said. "I imagined him as one of those YP company troublemakers up here for a good time in the summers. That's how he's been described to me—but, in fact, he's different. He could be sitting up there in Hayden Valley in a warm cabin, not learning a goddamn thing, and instead, he comes out and tests himself. I have a deep respect for this kid now, and it just about kills me to admit that. He's got more guts, more daring, and probably more stamina than anybody I know—even though I hear he's a little guy."

"He's not little, just short, but very heavily built," she smiled. "He's not muscle-bound like a weight lifter, he's thick. He'll tend towards fat when he's older. He's certainly got stamina, though."

"I'll say," the ranger agreed.

"But that's not what I'm asking. As far as we know, this whole thing has been spontaneous. What's the thing about him that drives surveillance wild?"

"He's unpredictable."

"Well, I've just decided he's not. He left Lake Lodge. What opportunity presented itself? The ice. That's Phase One. Having walked the ice, learning and playing to his heart's content, what opportunity presented itself?"

"Avalanche."

"Phase Two. And having climbed it? Phase Three, sliding down the west slope. He's not random, he just doesn't have any plans. We keep trying to predict the future, and he reacts to the present. Sliding down the mountain—pure recklessness according to all you guys—but then Ranger Downes follows him down the mountain! A couple days ago, Jimmy swore to me he would never climb that mountain in the winter—even if you paid him in gold, he claimed—but look what he just did today. Why is that? You rangers respect Gene Siegfried, but why?"

"He's living the greatest adventure," the ranger said, "He's got an opportunity none of us will ever have in our lifetimes, and he's doing it without hesitation."

"And who's he doing this for?" she asked. "Half of the 'adventures' he's indulged in, he doesn't bother reporting to Project Snow. He thinks he has secrets from us. Is he doing this for his own enjoyment, or for us and our precious experiment?"

Britt stared at the map, tracing with a silver-ringed forefinger the purple line of Siegfried's route and the dark wanderings of Downes and the other men. "I think he's doing it as a progression." When the ranger looked up, she added, "Each adventure is a step further down into savagery. He doesn't feel a challenge or sense a reward. Siegfried's adventures are stages along a long route to survival."

"So?"

"So … Gene Siegfried will not rejoin the East Entrance Road anywhere short of Fishing Bridge." Having decided that, she pushed away from the map and went back to bed.

The next morning, eighteen stiff, cold men stumbled out of their tents and made breakfast. Jimmy Downes expected that Siegfried would get a relatively late start—he was a notoriously late sleeper—and would emerge from the forest sometime after ten o'clock near Sylvan Lake, then proceed along the road to Fishing Bridge on the way back to Hayden Valley. Accordingly, Downes restrained his grumpy men until eleven o'clock and then sent four of the best skiers to pick up Gene's trail on the snow-covered road. Until Siegfried passed Lake Butte, they didn't dare start their snowmobiles, lest he hear the machines.

To his surprise, however, the four scouts ran across no fresh tracks by the time they reached Cub Creek. With the weather worsening by the hour, a decision had to be made, so Downes picked four men to return to Gene's last known position on Mount Avalanche to pick up his trail. Lake gave a poor weather report: light snow, windy conditions, decreasing visibility, and increasing cold, but the Lake Ranger also suggested Siegfried would not return to the roadway at all.

"If Dr. Chamberlain is right about Siegfried reacting to possibilities as they present themselves," he radioed," *he might be working his way northwest to Pelican Creek Valley. He's familiar with the valley, y'know."*

"You believe a *dude*, and a *woman* to boot?" a ranger laughed derisively from nearby. Downes shrugged. In the summer, such a route was difficult, if not impossible. There was rugged terrain between Mount Avalanche and Turbid Lake, and a dense, tangled forest blocked the way from the East Entrance road to Mount Chittenden and the valley. Only one route, the Jones Pass Trail, crossed this vast area, but buried under twelve feet of snow, it would be impossible to find. Winter's only advantage was that the forest's tangled blowdowns were now smoothed over with drifts, but Downes believed it was still a trackless wasteland.

For that reason, the ranger was inclined to reject the suggestion outright, but an hour later, the Avalanche team reported a trail going northwest toward the source of Clear Creek. Siegfried was, indeed, headed for Pelican Creek Valley.

Quickly ordering new dispositions, Downes decided fewer dangers would threaten a lone man in a sterile winter forest, so he decreed direct observation was to be abandoned. He ordered the four men dug in on Cub Creek to wait an hour before proceeding up that stream to cross Gene's trail; they were to follow him into Pelican Creek Valley. He then ordered the men on the mountain to help move the snowmobiles as soon as Siegfried was safely out of hearing. At the same time, he dispatched two men to Turbid Lake and took the rest with him to Squaw Lake.

Now, with four men tailing him and two teams ahead, Gene was sure to be seen, but it was slow, careful surveillance work. Downes himself waited at Squaw Lake, while the remaining men, including the bruised scout and Capland, were released and sent back to Lake Ranger Station for a rest. Late that afternoon, Gene emerged from the forest exactly as expected and moved into the northern reaches of Pelican Creek Valley to camp.

Next morning, under total surveillance, for Downes had ordered all of his tired men back into the field, Siegfried moved the length of Pelican Creek Valley, checked on buffalo sign—a small herd wintered there—then visited old haunts in the relatively snow-free Sulphur Hills. Continuing through without hunting, he then turned south toward Fishing Bridge.

After learning of his intention to cross the river at Fishing Bridge, Britt Chamberlain and the Lake Ranger threw on their winter gear and skied to the outlet of the lake, where they waited behind a snowdrift high above the west end of the bridge. Before long, Gene appeared out of the blowing snow. Although they never saw him clearly and certainly couldn't see his face or other details, Britt was left with an intuitive impression of strength and confidence, and she felt the oddest desire to rush downslope to hug him. How strange, she thought, that she would react that way to one of her subjects. She pulled out a notebook and recorded her impressions. When she looked up, he had disappeared into the blowing snow.

In contrast with the power and buoyance of the savage, however, was the pathetic condition of the surveillance team, which drifted back to the ranger station in disarray, each man covered with ice, bone-tired, and very hungry. Jimmy Downes, Reese, and the Indians were in the best shape, for they had spent the winter rotating surveillance shifts, but the others were hastily borrowed volunteers who were worn out now. The ranger station stank with sweat and coffee, nylon and wet wool. While a violent blizzard raged outside, the exhausted men slept wherever they could: on the floor, in chairs and desks, and even on the information counter in the reception area. Britt spent the night staring out the window.

The eternal winter dream was beginning again; the cold settled even more deeply over the park that night. The recorded low was minus twenty-eight degrees Fahrenheit. Starlight and moonlight peeked through forbidding, gray clouds scudding overhead, lighting the earth with temporary flashes of blue radiance.

Somewhere to the north, Britt knew Gene Siegfried was picking his way home to Hayden Valley through the storm. Visibility was good enough to distinguish distant hillsides, yet paradoxically, when she looked out the window, it was hard to see trees a few feet away. There was a surrealistic beauty to this night, hushed by the sad music of wind soughing through the piney combs over the ranger station. Undoubtedly thankful he was almost home in Hayden Valley, Gene slogged onward, just a dim, silent shadow in a lonely winter dream.

Towards morning, Reese joined her at the window. "You know we can't do this again," he said.

"I know," she replied, pulling a wool blanket around her shoulders. "I didn't have any idea it was going to be like this. In West Yellowstone, it's so cold it's reported on the national news every week, but I didn't understand it was worse on the Central Plateau. No," she said, "we can't ever do this again. Without knowing what's in his head, we stumble around endangering ourselves looking for tracks and guessing at his next move. Twenty people, snowmobiles, radios, resupply, hot coffee and chicken soup, and skis versus his snowshoes, and the closest we got to him in a week was a hundred yards. It scares me to death."

"Why's that?" he asked.

"Because every time he sets out from now on, we'll have fewer men, worse weather, more difficult conditions, and longer distances. He doesn't even know we're trying to monitor or protect him, and each time, we're less effective. We're failing him, y'know...."

CHAPTER 25

✻ ✻ ✻

The Winter March

ONE BRIGHT BUT cheerless day, a nagging dread deep in his bones drove Gene Siegfried outside the cabin, and he stood in the sunshine, unable to do anything but sigh and complain. He should pry firewood loose from the woodpile to thaw, he thought, but he couldn't bother. There was plenty of time for chores. Instead, plagued by ominous feelings of doom he couldn't explain, he soaked up the meager warmth of morning. Out in the valley, ravens circled around an old carcass, but otherwise the area was quiet ... perhaps too quiet, he thought. A feeling of fate clawed at him; something was very wrong, though he couldn't imagine what was.

The sunlight shot across the snow in a glare that could drive a man blind in hours. The drifts were damp on the surface and trees shook slushy snowballs from their branches. Out in the valley, the few running streams were muddier than usual, but it was not this good weather that forced him out into the sunshine. No, he decided, there was something else that made him so uneasy, but try as he might, he couldn't imagine its source.

In a black mood, he put on his snow mask and slung an elk robe over his back. Packing more rations than seemed necessary, he tied his snow-shoes on and set off on a hike into the valley. Before long, he knew his uneasiness wasn't just his man-sense. Every raven was in the air, and down by the river the winter geese were honking in alarm; to the northwest, a nervous band of buffalo was moving aimlessly from feed to water.

There was a storm coming—as he tramped across the clingy snow, he could feel its heaviness in the air—but it was still at least twelve hours away. When he looked up, the sky, though gray with clouds, had a slight greenish cast to it. What could that mean? What could have caused it?

For want of anything to do and certainly not intending to return to the cabin so soon, he snowshoed north along the river toward the Grand Canyon of the Yellowstone, an excursion he had been making often in the last few weeks. On the far side of Otter Creek, he encountered two fresh sets of ski tracks that preceded him across Chittenden Bridge. Here, he liked to pause to watch the river pick up speed as it neared the falls, and so he did today. There was as yet no sound, but a short distance away, he knew the mighty river skidded through two sharp curves to the brink of the Upper Falls, a one hundred-nine-foot drop.

Farther on, near where a spidery staircase named Uncle Tom's Trail led down to a viewing platform deep in the Canyon close to the base of the Lower Falls, Gene lost the trail of the two unknown skiers in a maze of tracks from snow coaches and winter dudes. Obviously in no mood to meet tourists, he hurried past the trampled parking lot to another lot farther on, from whence he could view the falls from Artist Point—and it was the closest Gene Siegfried ever came to accidentally stumbling upon the surveillance team shadowing him!

The two men on duty that morning had also been feeling antsy, and when they saw him come into the valley and start north, they knew exactly where he was headed, for he had made the trip fairly often. Barely beating him across the bridge, the men had frantically hidden themselves under a white bed sheet in a grove of pines not far from the brink of the falls. Siegfried, who had been following their tracks, came within thirty feet of them. They took two pictures. Lost in thought, Gene strode past their hiding place and headed toward Artist Point.

"Canyon?" one of the scouts radioed as soon as their subject was out of earshot.

"*Go ahead,*" Jimmy Downes answered.

"That was close."

"*He didn't spot you?*"

"Nope."

"*Good. Is he headed for the same place?*"

"Looks that way."

"*Then stay put. He's gone down there before and just sits for hours. No need to take a chance he'll spot you. If any dudes come along, keep them from visiting anywhere on that side of the canyon. Send them here, on the north rim. Don't let anyone take pictures.*"

"Roger," the scout answered, grinning at his partner, for guard duty was a lot easier than surveillance.

A few hundred yards away, Artist Point, an eroded parapet on the canyon's eastern wall, offered a panorama second only to the Snake River Overlook in the Tetons for changeability and freshness. Perched eight hundred feet above the river, the spot was bright and colorful in summer, but it was a sullen, dangerous aerie in the winter. Dirty snow streaked the mustard walls of the windy canyon, and ice clattered in the trees huddled on its frozen rim. Gene often sat here on one of the low stone benches, staring out at the canyon, thinking.

It was a fitting place for a savage's dark moods. Opposite him, the Lower Falls, twice the height of Niagara, droned in the distance, the noise sometimes a roar, sometimes a whisper, depending on how the wind carried the sound. Gene knew of another falls in the backcountry even higher, but nothing beat the Lower Falls in beauty. He had watched a huge ice beard, which choked the lower half of the mighty falls, grow steadily all winter, its deeply scored flanks alternately pigeon blue or porcelain. As he sat there looking around, he noticed a recent heavy snowfall had caked the upper margins of the cindrous rock face framing the falls, and thick snow banks overhung most of the canyon walls.

As was his custom, Gene shouted, "Hello!" into the canyon.

"*Helloelloellolololololo!*" the canyon answered, the cheery echo quite clear.

"Saa-vage!" he bellowed.

"*Savage avage ... vageageage,*" the echo rang back.

On a whim, he put his hands on the low wall framing the parapet and roared as loud as he could, "Siegfried!"

Strangely, there was no echo this time, but Gene wasn't surprised. Instead, he shook his head in disgust and listened for a while to the drone of the waterfall. His black mood deepened; he took a seat on one of the benches facing the falls. He sat there all morning, wrapped in a warm elk robe, staring vacantly at the canyon. The only sound to disturb him was the frigid wind gusting up out of the depths of the ochre canyon until, quite suddenly, there was a trickling of rock on the far side of the abyss, a mile distant. Gene jumped up to see the rockslide better, but as he put his reddened hands upon the retaining wall and leaned out to watch a tawny plume of dust and snow arrowing straight down into the gorge—all the while tinkling like broken dishes—a low howl rose out of the canyon to the north of him, a noise so loud it obliterated the roar of the falls. The second he glanced to the right, however, the sound came from his left, a bass rumble so vast it had actually been reflected off the face of Mount Washburn, six miles to the north! It moved through the wall in front of him and then ... CRACK ... it was gone.

It was an earth tremor, Gene realized in surprise, lifting his hands to better feel the tingling of his fingers. While he stood there, dozens of minor earth slides and avalanches cascaded into the canyon as the great earth masses, having twitched the geologic spine on a nearby fault, adjusted to a new order. Long after the tinkling of the other rock falls died away, a persistent, liquid drift of rock-studded ice and dirt to his left crept down the eastern wall of the canyon towards the fragile steel stairs of Uncle Tom's Trail. As he watched in horror, the slide twisted the steel girders and engulfed the platform, and one of his favorite places in Yellowstone was gone forever.

Not thirty seconds later, just as he was raising his eyes from the wreck of the trail, a black, saw-toothed crack broke across the right edge of the fall's icy cover, and the entire icy beard, sixteen stories high, leaned backward and collapsed into the base of the waterfall. Enormous chunks of ice plugged the foot of the falls, and cold water spewed into the air as a thick ice mist. In seconds, a rapidly spreading fog of clinging ice enveloped the entire scene. The roar was deafening. Pieces of ice the size of refrigerators were blown up out of the falls to crash like artillery shells into the canyon walls, starting more earth slides, and then, like the dust of some massive explosion, the mist spread down into the canyon and overflowed its walls. It was a perfect whiteout, both the snow of the ground and the mist in the air illuminated by the bright sunshine.

Time and space disappeared. Gene felt like he was floating as he frantically buckled on his snowshoes. The ice was so cold, it burned. He knew any exposed flesh was in danger of frostbite, and he hurried to protect himself. Blinded and confused, he had difficulty wrapping his furry robe around himself for protection, for the frozen mist quickly caked everything. There was no way to tell which way was up to safety, or which way straight down to death in the canyon, but somehow, he managed to keep a sense of direction. Ten minutes later, he struggled out of the pogonip and into the sunshine again. Badly iced and shaken by the experience, he decided to head for home, determined to stay put for a few days.

The surveillance men, who had been closer to the blast of the ice mist, lost each other in the whiteout. One sprained his knee falling over a blowdown and then broke his arm when he crashed into a tree; the other scout was frostbitten on his face and hands.

Unfortunately, the loss of these two good scouts would now lead, inevitably, to sloppiness and neglect by the other scouts. Already strained by the cumulative effects of boredom, overwork, cabin fever, and a recent simmering disagreement between Ranger Downes and his scouts, surveillance would grow worse and worse in the weeks after the earth tremor. Without fresh scouts to relieve the others, the inevitable, final breakdown of the team would cause surveillance of the Hayden Valley Test Subject (HVTS) to cease in the tenth month of the experiment.

The tremor didn't, however, relieve the uneasiness Gene felt. Only a few days afterwards, he spotted a winter-angry grizzly that had been shaken awake from its slumber. As the dangerous bear limped across the little meadow, its hair hanging in tatters along its gaunt ribs, there was a terrible desperation in its face as it stood on its hind legs at the edge of the trees and sniffed the air for scent of food. Not wanting any confrontation, which he knew the bear would win, Gene withdrew into the cabin and barricaded the door with firewood. As an added precaution, he unslung all his javelins from their scabbard and laid them nearby. Even so, as day passed into night and the wind rose to a shriek outside, he waited, expecting something to happen.

Was he being foolish? He began to wonder if this was just paranoia brought on by his snowy isolation. A winter bear was a dying bear. He knew it had lost the constipated plug in its bowels that slowed its metabolism for winter, and while asleep in its den it had digested too many precious bodily nutriments. Would it have the strength to attack him now, let alone the determination to plan such an attack? In his logical mind, he knew it would not, but an uneasy, nagging feeling gnawed at him. He had learned not to ignore his intuition. It was a powerful weapon in the wilderness. It had saved his life on more occasions than he cared to recall, but it didn't provide him with answers this time. There was something very wrong, but in the end, he threw himself down on his bed, wrapped in an elk robe. In the morning, the bear was gone, and even its tracks were buried under a light snowfall. There was nothing to indicate it had ever been there. In his heart, Gene knew he would never see it again, but the uneasiness he felt would not go away.

Two days later, he was late getting home from an unsuccessful hunt across the river. Night had fallen. The wind was picking up so much he had a hard time making his way back to the cabin in the meadow. Having snowshoed all day in the valley, he felt exhausted, but a small band of buffalo plowing through the drifts ahead of him blocked the easy way home. Circling far to the north to come around the buffalo, he had a particularly clumsy crossing of Trout Creek that left frozen slush all over his snowshoes. A short time later, a pack of coyotes dogged his trail for a while, and then a buffalo bull in a drift to his right ended up being just a savaged carcass.

The night was playing tricks with his vision, and he grew cautious and a bit fearful. Shadows danced in the trees, snow ghosts sprang up in the wind, beckoning him with their frosty fingers to come and party in the wind. Soon, the squeaking of his own footsteps seemed to echo in his mind. As he entered the little meadow, glad to be almost home—and safe—the hair on his neck rose up with a will of its own.

There really was, this time, something wrong....

Jinking to his left, he took cover behind a fallen pine at the edge of the forest. Quietly he pulled one javelin, then two from his scabbard; snapping the leather harness of a spear thrower out of his sleeve, he engaged one of the javelins and held it ready. From his vantage in the trees, he couldn't put his finger on what was wrong with this familiar scene, but then the moon played peek-a-boo between the clouds, and the picture changed. There was something different with the snow to the right of the cabin ... something had been digging there.

The bear, he thought. In the dead of winter, he on snowshoes and in the open, and the bear under cover of the verandah, picking its time! It was the exact reverse of his greatest fear. The bear had the cabin, and he would be alone in the snow.

"No, no, no," he muttered under his breath, yet there was this about his courage: the inevitability of the situation lent itself to a quiet determination, perhaps even a kind of fatalism. He pulled the remaining javelins from their scabbard, gripping them in his left hand like a sheaf of steel.

Thinking he might miss the bear with his first thrown javelin, he wanted the remaining spears to feel for its eyes as it bowled him over. Hopefully, if the damage weren't too great, there would be time to rise one last time with his axe.

Gene couldn't decide what to do with his snowshoes. He knew they would keep him mobile up to the first rush of the bear, but after that, they would be an entanglement. After worrying about it for several minutes, he decided to shed them and immediately sank thigh-deep into the snow. This might be an advantage, he thought grimly, for now he would be a lower target, yet the snow clung to him, and it was hard work coming around to the right to quarter the cabin's entrance.

The bear would have to turn to its left as it cleared the abatis out front. There might be time for two or three thrown javelins. Cautious now, Siegfried edged closer to a pine at the edge of the clearing before beginning the deadly trek across open snow. There was not a sound anywhere, no hint of what was to come. Wind swept across the meadow, and suddenly a dark shadow leaned towards him, flapped its noisy raven's wings and flew away into a taller tree. As it cawed, Gene nearly died of heart failure; he sank down in the snow and cursed the raven, but it ignored him and swooped to its customary perch in the moose antlers over the verandah.

Surely the bird wouldn't act this way if there were a grizzly nearby, Gene thought. He retrieved his snowshoes and walked boldly toward the cabin. He needed a fire and some meat to cheer him up, but as he reached the woodpile, his hackles rose straight up again, and an overwhelming feeling of doom seized him. Hurling himself to the right, he whirled around with his javelins ready. In the darkness between the pantry and the kindling box, the cabin door hung loosely from its hinges. He remembered barring it shut that morning when he had left.

The narrow walkway under the verandah between piles of firewood limited his attack, but he figured there was a space beside the kindling box where he could wedge his back. Getting there, just ten feet away, was the problem, for he couldn't see anything inside the cabin and wouldn't know when to expect the bear's rush. It was safer to crawl on his belly, so, covering his face with the bundle of javelins and trailing his ax behind him in his right hand, he readied himself for only one blow—a blow he hoped would split the bear's skull in half, killing it in its tracks.

"Mother of Jesus," he croaked, crawling slowly toward the dark doorway. Jamming the spears into the cabin, he tensed himself for an attack, but nothing happened. A lifetime seemed to pass as he waited for his death, and then he howled into the cabin in frustration. Jumping bravely inside to stab the empty darkness, moments later, he came flying out backwards, terrified. He threw open the lid of the kindling box and fumbled for his fire striker, but it wasn't there. He stabbed at the black doorway again and again, then kicked the door off his pantry and felt inside for his spare fire striker and a stone. They weren't there either, nor was the shelf he kept them on, nor some of his meat. The realization was slow coming to him.

A stone! He had to have a stone, but where? He remembered a piece of stone picked up along the river, two months before. He had put it on one of the logs of the woodpile—was it still there? Scrambling up the frozen wood, he shed his mittens and felt in the snow with his bare hands until he found it. Seconds later, piling some punk in front of the door, he struck sparks off his ax with the stone, then added kindling. These first few flames he carried by hand into the cabin and placed on the cold ashes of the fire pit. Before long, the rising light revealed all.

The intricately carved support beam bracing his roof had been chainsawed off at the floor and was gone. So were most of the sculptures on the west wall, and only a few pathetic half-beams held up the ceiling. The bed had been stripped and chain sawed for its carved legs, and all of his tools were gone, his precious tools! Also missing were his spare javelins, camp ax, knife, all his carefully tanned skins and the aluminum pot.

"My God, who could have wanted that?" he screamed out loud, rushing about the cabin touching things.

There was little of use still in the cabin. It seemed everything he had created during the long winter was gone. Who could do this to him? Screaming in rage, he went about collecting the things left, and in a way, he felt offended some of his minor works hadn't been taken. What was wrong with the carved handle of this maul? Wasn't it good enough for the thief? What about this incised stone? Wasn't it nifty enough to attract thieving eyes? Finally, a feeling of defilement flooded over him. Someone had soiled his things with dirty hands! The revulsion was the hardest to control. Shaking like a leaf, he sat on the edge of his fire pit and wept bitterly, and it was some time before he could wipe his face and think.

Nearly beside himself, he swore to get the thief if it were the last thing he ever did. Sitting on the floor beside the fire pit, he forced himself to analyze what he had learned. The thief had a chainsaw, there was sawdust all over the cabin floor. Gene had left about nine o'clock and was far away before the thief dared begin, lest Gene recognize the unmistakable chatter of the saw. It was cold outside, and since sound carried well in the cold, it must have been at least two hours before the man started. Since Gene had headed towards the canyon, the thief couldn't have gone the easy way north with his booty, he must have gone south to West Thumb, then either further south to Jackson Hole, or west to Old Faithful, or West Yellowstone.

With the aid of a firebrand, Gene continued his investigation outside. To his surprise, he found the tracks of two men—a large one and a small one—and two snowmobiles driven right up to the cabin. Both snowmobiles had sleds attached. Damn them both straight to hell! he thought. The tracks were still stark in the snow, even in the rising wind, so the men had left about two hours ago. How fast could they go? Not fast enough, he thought, if they had gone west. Nightfall caught them before they could reach Old Faithful, and someone was bound to question a chainsaw and carved logs on the machines. No, he decided, they had probably gone south and were camped somewhere by Lewis Lake at this very minute.

By now, the moon was peeking out of moving cloudbanks. A weather change was coming, and there would be wind and cold that night. The men, Gene decided, were not dudes. They knew how dangerous the south entrance country could get in the winter, so they wouldn't try it at night. After camping, they would have a hard day of it tomorrow in freshly drifted snow. There was a chance to catch them.

Having decided on a course of action, Gene jumped up, fed the fire and prepared his last buffalo roast to grill. While the meat thawed, he carefully stripped himself naked in order to dry the sweat stains in his clothes, and then, after a hearty meal of burnt, cooked, rare, raw, and still frozen meat, sliced from a roast too hastily cooked, he quickly packed a bag with jerky and tea. Feeling up in the rafters, he found a two pint bottle of whiskey Mack had given him. He drained half the bottle, and then pocketed the rest for later, when he'd really need it. Dressed again, he knew he was preparing for something that had never been done before, a dangerous night crossing of Hayden Valley and Mary Mountain during a dreaded mountain blizzard in order to strike for Nez Perce crossing by morning.

Snow was just beginning to filter in around the door, and the crackling fire was quickly losing heat. It would be easier to go north to Canyon and the winter keeper there, or south to the ranger station, but by the time he got there, roused the people, and contacted West Yellowstone, Gene knew it would be morning, and he would have to travel many more miles to meet a posse of rangers hurrying south. No, he told himself, West Yellowstone was his best alternative, but it would be difficult getting there.

Buckling up carefully, he snuffed the fire and opened the door. It was a snowy nightmare outside. It was, in fact, the coldest night of the winter. Lake Yellowstone Station, twenty miles south, recorded a low that night of forty-six degrees below zero, with lots of blowing snow. A single misstep would mean death, not to mention the hazards of a lost trail or the tricky, steep descent on the Nez Perce side of Mary Mountain. There were also the animals: buffalo driven on the wind, and perhaps that winter bear again. By now, the moon was gone; visibility was only a hundred feet, but as he crossed the meadow, he knew what worried him most was the stiffness of legs that had snowshoed all day and now faced this, the hardest test of his life.

He turned it into a mental game, moving even when the pain was intense. Move because you're alive, he told himself. Stroke, pull! He dug with his snow poles and stomped on, until finally he had it down to a mindless, mile-eating rhythm. His frozen breath iced his snow mask, icicles hung in his beard, and cold sweat ran down his pits, back, and belly, but he pushed on, vowing to catch the thieves tomorrow and make them pay.

CHAPTER 26

✳ ✳ ✳

West Yellowstone

THE AFTERNOON OF March 15, 1974, Britt Chamberlain was enjoying a luxurious bubble bath in the hotel's biggest tub when news swept through the winter-bound hamlet of West Yellowstone. "Siegfried's coming in," her landlady said through the door. "He's on the Madison Road, coming like a bear. It's finally over."

People were shouting all up and down the hall of the little hotel. As she hurried back to her room to dry her hair, she heard a dozen snowmobilers had seen him that morning, but he wouldn't talk to any of them. Hurrying to get dressed, she zipped herself into her snowsuit and ran out into the street for information. A snow coach rumbled past like a tank, stirring up feathery snow in its wake as it headed for the West Gate and the Madison Road. Three winter employees and a man from West Yellowstone were going to bring him in, someone said, but the men were gone just an hour before returning empty-handed.

"He insists on walking in," one of the men told her. "He should be here in two hours if he keeps that pace up." Looking her in the eye, he stammered, "H-he..." and he stopped, unable to describe what he had seen.

"I know," she said, not wanting a stranger to tell her the long experiment was over. She wanted to see it herself. Ten months, she thought bitterly. So close! If only he had lasted two more months.... Somehow, she was sad he hadn't finished the year, but she banished the thought and consoled herself with the fact that at the beginning of Project Snow none of the scientists thought he'd last even a week.

Two hours later, she stood with much of the winter population of West Yellowstone at the Park's West Entrance. A few people leaned against the iced tollbooths of the gate; others stood in front of the log uprights of the entrance itself or gathered in groups to talk. Released from school for the occasion, children were throwing snowballs and running around, and everyone, young and old alike, kept an eye on the road. No one had gone down the road in an hour, for everyone who had, returned in awe.

Britt Chamberlain and Doctor Garner were waiting with the towns-people, but Capland was off preparing a borrowed woodshed for a debrief-ing. A local doctor and nurse had volunteered to help with the exam, and rangers and the county sheriff were prepared for security and crowd con-trol. Several reporters, including two from Idaho were sitting nearby, but Britt made sure they were told to wait their turn. The local cub reporter cursed the cold from his perch astride a tollbooth. There was no sun, just a general grayness relieved by the white of the snow in the surrounding trees. The road to Yellowstone Park was hazy in the frozen mist.

"There!" someone said, pointing.

In the distance, a shadow in the gray snowmist was moving rhythmi-cally. Britt strained to see, and sure enough, just at the bend of the road exactly a mile east of where they were standing, something was moving toward them. As the apparition drew nearer, a man became more distinct. He was punching along at an efficient, practiced pace, a wonderful ex-ample of snowshoeing at its best, and in a little under twenty minutes, he stood before the West Entrance. No one spoke.

Nothing could have prepared Britt for this. He was beyond belief, and he chilled her to the bones. He looked like nothing less than the Old Man of the Mountains. With an elk robe thrown around his shoulders, he was nearly as wide as he was tall, a square brown-and-black figure of snow doom. Six steel javelins shone wickedly over his shoulder in their scab-bard, and the great axe hung loosely from his belt, but it was the face that frightened them the most. Children moved closer to their mothers, none of the reporters took a picture, and no one moved.

When he removed the fanged snow mask, Siegfried's wild, curly beard was frosted completely white, icicles hung from his mustache, and frost gleamed thickly from the ragged ends of his hair where it had blown loose from his fur hat. His ghastly facial scar throbbed purplishly in the light, and his eyes shone a venomous green, a startling color on that gray afternoon.

"Gene!" Britt called, her heart in her mouth, and the magic spell was broken. The crowd surged around their mountain hero to escort him into their little town.

It was an hour before she could squeeze into a cramped woodshed to see him. The shed had been chosen for its privacy, but of prime importance was its chilly interior, for the scientists did not want Siegfried overheated after such a long exposure to the bitter cold. It couldn't have been more than forty degrees inside the drafty shed, and frost streaked the damp, wooden walls. The owner, a wizened, old Montanan in jeans and a checked wool shirt, stood patiently beside a red-hot stove, stoking it with thin sticks of pine.

Britt's entrance was hardly noticed, and she unzipped her ski jacket and took off her hat, letting her long, blonde hair cascade over her shoulders. There was a clutter of greasy engine parts on the floor, a dusty, ancient Ford pickup in the corner, and stacks of firewood lining one of the walls. From a rafter, a rusted meat hook hung over the stained floor, the sure sign of a good hunting season last fall, and when Britt came around the stove and saw Siegfried standing naked in a cluster of doctors and rangers, the whole scene reminded her not so much of a physical examination as a crowd of veterinarians prodding a tired plow horse.

He was watching her, his eyes turned wordlessly toward her, and she was chilled by their expression. Looking away, she moved to a nearby tool bench to put her hat and coat next to a steaming urine sample and cuttings of hair and fingernails. Again she was drawn to those quiet, dreadful eyes of his. Although Gene Siegfried was shorter than anyone else in the room, including the old man by the stove, he was more solidly built than anyone she had ever seen. His burly chest rippled with corded muscles, his neck was thick, his arms powerful, and his short legs were like tree trunks. He had a bit of a pot belly too, she noticed, but it was not the loose gut of luxury, just the winter fat of a powerful bear, and in that cool room, not a single goose bump showed on his hairy, white skin.

He was stronger looking than she had ever seen him, but the changes were deeper than that. Now, his long, greasy hair was streaked with white, and gray was apparent in his beard and mustache. The strain of winter had taken a desperate toll. His wide, beautiful eyes were gone forever, replaced by emerald slits furrowed with powerful snow wrinkles. His jaw was set, and he had a knowing look in his eyes. His gaze probed her soul.

"Okay," Dr. Capland said at last, taking several electrodes off Gene's chest. "You can get dressed again."

Turning away from the savage, Capland put his arm around her shoulder and whispered, "He's going back. Somebody stole his tools and all his bedding. He wants us to replace these items and provide him with some kind of fire striker because he can't make one for himself now. The rangers say it's impossible to catch the thieves. Dr. Garner's got a couple of people going door-to-door asking for elk hides, and I believe they have a welder making a fire striker."

"Surely Dr. Garner won't let him go back!" Britt exclaimed. Couldn't they see what this experiment was doing to Gene? she wondered. Was she the only one with any sense, or was she the only one who didn't understand what was happening?

"I'm afraid the decision's been made," Capland said, glancing over his shoulder, "and we couldn't keep him here if we tried. Besides, he's doing well. He's healthy and strong. Look at him! He's got a lot of information for us." He searched her eyes, but there was no give in her resolve. "It's not long now until spring," he said lamely.

"You're crazy!" she answered defiantly. "This has got hold of us and won't let go. Don't you see that? How many times have you and I despaired over that man out there in the cold? Twenty-four hours a day! Winter like neither you nor I have ever experienced. What more can we gain from this? I'm speaking as a scientist now, not a woman. What more can we gain? We don't know, and that's why you're all willing to let him go back out and risk his life. Look how he's changed since last November. Look at his face. Do we have the right to do this to someone? Everyone in the street calls him 'The Savage.' They're going to <u>cheer </u>when we tell them he's going back. Is that fair? Can we expect empirical data at the end of this experiment that could possibly justify this? I hate what we're doing here. I HATE IT!" she hissed angrily.

The knot of men around Siegfried turned at her sudden exclamation. "I hate the cold, too," Gene said, misunderstanding her. Having slipped on his broken Levis and the rags of his thermal top, he was just then working on patiently darned socks. The wrecks that were once proud hiking boots were next, and then moose-hide snow boots, and all the while the researchers stood by, silently watching him.

Next, he pulled on tight leather snow pants, and smooth, white gaiters that covered his legs like a cowboy's chaps. There was an incredible style to these leather clothes, Britt noticed, for an artistic balance had dictated the workmanship. Although the style would be imitated everywhere from the gays of San Francisco to the fashion boutiques of Europe, the originals were the product of a winter spent alone, the leather artistically tailored for this one man and his unique challenge.

As he dressed, Gene began to talk of weather and snow, the characteristics of animals, the nature of fire, his problems with dampness, and the smell of sulfur in the cabin, all things the scientists wanted to know. Later, he inquired about his family in Colorado, baited Capland a bit, and snapped at the rangers, but he said nothing to Britt, and she was forced to wait by the old man and the red-hot stove.

People drifted in and out of the cramped shed—local politicians, rangers, and townspeople—and he had salt for all of them, for he was mountain folk too. Britt slowly realized Gene Siegfried had really become a symbol for these people's trials and wrinkled strength; he was their hero in a rugged mountain home. She watched it all but saw only the changes. This was no longer the happy-go-lucky college kid she had once known. Gene was a living legend now, confident in the role he had earned: a mountain man with a clear-air soul.

Many were the nights she had lain awake listening to the winds raging outside, worried sick over this savage of theirs, but now she understood she worried because no one else did. She could see the concern on his face, and she felt certain only she, of all the scientists and rangers gathered there, knew how he dreaded going back, though there was still this remarkable determination, that love of wilderness, and the challenge of being savage she had never understood.

In the evening, a housewife came in with a tray of food from the women in her church. Gene thanked her, checked with Dr. Garner to be sure it didn't break the rules of the experiment, and then invited those standing around to eat with him. Politely declining, most soon left for their own suppers, except the old man, the woman who brought the food, and Britt.

"You'll join me, won't you, Dr. Chamberlain?" he asked.

"Yes, I'd love to," she answered happily. Strangely, she hadn't wanted to leave as long as he was in town, and she was thrilled he wanted her to stay.

Glancing at the old man, who merely shook his head, Siegfried placed the big tray on a chopping block and unwrapped the tablecloth that covered it. Britt found a folding chair and a stool and placed them nearby.

"Have you seen Roxy lately?" Gene asked as he divided a piece of roast beef into three portions.

"Yes. As a matter of fact, I saw her last week." Anxious to begin her interview, Britt laughed, "She and I got drunk in the Mangy Moose down in Jackson." Helping herself to creamed corn, she decided to ask him a personal question. "What about you two? Roxy and Mack, that's an easy relationship to figure—they're just friends, aren't they? But what about you two?"

Wiping his hands on his pants, Gene smiled, "First of all, you've got Mack's and Roxy's relationship all wrong. Mack's always mooning over some girl, and he doesn't say much, but Roxy thinks the world of him, and sometimes when the three of us are together, those two will start talking, and it'll be an hour before I can get a word in."

"But they're not lovers?"

"No, just friends."

"What about you and Roxy?" Britt asked.

"Friends, but in a different way. Roxy and I could go camping, share a whole summer together or all winter cooped up in a keeper's cabin. We're friends."

"But there's nothing sexual between you?" she prodded teasingly, slightly relieved at the innocent look on his face. She noticed how clumsy with a knife and fork he was. He was out of practice, she decided, smiling to herself.

"No. We could go to a dance in Lake Lodge, Old Faithful for a movie, Roosevelt for a luau, or Bridge Bay with the boat-dockers for a beer bust, maybe even Family-Home-Evening with the Mormons at a bonfire on Yellowstone Lake, but we're not each other's type and I'm not certain either of us would want to be." He thought about it a moment, then confided, "The first year she worked here, Roxy picked up a boyfriend, and they were in love. They went out most evenings —but she ate her meals with Mack and me. In August that year, Roxy's boyfriend got killed in the Tetons in a climbing accident. I drove down to Jackson to get her, but she didn't talk on the way back. Mack didn't try to talk to her at all and avoided her for a couple days, but then they went down to the shore of the lake one evening and cried together. They shared it—that's the kind of friends they are."

Siegfried listened to the popping of wood in the stove, and then glanced at the old man feeding the fire. "Mack's Irish, you know," Gene abruptly added. "I believe the Irish have a feeling for death. They always know when it's coming and what to do. I appreciate that. Anyway, Mack, Roxy, and I all just good friends."

He finished eating without another word, and at that moment, another woman came in with a pot of coffee and a fruit pie. Britt poured five mugs, two for the women who didn't seem inclined to leave, one for the uncomplaining old man, and one for each of them. "What's going to happen to the three of you when this is over?" she asked.

"This is it for me and Roxy. Roxy's is getting too old for climbing mountains all her life. I think she's about to give it up. It's time for her to get some kind of career going. Of course, she'll never be a flatlander again—she's thinking of Utah, or northern California—she's from California originally y'know."

"Yes, I know."

"Mack's the one we're worried about. Getting a college education is a big deal to him. None of his family's ever done that, but this winter off from school is going to delay him, and he doesn't seem to know what to do with the rest of his life. Roxy and I think he's never going to get Yellowstone out of his system. He may turn into one of the perennial seasonals."

"What do you mean?"

"He'll work tourist seasons here, then hangout at his family's ranch down in Jackson Hole or maybe work the ski area. This wouldn't be unusual. There's a kind of seasonal that works the summers here and the winters in Florida. Some don't work the winters at all; they just draw unemployment. Being seasonal can get in your blood. Some people really like the lifestyle. If Mack doesn't finish college, he could end up being seasonal."

"What about you?" she asked.

"I think that's going to be decided for me, don't you? Those people out there aren't going to leave me alone. I'm going to be in the public eye for a couple of years. Roxy's brother has a friend who's into celebrity management; I'll get him to help, and I think I'll be famous until people forget me. After that, I'll go to school and get an art degree—despite my father's wishes. I'd like to move to Jackson and be a sculptor. I don't want to become what others want, I just want to make beautiful things and be paid what I'm worth."

The women began to gather up the dishes, and Gene thanked them for the meal. The old man by the fire stirred too and said his wife probably had his dinner waiting. "Watch the fire," he grumped. "I may be back."

"I'll take care of it," Gene promised, helping the old man into his coat. "Leave no tracks."

"Eh?" the old man grunted from the door.

"See you later."

"Yeah," the man waved as he went out. Fresh snow flurries blew in the opened door, and the shed chilled perceptively.

"Leave no tracks," Britt repeated softly. "I've heard Roxy say that too. What does it mean?"

"It means a lot of things, I guess," Gene remarked, getting up to stoke the fire. "Picture this: a grassy meadow full of flowers on the way to some scenic wonder. One day, an adventurer walks across the meadow on his way to see the sights. That doesn't hurt. Grass and flowers stepped on, spring up later; ants that have been crushed in the hiker's footprints un-kink their legs and go on with their business. The man has, in effect, left no tracks. In hours, his passage is erased.

"The damage comes when someone repeats his passage, perhaps walking back the same way he went in, or maybe a file of people following a leader. Now, there's damage. Flowers are kicked off their stems, branches are broken off the sagebrush, small stones overturned, and a tendency is started."

"What's that?" she asked.

"A tendency," he explained, "is not a trail, but the grass is a little short-er. Before you know it, there's a real trail where there was none before—not a dug-in-the-earth Park Service trail—just one trampled through the grass. Over the years, the trail is eroded below the ground surface, and it becomes too narrow and deep for human feet, so parallel tracks are cre-ated, especially when it gets mushy in the spring. Somebody lays logs to bridge the mud, and pretty soon, the seepage is diverted. One day, some smart guy takes his motorcycle up it. Flowers get picked for twenty yards on either side, branches are broken off for firewood, and fire pits scar the earth every few yards. Boy scouts go marching down it, then children's groups, and the Park Service is obliged to come in to construct bridging and drainage. Soon, it's marked on maps."

"That's not a pretty picture," Britt said.

"No, it's not," he said sadly, "but it's inevitable. Look at Rocky Mountain National Park or Yosemite in California. What's happened there will happen in Yellowstone, and when it happens here, Alaska is next."

"So when you say 'leave no tracks,' you're making some kind of low-impact environmental statement?"

"Since I said 'tracks,' I dealt with it on a literal level, but I was thinking of several things. Let's say you move into a new city, get an apartment, a phone, and a new job. What'll happen? You'll have paperboys banging on your door asking you to subscribe, people are going to solicit donations or try to get your vote. After you get a credit card, you find the credit card company hustles cameras and mattresses. When you get on their mailing lists, believe me, it's time to move."

"That's all part of city life," Britt smiled.

"City life is when you can't escape being hustled by religious fanatics and whores, but in your own home, you can avoid unsolicited hustling. Hang up the phone and close the door. Don't clutter up your mind with other people's details. You don't have to leave tracks across your soul, because before long, you're going to be raped by four-wheel-drives and people bridging your low places."

"Isn't that what's happened between you and your father?" she asked, remembering what Roxy had told her of Siegfried's own search for identity.

"All my life," Gene said, "my dad has told me what to do. Although he's right sometimes, I've been miserable trying to be an engineer or an accountant. There's a well-beaten trail through my head where he's been marching through! Look at Roxy, too. Her parents never tried to mold her, they only let her know how disappointed they are, and look how aimless she's been. Neither of us has to be this way. We can say no."

"So, 'leave no tracks' is a manifesto."

"It's an alternative."

Wondering how much of Siegfried's resolve had formed during the experiment, Britt was pleased his plans for the future definitely pointed to going his own way, and she knew he would do well. Probably, she thought cynically, he would be the only one to come out of Project Snow with an enhanced reputation.

Dr. Capland, the old man who owned the shed, and two rangers came in out of the cold and interrupted their conversation. "Well, Gene," Capland said as he took off his coat, "This is all we could put together on short notice. It's got me worried that your entire survival depends on a few tanned hides and a bent piece of metal—you sure this is what you want?"

"Yes," Gene answered, rising from his chair and pawing through the bundles. There were five elk hides, a loop of steel for his fire striker, a dime store camp ax that had never been sharpened, a thimble that was too small, a good butcher knife, a two-way radio with extra batteries, and an assortment of large sewing needles.

"Perfect!" he declared, but Britt could see he was as enthusiastic over the supplies as a poor child getting used clothes from Goodwill for Christmas.

"What can you tell us about the two men?" one of the rangers asked. "How close to the cabin did they drive their machines? Did they show any familiarity with the area? How experienced were they?"

For about the twentieth time, Gene repeated his story, and both rangers nodded. "You see?" said the second ranger to the first, "I think this means they'd been in the cabin before. They knew where it was, knew he'd be gone, and how far he'd go. They knew exactly what they wanted and brought a chainsaw to get it. Neat operation. That's why it'll be hard to catch them."

The ranger then asked when Gene had first discovered the theft; he seemed astounded to learn that it was just the night before.

"I left about ten o'clock last night with what you see here," Gene said, indicating his coat, snowshoes, and weapons. "I stopped about six this morning in the Nez Perce country to boil tea in a piece of old hide—hey, that reminds me—can you get me a cooking pot? They even stole my old aluminum pot because I had scratched some of my designs on it."

Capland nodded wearily, but the old man at the fire chimed in, "I've got an enamel pot right here you can have. Just give it back to me in May."

"I will," Gene promised as he added the black pot to the stack. "I had to rest my legs awhile last night. My left leg's real sore after walking all day yesterday and all night. I've cramped up a bit. After a couple hours sleep, I came in."

"How many miles would you say that is?" one of the rangers asked the other.

"At least twenty-five miles, plus what he did yesterday. Fifteen or sixteen hours on the trail, in addition to his rest period—that's damn good time."

"Well … I was mad," Gene said in embarrassment. "When people started offering me rides, I figured if I'd come this far, I might as well finish it on my own." Britt saw a flash of pride in Siegfried's eyes, for it was quite an accomplishment.

The door of the shed banged open again, and Doctor Garner limped in. "Goddamn! Leave this place for a couple hours, and you let the fire go out. Siegfried! Get up out of that chair and let an old man sit down. Go feed the fire." Garner's eyes were friendlier than his voice, and Gene did it without complaint, but the two rangers, who had never met the crotchety old man before, exchanged surprised looks.

"Anything else, Doctor Garner?" Gene said after stoking the fire. He sat down on the cold dirt floor before the old man could answer. "We were just talking about the guys that ripped me off."

"It looks like your hunch about the south entrance is right," Garner said. "Nobody in West Yellowstone saw anyone unusual coming out of the park, but the South Entrance reports two men exited the park about eleven this morning. Of course, Grand Teton National Park and the Teton County sheriff have been alerted, but they haven't found anything yet. A guy at Flagg Ranch says he saw two men loading snowmobiles on a trailer with Wyoming plates. Unfortunately, Red Reese—who's in charge of security, and Jimmy Downes, our liaison to the Park Service—both took the week off. Neither can be contacted, so we're sort of operating in the blind."

"I'd like to get in touch with my friends at Snow Lodge to let them know I'm all right," Siegfried said. "They'll be worried about me after all this publicity—"

"No. We're not revealing the reason for the trip to West Yellowstone at this time," Garner said apologetically. "We have several reasons for this. First, it doesn't make any of us look good. Secondly, we don't want people to know how vulnerable you and your cabin are. Third, if people were to find out you were so desperate, there might be some hue and cry to call off the experiment. Dr. Chamberlain believes we've learned enough, and I'm sure she's been filling your head with nonsense and dangers—"

"Dr. John Garner, you know I have not!" Britt exploded angrily. "You know how—"

"Yes. I know. I was just spouting off," Garner soothed her. "You're extremely professional, and I'm sure you haven't tried to influence Gene, but I know you're concerned—I am too, to be honest. Perhaps I say that too rarely, but I worry too."

"Thank you," Siegfried replied. "But if you're not going to tell anyone the reason I came in, what are you going to tell the reporters?"

"This was your regularly scheduled midwinter physical."

"Of course. It fits, doesn't it?" Gene laughed. "That's why the reporters didn't ask any serious questions today, isn't it? They're waiting for a briefing tomorrow, aren't they?"

"Yes." Garner said, looking embarrassed, but it was hard for Britt to tell what Capland thought of it; he had his back turned, feeding the fire. "We want you to say this visit to West Yellowstone was planned all along. We'll set the record straight in the spring."

"What time is the briefing tomorrow?"

"Ten o'clock. We didn't want the networks to find out about your facial injury, but it can't be helped now. The media will be swarming into West Yellowstone tonight."

Gene didn't seem to like it; Garner, Britt, and the rangers didn't like it either, and they hastily changed the subject. Sometime later, the weather thickened. Great handfuls of snow began to fall, and strong winds swayed the pines. By nine o'clock, another dreaded Yellowstone storm was in full blow. The rangers and the old man by the fire went home for the night, and then Dr. Garner got restless, so Capland walked him home too. Only Britt remained.

"I'm going to sleep awhile," Gene announced. "Will you stay?"

"Yes, Gene, I will. Someone brought some quilts. Take a couple and make a bed on the tool bench. Here's a wool blanket to put over—"

He was asleep before she could cover him, the quiet, unmoving sleep of a man who had learned not to waste body heat by rolling around under the covers. Sitting nearby in an old chair, Britt brought her journal up to date, smoked some cigarettes, fed the fire, and watched. Somehow, this strange young man had become her friend. She knew he was content with her there and trusted her to feed the stove. There was a closeness between them that, as a scientist, she could never explain. She could _feel_ with him.

Britt knew Gene dreaded going back, but she also understood he desired nothing less. God, how he had aged during the experiment, she thought. He looked so old and worn now. Looking at his hair, she was moved to tears by the streaks of gray in it. How old was he? Just in his mid-twenties. And that scar—he would have it the rest of his life. What about the mottling on his hands and neck from sitting so close to a fire? Would it ever go away? And where was his silver rosary? Had he lost it in the snow? Had it, too, been stolen, or was it hanging on a peg back in the cabin? Worse, had he lost his faith and was no longer wearing the rosary? Every time she'd seen him before, he had been wearing it.

"You know," she whispered softly as she reached out to touch his hair, "I have never known anyone with greater courage." And then, overcome with emotion, she stepped away and wept silently in the shadows near the stove.

Before long, the wind changed its pitch. His eyes opened like he had never slept, but it was minutes before he spoke. "That's a blizzard outside; it's going to keep this up for several days. Reporters won't be able to travel through this. We can forget a briefing today."

Never questioning him, Britt watched as he got up and put on his heavy snow shirt, then laced a leather band to his wrist.

"What's that?" she asked, desperate to say something, for she felt a lump in her throat. It was 5 in the morning, March 16, 1974.

"It's my latest spear thrower," Gene answered, stretching out two straps, one for his hand, and the other with an ivory hook for a javelin's butt. "It does the same thing as a solid shaft. I get real good distance with it."

After feeding the straps of the spear thrower up his sleeve, Gene put on his coat, its furry collar fluffed up around his neck. Looking frighteningly huge again, Siegfried looped a rope around a large bundle, slung it and the noisy cooking pot on his back with his javelins, then stuck a small kitchen knife one of the women had given him in his pocket. Time to go, and Britt was very sad.

"Here," he said. "Too heavy to carry back, and I can make another."

It was a small elk leather bag, well sewn with sinew. Its flap was made from the tanned face of a coyote. "Thanks," she said, embarrassed at the gift. "Coyote," she said. "You've been harassed by them...."

Ignoring her comment, Siegfried said, "The gift's for you, not the project."

"I understand," she said, tucking it in her pocket.

Gene pulled a half-full pint of whiskey from a pocket, looked at it a long minute, then swigged it down. "A friend gave that to me," he said, "for such a day as this...." His voice was thick with emotion, and he waggled the empty bottle apologetically.

"It's okay, Gene. I understand. It doesn't break the rules."

He tossed the little bottle into the trash. "I don't even like whiskey.... But I know it works."

It was dawn outside. The wind lessened, and the temperature plunged, but the chill was in her soul, not her body, as she shrugged into her own gear and followed him out into the grayness of the morning. Should they lock the shed? No. Probably no one stole anything in West Yellowstone. The snowy streets were empty. No one was moving this time of morning.

After kneeling outside the door to put on his snowshoes, Gene straight-ened up with great difficulty.

"You're sore," she said, unslinging a camera for a last picture of him.

"You betcha," he admitted. "And tired too."

Neither of them said another word as they squeaked through the snowy desertion of West Yellowstone to the tollbooths and archways of the West Entrance. Britt stopped there with him, the long terrible road stretching east into the wilderness. Yellowstone Park was gray with frost smoke fill-ing the shadows of the black forest and fresh snow drifting across the road. The storm was getting worse by the minute.

This was their goodbye, yet neither of them said it. Instead, Britt caught him looking up at her. She watched his eye move to her lips, lin-ger at her cheek, then settle on her forehead. There was no way he could stretch up that far, no way she could bend gracefully for the kiss, but at the thought, their eyes met, and the moment was lost.

She thought his beard moved slightly around the mouth. His eyes crinkled with humor, then he turned away, slipped on his snow mask and hat, and clumped off into the snow.

Twenty minutes later, at the bend in the road, he stopped and turned around. Britt was still at the West Gate, waiting for a last sighting of him. He probably had a hard time seeing her, but yes, here she was, waving like a fool from in front of the tollbooths. He stared at her a long while. She imagined he might shout something, but instead, pulling off his right mitten, he freed his hand, drew his axe from his belt, and raised it straight above his head.

She understood the message immediately. Despite her earlier skepti-cism, she had never been so proud of anyone before. For the first time since the experiment began, she believed he was right for going back into the wilderness, and she was confident he would be okay. He had proven that, given the time, a human being could build the tools he needed to survive a snowy winter. When the experiment ended in two months, he would make more money with endorsements, a memoir, personal appear-ances, and televised interviews than any of the researchers. A lump rose in her throat, and she tore off her right glove, raised her arm in answer and shouted his name. Of course, at that distance he couldn't have heard her, but he probably understood how she felt.

As Britt watched, the snow settled in around him, and Gene vanished into the grayness of the storm. He had triumphed. He had proven himself beyond anyone's expectations. She was sure now that Siegfried would take no more chances. Warm tears running down her face, she opened her fist and let her hand sink to her heart in farewell.

For lack of anyplace better to go, Britt returned to the shed fifteen minutes later. Fishing the whiskey bottle out of the trash, she put it in her pocket. No one must know, she knew. Should she stoke the fire? Put things away? She didn't know, but as she looked around she spotted four folded elk hides on the workbench that Gene had rejected as being too poorly tanned, plus the welder's fire striker that wouldn't spark, and a thimble too small for his fingers. After his hazardous trek to West Yellowstone, Gene was returning to Hayden Valley with only two elk hides, a cooking pot, a small store-bought kitchen knife, and a two-way radio.

CHAPTER 27

※ ※ ※

Mack Simms

A RANGER SPOTTED Gene Siegfried in Hayden Valley late the next morning. This fact became the basis for West Yellowstone's short-lived Winter March Festival, which featured an annual snowshoe race to Hayden Valley and back, timed to resemble Gene's actual trip and rest periods. In the years the festival was held (1979-1984), Britt Chamberlain was twice asked to appear as grand marshal of the Snow Parade, but she could not find the time. Neither could the winter tourists. In the end, few snowshoers matched Gene's "record," and none did it in the same kind of weather.

As Britt was to discover, however, there were other facets of the Winter March that were quite confusing. That spring, she spotted a few of the Siegfried Sculptures for sale in an art gallery in Jackson, Wyoming. When she confronted the owner, he retorted, "These are not stolen. I do not deal in stolen merchandise. I paid good money for them."

"They are the property of Gene Siegfried, Project Snow, and the National Park Service," she replied evenly.

"Get out of my shop," the man yelled, pointing at the door.

Hardly able to contain her rage, she marched out of the gallery and straight to the sheriff, but it was only after ten months of legal wrangling that the sculptures were returned to the Park Service. Today, they are on semi-permanent display in Cody, Wyoming.

Another part of the story, however, soon occupied Britt's speculations. Three weeks after the Winter March, she heard a rumor about two locals having a drink in the bar of the Wort Hotel in Jackson. A third man entered the saloon, pulled an old-fashioned pistol out of his ski jacket, called the men by name, then warned them never to bother Gene Siegfried again. To emphasize his point, he reportedly blew a hole in the bar near one of the men's hands. The acrid smoke from the black-powder pistol eddied in the bar for an hour.

"I've known the Simms family all my life," an eyewitness told Britt. "I'd swear that was Ora Simms' youngest boy."

"You mean Mack Simms?"

"You betcha. That's exactly who I mean," the man said.

Unfortunately, the Simms family was well thought of in northwestern Wyoming. Before long, people were claiming it wasn't Mack at all; it had to be someone else. When Britt sought out her eyewitness, he declared, "I didn't get a good look. It could have been anybody."

Perhaps the story was too melodramatic in a western sense to be true, but Britt felt there was something to it. Intrigued, she spoke with dozens of natives, but she never found another eyewitness. Did Mack know something? Had he recognized who might have stolen Gene's things? What did he know? And when did he know it?

In the end, no one was implicated in the theft from the cabin. One obvious clue never occurred to Britt until it was too late. She neglected to check the bar, and in 1980, the Wort Hotel burned to the ground, so she never learned if the bar had a hole in it.

She was convinced, however, that if Mack knew the perpetrators, he would come forward to accuse them publicly. She began to believe the story was malicious gossip, but then Mack disappeared from Snow Lodge for two days in mid-April 1974. Upon his return, he was busted by rangers for taking a Yellowstone Park Company snowmobile. After being fired for "unauthorized use of a company vehicle and unexcused absence from work," he was taken into custody by the rangers. When the snowmobile was searched, rangers found camping gear and a muddy shovel. Arrested for stealing the snowmobile, Mack was ordered to pack his belongings. To everyone's surprise, he had a .44 caliber black-powder 1860 Colt Army replica pistol in his room. One chamber in the cylinder had been fired.

Butch Denny

Charged with possession of a firearm in a national park, Mack was handcuffed, bundled into a snow coach with his gear, and shipped out before his friend Roxy could talk to him.

"Mack! What's going on?" she screamed, running after the rangers' snow cat as it roared away. "Why? Why?" she hollered after it, then she sank to her knees and began to cry.

"He wouldn't talk," she told Britt on the phone that night. "He wouldn't even look at me. I've never seen him like this. There's something really wrong. It's not like Mack at all. I don't understand what's happening."

"I'll call ranger headquarters at Mammoth to get some information," Britt promised.

"Would you?" Roxy asked in relief.

"Sure," Britt said, though it would be difficult. She was barely getting along with Jimmy Downes and the other rangers now, but she managed to learn from someone that Mack had been fined two hundred dollars and had his weapon confiscated. Helped to get his car out of storage from the company warehouse, the young man had driven quickly away. He never told Roxy goodbye nor offered an explanation.

CHAPTER 28

❄ ❄ ❄

The Straggler

THERE HAD BEEN a time when the experiment was an enjoyable game played primarily for the intellectual amusement of theoretical scientists, but now, Project Snow was neither entertaining nor stimulating. After the breakdown of surveillance, and in the absence of hard facts and firm data, the researchers had little choice but to wait for the conclusion of their project. In the meantime, they prepared for their final meetings with the subject, arranged notes, and drew preliminary conclusions.

Most of the staff took off until spring, but Doctor Garner stayed on, spending his time in front of a blazing fireplace in the home where he had rented a room. Dr. Capland also stayed in West Yellowstone, though he had been driven nearly insane by the confinement. He passed his time in a drugstore reading pharmacy books and talking with the pharmacist.

"So what do you think's going to happen? the druggist pestered one day.

"That kid's going to make it," Capland declared, and then a debate was on. Every customer that came in was asked the same question, and again and again Dr. Capland and the druggist would get into it. Finally, a bet of a hundred dollars was made. "Easy money," Capland said to himself as he trekked home in the snow that evening.

The general malaise affected Dr. Britt Chamberlain too. A corner of her room was stacked with paperbacks of every sort, but her chief pursuit—outside of a minor flirtation with a local civil servant—was taking baths. Trotting down the hall to the hotel's bathroom, she would fill the claw-footed iron tub with warm water and read. Twice, she visited Roxy down at Old Faithful; she also went up to Bozeman to shop, but even spending money was no fun anymore, for she had little need of anything. Offers poured in from universities and think tanks across the country, and though she considered each one, she resolved to choose her next project more wisely.

Meanwhile, the weather remained uniformly awful. Terrible cold and steady snowfalls, poor visibility, and the ponderous shifting of the seasonal winds took all the joy out of this endless winter. Snow dudes were fewer and further between as the romance of Yellowstone-in-the-snow diminished. Visitation was at its lowest point in three winters, yet the work at Snow Lodge was never done for long.

Roxy worked harder and volunteered for more, in part because of an uneasiness coming over her, but also due to growing friction among the employees of Snow Lodge. Petty jealousies, poor management, and difficult conditions had destroyed the camaraderie of earlier in the season. To distance herself from the others, Roxy became a geyser watcher, one of that lonely breed who hang out on misty boardwalks waiting for the rarest eruptions.

As boredom and restlessness increased during the late winter, so too did the number of catastrophes, for the end of the season is more deadly than its beginning. A ranger slipped and broke his hip during an afternoon excursion to the Hoodoos. A lifelong resident of Montana was found sitting in the lee of his broken snowmobile, frozen to death. A few miles south of Cody, Wyoming, two college students returning home for the weekend were killed in a car accident caused by icy roads. A family living near Henry's Lake, Idaho, was gassed by a stove that had given them no previous trouble. In Bozeman, a man had a heart attack while shoveling snow; he died on his own front porch. In the Tetons, a skier was reported missing in an avalanche. The suicide rate was up slightly over any previous winter; liquor stores were doing a good business; and a travel agency offering trips to "sunny Mexico" signed sixteen people in two days.

The northern Rockies—despite immense mineral wealth, scenic beauty, and romantic legends—is sparsely populated. The reason is not so much winter's harshness as April's hopelessness. The winter seems to drag on and on.

If there were any justice in this world, Gene Siegfried should have also been comfortably bored and blue. Instead, he was like a punch-drunk boxer reeling under the continuous blows of winter. Storm after storm swept the Central Plateau. Temperatures cold enough to crack trees and days of wind and drifting snow confined him to the cabin. Flour snow sifted through every gap and covered all his steel with rust. The few remaining herbs suspended from the ceiling were plastered with ice, but they had long ago lost their efficacy, and he no longer bothered to use them. Lake Station recorded average snow depths of more than five feet, but drifts everywhere in the forests were much deeper.

Then, in late March, the banshee of all storms, the most terrible blizzard in five years rose over the northern horizon. It was as if winter had been rehearsing for this, and there was a ferocity of hiemal wrath so cold, so cutting, that as Gene huddled miserably over a guttering fire, he began to wonder if life itself weren't dreary compared to the peace of everlasting chill. The storm lasted three days, which for him were the longest of the winter, but even as his fire spluttered lower and the cold bent his back, while wildlife cowered deeper into the trees looking for shelter and even the desperate predators hid, he hoped for a respite.

Relief there was, too, for after the blizzard reluctantly released its bony grip on the valley, clearing skies did not radiate the meager warmth of a dying world into space. Instead, a Chinook broke the chill, and a light haziness held some heat to a grateful earth. Temperatures rose to freezing for the first time in four weeks. What little snow that had fallen was soon blown away, and snowdrifts solidified and packed down. Travel would be easier in the hard snow, Gene told himself as he grumped out of his cabin, but there wasn't anywhere to go, and besides, he no longer had the surpluses of food, leather, and fat to fuel more adventures.

Since his desperate trip to West Yellowstone, he had only the barest essentials and a new resolve to stay close to the valley's southern margin. The Gene Siegfried that emerged from his cabin the day after the terrible blizzard was not the one who had entered it weeks before. His mouth had grown thin and bitter, his eyes narrower and more determined. A lot of gray showed in his hair and beard now. He was stooped and beaten by the cold, and his winter wrinkles were deep and permanent. Only his mind remained active.

This was the period of winter most hazardous to a lone man, and he knew there were dangers all around. Reminding himself good fortune comes slowly, but disaster happens in a heartbeat, he consciously tried to take better care of himself. Ground blizzards were likely, early April would bring the fiercest storms of all, and there would be wind and blowing snow every day. Whiteouts and accidental dunkings were continual dangers, but worse than any of these, he expected the first ravening spring bears to appear soon.

In the meantime, the buffalo were on the move. Most of the cows and younger bulls had gone over Mary Mountain to the sheltered calving along the Nez Perce, but the bigger bulls had banded together, wavering in their desires to follow. The remaining buffalo still in Hayden Valley had left the lowlands along the river or around the thermal zones and were now in the shelter of the southern and western trees. What remained of the easier grazing near Sulphur Mountain, the hot springs, and down by the river now stank of death. Disembodied bones, clumps of hair, and bleaching skulls littered such places, and the thermal zones were haunted by scavengers searching for the gift of meat and blood. From an animal on the hoof to scattered bones in the snow was a matter of three days, Gene observed, which was a sign of how desperate times were. Frightened at a visceral level by images of death all around him, he resolved to avoid such places.

Another reason to be cautious was that the devil bull was on this side of the valley now. One afternoon, he thought he saw it under the branches of a back-scratching pine a few hundred yards west of the cabin, but in the shade, it was hard to identify. Cautiously, he circled past lest his scent be carried to it on the breeze. The rogue would have to be shot before the next tourist season. Nursing its grudges as it did, the bull was dangerous, and in its obtuse mind, the merest sight of a human would set it off on a vengeful spree among the innocent tourists. Gene must stay clear—he could not afford to confront the dangerous buffalo again. Sadly, this meant he couldn't hunt Mary Mountain or approach the warmth of the thermal zones, for the straggler might be lurking there. Instead, he must stay close to the cabin for the remainder of the winter.

Unfortunately, the cabin was not very comfortable. The vandalized western wall, which hadn't been too strong anyway due to a sulfurous seepage and the lingering warmth of volcanic fires somewhere in the hellish depths below, was definitely unsound. The added weight of the recent snows, the expansions of freezings and thaws, and the movement of the alluvium behind the wall had caused the posts to separate and creep inward. The logs became disarrayed, and one day, as Gene was boiling bones for his dinner, the biggest roof beam slid between two of the posts, spraying him with muddy gravel and extinguishing the fire.

To fix the damage, he decided to work on his roof the next morning. The dirt and rocks insulating the cabin were so solidly frozen that he found their removal difficult, especially with the sticks and stones he had embedded in the roof the previous fall. To counter this, he built a fire in his firepit to warm the structure through and through, but then he was forced to store all of his belongings under the verandah because of dripping water. The kindling box was empty and the pantry nearly so, so he broke them up and stacked them and the remaining firewood along the front wall to support the verandah's roof.

The good weather wouldn't last long, and he had to work fast. The roof became more vulnerable as it was exposed, but Gene stacked the loose rock and mud nearby to throw back in a moment's notice. It took a day of hard labor to strip the mound and uncover the western wall, but finally, late the second morning, the cabin lay open in the weak winter sunshine.

Making the cabin very vulnerable, Gene uprooted three big stakes from the western abatis and tied them into a tripod; he slung a braided leather cable over the tripod and around the butt of the cracked beam, then tied the leather into a loop. As he prepared to winch the beam up by twisting the loop with a stick, the raven, which hadn't been closer to the cabin in the last week than a pine overlooking the meadow, landed on the roof.

"Hey, Munin," Siegfried greeted it. Grateful for the bird's company, he thought about giving it his last smoked trout, but it had been eating well. Stinking of a dozen carcasses, it appeared to have a mate, a bird he dubbed Hugin, which did not come nearer than the opening to the valley.

Pawing through his trash, Gene found several rotten strips of fat and flesh he had scraped from a skin; he hung the tidbits in the moose antlers where the raven could reach them. Cawing for more and better, the bird grumpily swallowed the greasy bits whole, then it pecked the leather loop and tossed it onto the roof.

"Don't do that," Gene laughed, waving the bird away. Replacing the loop, he winched the roof high enough to clear the ruined western wall, much of which collapsed as soon as the weight was lifted away. For the first time, he could see how rotten the structure had become. The combination of damp heat and sulfur compounds in the ground water had eaten away the footings of all of the posts, and the chain-sawing by the thieves had further weakened the wall. Pursing his lips thoughtfully, Siegfried realized the damage would be hard to fix. He wondered how much time he had before the next storm.

Strength didn't matter anymore, for the cabin had to last only another two months, so he attempted to solve the problem by building a light, double wall of poles. When finished, the new wall was actually stronger than the original, but unfortunately, the roof was not as tight as before. Some light poles were shaken loose by the movement and wedged themselves between the beams. Sticks slipped into the interior of the cabin, and many holes appeared. The roof needed extensive repairs before it could be re-covered with rocks and soil.

Disappointed, Gene decided to collect poles and add braces inside the cabin between the new wall and the roof, but before he could begin, he needed to sharpen his axe, for its edge was nicked from all the recent work. Though the temperature was just above freezing, he worked up a sweat; he shed his vest and long shirt, hanging them to dry in the woodpile. Soon thereafter, a change in the wind caused him to look up. To his surprise, the northwestern sky was gray lead, and the banshee wind was coming around again. Sighing, he leaned against one of the posts of the verandah and watched the storm develop. He was feeling depressed. Would this winter never end? he wondered. He had a notion to give up the work entirely and go hunting for fresh meat, but there was work waiting, and he had to finish the roof before the new snow. He stuck his axe into a column of the verandah, stripped off his elk leather shirt, hung it beside the axe, and went back up onto the hillside to work on the roof. It was the first time in seven months he was separated from his axe.

The raven reappeared, cawing excitedly while looking to the west, but there was no time to bother with the noisy bird, and besides, Gene could see the storm himself, approaching from the northwest. If he hurried, he could finish covering the roof before snow fell, but he knew there wouldn't be time to replace the stakes of the outer abatis.

With no time to hunt for more poles in the forest, Gene decided to pack large stones into the gaps and then throw dirt onto the roof. If he worked steadily, he might be done in three hours. After hammering rocks between the logs, he stamped his foot on the roof, and it sounded satisfyingly solid—but far away inside the cabin, the vibration caused a pole to slip between two beams and fall across the fire pit. As he tossed more stones against the wall, sparks popped away into the cabin's interior. The coals grew lively with the added fuel, and the pole bent as hungry flames devoured it.

Gene was oblivious to the danger as he shoveled dirt onto the roof. Though a breeze from nowhere chilled his sweaty back, he ignored it in his hurry to beat the approaching weather. The raven clucked disapprovingly, then glided away from its perch in the moose antlers to a roost in a pine overlooking the meadow. Inside the cabin, the pole broke into two flaming brands. Embers were dredged up out of the pit by the shifting wood, and sparks flew onto the dry poles covering the floor.

The snap of the sparks finally alerted him to the potential fire, but as he straightened from his work at the edge of the cabin wall, Siegfried knew the danger was already upon him. His eyes widened with horror. His fate was <u>behind</u> him, not below, for three feet from his back, the devil bull stood patiently waiting, bent on revenge. The buffalo had been stalking his sweaty scent in the wind, silently inching closer across the meadow, nursing its hatred of the man-thing that had humiliated it.

The bull inclined its massive head to the left and the right to fix its target. Its black tongue drooled out of its mouth, and each of its glittering, hateful eyes focused separately on the middle of the man's back.

Gene didn't need to see the horns curling around his shoulders; he barely realized the buffalo's presence before he felt the heat of its eyes on him. He heard its tail snap in the wind like a whip, and he sensed its cloven hooves dig into the snow for better purchase. As he began a slow motion leap for his life, the bull's first hook grazed him in the back and flipped him head over heels onto the rocky cabin roof. Knowing he was badly hurt, Gene somehow sorted himself out and rolled over to face the enormous buffalo.

He was lucky the first blow was only glancing, but several of his ribs were broken; the wind had been knocked out of him, and he struggled to suck some air in again. Get away! Get away! rang in his head. Get on your feet! But he could move only as in a bad dream.

The only real sound came from the buffalo bull. It hooked left and right with such violence the vertebras in its neck popped, and then a deep rumble echoed from its cavernous chest. Muscles stiffened like cable in its hindquarters as it tensed to leap after its puny foe.

Even so, as it hopped onto the roof, the mighty buffalo's natural agility failed it. In the perverse way of sheer luck, one of its front hooves plunged between two roof beams, and the buffalo crashed down so close its bearded chin was only an inch from Siegfried's knee. An ominous popping and crackling came from below, but ignoring the sound of the fire, Gene raised his right fist in a pitifully defiant gesture and punched the madly scrambling bull right on its slavering nose. That was the last insult! Roaring in fury, the bull wrenched itself to its knees—and at that moment, the largest beam snapped its pinning and broke in two, and man and beast were thrown helplessly into the fiery pit as the entire roof of the cabin collapsed.

Almost a minute of silence followed the cave-in, and then all hell broke loose. From the twisted wreckage, an unholy roar boomed, and the first red blaze burst forth, quickly followed by a maelstrom of sulfurous smoke and noise. The horned demon slashed among the rising flames, and there was an ominous snapping of wood and bone as the smoke of the rising inferno obscured the ruined cabin. Whether the sulfur-stained walls or the dry poles on the floor were the first to catch fire hardly mattered. In moments, the cabin was fully engulfed in flames. Fire blew out the shattered doorway to the still-standing roof of the verandah; the wind of the fire tore through the woodpile like a blowtorch, an odd contrast to the first downy snowflakes of the approaching storm.

Unbelievably, however, from all this destruction, past the hooking horns and kicking hooves of the frantic devil bull, Gene Siegfried reached a scalded arm out of the smoke and grabbed what remained of the door-jamb. Pulling himself on his belly out of the wreckage, he got clear of the burning cabin. Gene's left elbow was dislocated. His hair was smoldering. He had lost all his front teeth but one, and his lower lip was split all the way to the chin. In the firelight, his eyes had gone ruby red, and his face was stiff as a mask. With tears washing down his cheeks, he struggled to stand up, truly a savage now. Strangely, he felt no pain at all, and he did not hesitate. Slipping back into his shirt, he wrenched the axe from where he had stuck it in the column of his porch, glared at the steel of its blade, and then he made a sound, a sound from deep in his being, but it was not a human sound.

The burning cabin backlighted him; greasy smoke rose to meet the rising wind. Far away, something set the wintering geese along the river to honking, and their trumpeting rose and faded eerily in the cold air. Logs collapsed into the fiery cabin, embers flew away in the wind like an angry red rainbow, and then the devil bull challenged him from the fire, roaring in fury and death. Turning towards the cabin, Gene Siegfried answered the bull's challenge.

Three times the raven squawked from its perch in the dead pine, its dark eyes mirroring the reflection of the hungry flames below, and then it turned its face into the wind and soared away into the valley. It was soon joined by the other raven, and together, the two birds roosted somewhere to the northeast by the Grand Canyon of the Yellowstone. Meanwhile, the snow line of the advancing storm crossed the rolling hills of Hayden Valley and obscured the rising smudge of black smoke to the west.

CHAPTER 29

Full Circle

Two months before the first human could detect it, spring began to drip, and as the snow began to melt, the muddy ashes and bloody snow of spring were scarred with the ghosts and tracks of winter past. The soil turned to mud, and billions of newly awakened seeds stretched roots into the muck for precious water. Rivers that had run black all winter were now coffee-colored. In late April, the icy beard of the Lower Falls collapsed and was washed away; at the same time, the ice on Yellowstone Lake began to crack and heave.

Although fresh, new green nubbins and early shoots tempted the grass-eaters, the change in the weather was already too late for some. More animals die at the promise of spring than at any other time of year, yet it was their death that brings hope to others. The wreck of a weakened elk would provide the warmth of a full belly to emerging bears, mice, and worms.

For humankind, the first sign of spring was the opening of the park's roads. Due to the enormous interest in the triumphant return of the savage, tourists were expected earlier than usual; in mid-April, rotary snowplows' rusty blades were polished on the deep drifts of the Golden Gate near Mammoth Hot Springs. Every day after that, plows worked at the face of the snow, and mile by painful mile, the cracked and sodden asphalt was exposed to the sun.

Winterkeepers could hear the roar of the snowplows two days before their cabins were delivered from the grip of winter. For the keepers at Old Faithful, the coming of the plows brought peace, for the noisy snowmobilers were cut off by the advance of open roads. For more isolated winterkeepers, the plows brought mail, fresh supplies, and relief from the loneliness of winter. Some sections of road had to be re-plowed after spring storms, but it was good work, sweat-down-the-pits-and-numb-fingers work, and each weary mile of open road was a triumph.

The plow crew that cut across Hayden Valley expected Gene Siegfried to come across the snow to greet them at any moment. Having been warned to let him make the first overtures, the crew watched in vain, for he never showed himself, and the men had no time to look for him. Every day after that, a few vehicles drove through the valley on the way to the plowing of the Sylvan Pass, but still he kept to himself.

It worried Britt; it probably concerned Doctor Garner and Bill Capland too, for they remarked on the single-mindedness of their subject. "I don't think," Britt said one day, "that Gene's privacy should be invaded until the end of the experiment."

"Why not?" Garner asked.

"Because of the isolation he's gone through. I think he'll feel strange being thrown into a spotlight after all these months. We must be sensitive to his feelings."

After some reflection, Garner agreed, "You might be right. If he wanted contact, he's had an opportunity. We'll wait."

Due to this decision, Red Reese and Jimmy Downes angrily withdrew from the experiment. "I don't feel this is the Siegfried I've been watching so long," Downes wrote in his resignation. "I believe he's starved for human contact. We should reestablish surveillance."

"You're wrong," Britt said as she accepted his resignation. "It's my opinion the end of the experiment and the loss of the independence he's enjoyed up to this point conflicts him. He'll have difficulty adjusting to the media attention he'll soon face. We must give him a chance to re-adapt to society at his own pace."

With the opening of the park's roads nearly complete, other preparations were soon underway. In those areas scheduled for early opening, carpenters removed shutters and patched roofs. Level floors had tilted, doors were stuck, broken pipes gushed rusty water, steam leaks twisted wood tightly where it should have been loose and loosened it where it should have been tight. All over the park, buildings groaned and popped, haunting the men working in their lonely halls.

Roxy disappeared in the rush, but Britt learned the younger woman was now the Head Housekeeper at Old Faithful Inn. Hurrying to meet the early opening date, Roxy was busily training a crew of maids and houseboys struggling to open each wing of the Inn on schedule. Meanwhile, warehouses were stocked, trucks brought in fuel, and equipment uncovered. As laundry workers put their operation in order before the crush of millions of pounds of linens, food service had to provide meals almost from the first day. Dormitories were opened, the bus fleet readied, and personnel clerks processed hundreds of new summer employees. Everywhere there was haste and work aplenty.

By the end of April, the entire figure-eight road system was open for traffic except over Dunraven and Sylvan Passes. Old Faithful Inn and Mammoth Hotel opened their doors, followed a week later by Lake Lodge. The first influx of visitors was so heavy Hamilton Stores opened their Lake store early, and Yellowstone Park Company's boat division trucked in its two cruisers and put them into icebound anchorage at Bridge Bay. By mid-May, half of the park's concessions were in operation.

Doctor Garner asked the Park Service to reopen the Canyon Village Test Center, but he was brusquely informed he would have to rent other quarters instead. Stretched thinly due to the unexpected rush, rangers were having a hard time of it in Hayden Valley. Several adventurous groups of hikers tried to scour the valley for Gene, but luckily, none got very far, and the Park Service was quick to prosecute. Posting signs at each end of the valley warning of an "unusually high concentration of grizzlies," due to "poor feed conditions, and the "imminent mating season," rangers warned tourists to stay in their cars.

On May eighth, a meeting was held at Mammoth Hotel to discuss Gene's return. Britt Chamberlain, the press, the Park Service, a Congressman from Montana, and members of three conservation groups were present. After hours of discussion—plus a frustrating soliloquy by a radical—it was agreed:

1.) Gene would be allowed to return to civilization at any place and in any manner he chose. Britt argued, "He might need adjustment time, but if he chooses to come back with the fanfare of a public welcome, I urge that it, too, be arranged."

2.) It was possible he had lost track of time and might be several days early or late. If he came in early, the conferees agreed it would count as a full year, but if he were late, no one would hurry him. He could come in when _he_ wanted.

3.) In her capacity as representative of Project Snow, Britt promised that shortly after his return, a news conference would be held. Data not previously released to the public would be made available, and then a news conference would be scheduled after Siegfried had undergone a complete physical. He could, at his option, participate in either or both of the conferences.

On May tenth, the weather turned bad. Hail, sleet, rain, and snow all came that day, and six inches of wet snow fell that night. The next day, snow hung in the air, and the dismal skies foretold more damp weather. The fireplaces at Old Faithful Inn were surrounded by reporters, one of whom collected anecdotes from people who knew, or claimed to know, Gene Siegfried; this article, published on May twelfth, quoted a friend of Gene's as saying, "He won't finish the experiment in Hayden Valley. He'll come in at Old Faithful, for this is the heart of Yellowstone."

The morning of May fifteenth dawned clear and rosy, a day of promise, and three distinct groups met to wait for Gene's return. Most of the original crowd from the year before gathered again in the parking lot in Hayden Valley. Conspicuously absent were Gene's friends, Mack and Roxy, but a dozen quarrelsome reporters took their places. There were also a dozen tourists, four of whom unfurled two banners: one, an innocuous "Welcome Home Gene" and the other ominously proclaiming, "The Senseless Slaughter of Our Wildlife is Finished at Last!"

Garner and Capland hoped to intercept Siegfried and whisk him to their new headquarters; they waited outside the locked and shuttered research center near Canyon Village. Nearby, detailed by the Park Service to keep Garner away from the former test facility, Rangers Reese and Downes sat in an official truck, reluctant to come any closer to the old man. Britt Chamberlain, for want of a better place, sat on the benches facing Old Faithful Geyser, unaware Roxy was waiting only a short distance away at Old Faithful Inn.

The morning passed pleasantly. It was warm outside, and water dripped everywhere. In the forest, clods of snow shaken from the trees pelted the ground like hail. The afternoon was cloudy, and the crowds grew restless. As the evening grew breezy, the tourists drifted away to their accommodations.

The sixteenth passed much the same way, with pretty nearly the same faces in the same places, waiting almost as patiently as before. In the afternoon, however, a rumor swept the crowd at Old Faithful that Gene Siegfried had been spotted sitting high above the geyser basin on Observation Point. Someone in the crowd began to shout, "SAA-vage! SAA-vage! SAA-vage!" Hundreds picked up the haunting chant. Sitting among the tourists, her heart filled with a complex stew of emotions, Britt was embarrassed how easily her eyes misted with tears. She wrote in her journal that even after it became obvious he wasn't really there, the chanting fed on itself for two hours, the sound echoing between the mountains.

By the seventeenth, most people were angry. Rangers charged three determined groups in Hayden Valley with hiking in a clearly marked bear-hazard zone. With tempers flaring at Old Faithful, Britt found it less upsetting to sit on the high balcony of the Inn. Tourists felt gypped, the news services fumed at the delay—and then the rules broke down.

NBC succeeded in fielding a reporter in Hayden Valley on the eighteenth. When other networks prepared to follow, the Park Service agreed to a guided outing to the cabin. By this time, Dr. Garner, Ranger Reese, and others were convinced the experiment would end at Old Faithful, but when they joined Britt on the Inn's viewing platform, Gene's friend Roxy was tending to her duties inside the labyrinthine hotel.

Each network assigned a camera crew and a reporter to the expedition into Hayden Valley, which also included the wire services, local newspapermen, a morose Douglas Paine Hanson, and a dozen rangers and naturalists. After gathering in the Trout Creek pullout, they marched into the valley along the old service road. With miles of wilderness, dozens of spring bears, and rotten snow around them, the rangers were strict about keeping together, so progress was slow. Some of the dudes joked they might encounter grizzlies, but the rangers said they would see little wildlife with such a noisy group.

The excursion traveled five miles down the road to the farthest tributary of Trout Creek, then southwest along the stream to the little meadow, but as the group came through the trees, they realized there wasn't a cabin set into the rise any more. All traces of the cabin were gone! The only thing left was a muddy depression newly planted with grass and sprigs of sagebrush. A short distance away, a blackened beam was set in the ground, a grisly buffalo skull wired to it.

The reporters demanded an explanation, but the rangers were as mystified as anyone. They were in the eye of a storm; they didn't comprehend the lengths to which people would go to get the story. To most, destroying the cabin and returning the site to nature was wrong. Stories began to circulate that Gene Siegfried was dead; for his part, Douglas Paine Hanson decided Gene had decided to remain in the wilderness forever. Some others wondered if he weren't already back in civilization and hiding out of embarrassment. Some felt after all he'd been through, he might be insane. Rumors snowballed, and the Park Service grew defensive.

The days of the mystery grew into a week, then another. Project Snow's funding was exhausted, and Dr. Garner let all the technicians go. Almost immediately, the Park Service launched an attack on the Project. While its official policy had been weary, yet patient, agreement, the Service had already prepared to disavow the entire experiment. On May 30th, the Superintendent issued a statement minimizing the role of Yellowstone National Park in the project. Conservationists attacked Project Snow before a Congressional hearing; newspapers reevaluated the meager data obtained in the experiment; and key figures denied responsibility for approving either the project or its locale. Two weeks stretched into three; Dr. Capland grew restless and left, promising to return if needed.

Meanwhile, tourists poured into the park in unprecedented numbers. Question-mark T-shirts became common. A hastily prepared brochure published in West Yellowstone detailed Gene's arduous survival story and challenged all comers to a snowshoe race the next winter. Shipped to Chicago from Wyoming ranches, buffalo steaks reached an all-time high of nine dollars a pound. Leathers and furs were chic, and a Parisian designer released a collection of "Wilderness Experience" fashions to honor the savage, but still something was missing: the man himself.

Every day it didn't rain, crowds formed at Alum Creek and at Old Faithful. A month passed, and park employees were sick of answering questions from the dudes, but it was all <u>they</u> talked about too. Dozens of the bolder ones combed the valley for some sign.

On June sixteenth, the Park Service informed Doctor Garner the cabin would be excavated to search for clues. Intrigued, Britt joined Garner at the site. By this time, the buffalo skull was gone; it was located nearby, its horns sawn off by vandals. Someone had dug a hole in the center of the cabin site, but they had probably found little, if anything, of value. The rangers were more thorough. Digging all around the beam that had supported the skull—for some thought it marked a grave—they found nothing. Next, the men cleared the verandah and pantry. All the front wall of the cabin had been burned to stumps, and only remnants of the other walls remained, but these were to become part of the Park Service's collection of "Siegfried Sculptures."

Nearing the floor of the former cabin, however, a digger discovered ribs. Overcome with emotion, Britt Chamberlain sat on a nearby log, her head in her hands. When Garner and a ranger approached, she asked, "Is he...?"

"No, it's not him," Garner told her. "The ribs are too large. It's a buffalo." Pulling her to her feet, the old man helped her over to the excavation.

By this time, quite a few bones had been uncovered. "Pretty big buffalo, but headless," a ranger shouted, tossing up a vertebra from the neck of the carcass to a naturalist at the edge of the hole. Comparing it to bones still attached to the back of the skull, the naturalist declared them a match.

Although they had intended to open the cabin site for answers, more questions had arisen. Where had the buffalo come from, and why was it beheaded in the middle of the wrecked cabin? Why was the cabin so badly burned, and then carefully buried? Had Siegfried withdrawn into the deeper wilderness like Hanson was saying? What did the skull on the post mean? There were no other bones nor any sign of a man; a few of Siegfried's minor tools were recovered from the ruins, but not his axe nor his javelins.

Surprisingly, the excavators didn't bother to rebury the hole, but left it a sore on the landscape. A few days later, Britt Chamberlain returned alone to the site with a shovel she had bought in West Yellowstone; the monument to her success is that, today, there is a controversy over the actual location of the cabin.

Doctor Garner stayed on another week, then, in early July, he went home to Houston, Texas, to write his preliminary report on Project Snow.

On July second, Britt journeyed to Old Faithful to invite Roxy to West Yellowstone for the Fourth of July. A lot had happened in the year since she had first met Roxy in the Lariat Saloon. She had come to love these mountains. She had hiked and fished, and Roxy had been her mentor, helping her and stimulating her interest. Britt felt she had to give Roxy an explanation as to why she, too, had decided to leave.

Old Faithful Inn was busy as usual. The heavy red doors of the *porte cochere* were propped open to reveal hundreds of dudes milling about, gawking at the unbelievable log construction. Above her head as she entered the lobby, convoluted beams grappled upward like a dream fantasy, the blackened ceiling soaring out of sight. Souvenir shops were busy, cash registers were clanging away, and there was a hubbub of voices mixed with laughter from the bar and the tinkling of dishes from the restaurant. A few tourists sat along the railings of the galleries on the second and third floors; children ran up and down the wide stairs.

Down one of the vast halls of the Inn, Britt knew she would find Roxy, but it took an hour's search before she located her office on an upper floor. Busy on the phone, Roxy was surrounded by maids working on a load of clean linens from the laundry.

"Talk to you in a while," the younger woman promised.

Feeling very depressed, Britt considered sitting in one of the comfortable chairs along the second-floor gallery, but something drew her outside to the balcony above the *porte cochere*. Shivering in a chill breeze, she found a wicker chair that conformed well in the seat; she sat down and put her feet up on the railing. In the distance, Old Faithful was about to erupt; she could hear the tourists as they jostled for the best vantage points, yet she knew mixed in with all those interested in the eruption were plenty of skeptics. Old Faithful rumbled ominously, and the first super-heated spray shot twenty feet in the air and then drifted away in the wind.

"I guess you're getting ready to leave," Roxy said from behind her.

"How'd you know?" Britt asked, turning to smile up at her friend.

"It's a tradition. If you don't come here as a savage, you're doomed to do it later as a dude." Pulling another chair over to the railing, Roxy, who had bags under her eyes and looked a bit fat in the ass, sat down beside her. "Where you going from here?"

"Back to UCLA for now. When this is finished, I'll collect my notes and write about Project Snow," Britt answered sadly.

"Why do you think it's not over?" Roxy asked. "What if this is all there is?"

"You mean that I ... I mean that <u>we</u> ... never know?"

"I don't know what I mean," Roxy sighed, combing her fingers through her tangled hair. "What if there is nothing else? What if the buffalo skull on the post was a sign? What if Gene freaked and retreated into the wilderness forever? What if he finished his year and left to start a new life without telling us? What if he's dead?"

"I think you have something to tell me," Britt answered, sadness sweeping over her.

"I don't know anything for sure. I've lost two of the best friends of my life, and I don't understand why, with either of them." Roxy looked old in the sunshine. A gentle breeze snatched at her coarse hair; her brown eyes crinkled crow's feet as she stared away into infinity. Changing the subject, she asked, "Do you know anything of the Tao?"

"No. I've never read it," Britt said.

"Profit from what is there; usefulness from what is not." Roxy said, looking thoughtful. "We've got to find meaning in this, but what if this is all we learn? What if the buffalo skull on the post was it, and we don't get it?"

"What if it means nothing at all?" Britt suggested, unsure what her friend was getting at. "What if it was a barbaric sacrifice or simply a triumphant gesture?"

"Did you read the Denver Post today?" Roxy asked, ignoring her. "It said this is the biggest mystery since Amelia Earhart's disappearance."

"People are losing their perspective."

"Sure," Roxy agreed, "but look at the weirdoes trying to find Gene. They're hyping this and in two years no one will be able to tell fact from fiction. Don't you think you've got to figure it out now, before it becomes a legend later?"

"What if there's nothing to figure out?" Britt asked.

"Everything means something in a mystery," Roxy said. "But I can't, for the life of me, figure it out. I do know it's not like Gene to bury his cabin and destroy all trace of his life there, yet leave a monument."

"What are you saying?" Britt asked uneasily.

"Look out there," Roxy pointed. "What do you see?"

"People lining up for Old Faithful's next eruption, the geyser basin, the Firehole River—"

"Do you believe this will be here fifty years from now? What's the use of educating people on the fragility of precious thermal features, if they are going to be exposed to crackpots throwing pennies into them for good luck? What's the good of protecting whooping cranes in Texas, if some delinquent with a .22 can wipe out the entire species in an afternoon? Do you think captive breeding programs of rare animals will restore even one 'natural' population—?"

"Stop it. I can't believe you're saying this." Feeling like a drowning person gasping for air, Britt said, "You love this place too much to say such things."

"Yes, I do," Roxy admitted sadly. "That's why it's easier to ignore truth."

"But it's not true."

"The last time I saw Gene," Roxy said, changing the subject, "was four months ago. Mack and I had driven a snowmobile to Dragon's Mouth and skied over to his cabin. It must have been awful cooped up all winter. Gene had concluded everything he loved was doomed. The urban sprawl can't be stopped. Development eats up farmlands while conservationists battle for wilderness areas. Vacationers are guided through national parks like hallowed museums, and each one picks up a souvenir—a rock here, a flower there. Every year, there is less, so the souvenirs become more precious than ever. People destroying what they most yearn for, depriving themselves by depriving each other, and finally, when everyone's forgotten the allure of wilderness, when all that's left are a few trees in a barren landscape and mosquitoes are the only wildlife...."

"STOP IT!" Britt shouted. "So what if Gene brooded out there? There are millions like you who will protect the wilderness. Sure, maybe a few species are doomed. Maybe there's no place in this world for elephants in Africa, or tigers in India, or grizzlies in Yellowstone, but it's not like you to suggest it's not worth trying!" She was fuming, but Roxy seemed to smile. "God, I don't know you at all," Britt said. "Maybe you're just bullshitting me."

"No. I'm not bullshitting. It's what Gene thought," Roxy said. "But it has to do with something I've been thinking lately. Did you ever hear of Frederick Jackson Turner?"

"No," Britt snapped. "Who's he?"

"He was a historian who wrote about the end of the frontier and its effect on Americans. You and I have lived our whole lives without a frontier, but think of it: always a possibility over the next hill until there wasn't anywhere new to go. There was a point when the frontier was settled."

"What does Turner have to do with this?" Britt asked in exasperation.

"After the census of 1890," Roxy said, "there wasn't a definable frontier anymore. It was the starting point in Turner's research. That's what this is about, I think. We're living the end. Like the census of 1890 for Turner, the conclusion of Gene's year will be someday be seen as the end of wilderness by some future historian."

They were quiet then, the two women. In the distance, Old Faithful surged once, twice, three times before wrenching itself high into the air in the grandest display Britt had ever seen. Tourists snapped pictures, and she could hear the same hackneyed expressions of awe and disappointment. Turning for Roxy's reaction, she was surprised the younger woman had risen to go back to work.

"I shouldn't have let Gene leave West Yellowstone in March," Britt admitted as she got to her feet. "I was the last to believe in him, but I should have been the first to stop him. I thought he was going to make it."

"I did too."

Embarrassed by the tears filling her eyes, Britt asked, "You _do_ know something, don't you? It has to do with that muddy shovel on Mack's snowmobile the day he was busted at Snow Lodge. Where the hell did he find mud in the middle of winter? It was Mack who buried the cabin and hung the buffalo skull on the post, wasn't it? Do you know what he found out there in Hayden Valley?"

An ashen raven clucked three times from a nearby pine, the sound like the winding of an old alarm clock. Roxy bit her lower lip all the way to blood. "There wouldn't have been much left," she said sadly before she hurried back into the Inn to work, to forget.

Rangers opened Gene's cache in September 1974 and recovered a few tools and minor artworks. Other than these items, the cache was empty, not a scrap of meat nor fish left. It indicates Siegfried's probable desperation in the last weeks of his life, and it may explain why he was so often out hunting in bad weather.

NASA (the official sponsor of the experiment) and the National Park Service disavowed cooperation with Project Snow, but in Congressional hearings held later that year, they were both heavily criticized. In the end, Gene Siegfried's disappearance between April 7th and April 17th, 1974 was blamed on three factors: his propensity to random adventuring, the unexpectedly harsh springtime weather, and the failures of the surveillance team to monitor and provide assistance. Jimmy Downes, former head of surveillance, was fired by the Park Service. Ranger Red Reese, former chief scout, was transferred out of the mountains he so loved to Glen Canyon National Recreation Area in Arizona. He committed suicide in 1977.

Mack Simms took over management of his father's ranch in 1976. In 1979, he combined this property with his new in-law's operations, and he worked there until 1994 when a tractor accident with a post-hole auger took one of his legs. He sold out and moved to Scottsdale, Arizona. He never granted an interview and died alone in 2003. The Simms Ranch exists today as an entity, but a conglomerate bought up most acreage and developed condominiums and five-acre "ranchettes" overlooking Jackson Hole, Wyoming.

Today, Roxy owns several Nissan dealerships in Arizona and southern California. She has consistently declined to grant interviews related to this story.

Douglas Paine Hanson never returned to Yellowstone, but he continued writing about outdoor sports and conservation. His memoir *The Wild Geese Haven't Called For Me Yet*, published in 1996, is listed by the Montana State Director of Public Instruction as recommended reading for fifth through eighth graders. Hanson's many influential articles await being collected by an editor and republished for posterity.

After months of discussion, and based on the testimony of Project Snow's Indian scouts—especially the man who personally witnessed Gene's encounter with the grizzly bear—the Apsaalooké, the Crow Indian Nation, awarded Gene Siegfried an exceptional honor for his courage and spirit during the long experiment. Gene's family accepted the award in a tearful ceremony at the Crow Agency, Montana, in July 1976.

In March 1984, Eugene Carl Siegfried was posthumously awarded a Presidential Commendation in Environmental Leadership. The award was controversial with conservationists and environmentalists at the time and is rarely cited now.

The National Park Service continues to encourage research in protected areas—as it should—but the application process and oversight is intense.

Project Snow never released any substantive data. All researchers associated with the project cooperated with Congressional hearings and then were silent. Dr. Britt Chamberlain and Dr. John Garner, who have both since passed away, denied requests for interviews.

In 1988, a Park Service patrol accompanying photographers recording the Great Fires of the Yellowstone found a rusted, riveted axe head three hundred eighty yards northeast of the former cabin site. Its identification was verified from measurements.

No other trace of Gene Siegfried was ever found.

The axe, artworks, and photographs of Project Snow and the adventures of The Savage are available today for research, and are, as The Siegfried Collection, on occasional display in Cody, Wyoming.

—THE END—

Butch Denny
OFI/YNP

#1 The Siegfried Axe. "Restored" by a well-meaning Livingston, Montana farrier/blacksmith in 1988. After polishing away the rust and replacing its broken handle with a lathed oak handle of similar dimension, plus two steel hammer wedges, the smith's axe weighs 1.6 ounces more than it did originally. Carried in "mountain man" gatherings in Montana, Idaho, and Wyoming from 1989-96, the axe passed through a variety of owners after the smith's death in 1998. It was purchased from a fur and trap shop in Bridger, Montana in 2003. — Siegfried Collection, donated by the author.

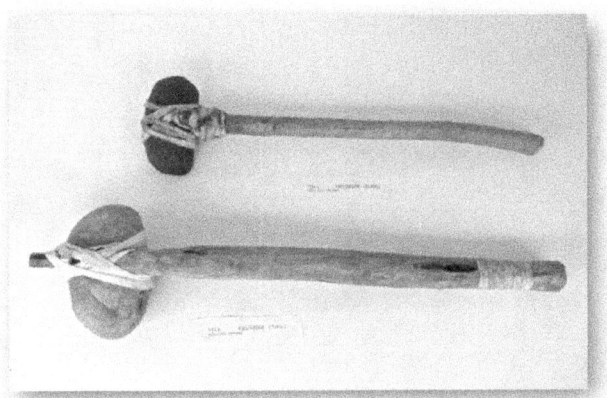

#2 Camp crushers. Gene made several to tenderize meat, hammer sinew, break bone to remove marrow, and crush roots and leaves. The upper crusher was heavily used. It was stolen from the cabin and only recovered after litigation. The lower example was unused and found in the cache by rangers in 1974. —Siegfried Collection

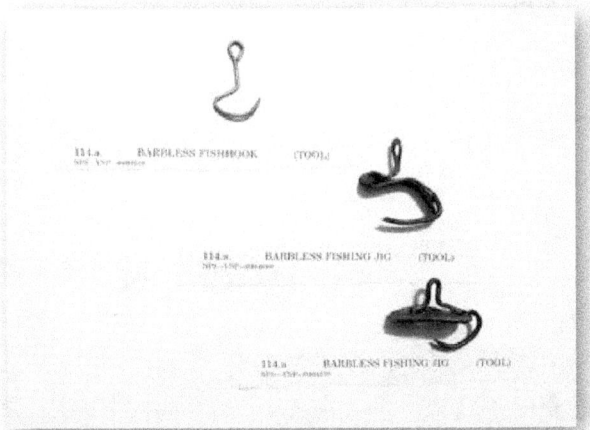

#3 Fishing jigs and hook

Every fisherman asks the same question. The answer is in an inventory of the Siegfried Cache, secretly opened and inventoried by rangers in September 1973. There were 42 pounds of dried trout therein. —Siegfried Collection

#4 Chisel dart and light javelin head. The chisel head was meant for target practice. Several examples have been recovered. This particular specimen was stolen from the cabin. Considerable litigation failed to recover it. The meaning of the three "dots" and two "slashes," repeated on the reverse side, is unknown. The "light javelin" head was recovered from the carcass of the elk bull at Ebro Springs; it passed into private ownership. —From a collection in Nagasaki, Japan.

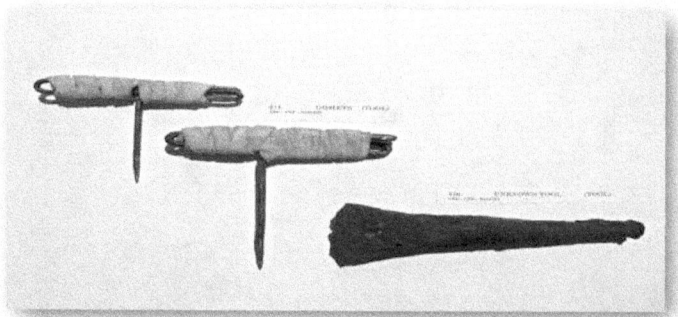

#7 Gimlet and awl
Made from round "bar" stock. Both handles from elk rawhide and heavily used. —Siegfried Collection

#8 Hand Axe. Thought to have been a recovered pneumatic hammer chisel, this tool was used as a cold chisel during the forging process. Possibly mated to a carriage bolt later, it was used as a hand axe in butchering and food preparation. Badly burned during the cabin fire, this hand axe was recovered during excavation of the cabin in 1974. —Siegfried Collection.

#5 Detail of an antler carving. Some see this as a self-portrait. — From a private collection in Nagasaki, Japan.

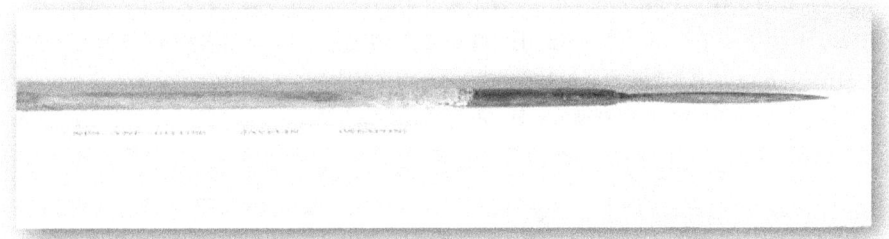

#6 "Heavy" javelin. During Project Snow, researchers secretly marked the javelins and darts. This example was used when Gene faced the grizzly bear west of Canyon Village in 1973. He also carried it to West Yellowstone in March 1974, and it is considered his favorite weapon. It was made using a pipe nipple, a carriage bolt, and a salvaged broom handle. Its handle is wrapped with catgut (elk intestine.) The first mark is the "short stab," a marking deemed best for close-in work. The second wrapping is the balance point, named the "long stab." The javelin was meant for use with an atlatl, not by hand. Its shaft is stained with blood. It weighs 11 ounces. In 1975, the Park Service tested it. Its hand-cast effective range (60% accuracy in a 12-inch target) is 30 feet. Its range with an atlatl and 60% accuracy is 25 yards. Maximum range is 80 yards. This is the most famous of the javelins Siegfried made. After passing through several owners and some litigation, the javelin is now part of the Siegfried Collection. It is on permanent display at the Hayden Valley Museum and Visitor's Center.

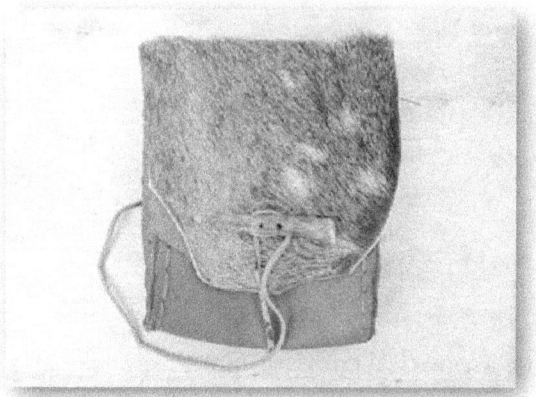

#9 "Lunch pack."
Lost in a sudden dunking near the Yellowstone River in January 1974, the lunch pack contained 11 ounces of dried elk jerky, 2 ounces of roots and herbs, and a small fire striker and stone. From a private collection in Düsseldorf, Germany

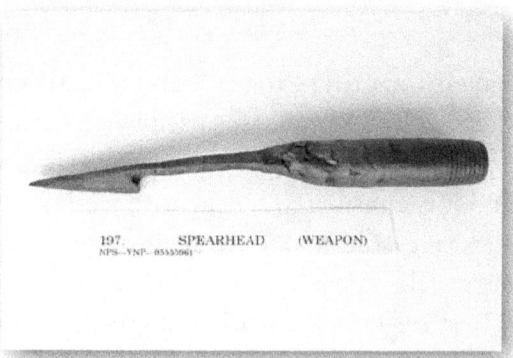

10 **"Banderillero."** Siegfried is known to have carried two in his hunting expeditions, but only one is known to have been used. This example was thrown— and lost in the snow— during the desperate fight with the devil bull. It was found using a metal detector in 1975. It is now part of the Siegfried Collection.

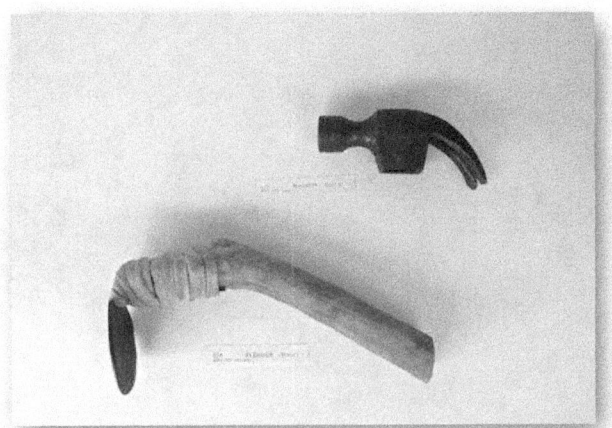

#10 **Claw Hammer Head.** Gene found this antique hammerhead in the landfill north of Fishing Bridge and used it in his forging operations in the Sulphur Hills. Burned in the cabin fire, the hammerhead was found in the excavation of the cabin.

#11 **Flensing tool.** Gene made at least four of these. This example, nearly new, was stolen from the cabin. After a threat of litigation, it was turned over to the Park Service. Strangely, it has never been on exhibit in the Siegfried Collection. It is in permanent "storage" with dozens of other tools and a large number of woodcarvings at Park Service Headquarters in Mammoth, Wyoming.

#13 **Gene Siegfried's Rosary.** Worn by Mack Simms the rest of his life.
—Courtesy of the Simms Family, Jackson, Wyoming

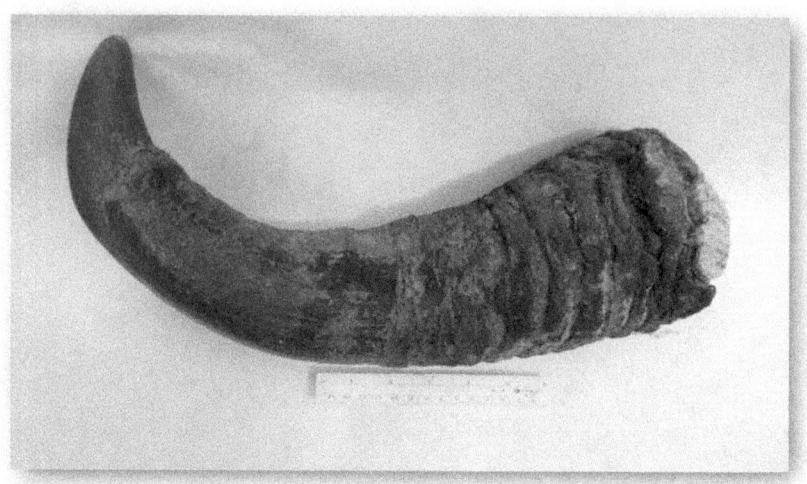

#12 **Buffalo Bull's Horn.** Vandalized from the skull hanging near Gene's cabin, this exceptional specimen was displayed in a bar in Butte, Montana for many years. —From the author's collection.

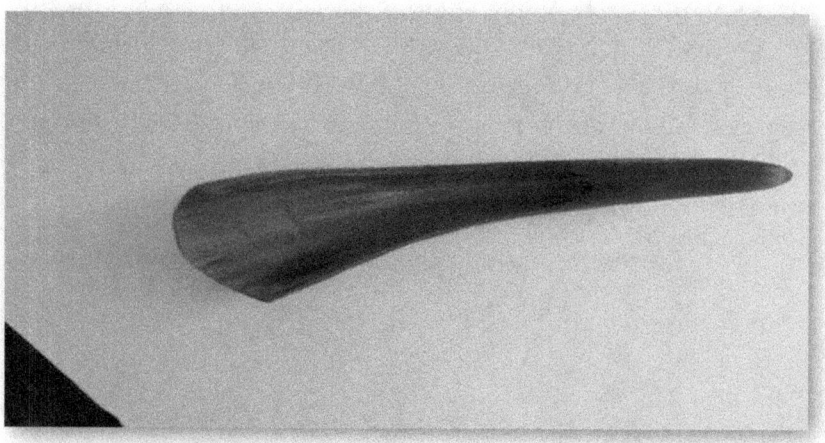

#14 **Buffalo Horn Scoop.** Stolen from the cabin prior to carving. —Private collection, Salt Lake City, Utah

#14 **Mystery Shirt.** Vintage Question-Mark t-shirt bought at a head-shop in West Yellowstone, Montana, in July 1974. These shirts were ubiquitous in the mountain country until the late 1970s.

—From the author's collection.

—Last words—

In a parting comment to Dr. Britt Chamberlain at West Yellowstone, Montana, before he clumped away forever into the snow, Gene Siegfried said, "You know, I'm glad I did this." She immediately recorded it in her journal but referred to it only once, in a presentation to the American Society of Research Professionals in Houston, Texas, on December 12, 1982.

www.ingramcontent.com/pod-product-compliance
Lightning Source LLC
Chambersburg PA
CBHW070217030726
47505CB00006B/1712